KU-736-038

Liane Moriarty is the Australian author of nine internationally bestselling novels, including the number one *New York Times* bestsellers *The Husband's Secret*, *Big Little Lies* and *Truly Madly Guilty*. Her books have sold more than twenty million copies worldwide, including three million in Australia and New Zealand.

The Husband's Secret was a number one UK bestseller, an Amazon Best Book of 2013 and has been translated into over forty languages. *Big Little Lies* and *Truly Madly Guilty* reached number one on the *New York Times* bestseller list in their first week of publication – the first time this has been achieved by an Australian – with *Nine Perfect Strangers* going straight to number one in Australia on publication, breaking sales records of the time. Liane is also the author of the Space Brigade series for children. She lives in Sydney with her husband, son and daughter.

Also by Liane Moriarty

apples
never
fall

LIANE
MORIARTY

PAN
Pan Macmillan Australia

Pan Macmillan acknowledges the Traditional Custodians of country throughout Australia and their connections to lands, waters and communities. We pay our respect to Elders past and present and extend that respect to all Aboriginal and Torres Strait Islander peoples today. We honour more than sixty thousand years of storytelling, art and culture.

The characters in this book are fictitious and any resemblance to real persons, living or dead, is purely coincidental.

First published 2021 in Macmillan by Pan Macmillan Australia Pty Ltd
This edition published 2022 in Pan by Pan Macmillan Australia Pty Ltd
1 Market Street, Sydney, New South Wales, Australia, 2000

Copyright © Liane Moriarty 2021

The moral right of the author to be identified as the author of this work has been asserted.

All rights reserved. No part of this book may be reproduced or transmitted by any person or entity (including Google, Amazon or similar organisations), in any form or by any means, electronic or mechanical, including photocopying, recording, scanning or by any information storage and retrieval system, without prior permission in writing from the publisher.

A catalogue record for this book is available from the National Library of Australia

Typeset in Bembo Regular by Post Pre-press
Printed by IVE

MIX
Paper from responsible sources
FSC® C018183

The paper in this book is FSC® certified. FSC® promotes environmentally responsible, socially beneficial and economically viable management of the world's forests.

For my mother,
with love

prologue

The bike lay on the side of the road beneath a grey oak, the handlebars at an odd jutted angle, as if it had been thrown with angry force.

It was early on a Saturday morning, the fifth day of a heat-wave. More than forty bushfires continued to blaze doggedly across the state. Six regional towns had 'evacuate now' warnings in place but here in suburban Sydney the only danger was to asthma sufferers, who were advised to stay indoors. The smoke haze that draped the city was a malicious yellow-grey, as thick as a London fog.

The empty streets were silent apart from the subterranean roar of cicadas. People slept after restless hot nights of jangled dreams, while early risers yawned and thumb-scrolled their phone screens.

The discarded bike was shiny-new, advertised as a 'vintage lady's bike': mint green, seven-speed, with a tan leather saddle and a white wicker basket. The sort of bike you were meant to imagine riding in the cool crisp air of a European mountain village, wearing a soft beret rather than a safety helmet, a baguette tucked under one arm.

Four green apples lay scattered on the dry grass beneath the tree as if they had spilled and rolled from the bike's basket.

A family of black blowflies sat poised at different points on the bike's silver spokes, so still they looked dead.

The car, a Holden Commodore V8, vibrated with the beat of eighties rock as it approached from the intersection, inappropriately fast in this family neighbourhood.

The brakelights flashed and the car reversed with a squeal of tyres until it was parked next to the bike. The music stopped. The driver emerged, smoking a cigarette. He was skinny, barefoot and bare-chested, wearing nothing but blue football shorts. He left the driver's door open and tiptoed with balletic, practised grace across the already hot asphalt and onto the grass, where he hunkered down to study the bike. He caressed the bike's punctured front tyre as if it were the limb of a wounded animal. The flies buzzed, suddenly alive and worried.

The man looked up and down the empty street, took a narrow-eyed drag of his cigarette, shrugged, and then grabbed the bike with one hand and stood. He walked to his car and laid it in his boot like a purchase, deftly popping off the front wheel with the quick-release lever to make it fit.

He got back in the car, slammed the door shut and drove off, rapping the beat to AC/DC's 'Highway to Hell' on his steering wheel, pleased with himself. Yesterday had been Valentine's Day, apparently, and he didn't believe in that capitalist shit but he was going to give the bike to his wife and say, Happy late Valentine's Day, babe, with an ironic wink, and that would make up for the other day and odds were he'd get lucky tonight.

He didn't get lucky. He got very unlucky. Twenty minutes later he was dead, killed instantly in a head-on collision. A semi-trailer driver from interstate didn't see a stop sign concealed by an overgrown liquidambar. Local residents had been complaining for months about that sign. It was an accident waiting to happen, they said, and now it had happened.

The apples rotted fast in the heat.

chapter one

Two men and two women sat in the far corner of a café underneath the framed photo of sunflowers at dawn in Tuscany. They were basketball-player tall, and as they leaned forward over the mosaic-topped round table, their foreheads almost touched. They spoke in low, intense voices, as if their conversation involved international espionage, which was incongruous in this small suburban café on a pleasant summery Saturday morning, with freshly baked banana and pear bread scenting the air and soft rock drifting languidly from the stereo to the accompaniment of the espresso machine's industrious hiss and grind.

'I think they're brothers and sisters,' said the waitress to her boss. The waitress was an only child and intrigued by siblings. 'They look really similar.'

'They're taking too long to order,' said her boss, who was one of eight and found siblings not at all intriguing. After last week's violent hailstorm, there had been blessed rain for nearly a week. Now the fires were under control, the smoke had cleared along with people's faces, and customers were finally out and about again, cash in hand, so they needed to be turning over tables fast.

'They said they haven't had a chance to look at the menus.'

'Ask them again.'

The waitress approached the table once more, noting how they each sat in the same distinctive way, with their ankles hooked around the front legs of their chairs, as if to prevent them from sliding away.

'Excuse me?'

They didn't hear her. They were all talking at once, their voices overlapping. They were definitely related. They even sounded similar: low, deep, husky-edged voices. People with sore throats and secrets.

'She's not technically missing. She sent us that text.'

'I just can't believe she's not answering her phone. She always answers.'

'Dad mentioned her new bike is gone.'

'What? That's bizarre.'

'So . . . she just cycled off down the street and into the sunset?'

'But she didn't take her helmet. Which I find very weird.'

'I think it's time we reported her missing.'

'It's over a week now. That's too long.'

'Like I said, she's not technically –'

'She is the very definition of missing because *we don't know where she is.*'

The waitress raised her voice to a point that was perilously close to rude. 'Are you ready to order yet?'

They didn't hear her.

'Has anyone been over to the house yet?'

'Dad told me please don't come over. He said he's "very busy".'

'Very *busy*? What's he so busy doing?'

The waitress shuffled alongside them, in between the chairs and the wall, so that one of them might see her.

'You know what could happen if we reported her missing?' The better-looking of the two men spoke. He wore a long-sleeved linen shirt rolled up to the elbows; shorts and shoes without socks. He was in his early thirties, the waitress guessed, with a goatee and the low-level charismatic charm of a reality star or a real estate agent. 'They'd suspect Dad.'

'Suspect Dad of what?' asked the other man, a shabbier, chunkier, cheaper version of the first. Instead of a goatee, he just needed a shave.

'That he . . . you know.' The expensive-version brother drew his finger across his neck.

The waitress went very still. This was the best conversation she'd overheard since she'd started waitressing.

'Jesus, Troy.' The cheaper-version brother exhaled. 'That's not funny.'

The other man shrugged. 'The police will ask if they argued. Dad said they *did* argue.'

'But surely –'

'Maybe Dad did have something to do with it,' said the youngest of the four, a woman wearing a short orange dress dotted with white daisies over a swimsuit tied at the neck. Her hair was dyed blue (the waitress coveted that exact shade), and it was tied back in a sticky wet tangled knot at her neck. There was a fine sheen of sandy sunscreen on her arms as if she'd just that moment walked off the beach, even though they were at least a forty-minute drive from the coast. 'Maybe he snapped. Maybe he finally snapped.'

'Stop it, both of you,' said the other woman, who the waitress realised now was a regular: extra-large, extra-hot soy flat white. Her name was Brooke. Brooke with an 'e'. They wrote customers' names on their coffee lids, and this woman had once pointed out, in a diffident but firm way, as if she couldn't help herself, that there should be an 'e' at the end of her name.

She was polite but not chatty and generally just a little stressed, like she already knew the day wasn't going to go her way. She paid with a five-dollar note and always left the fifty-cent piece in the tip jar. She wore the same thing every day: a navy polo shirt, shorts and runners with socks.

Today she was dressed for the weekend, in a skirt and top, but she still had the look of an off-duty member of the armed forces, or a PE teacher who wouldn't fall for any of your excuses about cramps.

'Dad would *never* hurt Mum,' she said to her sister. 'Never.'

'Oh my God, of course he wouldn't. I'm not serious!' The blue-haired girl held up her hands and the waitress saw the rumpled skin around her eyes and mouth and realised she wasn't young at all, she was just dressed young. She was a middle-aged person in disguise. From a distance you'd guess twenty; from close up, you'd think maybe forty. It felt like a trick.

'Mum and Dad have a really strong marriage,' said Brooke with an 'e', and something about the resentfully deferential pitch of her voice made the waitress think that in spite of her sensible clothes, she might be the youngest of the four.

The better-looking brother gave her a quizzical look. 'Did we grow up in the same house?'

'I don't know. Did we? Because I never saw any signs of violence . . . I mean, *God!*'

'Anyway, I'm not the one suggesting it. I'm saying *other* people might suggest it.'

The blue-haired woman looked up and caught sight of the waitress. 'Sorry! We still haven't looked!' She picked up the laminated menu.

'That's okay,' said the waitress. She wanted to hear more.

'Also, we're all a bit distracted. Our mother is missing.'

'Oh no. That's . . . worrying?' The waitress couldn't quite work out how to react. They didn't seem *that* worried. These people were, like, all a lot older than her – wouldn't their mother therefore be properly old? Like a little old lady? How did a little old lady go missing? Dementia?

Brooke with an 'e' winced. She said to her sister, 'Don't tell people that.'

'I apologise. Our mother is *possibly* missing,' amended the blue-haired woman. 'We have temporarily mislaid our mother.'

'You need to retrace your steps.' The waitress went along with the joke. 'Where did you see her last?'

There was an awkward pause. They all looked at her with identical liquid brown eyes and sober expressions. They all had the sort of eyelashes that were so dark they looked like they were wearing eyeliner.

'You know, you're right. That's exactly what we need to do.' The blue-haired woman nodded slowly as if she were taking the flippant remark seriously. 'Retrace our steps.'

'We'll all try the apple crumble with cream,' interrupted the expensive-version brother. 'And then we'll let you know what we think.'

'Good one.' The cheaper-version brother tapped the edge of his menu on the side of the table.

'For breakfast?' said Brooke with an 'e', but she smiled wryly as if at some private joke related to apple crumble and they all handed over their menus in the relieved, 'that's sorted, then' way that people handed back menus, glad to be rid of them.

The waitress wrote *4 x App Crum* on her notepad, and straightened the pile of menus.

'Listen,' said the cheaper-version brother. 'Has anyone called *her*?'

'Coffees?' asked the waitress.

'We'll all have long blacks,' said the expensive-version brother, and the waitress made eye contact with Brooke with an 'e' to give her the chance to say, No, actually, that's not my coffee, I always have an extra-large, extra-hot soy flat white, but she was busy turning on her brother. 'Of course we've called her. A million times. I've texted. I've emailed. Haven't you?'

'So four long blacks?' said the waitress.

No-one responded.

'Okay, so four long blacks.'

'Not Mum. *Her*.' The cheaper-version brother put his elbows on the table and pressed his fingertips to his temples. 'Savannah. Has anyone tried to get in contact with her?'

The waitress had no more excuses to linger and eavesdrop.

Was Savannah another sibling? Why wasn't she here today? Was she the family outcast? The prodigal daughter? Is that why her name seemed to land between them with such portentousness? And *had* anyone called her?

The waitress walked to the counter, hit the bell with the flat of her hand and slapped down their order.

chapter two

Last September

It was close to eleven on a chilly, breezy Tuesday night. Pale pink cherry blossoms skittered and whirled as the taxi drove slowly past renovated period homes, each with a mid-range luxury sedan in the driveway and an orderly trio of different-coloured wheelie bins at the kerb. A ring-tailed possum scuttled across a sandstone fence, caught in the taxi's headlights. A small dog yelped once and went quiet. The air smelled of wood smoke, cut grass and slow-cooked lamb. Most of the houses were dark except for the vigilant winking of security cameras.

Joy Delaney, at number nine, packed her dishwasher while she listened to the latest episode of *The Migraine Guy Podcast* on the fancy new wireless headphones her son had given her for her birthday.

Joy was a tiny, trim, energetic woman with shiny shoulder-length white hair. She could never remember if she was sixty-eight or sixty-nine, and sometimes she even allowed the possibility that she was sixty-seven. (She was sixty-nine.) Right now she wore jeans and a black cardigan over a striped t-shirt, with woolly socks. She supposedly looked 'great for her age'. Young people in shops often told her this. She always wanted to say, 'You don't know my age, you darling idiot, so how do you know I look great for it?'

Her husband, Stan Delaney, sat in his recliner in the living room, an icepack on each knee, watching a documentary about the world's greatest bridges while he worked his way through a packet of sweet chilli crackers, dipping each one into a tub of cream cheese.

Their elderly Staffordshire terrier, Steffi (named after Steffi Graf, because as a puppy she'd been quick on her feet), sat on the kitchen floor next to Joy chewing surreptitiously on a fragment of newspaper. Over the last year Steffi had begun obsessively chewing on any paper she could find in the house, which was apparently a psychological condition in dogs, possibly brought on by stress, although no-one knew what Steffi had to be stressed about.

At least Steffi's paper habit was more acceptable than that of her neighbour Caro's cat, Otis, who had begun pilfering clothing from homes in the cul-de-sac, including, mortifyingly, under-wear, which Caro was too embarrassed to return, except to Joy, of course.

Joy knew her giant headphones made her resemble an alien but she didn't care. After years of begging her children for quiet she now couldn't endure it. The silence howled through her so-called empty nest. Her nest had been empty for many years, so she should have been used to it, but last year they'd sold their business, and it felt like everything ended, juddered to a stop. In her search for noise, she'd become addicted to podcasts. Often she went to bed with her headphones still on so she could be rocked to sleep by the lullaby of a chatty, authoritative voice.

She didn't suffer from migraines herself, but her youngest daughter did, and Joy listened to *The Migraine Guy Podcast* both for informative tips she might be able to pass on to Brooke, and also as a kind of penance. Over recent years she had come to feel almost sick with regret for the dismissive, impatient way she'd first responded to Brooke's childhood headaches, as they used to call them.

'Regret' can be my memoir's theme, she thought, as she tried to shove the cheese grater into the dishwasher next to the frypan. *A Regretful Life*, by Joy Delaney.

Last night she'd been to the first session of a 'So You Want to Write a Memoir' course at the local evening college. Joy didn't want to write a memoir but Caro did, so she was keeping her company. Caro was widowed and shy and didn't want to go on her own. Joy would help Caro make a friend (she already had her eye on someone suitable) and then she'd drop out. Their teacher had explained that you began the process of writing a memoir by choosing a theme, and then it was simply a case of finding anecdotes to support the theme. 'Maybe your theme is "I grew up on the wrong side of the tracks but look at me now",' the teacher said, and all the ladies in their tailored pants and pearl earrings nodded solemnly and wrote *wrong side of the tracks* in their brand new notebooks.

'Well, at least your memoir's theme is obvious,' Caro told Joy on the way home.

'Is it?' said Joy.

'It's *tennis*. Your theme is tennis.'

'That's not a theme,' said Joy. 'A theme is more like "revenge" or "success against the odds" or –'

'You could call it *Game, Set and Match: The story of a tennis family*.'

'But that's . . . we're not tennis *stars*,' said Joy. 'We just ran a tennis school, and a local tennis club. We're not the Williams family.' For some reason she found Caro's comment annoying. Even upsetting.

Caro looked astonished. 'What are you talking about? Tennis is your family's passion. People are always saying, "Follow your passion!" And I think to myself, Oh, if only I had a passion. Like Joy.'

Joy had changed the subject.

Now she looked up from the dishwasher and remembered Troy, as a young boy, standing right here in this very kitchen, racquet gripped like a weapon, face rosy with rage, his beautiful brown eyes full of blame and tears he would not let himself cry, shouting, 'I *hate* tennis!'

'Ooh, sacrilege!' Amy had said, because her role as the oldest child was to narrate every family argument and use big words the other kids didn't understand, while Brooke, still little and adorable, had burst into inevitable tears, and Logan's face became blank and moronic.

'You don't hate tennis,' Joy had told him. It was an order. She had meant: *You* can't *hate tennis, Troy.* She'd meant: *I don't have the time or the strength to let you hate tennis.*

Joy gave her head a little shake to dislodge the memory, and tried to return her attention to the podcast.

'. . . *zigzag lines that float across your field of vision, shimmering spots or stars, people who have migraine aura symptoms say that . . .*'

Troy hadn't really hated tennis. Some of their happiest family memories were on the court. Most of their happiest memories. Some of their worst memories were on the court too, but come on now, Troy still *played*. If he'd really hated tennis he wouldn't still be playing in his thirties.

Was tennis her life's *theme*?

Maybe Caro was right. She and Stan might never have met if not for tennis.

More than half a century ago now. A birthday party in a small, crowded house. Heads bounced in time to 'Popcorn' by Hot Butter. Eighteen-year-old Joy gripped the chunky green stem of her wineglass, which was filled to the brim with warm moselle.

'Where's Joy? You should meet Joy. She just won some big tournament.'

Those were the words that unfastened the tight semicircle of people surrounding the boy with his back against the wall. He was a giant, freakishly tall and big-shouldered, with a mass of long curly black hair tied back in a ponytail, a cigarette in one hand, a can of beer in the other. Athletic boys could still smoke like chimneys in the seventies. He had a dimple that only made an appearance when he saw Joy.

'We should have a hit some time,' he said. She'd never heard a voice like it, not from a boy of her own generation. It was a voice so deep and slow, people made fun of it and tried to imitate it. They said Stan sounded like Johnny Cash. He didn't do it on purpose. It was just the way he spoke. He didn't speak much but everything he said sounded important.

They weren't the only tennis players at that party, just the only champions. It was destiny, as inevitable as a fairy tale. If they hadn't met that night they would have met eventually. Tennis was a small world.

They played their first match that weekend. She lost 6–4, 6–4, and then went right ahead and lost her virginity to him, even though her mother had warned her about the importance of withholding sex if she ever liked a boy: 'Why buy a cow when you can get the milk for free?' (Her daughters *shrieked* when they heard that phrase.)

Joy told Stan she only went to bed with him because of his serve. It was a *magnificent* serve. She still admired it, waiting for that split second when time stopped and Stan became a sculpture of a tennis player: back arched, ball suspended, racquet behind his head, and then . . . *wham*.

Stan said he only went to bed with her because of her decisive volley, and then he said, that deep slow voice in her ear, *No, that's not true, your volley needs work, you crowd the net, I went to bed with you because as soon as I saw those legs I knew I wanted them wrapped around my back*, and Joy swooned, she thought that was so wicked and poetic, although she did not appreciate the criticism of her volley.

'. . . *this causes the release of neurotransmitters . . .*'

She looked at the grater. It was covered in carrot, which the dishwasher wouldn't wash off. She rinsed it in the sink. 'Why am I doing your job for you?' she said to the dishwasher, and thought of herself in pre-dishwasher days, standing at this sink, rubber gloves in hot dishwater, a skyscraper of dirty plates by her side.

Her past kept bumping up against her present lately. Yesterday she'd woken from a nap in a panic, thinking she'd forgotten to pick up one of the children from school. It took her a good minute to remember that all of her children were adults now: adults with wrinkles and mortgages, degrees and travel plans.

It made her wonder if she had dementia. Her friend Linda, who worked at a nursing home, said a wave of restlessness swept through the place at school pick-up time each day as the elderly ladies became agitated, convinced they should be rushing to collect long-since-grown children. Hearing that had made Joy teary, and now the exact same thing had kind of happened to her.

'It's possible my superior intellect is masking my dementia symptoms,' Joy had told Stan.

'Can't say I've noticed,' said Stan.

'My dementia symptoms? Or my superior intellect?'

'Well, you've always been demented,' he'd said, and then wandered off, probably to climb a ladder, because his sons had informed him that seventy was too old to climb ladders, so he liked to find excuses to climb them as often as possible.

Last night she'd listened to a very informative podcast called *This Dementia Life*.

The cheese grater refused to join the frypan in the dishwasher. She studied the two items. It felt like a puzzle she should be able to solve.

'. . . *trigger a change in the size of the blood vessels* . . .' said the Migraine Guy.

What? She was going to have to rewind this podcast and start again.

She'd heard that retirement caused a rapid decline in brain function. Maybe that's what was going on here. Her frontal lobe was atrophying.

They had thought they were ready to retire. Selling the tennis school had seemed like the obvious next step in their lives. They couldn't keep coaching forever and none of their children were interested in taking on the business. In fact, they were insultingly disinterested. For years Stan had nursed a wild hope that Logan might buy into Delaneys: that old-fashioned idea of the eldest son becoming his proud successor. 'Logan was a great coach,' he'd mutter. 'He got it. He really *got* it.'

Poor Logan had looked completely aghast when Stan had diffidently suggested he might like to buy the business. 'He's not very *driven*, is he?' Stan had remarked to Joy, and Joy had snapped at him because she couldn't bear to hear criticism of her children, especially when that criticism was valid.

So they sold up. To good people for a good price. She hadn't anticipated this sense of loss. She hadn't realised how much they were defined by Delaneys Tennis Academy. Who *were* they now? Just another pair of boomers.

Thank God for their own tennis. Their most recent trophy sat, heavy and proud, on the sideboard, ready to show off when everyone was together on Father's Day. Stan's knees were paying for it now, but it had been a good solid win over two technically excellent players: she and Stan had held the net, attacked the middle and never lost their cool. They still had it.

In addition to tournaments, they still played in the Monday night social comp that Joy had established years ago, although that had recently got depressing because people kept dying. Six months ago Dennis Christos had died on the court while he and his wife, Debbie, played against Joy and Stan, which had been terribly traumatic. Joy believed poor Dennis's heart couldn't take the excitement of thinking he was going to break Stan's serve. She secretly blamed Stan for making Dennis think it was a possibility. He'd *deliberately* let the game get to love–40 for his own pleasure. It was taking a lot of willpower for her not to say, 'You killed Dennis Christos, Stan.'

The truth was, she and Stan weren't suited to retirement. Their six-week dream holiday to Europe had been a disaster.

Even Wimbledon. Especially Wimbledon. When the plane landed back in Sydney they'd both been giddy with relief, and they'd admitted that to no-one, not to their friends or their children, not even to each other.

Sometimes they tried to do things that their other retired friends did, like 'a lovely day at the beach', for example. Joy cut her foot to shreds standing on an oyster shell and they got a parking ticket. It had reminded her of those occasions when she had got it into her head that she and Stan would take the children on a *lovely picnic*, and she'd tried so hard to pretend they were a lovely picnicking family but something inevitably went wrong, there was always someone in a bad mood, or they got lost, or it rained just as they arrived and the drive home was silent and resentful, except for the regular sniffles of whichever child felt he or she had been unjustifiably admonished.

'We've actually become quite *romantic* since retirement,' one annoyingly chipper friend told her, which made Joy want to gag, but the other week she bought two banana milkshakes at the food court, as a kind of fun gesture because she and Stan used to buy them for breakfast at small-town milk bars when they used to travel together for regional tournaments in the early years of their marriage. They'd save on motels by sleeping in the car. They had sex in the back seat.

But it was clear that Stan didn't even *remember* their banana milkshakes, and then on the way home he dramatically and unnecessarily slammed on the brakes when someone pulled out in front of them, and Joy's milkshake went flying, so their car now permanently and disgustingly smelled of sour milk: the sour smell of failure. Stan said he couldn't smell a thing.

They needed different personalities to retire with grace and verve like their friends. They needed to be less grumpy (Stan did) and have a wider variety of interests and hobbies beyond tennis. They needed grandchildren.

Grandchildren.

The word alone filled her with the kind of giant, complicated

16

emotions reserved for the young: desire, fury and worst of all, spiteful, bitter envy.

She knew one tiny grandchild was all it would take to stop the silence roaring, to make her days splutter back to life again, but you could not ask your children for grandchildren. How demeaning. How ordinary. She believed herself to be more interesting and sophisticated than that. She was a feminist. An athlete. A very successful businesswoman. She refused to be that particular cliché.

It would happen. She just had to be patient. She had four children. Four tickets in the raffle, although two of her four children were single so perhaps they didn't count as tickets just yet. But two were in solid, long-term relationships. Logan and his girlfriend, Indira, had been together for five years now. They weren't married but that didn't matter. Indira was wonderful and the last time Joy saw her, she definitely had a mysterious, secretive look about her, almost as if she wanted to tell Joy something but was holding off: maybe until she got to twelve weeks?

Brooke and Grant were happily married, settled with a mortgage on a proper house and a family car, and Grant was older, so it could be on the cards soon. If only Brooke hadn't opened up her own physiotherapy practice. It was admirable – Stan *glowed* with pride whenever anyone mentioned it – but running your own business was stressful, and migraine sufferers had to manage their stress. Brooke was *too* driven. But surely she'd want a baby soon. Brooke always knew the latest medical guidelines so she would know you shouldn't leave it too late.

Joy secretly hoped her children might find a creative way to tell her about their pregnancies, like other people's children were always doing on YouTube. They could, for example, wrap up an ultrasound picture, and then film Joy's reaction as she opened it: bewilderment followed by understanding, hand clapped across her mouth, tears and hugs. They could post it on their social media! *Joy finds out she's going to be a grandma!* It might go viral.

Joy dressed extra nicely every time her children visited, just in case.

(She would never share that fantasy with anyone. Not even the dog.)

The Migraine Guy spoke seductively into Joy's ears: '*Let's talk about magnesium.*'

'Good idea. Let's do that,' said Joy.

There was no way for the frypan and grater to fit together. There was no solution. The grater would have to miss out. It was clean anyway. She straightened up from the dishwasher to discover her husband standing right in front of her, like he'd teleported himself.

'Jesus – bloody – what the –?' she shrieked.

She pushed her headphones down onto her neck and put her hand to her thumping heart. 'Don't creep up on me like that!'

'Why is someone knocking on the door?' Stan's lips were orange from the chilli crackers. There were damp circles on the knees of his jeans from the melting icepacks. It was aggravating just to look up at him, especially because he was looking down at her with an accusing expression, as if the knock on the door was her fault.

Steffi sat herself down next to Stan, ears pricked and alert, eyes shining with the glorious possibility of a walk.

Joy's eyes went to the clock on the kitchen wall. It was far too late for a delivery or a market researcher. Too late for a friend or family member to drop by, and no-one really did that anymore, not without calling first.

Joy considered her husband. Maybe *he* was the one with dementia. She knew from her research that the spouse must be patient and kind.

'I didn't hear anything,' she said, patiently and kindly. She would be an excellent carer, although she might waitlist him at a nice nursing home sooner rather than later.

'I heard a knock,' insisted Stan, and his jaw shifted back and forth in that way that indicated annoyance.

But then Joy heard it too: *thump, thump, thump.*

Like someone banging a closed fist on their front door. Their doorbell had been broken for years and people often knocked impatiently after they gave up on the bell, but this had the quality of an emergency.

Her eyes met Stan's and without saying a word they both headed for the front door, not running but walking fast down the long hallway, quick, quick, quick. Steffi trotted along beside them, panting with excitement. Joy's socks slipped on the floorboards and she felt that all three of them, man, woman and dog, shared an invigorating sense of urgency. They were needed. There must be a crisis of some sort. They would fix the crisis, because even though there were no children living at home, they still had that mindset: *We are the grown-ups. We are The Fixers.*

Maybe there was even pleasure in that rapid walk to the door because it had been a while since any of the children had asked for money or advice, or even a lift to the airport.

Bang, bang, bang.

'Coming!' called out Stan.

Fragments of memories flashed through Joy's mind: Troy arriving home from school when he was around eight or nine, hammering on the door and hollering, *'FBI! Open up!'* He did this for years every time he came to a door, thought he was so funny. Amy frantically ringing the bell, back when it worked, because she'd lost her house key yet again and was always in a hurry to get to the bathroom.

Stan got there ahead of her. He *click-clacked* the deadlock with an efficient twist of his wrist and threw open the door.

A sobbing young woman lurched forward as though she'd been resting her forehead on the door and fell straight into Stan's arms, like a daughter.

chapter three

'Hello there,' said Stan, stunned. He clumsily patted her shoulder.

For the first fraction of a second Joy assumed it *was* one of their daughters, but this girl barely came up to Stan's chest. Joy's children were tall: the boys were six foot four, Amy was six foot and Brooke was six foot one. They were all broad-shouldered, dark-haired, olive-skinned, scarlet-cheeked and dimpled, like their father. ('Your children all look like giant Spanish matadors,' Joy's mother used to say, chidingly, as if Joy had picked them off a shelf.)

This girl was petite, with straggly dirty-blonde hair and blue-veined mottled white skin.

'I'm sorry.' The girl stood back, took a shuddery breath, sniffed and tried to arrange her mouth into the shape of a smile. 'I'm *so* sorry. How embarrassing.'

She had a fresh, deep cut just beneath her right eyebrow. Trails of shiny-wet blood trickled down her face.

'It's fine, darling.' Joy took a firm hold of the girl's stick-thin upper arm in case she fainted.

She would call her 'darling' until she remembered her name. Stan would be no help. She could sense his eyes trying to meet hers: *Who the heck is this?*

The girl had a tiny seed-like piercing in her nose and a tattoo of a green vine curled around her pale forearm. She wore a threadbare long-sleeved shirt with a spatter of old grease stains on the front and ripped blue jeans. There was a silver key on a chain around her neck. Her bare feet were purple with cold. She was vaguely, blurrily, not-quite familiar.

It would be helpful if the girl said her name, but young people always assumed that they'd be remembered. It happened all the time. A young stranger would make a beeline for them, waving delightedly: 'Mr and Mrs Delaney! How *are* you? It's been ages!' Joy would have to bluff her way through the conversation while simultaneously flicking through her mental database: A tennis kid? A club member's grown-up child? One of the children's friends?

'What happened to you?' Stan gestured at the girl's eye. He looked frightened, suddenly elderly. 'Is someone out there?' He peered over her shoulder onto the street. It would never have occurred to Joy that there would be someone out there.

'There's no-one out there,' said the girl. 'I came in a cab.'

'It's okay, sweetheart, we'll get you fixed up,' said Joy.

This was very confusing but it would all become clear. Stan always wanted everything instantly clarified.

Joy guessed the girl to be in her late twenties, the same age as Brooke, but she didn't look like one of Brooke's friends, who were busy, polite young women with a lot on their minds. This girl had the grungy look that Amy favoured, so it seemed most likely she was one of Amy's friends. This made it difficult, because Amy moved in a variety of eclectic circles. Someone from that amateur theatre group Amy had been so enthusiastic about for at least a week? A university friend? From her first abandoned degree? Second?

'How did you hurt yourself?' asked Joy.

'My boyfriend and I got in an argument,' said the girl. She swayed and pressed the heel of her hand to her bloody eye. 'I just ran out of the apartment onto the street and jumped in a cab . . .'

'Your *boyfriend* did this to you?' said Stan. 'You mean he hit you?'

'Sort of,' said the girl.

'Sort of? What does that mean?' said Stan. The man could be so *abrasive* at times. 'Did he hit you or not?'

'It's complicated,' said the girl.

'No, it's not. If you've been assaulted, we should call the police,' said Stan.

'*No.*' The girl shifted from Joy's grip. 'No way. I don't want the police involved.'

'We don't need to call the police, darling, not if you don't want,' said Joy. 'It's your choice. But come and sit down.'

If the girl didn't want to call the police then that was fine with her. She didn't want police here.

As they passed under one of the hallway downlights, Joy saw that the girl was older than she'd first thought. Maybe her early thirties? *Think, think, think.*

Could she be one of the boys' ex-girlfriends? There had been a few years where it had been hard to keep track of all the young girls sashaying about their house. Both boys had long-term relationships with tanned blonde girls in white sneakers called Tracey. Stan could never tell which Tracey was which. Both Traceys ended up crying at Joy's kitchen table on separate occasions while Joy chopped onions and murmured comfortingly. Logan's Tracey still sent Christmas cards.

But this girl didn't look like one of the girlfriends. Troy went for glossy princesses and Logan went for sexy librarians and this girl was neither.

'Then I realised I didn't have any money,' said the girl as they walked into the kitchen, and she stopped and tipped back her head to study the high ceiling as if it were a cathedral. Joy followed her gaze as it travelled around the room to the sideboard crammed with framed family photos and ornaments, including the pair of horrible sneering china cats that had belonged to Stan's mother, and lingered on the bowl of fresh fruit sitting on the table: shiny red apples and bright yellow bananas. Was the child hungry? She was welcome to all the bananas. Joy didn't know why she kept buying them. It was as if they were for display purposes only. Most ended up mushy-soft and black and then she felt ashamed throwing them away.

'I was just completely empty-handed. No wallet, no phone, no money: nothing.'

'Sit down, darling.' Joy pulled out a chair at the kitchen table.

Stan had stopped barking questions, thank goodness. He silently took down the first-aid kit from its place in the cupboard above the refrigerator where Joy couldn't reach it without standing on a chair. He put it on the table and opened the lid because Joy always struggled with the stiff lock. Then he went to the sink and got the girl a glass of water.

'Let's take a look at this.' Joy put on her glasses. 'Is it very painful?'

'Oh, it's fine. I have a high pain threshold.' The girl lifted the glass of water with a shaky hand and drank. Her fingernails were ragged. A nail biter. Amy used to be a terrible nail biter. The chill of the cold night air radiated off the girl's skin as Joy cleaned the wound with antiseptic.

'So you realised you didn't have your purse,' prompted Joy as Stan sat down, put his elbows on the tabletop, clasped his hands together and rubbed his nose against his knuckles, frowning heavily.

'Yeah, so I was freaking out, thinking, how am I going to pay the fare, and the driver wasn't one of those friendly cabbies, you know, I could just tell, he looked like he could be the type to be mean, even aggressive. So we were just *driving* randomly, and –'

'Driving randomly?' interrupted Stan. 'But what destination did you give the driver when you got in the cab?'

Joy shot him a look. Sometimes he didn't realise how he could come across to people.

'I didn't give him an address. I wasn't thinking. I said, "Head north." I was trying to buy myself time while I worked out where to go.'

'Did the driver not even notice you were hurt?' asked Joy. 'He should have taken you straight to the nearest hospital without charging you a cent!'

'If he did notice, he didn't want to know about it.'

Joy shook her head sadly. People these days.

'But anyway, then, for some reason, I don't know why, something made me do it, I put my hand in the pocket of my jeans and I couldn't believe it! I pulled out a twenty-dollar note! It was so random! I never find money like that!'

The girl's face lit up with childlike pleasure as she remembered the moment she'd found the money.

'Someone was looking out for you,' said Joy. She cut a piece of gauze from the roll.

'Yeah, I know, so as the fare got closer to twenty dollars, I started giving the cabbie random directions. Like, turn left. Second right. I don't know, I was kind of delirious. I was just following my nose. Wait. Did I make that up? Following your nose. It sounds funny now I say it. How do you follow your nose?'

The girl looked up at Joy.

'No, that's right,' said Joy. She tapped her own nose. 'Following your nose.'

She looked over at Stan. He was pulling on his lower lip the way he did when he disapproved of something. He never followed his nose anywhere. You need a game plan, kid. You don't just hit the ball and hope to win, you *plan* how you're going to win.

'The moment the fare clicked over to twenty dollars I shouted, "Stop!" And I just got out of the car. It's so cold outside tonight, I didn't realise!' The girl shivered convulsively. 'And I've got bare feet.' She lifted her dirty foot and pointed at her toes. 'I was just standing there in the gutter. My feet felt like blocks of ice. I thought, You idiot, you stupid, *stupid* idiot, what now? And then I started to feel dizzy and I looked at the houses and yours seemed the friendliest, and the lights were on, so . . .' She tugged on the sleeves of her shirt. 'So here I am.'

Joy paused, the gauze midair. 'So . . . but . . . so are you saying, we don't, you don't . . .' She tried to think of a more elegant way to put it, but couldn't. 'You don't know us?'

She saw now that she'd been kidding herself thinking the girl was familiar. She was only familiar in the way everyone seemed familiar these days. They'd just let a stranger into the house.

She checked for signs of criminal tendencies and found none, although she wasn't exactly sure how those tendencies would manifest themselves. The nose stud was really quite pretty. (Amy had the most dreadful *lip* piercing a few years back, so Joy wasn't too concerned by a nose piercing.) A tattoo of a leafy green vine wasn't exactly intimidating. She seemed fine. A bit flaky perhaps. But she was sweet. This girl couldn't be dangerous. She was too small. As dangerous as a mouse.

'You didn't have any friends or family you could go to?' asked Stan.

Joy gave him another look. It was true she wanted to ask the same question but there had to be a nicer way.

'We've only just moved down here from the Gold Coast,' said the girl. 'I don't know a single person in Sydney.'

Imagine, thought Joy. You're all alone, without money, in a strange city and you can't go back home, what *can* you do except throw yourself on the mercy of strangers? She couldn't imagine herself in the same situation. She had always been cushioned by people.

Stan said, 'Do you . . . maybe want to call someone? Your family?'

'There isn't really anyone . . . available, right now.' The girl lowered her head, so that Joy could see her poor defenceless thin white neck between the clumpy strands of her hair.

'Look up at me, darling.' Joy pressed the gauze over the cut. 'Finger there.' She guided the girl's hand to the gauze, taped it in place with a strip of adhesive, and sighed with satisfaction. 'There you go. All fixed.'

'Thank you.' The girl looked at Joy with clear pale green eyes framed by the fairest eyelashes Joy had ever seen. They looked like they'd been dusted with gold. Joy's children all had those dark matador eyelashes. Joy herself had very ordinary eyelashes.

The girl was unexpectedly pretty now that the blood had been cleared up. So pretty, and so very skinny and dirty and tired. Joy felt an overwhelming desire to feed her, run her a bath and put her to bed.

'I'm Savannah,' said the girl, and she held out her hand for Joy to shake.

'Savannah. That's a pretty name,' said Joy. 'I have a friend called Hannah. Quite similar! Well, not that similar. *Savannah*. Where do I know that name from? I know, I think Princess Anne has a granddaughter called Savannah. She's a cute little girl, a bit wicked! I don't think she's Princess Savannah, I don't think she has a title at all. Not that you'd be interested in that. I've just always had a special interest in the Royal Family. I follow them on Instagram.'

She couldn't seem to stop talking. It happened when she felt upset or shocked, and she realised that she possibly did feel a little upset and shocked, right now, by the blood and the story of violence she'd just heard. She saw she was still holding the girl's small icy-cold hand, and gave it a quick comforting squeeze before releasing it.

'There's another Savannah I'm thinking of, besides the royal one, I'm sure there is . . . Oh, I know! My youngest daughter, Brooke, has a friend who just had a baby, and I'm ninety per cent sure she called her Savannah, or it could have been Samantha.'

She remembered the baby's name was actually Poppy, which was nothing at all like Savannah or Samantha, so that was embarrassing, but no need to mention it. 'Brooke herself isn't ready to have a baby yet, because she's started her own physiotherapy practice, which is exciting.'

Not exciting at all, infuriating, but as her grandfather used to say, 'Never spoil a good story with the facts.'

'She's very busy focusing on that. It's called Delaney's Physiotherapy. I have a card somewhere. She's really very good. Brooke, I mean. My daughter. Very calm and patient. It's interesting because we never thought –'

'Joy,' interrupted Stan. 'Take a breath.'

'We never thought we'd have anyone medical in our family . . .' Joy trailed off. She put her hand to her neck and felt the headphones that were still sitting there like a giant statement necklace. 'I was listening to a podcast,' she explained, idiotically. In fact, she could hear the tinny disembodied voice of her podcast host, still chatting obliviously on, unaware that Joy was no longer listening.

'I like podcasts,' said Savannah.

'We never said *our* names! I'm Joy!' Joy switched the headphones off and put them on the table. 'And this is my grumpy husband, Stan.'

'Thank you for fixing me up, Joy.' Savannah gestured at her bandaged face. 'Even though you're not a medical family I think you did a tip-top job!'

Tip-top. What a funny word. A blast from the past.

'Oh, well, thank you,' said Joy. 'I never – well.' She made herself stop talking.

'I had a good feeling about this house.' Savannah looked around her. 'As soon as I saw it. It just felt very warm and safe.'

'It is safe,' said Joy. She avoided looking at her husband. 'Would you like something to eat, Savannah? Are you hungry? Have a banana! Or I have leftovers from dinner I could heat up.' She didn't give the girl time to accept the offer before she rushed into the next. 'And then you'll stay the night, of course.'

She was so glad her cleaning lady, Good Old Barb, had been today and that together they'd vacuumed and dusted Amy's old bedroom.

'Oh,' said Savannah. She looked uneasily over at Stan and then back again at Joy. 'I don't know about that. I could just . . .'

But it was clear there was nowhere else for her to go at this time of night and there was no way in the world that Joy was sending this tiny barefoot girl back out into the cold.

chapter four

Now

'We're trying to track down that girl who stayed with Mum and Dad last year.'

The beauty therapist, dressed in immaculate white, knelt at her client's enormous feet as she gently guided them into a footbath filled with warm scented water, floating rose petals and smooth oval-shaped pebbles manufactured to look like they came from a mountain stream.

'She turned up on their doorstep. Late one night.'

The client, who was booked in for the Deluxe Power Pedicure, 'a luxury experience for the busy executive', wiggled his feet against the stones and kept talking, fortunately at an acceptable volume. He'd politely asked the beauty therapist if she minded if he made some calls while he had his pedicure. Most people just started randomly shouting.

'She's probably got nothing to do with it,' he said. 'We're just calling everyone Mum knows.'

The client's phone was in the pocket of his slouchy soft white shirt. He wore AirPods. The therapist's dad said people wearing AirPods looked like peanuts. (Her dad had recently turned fifty and it was cute the way he thought his opinions still had value.)

The client didn't look like a peanut. He was very attractive.

'It's just strange for Mum not to be in touch for this long. Normally she calls me back within two minutes all breathless and horrified that she missed the call.'

The beauty therapist scrubbed apricot kernel exfoliator into the heel of his right foot in hard vigorous circles.

'I know, but it's not like she disappeared without a word. She texted us all on Valentine's Day.' He paused. 'I'll tell you exactly what it said. Hold on a sec.'

He scrolled through his phone with his thumb. 'Here it is.' He read out loud, '"Going OFF-GRID for a little while! I'm dancing daffodils 21 dog champagne to end Czechoslovakia! Spangle Moot! Love, Mum." Heart emoji. Butterfly emoji. Flower emoji. Smiley face emoji. "Off-grid" was in capitals.'

The beauty therapist's mother used a lot of emojis in her texts too. Mothers loved emojis. She wondered what all that 'dancing daffodils' stuff could possibly mean.

'It just means she was texting without her glasses,' said the client to the person on the phone, who must have been wondering the same thing. 'Her texts are always filled with weird random phrases.'

The beauty therapist tried to massage his calf muscle. It was like trying to massage granite. He must be a runner.

'Yeah,' he said. 'I'm going over there now to talk to Dad to see if I can find out more, not that he'll tell *me* anything –'

At that moment his foot gave a sudden spasm, the toes splayed at an unnatural angle.

'*Cramp!*' he cried. The beauty therapist swerved her head just in the nick of time.

chapter five

Last September

Joy closed their bedroom door with a gentle, apologetic click, as if Savannah would overhear and know they were only closing it because she was there. They had always slept with their door wide open throughout their married life: so that small anxious children could hurtle straight into their bed after nightmares, so that they could hear teenagers crashing through the house, drunk but thankfully home alive, so that they could rush to administer medication, advice, comfort, so that they could leap from their beds each morning and run straight into the action of their busy, important lives.

Once, closing the bedroom door had been a signal that someone thought sex might be a good idea. Now it was a signal that they had a guest.

An unexpected guest.

Savannah was hopefully warm and comfortable in Amy's old bedroom, wearing an old pair of Amy's pyjamas. Amy, their eldest, their 'free spirit' as Joy liked to call her, their 'problem child' as Stan liked to call her, was turning forty next year, and she hadn't officially lived at home for two decades, but she still used her old bedroom as a kind of permanent storage unit, because she never seemed to settle at one address long enough to properly relocate her possessions. It was admittedly strange behaviour for a nearly forty-year-old, and there had been a time when Joy and Stan had talked about putting their foot down, and friends had suggested they should do so, as if it were possible to use sheer force of will to mould Amy into a regular person. Amy was Amy, and right now she had a job and a phone number, her fingernails were generally clean and her hair (albeit currently dyed blue) did not look like it was crawling with lice, and that was all Joy wanted from her, although it would be nice if she combed her hair occasionally.

'Is she in bed?' asked Stan as he came out of the bathroom, wearing boxers and a V-necked white t-shirt, from which sprang white chest hair. He was still a big, muscly, overbearing man, but he always looked vulnerable to Joy in his pyjamas.

'I think so,' said Joy. 'She seemed sleepy after her bath.'

She had insisted on running a bath for Savannah. The taps were tricky to manage. She'd added some of the peach-scented bubble bath someone had given her for Mother's Day, and laid out two of the fluffiest guest towels she could find, and it had been so pleasing to see Savannah come out of the bathroom, pink-cheeked and yawning, the tips of her hair wet, Amy's dressing-gown trailing on the floor behind her.

Joy could hear the rounded notes of contentment in her voice. It was the long-ago primal satisfaction of feeding and bathing a hungry, tired, compliant child, and then tucking that clean, pyjama-clad child straight into bed.

'Amy's dressing-gown was so *long* –' Joy stopped. What the heck? Her mouth dropped.

'Oh my word,' she said. 'You didn't.'

A pile of random objects was crammed, higgledy-piggledy, on top of their chest of drawers: Stan's ancient laptop that she was pretty sure was broken, her iPad that she never touched, their desktop computer, *including* the monitor, their ten-year-old television, a calculator, and an old jar of twenty-cent coins that probably had a total value of ten dollars, if that.

'I'm just being cautious,' said Stan defensively. 'We don't know anything about her. She could rob us blind in the night and we'd feel like real dickheads calling the police in the morning. "Oh yes, that's right, Officer, we fed her dinner, ran her a bubble bath, put her to bed, and lo and behold, we woke up this morning and all our worldly possessions have gone."'

'I can't believe you crept around the house unplugging all our worldly possessions.' She ran her fingers over the snarl of dusty electrical cords that dangled off the chest of drawers.

Oh my Lord, there was his precious laminator, which Troy got him last Christmas, thus beginning Stan's obsession with laminating anything he could find: instructions for using the TV remote (admittedly helpful), the article in the local paper about the sale of Delaneys, inspiring sporting quotes he printed out from the internet and wanted to remember. He'd laminate Joy if he got the chance.

'Wait, is that the DVD player? Stan. She wouldn't take the DVD player. No-one uses DVD players anymore.'

'We do,' said Stan.

'People her age don't watch DVDs,' said Joy. 'They all stream.'

'You don't even know what streaming means,' said Stan.

'I do so,' said Joy. She went into the bathroom to clean her teeth. 'It's just watching Netflix on TV, isn't it? Isn't that what streaming means?'

He had no right to pretend he had superior knowledge about technology. He was a man who didn't own a mobile phone, as a matter of principle and stubborn pride. He loved it when people were shocked to discover he had never owned one, never *would* own one. He truly believed it made him morally superior, which drove Joy bananas because, excuse me, he was not. The way he talked about his 'stance' on mobile phones, you would think he were the lone person in the crowd not giving the Nazi salute.

Before their retirement he told people, 'I don't need a phone, I'm a tennis coach, not a surgeon. There are no tennis emergencies.' There were *so* tennis emergencies, and more than once over the years she'd been furious when she couldn't contact him, and she was left in a tricky situation that would have been instantly solved if he'd owned a phone. Also, his principles didn't prevent him from happily picking up the landline and calling Joy on *her* mobile when she was at the shops, to ask how much longer she'd be, or to please buy more chilli crackers, but when Stan was gone, *he was gone*, and if she thought about that too much and all it implied she could tap into a great well of rage, so she didn't think about it.

That was the secret of a happy marriage: step away from the rage.

She put on her nicest pyjamas seeing as there was a guest in the house and hopped into bed next to Stan. Her movements felt theatrical, as if she were being observed. They lay in silence for a few moments, flat on their backs, the quilt tucked under their elbows, like good children waiting for bedtime stories. The light was out, their lamps were on. There was a framed wedding photo on Joy's bedside table. Most of the time she looked right through it as though it were a piece of furniture but sometimes, without warning, she could glance at it and feel the exact moment the photo was taken: the scratchy lacy neckline of her dress, Stan's hand insistently, inappropriately low on her back, the casual expectation that this wild happiness would always be instantly available, because she'd got the boy, the boy with the deep voice and huge serve, and next would come trophies, babies, picnics and fancy restaurants on special occasions, maybe a dog. Everything at that time had rippled with sex: tennis, training, food, the very clouds in the sky.

For years she'd been so confused when people talked about knowing the day their babies were conceived. How could they possibly know? She'd blissfully, adorably believed that all couples had sex every day.

She knew the exact day that her youngest daughter was conceived.

By then she got it.

Joy waited for Stan to pick up his book or turn on the radio or turn off the light, but he didn't do any of those things, so she decided he was up for a chat.

'I'm glad I had that leftover chicken casserole to give her. She seemed starving.'

Savannah had eaten like a wartime refugee. Halfway through her meal she'd begun to cry – great convulsive sobs, but even as the tears streamed down her face, she'd continued to eat. It had been unsettling and distressing to watch. Then she'd eaten not one, but *two* bananas!

'It wasn't an especially good casserole. It needed more . . . flavour, I guess.' Joy always overcooked chicken. She had a terror of salmonella. 'I've still got enough left to give some to Steffi for breakfast.'

Joy preferred not to embarrass Steffi by offering her dog food as Steffi didn't appear to know she was a dog. She chatted at length with Joy each morning after breakfast, making strange, elongated whining sounds that Joy knew were her sadly unintelligible attempts at English. The one time they'd taken her to the local dog park, Steffi had been appalled and sat at their feet with an expression of frozen hauteur on her face, as if she were a society lady at McDonald's.

Stan punched his pillow and settled it behind his head. 'Steffi would prefer a copy of the *Sydney Morning Herald* for breakfast.'

'She makes me think of the little match girl,' mused Joy.

'Steffi?'

'No, Savannah.'

After a moment Stan said, 'Remind me who the little match girl is? What match are we talking about? Did she win?'

Joy snorted. 'It's a fairy tale about a little girl trying to sell matches on a freezing night. My mother used to read it to me. I think the little girl freezes to death in the end.'

'Trust your mother to pick a fairy tale with a corpse at the end.'

'I *loved* that story,' said Joy.

Stan reached for his reading glasses and book. He wasn't a reader, but he was trying to read this novel Amy had given him for Christmas because she kept asking, 'What do you think of the book, Dad?' Stan had confided to Joy that he had to keep starting again because he couldn't make any sense of it.

'It's horrible to think of her boyfriend hurting her like that,' said Joy. 'Just horrible. Imagine if that was one of our girls.'

He didn't answer, and she kicked herself for suggesting he imagine his own daughters in a situation like that. When Stan was fourteen, he'd witnessed his father throw his mother across the room, knocking her unconscious. It was, supposedly, the first and only time his father had done anything like that, but it must have been a terrible thing for a teenage boy to see. Stan refused to talk about his father. If the children ever asked questions about their grandfather he'd say, 'I can't remember.' Eventually they'd stopped asking.

Stan said, 'Our girls are athletes, and they grew up with brothers. They'd never put up with it.'

'I don't think it works like that,' said Joy. 'It starts out small. You put up with little things in a relationship and then . . . the little things gradually get bigger.'

He didn't answer, and her words floated for too long above their bed. *You put up with little things . . . and then the little things gradually get bigger.*

'Like the frog getting boiled to death,' said Stan.

'What?' Joy heard herself sound a little screechy.

Stan kept looking at his book. He flipped a page in the wrong direction and for a moment she thought he wasn't going to answer her, but then he said, his eyes on the page, 'You know that theory: if you put a frog in warm water and keep slowly turning up the heat, it doesn't jump out because it doesn't realise it's slowly being boiled to death.'

'I'm sure that's an urban myth. I'll Google it.' She reached for her phone and glasses.

'Google it quietly,' said Stan. 'I need to focus. This bloke just spent *three* pages yabbering on about his memory of someone's smile.'

'Let me read it,' said Joy. 'I'll summarise it. Give you the gist.'

'That's cheating,' said Stan.

'It's not a test,' sighed Joy, but Stan seemed to think it was a test, set by Amy, to prove his love. There had been a lot of tests set by Amy over the years to prove their love.

Joy didn't bother to Google the poor boiling frog. She flicked through her text messages and thought about texting one or all of the children to let them know that a stray girl had turned up on their doorstep, but she had a feeling this news might be met with disapproval or even dismay. Since they'd sold the tennis school, their children had become increasingly vocal about how they thought Joy and Stan should be leading their lives. They dropped suggestions about package holidays, retirement villages, cruises, multivitamins and sudoku. Joy tolerated this intervention while never once mentioning the conspicuous lack of grandchildren in her life.

There was one new text from Caro sent earlier in the night: *Have you done your homework?* She meant the memoir-writing course homework. They had to do an 'elevator pitch' where they wrote their life story in just a few paragraphs. She would have to do it, even though she wasn't going to complete the course. She didn't want to hurt that peppy little teacher's peppy little feelings.

No point answering Caro now; she'd be asleep. Savannah would never have chosen *Caro's* house as a safe haven because all the lights went off reliably at nine pm each night.

Instead, Joy clicked on an article that her phone predicted would 'interest her': *Forty Sweet Father/Son Moments between Prince William and Prince George.*

She was on the seventh sweet moment between Prince William and Prince George when Stan gave up on the book with a heavy sigh and picked up his iPad, which Troy had given him as a birthday present a few months back. Everyone assumed Stan wouldn't use it on principle because wasn't an iPad pretty close to an iPhone? But apparently not. Stan loved the iPad as much as he loved his laminator. He read the news on his iPad every day because he could make the font nice and big, which he couldn't do with a newspaper. Troy was inordinately pleased by the success of his present. It was important to him to always win the competition for best gift.

Joy looked over Stan's shoulder to see what he was reading and scrolled through the same news site on her phone, so she would have read the same articles and would be prepared to set him straight if he attempted to set her straight on a particular issue.

'Stop mansplaining, Dad,' Amy once said at a family dinner.

'He's Stan-splaining,' Joy had said, and that got a good laugh.

Her thumb stopped.

That specific combination of letters was so familiar it jumped out from the screen as if were her own name: *Harry Haddad*.

She waited. It took ages. She wondered if he was going to miss it. But then, finally, his body went still.

'You see this?' He held up the iPad. 'About Harry?'

'Yes,' said Joy. She kept her tone neutral. It was important to maintain the pretence that their former star student, Harry Haddad, was not a touchy subject, not at all, and that she wasn't trying to change the subject or, God forbid, offer comfort or sympathy. 'Just saw it then.'

'I knew it,' said Stan. 'I knew this day would come. I knew he wasn't done.'

'Did you?' If this were true, which Joy doubted, he'd never once mentioned it, but she didn't say that. 'Huh. Well. That's going to be very . . . interesting.'

She waited a moment and then carefully placed her phone facedown on her bedside table, next to her headphones. Her glittery metallic phone case, also a gift from Troy, shimmered like a disco ball under the bedside lamp.

She yawned. It started out fake and ended up genuine. She stretched her arms above her head. Stan turned off his iPad and took off his glasses.

'I wonder what time Savannah will wake up,' she said as she switched off her light and turned on her side. Thank God this poor young girl had chosen to knock on their door, tonight of all nights. She would be a distraction from Harry bloody Haddad. 'Did she seem like a morning person to you?'

Stan said nothing. He put down his iPad, switched off his lamp and rolled onto his side, taking the covers with him as usual. She wrenched them back as usual. His back was warm and comforting against hers, but she could feel the tension that gripped him.

Finally he spoke. 'I don't know if she's a morning person or not, Joy.'

★

Down the hallway their unexpected guest lay flat on her back in the neatly made-up single bed, wide awake and staring dry-eyed at the darkness, hands clasped like those of a corpse or a good little girl, her bedroom door pulled wide open as if to show she had nothing to hide from anyone.

chapter six

Now

Barb McMahon grimly dusted the framed picture of Joy and Stan Delaney on their wedding day and thought what a good-looking couple they'd been. Joy's dress had a high neckline and billowing sleeves. Stan wore a ruffled wide-lapel shirt and purple bell-bottom trousers.

Barb had been at that wedding. It was a big raucous affair. Some guests thought the bride and groom an odd couple: Stan the giant, long-haired lout and Joy, the tiny blonde fairy princess, but Barb thought they were probably just jealous of the couple's obvious sexual chemistry, so obvious it was almost indecent, not that anyone would have used the phrase 'chemistry' back then because she was pretty sure it was invented by the people who made *The Bachelor*.

Barb had married Darrin a year after that wedding, and she didn't remember much chemistry, just a lot of earnest conversation about savings goals. When Darrin died of a stroke ten years ago, Barb started cleaning to bring in extra cash. She generally only cleaned for friends, people like Joy of her own circle and generation. Barb's daughter thought that was weird. *Doesn't it make you uncomfortable, Mum?* It didn't make her at all uncomfortable. Why should it? Barb *preferred* to clean for friends, and friends of friends, the sort of women who had never had a cleaner before and felt embarrassed by the luxury of it, so they liked to work alongside you, chatting at the same time, and Barb liked that too because it made the time fly.

But Joy wasn't here today, so time wasn't flying.

'She's away,' Stan had said.

He looked terrible without Joy there to look after him. He probably couldn't boil an egg. His jaw was covered in snow-white stubble and there were two long scratch marks, like a railway track, down the side of his face.

'Away?' Joy never went *away*. Where would she go? 'When did she go away?'

It was on Valentine's Day, according to Stan. Eight days ago.

'She never mentioned she was going away,' said Barb.

'It was a last-minute decision,' Stan had said tersely, as if Joy were in the habit of making last-minute decisions.

Very odd.

Barb put down the framed photo with a regretful sigh, plugged in the vacuum cleaner and tried to remember if they were due to vacuum under the bed. How long had it been? Joy liked to make sure they pushed the bed to one side and gave it a good clean at least once a month.

She got down on her hands and knees and peered under the bed. Not much dust. She'd leave it until Joy was back. She was about to stand up again when something caught her eye. A sparkle.

She dropped flat on her stomach and reached out with her fingertips. She had a good reach. Joy used to tell her that when she played in the afternoon ladies' tennis comp.

She pulled the object towards her. It was Joy's mobile phone. She recognised it immediately because of the glittery phone case, like one of those Glomesh evening bags they all used to love in the seventies.

She got back up and sat on Joy and Stan's bed, panting a little from the effort. The phone was dead.

So Joy had gone away *without her phone*? There was a sick feeling in her stomach.

She walked out into the kitchen where Stan was sitting at the table with his son Troy. They weren't talking. They looked like two strangers forced to share a table in a food court, although there were no cups of tea or food on the table.

Troy was holding Joy's precious headphones, which gave Barb a strange, chilly feeling. It felt too intimate, like he was holding something that was part of his mother: a wig or dentures.

'Hi, Barb,' said Troy brightly. 'Haven't seen you for ages. Love the new haircut. How is –'

'I just found your mother's phone.' She held it up. Troy's smile vanished as fast as if she'd slapped him. His eyes flew to his father.

Stan said nothing. Not a word. He didn't even look surprised. He just stood and dully held out his hand for the phone.

'I have to say, I found Stan's reaction quite peculiar,' Barb would later tell people. Then she'd pause and let her cheeks collapse with the dreadful gravity of her inside knowledge. 'Even, you might say, suspicious.'

chapter seven

'Troy just called to say Barb found Mum's phone under the bed.'

The physiotherapist's voice carried out to where her patient sat reading a health and fitness magazine. It was the patient's third rehab visit after surgery for a ruptured anterior ligament following a clumsy fall while jogging. The patient hadn't rung the bell on the reception desk when she arrived fifteen minutes early, just in case Brooke – that was the physio's name, she was very nice, very caring and calm – was seeing another patient.

She wanted to be helpful because she knew Brooke had only just started out and didn't have a receptionist yet.

At their first consultation, the two of them had bonded over their shared experience of debilitating migraines.

Brooke Delaney said she'd decided to become a physiotherapist after seeing one as a child. 'He said he might be able to help my migraines if they were caused by upper neck tension,' she said. 'My neck wasn't the culprit, but it still felt like he was one of the few people in the medical profession who took me seriously. You know how people think you're exaggerating your pain? Especially when you're a little girl.'

Oh, the patient knew *all* about that.

She turned a page of her magazine and tried not to listen to what was clearly a private conversation.

'So that explains why Mum isn't answering our calls.' Brooke's voice was looser and louder and also somehow younger than the soothing well-modulated tone she used when addressing her patients. 'We just feel like this might be more serious than we first thought.'

Goodness me. The patient closed her magazine. She wished now that she had rung the bell.

'I know. Off-grid means off-grid, but it just doesn't seem like her to leave her phone behind.'

Pause.

'Sure, but you know how you said you and Mum argued the last time you talked?'

Pause.

'Yes. Yes, I know, Dad, but I just wondered . . . I just wondered, was it a very *bad* argument?'

There was a seismic tremor of emotion on the word 'bad'.

The patient stood. She tossed the magazine back into the basket. This was not a call that should be overheard.

Everyone had secrets. The patient had not, in fact, been jogging when she ruptured her ligament. She'd never jogged in her life. She'd fallen out of a taxi after two glasses of champagne and three espresso martinis at a fiftieth birthday lunch. She suspected that Brooke Delaney knew she hadn't been jogging, and she appreciated the fact that she didn't push the point.

The patient quietly got up and left the office. She would come back in fifteen minutes. She didn't need to know her lovely physiotherapist's possibly terrible family secrets.

chapter eight

Last September

Brooke Delaney drove to work on Monday morning with breakfast radio on low, her window shield shades tilted down. Occasionally she moaned softly, for effect. For whose effect, she didn't know. Her own, presumably. She wore polarised sunglasses but the morning sunlight pouring through her tinted car windows still felt hurtful, in an unspecified way, like a mild insult from a stranger.

She stopped at a pedestrian crossing to let a little schoolgirl cross. The girl waved her thanks like a grown-up and walked hurriedly, gratefully. Flat feet. She broke Brooke's heart. *You are fine*, Brooke told herself as her eyes filled with tears and she put her foot on the accelerator. You feel strange and teary and fragile and surreal but you are fine.

She touched her forehead. The ache is just the memory of the pain, not the pain itself.

The migraine had attacked with a brutal blow to her right eye early Saturday morning. She was braced for it. She'd known the fucker was coming, so she'd cancelled her plans in anticipation. She'd spent the weekend alone in her bedroom, the blinds down, a cold cloth on her forehead. No-one but her and her migraine.

It was her first migraine since Grant had moved out six weeks ago. No-one to bring her icepacks or glasses of chilled water, no-one to check in or care or lay a firm hand on her forehead. But she'd got through it on her own. A migraine wasn't child-birth. Although she'd read a survey that showed women who had experienced both rated their migraine pain as the higher of the two, which was oddly cheering to hear.

She remembered her friend Ines talking about how, after her divorce, she'd constructed a desk from an IKEA flatpack on her own while playing 'I Am Woman', but then, after she was done, all she'd wanted to do was call her ex and tell him about it.

Brooke felt the same desire to call Grant and tell him she'd got through a migraine on her own. How pathetic. Her migraines were no longer of interest to him. Perhaps they never had been of interest to him.

'Are you *postdrome*, my darling?' her mother would say if she saw her this morning, because now, thanks to her podcasts, she recognised symptoms and spoke the lingo with jaunty ease.

Brooke wanted to snap: You don't get to use the lingo, Mum, if you've never had a migraine.

But her mother would be so remorseful, and Brooke couldn't stand it. She knew her mother wanted exoneration, and she didn't think she was deliberately withholding it, but she certainly wasn't giving Joy what she needed.

'The thing is,' Joy would say, 'I was so busy that year, the year the headaches started, I mean the migraines, when your migraines started, that was a really bad year in our family, a terrible year, our "annus horribilis", as the Queen would say, I might be mispronouncing it, my grumpy old Latin teacher, Mr O'Brien, would know how to pronounce it, he drowned, the poor man, on Avoca Beach, not swimming between the flags apparently, got caught in the rip, so no-one to blame but himself, but still, anyway, that year, that bad year, there was just a lot . . . and we thought we might lose the business, and *both* your grandmothers were so sick, and I had *no idea* what you were going through –' And Brooke would cut her off, because she'd heard all this so many times before, right down to the drowning of the Latin teacher.

'Don't worry about it, Mum. It was a long time ago.'

Her mother had too much time on her hands. That was the problem. She was going a little dotty. She spent hours looking at old photos and then ringing her children to tell them how little and cute they'd been and how sorry she was for not noticing it at the time.

The truth was, Brooke didn't even remember her mother dismissing her migraines. She had no memory of the 'unforgivable' time when Joy yelled at Brooke for coming down with a migraine when they were running late.

What she remembered was the extraordinary, astonishing pain, and her fury with her mother for not fixing it. She didn't expect her dad or the doctors to fix it. She expected *her mother* to fix it.

Brooke managed her migraines now: efficiently, expertly, without resentment. Watch for the symptoms. Get on to the medication fast. This had been the first in six months. She was responsible for the incarceration of a monster, and sometimes the monster broke free of its shackles.

'*Last Tuesday, retired tennis star Harry Haddad revealed that he is planning . . .*'

The radio announcer's words slid into her consciousness. She flicked up the volume.

'*. . . a return to professional tennis next year. The three-time grand slam champion retired after a serious shoulder injury four years ago. He announced his plans on social media last Tuesday and today posted a picture of himself working out under the guidance of his newly appointed coach, former Wimbledon champion Nicole Lenoir-Jourdan. Haddad, who is reportedly soon to release his autobiography, is obviously hoping for one last exciting chapter in the story of his incredible career.*'

'Oh for God's sake, *Harry*,' said Brooke.

She changed the radio station to show her disapproval. He was making a mistake. His shoulder would never be the same and Nicole wasn't the right fit. Former greats didn't necessarily make great coaches. Nicole Lenoir-Jourdan was a beautiful, single-minded player but Brooke suspected she didn't have the patience for coaching.

She tapped her fingers against the steering wheel and murmured, 'C'mon, c'mon,' to the traffic light. Her dad had no patience with traffic lights either, or children who took too long to put on their shoes, or romantic scenes in movies, but he had all the patience in the world when it came to coaching.

Brooke remembered how he used to watch and analyse a student, eyes narrowed against the glare – he refused to ever wear sunglasses on the court; it had been a historic moment when he let Brooke wear them in a fruitless attempt to combat the migraines – and then he would beckon the player to the net, holding up one finger while he thought it out: What do I need to say or do to make it click in this kid's head? He never gave the same lesson twice.

Brooke's mother had been good with the group lessons, keeping the little kids running and laughing (*she* wore glamorous oversized sunglasses when coaching, although never when playing), but she didn't have the passion or patience for one-on-one coaching. She was the businesswoman, the brains behind Delaneys, the one to start the pro shop, the café, the holiday camps.

Joy made the money and Stan made the stars, except they'd lost their shiniest star: Harry Haddad.

Stan could have taken Harry all the way and much further, although some would argue that three grand slams were as far as he was ever going to get. Not her dad. He believed Harry could have flown as high as Federer, that *Harry* would be the Australian to finally break the Australian Open drought, but they would never know what could have happened in the parallel world where Harry Haddad stuck with his childhood coach, Stan 'the Man' Delaney.

The light changed and she put her foot on the accelerator,

thinking of her poor parents and how they'd be feeling about this news. They must surely know. The announcement was made last Tuesday. If they hadn't seen it on the news, someone in the tennis community would have told them. It was strange that her mother hadn't called to talk about it, and to worry about Brooke's dad and how he'd feel seeing Harry back on the court.

It was painful to watch her dad watch Harry Haddad play tennis on television. He quivered with barely contained tension through every point, his shoulders up, his face a heartbreaking combination of pride and hurt. The whole family had complicated feelings about their most celebrated student. Multiple Delaneys Tennis Academy players had done well on the circuit, but Harry was the only one who'd made it all the way to the Promised Land. The only one to kiss that magical piece of silverware: the Gentlemen's Singles Championship Trophy at Wimbledon. Not once, but twice.

Brooke's dad had discovered Harry. The kid had never held a racquet, but one day Harry's dad won a one-hour private tennis lesson at Delaneys Tennis Academy in a charity raffle and decided to give the lesson to his eight-year-old son. The rest, as Brooke's mother liked to say, was history.

Now Harry was not just a beloved sporting icon but a high-profile philanthropist. He'd married a beautiful woman and had three beautiful children, one of whom had been very ill with leukaemia, which was when Harry became a passionate advocate for childhood cancer research. He raised millions. He was saving lives. How could you say a bad word about a man like that? You couldn't.

Except Brooke could, because Harry hadn't always been a saint. When he was a kid, back when Brooke and her siblings knew him, he was a sneaky, strategic cheat. He used cheating as a tactic: not just to score points but to rattle and enrage his opponents. Her dad never believed it. He had always suffered from tunnel vision when it came to Harry, but then again, nearly all adults used to have tunnel vision when it came to Harry. All they saw was his sublime talent.

While playing a match against Brooke's brother Troy when they were teenagers, Harry kept blatantly calling balls out that were plainly in. Troy finally snapped. He chucked his racquet, jumped the net and got in a couple of good hits. It took two adult men to drag Troy away from Harry.

Troy was banned from playing for six months, which was better than he deserved according to their father, who took a long time to forgive Troy for shaming him like that.

And then, just two years later, Harry Haddad betrayed Stan Delaney when he dumped him as a coach after he won the Australian Open Boys' Singles. Brooke's dad was blindsided. He had assumed, with good reason, that he was taking Harry all the way. He loved him like a son. Maybe more than his own sons, because Harry never questioned a drill, never rebelled, never sighed or rolled his eyes or dragged his feet as he walked onto the court.

It was supposedly not Harry's but his father's decision to leave Delaneys. Elias Haddad, Harry's photogenic, charismatic father, was his manager, and there in the player's box at every match with a beautiful new girlfriend by his side. Brooke and her siblings never believed that Harry wasn't involved in the decision-making process to dump their dad, in spite of the heartfelt card he sent their father, or the earnest, disingenuous way he spoke in fawning magazine profiles about his gratitude for his first-ever coach. Her dad never let himself get that close to a player again. He was beloved by his students and he gave them his all, except he kept his heart safe. That was Brooke's theory, anyway.

Brooke drove into the busy car park of The Piazza, as her local shopping village was now called after its recent redevelopment. Everyone enjoyed mocking the 'Tuscan hilltop town' theme but Brooke didn't care much either way. The new Italian deli was great, the café had put up some nice photos of Tuscany, the hanging baskets of artificial flowers seemed almost real if you didn't look too closely, and at least the fake cobblestones didn't catch heels like real cobblestones.

'Although the occasional twisted ankle would probably be good for *your* business, nudge, nudge, wink, wink, hey, Brooke?' the local MP had said on opening day last month, after he'd cut the ceremonial ribbon with a pair of giant novelty scissors. The MP was one of those men who gave everything he said a vaguely sexual connotation.

If this trial separation maintained its momentum and rolled all the way towards a divorce, which it seemed to be doing, Brooke would have to *date*. She'd have to put on lipstick and endure vague sexual connotations over coffee.

She pulled into her favourite parking spot, turned off the ignition and looked at her bare left hand on the steering wheel. No indentations to mark her missing wedding and engagement rings. She never wore them to work anyway, and often she'd forgotten to wear them on the weekend, which was maybe relevant, but probably not. She was looking for signs she'd missed.

Brooke's clinic, Delaney's Physiotherapy, was a two-room office she rented in between the café and the fruit and veg shop. The previous tenant had been a tarot card reader whose customers still sometimes turned up hoping for an 'emergency reading'. Just last week a guy in a paisley shirt and tight pants had said, 'Oh, well, if you can't read my cards you might as well check out this dodgy knee of mine.' Brooke had predicted surgery in his future.

'*Brrrr! It sure doesn't feel like spring yet!*' said the weather reporter.

Brooke fixed a stray eyelash in her rear-vision mirror. Her eyes were red and watery. She would tell today's patients she had allergies. Nobody wanted a physio with migraines.

Nobody wanted a wife with chronic migraines. A daughter or a sister with migraines. Or even a friend with migraines. All those cancellations! Brooke let the self-pitying train of thought unravel only so far before she snipped it short.

'*Who's looking forward to the last few weeks of the snow season?*' said the weather reporter.

'I am,' said Brooke. Spring skiing meant torn and strained knee ligaments, back injuries, wrist fractures.

Please God, let there be injuries. Just enough to get that cash flow flowing.

God replied in the same aggrieved way Brooke's mother answered the phone when her children left it too long without checking in: Hello, stranger.

Forget I asked, thought Brooke. She turned off the radio, undid her seatbelt, and sat for a moment. Her stomach roiled. Mild nausea was expected the day after a migraine. Come on, she told herself, like she was a toddler. Out you get.

Even on a good day, when she wasn't postdrome, when she had arrived somewhere she actually really wanted to be, she always experienced this resistance to getting out of the car. It was a little weird but it wasn't a thing. Just a quirk. No-one noticed. Well, Grant noticed, if they were running late, but no-one *else* noticed. It dated back to her days of competitive tennis. She'd arrive at a tournament and be paralysed by her desire to stay in the warm musty cocoon of the car. But she always did move in the end. It was *not* a thing. She was not her sister.

No rush. She had half an hour before her first appointment.

She hugged the steering wheel and watched a big-bellied man pick up a hefty box from outside the post office without bending his knees. That's the way, buddy, strain those back muscles.

When she'd taken on the lease for the clinic, she'd known about the planned redevelopment and been offered a substantially reduced rent as a result, but she hadn't anticipated that months would slide by with delay after delay. Business slowed for everyone. The overpriced patisserie closed after forty years of business. The hairdressers' marriage broke up.

It was stressful and Brooke needed to manage stress in order to manage her migraines. Migraine sufferers shouldn't start new businesses or separate from their husbands and they certainly shouldn't do both at the same time. They should move gingerly through their days, as if they had spinal cord injuries.

Brooke had just managed to keep her fledgling practice afloat, barely. There was a period where she didn't have a single patient for twenty-three days in a row. The words, 'You need more money, you need more money, you need more money' buzzed in her ears like tinnitus.

But now the renovations were complete. The diggers, trucks and jackhammers were gone. The car park was full every day. The café that had replaced the patisserie bustled. The hairdressers were back together and booked up six weeks ahead.

'It's now or never,' her accountant had told her. 'This next quarter will be make or break.'

Her accountant reminded her of her dad. He used to grab her by the shoulders and look her in the eyes. *Leave it all on the court, Brooke.*

She could not have her business fail at the same time as her marriage. That was too many failures for one person.

She was leaving everything on the court. She was giving it her all. She was being the best she could be. She was writing free articles for the local paper, doing letterbox drops, studying her Google analytics, contacting possible referring doctors, contacting every contact she had, even God, for God's sake.

'If it doesn't work out, the door is always open,' her old boss had said when she handed in her notice. New clinics failed all the time. Brooke had two friends who'd had to cut their losses and close up shop: one cheerfully, and one devastatingly.

She put her hand on the car door. *Out you get.*

She opened the door and her phone rang. At this time of day it had to be business-related. Friends and family didn't call before nine.

She answered at the same time as she registered the name on the screen: *Amy.* Too late.

'Hi,' she said to her sister. 'I can't talk.'

Brooke once had a boyfriend who could always tell which family member she was talking to on the phone just by the tone of her voice. *Amy*, he would mouth if he heard her now. 'When it's Amy you sound pompous and put upon,' he told her. 'Like you're the school principal.'

'Is everything okay?' She tried not to sound like the school principal.

The problem was that she didn't really feel like the school principal at all when she spoke to Amy; what she felt like was the baby of the family, the one who always did Amy's bidding, because Amy was the revered, adored boss of the family, and they all used to do what she commanded, even the boys. That was fine when they were children, when Amy was the best at coming up with ideas for games and finding loopholes in the rules set by their parents, but now they were grown-ups, or at least Brooke was a grown-up, and she was not taking instructions from someone with no career, no driver's licence, no fixed address and precarious mental health. Yet as soon as Brooke heard Amy's voice she could sense an involuntary reflex, as irresistible and unmistakeable as the knee-jerk reflex, to please and impress her big sister and consequently, in her fruitless attempt to resist and conceal that reflex, she ended up sounding like the school principal.

'Why did you answer, then? If you're busy?' Amy sounded breathless.

'I accidentally answered.' Brooke leaned back against the car door. 'Are you running for a bus or something?'

'I just finished a run.'

'Good for you. Did you stretch first?'

She knew her sister's hamstrings as well as her own. Her family's bodies were the first ones she'd practised on when she was studying. She felt a sense of ownership of all their problems: Amy's hamstrings, her dad's knees, Logan's shoulder, Troy's calf issues, her mother's knotted-up lower back.

'I sure did,' said Amy.

'Liar.' She started walking towards the café with the phone to her ear. She was aware of an irrational but fierce sense of competitiveness because Amy had been for a run and Brooke had done no exercise this weekend thanks to the migraine. It made no sense. Brooke was younger and fitter than Amy. Yet as soon as she knew her sister was out for a run Brooke felt a wild desire to be running too: faster, longer.

'How are you?' asked Amy. Brooke heard a seagull's squawk. She'd been running on the beach. Damn her. So typical. Brooke was in a suburban car park worrying about cash flow, and Amy was running on a beach, probably about to eat eggs Benedict for breakfast.

'I'm fine,' said Brooke. 'Well, not great. I had a migraine on the weekend.'

A woman walked out of the café carrying a cardboard tray of coffees. She lifted the tray in clumsy greeting, and Brooke waved back. Right hip pain. Brooke monitored her gait which was unfortunately perfect. The patients who were diligent with their exercises got better and didn't need her anymore.

'I'm sorry,' said Amy. 'Did Grant look after you?'

'He was away. Camping. The Blue Mountains. With some old friends from – just some old friends.' She made herself stop. Apparently the trick for a good lie was not to give too much unnecessary detail.

'Oh no! You should have called. I could have brought you soup! My local Chinese takeaway does the best chicken and sweet corn soup you've ever tasted!'

'It's fine. I was fine. Anyway, what's up?' Brooke put her key in the glass door. The sight of her logo on the door gave her a complicated sensation of pleasure and pride and fear. It was two stick figures of a woman and a man holding the name 'Delaney's Physiotherapy' above their heads like a banner. Logan's girlfriend, Indira, who was a graphic designer, had created it for her, and Brooke loved it. She imagined someone scraping her logo off the door, optimistically replacing it with a brand new logo for their own dream business.

'Sorry,' said Amy. 'I won't take long. Got any patients today?'

'Yes,' said Brooke shortly. She would never admit her fears for the clinic to Amy. That wasn't the way their relationship worked. She always needed her big sister to see that *this* was

how a grown-up lived her life, and Amy was always gratify-
ingly impressed, although there was a certain detachment to her
admiration, as if Brooke's perfectly normal choices (get a degree,
get married, buy a house) were just not possible for her.

'Oh, well, that's great, good for you. Listen, so I only just
heard about –'

Brooke cut her off.

'About Harry's comeback plans? Yes, I only just heard about
it too. I assume Mum and Dad know, although I'm surprised I
haven't heard from them. I don't think he'll have the mobility –'

'No, I'm not talking about Harry. I'm talking about the girl.'

Brooke paused. What girl? Some other ex-student?

'I couldn't sleep last night thinking about it,' said Amy.
She was speaking in that irritating singsong voice that meant she
might be about to cry or yell or have some kind of meltdown.
'Have you met her yet? I don't know, I just feel quite weird about
it, don't you? The whole situation is just so . . . random, don't
you think?'

As Brooke listened to her sister she switched on the lights.
There was a reception counter and empty desk ready and waiting
for the office manager she couldn't yet afford to hire. The walls
were painted an encouraging, calming Sea Breeze. She'd spent
hours trying to decide between Sea Breeze and Deep Ocean
Blue as if the right wall colour would affect patient outcomes.
She'd mounted full-length mirrors so patients could check their
form as they did their exercises, although this meant she had to
keep seeing her own reflection. It didn't matter when patients
were there. It was just when she was alone that she hated seeing
her own face. The new rented equipment sat there ready and
waiting and costing her money: one exercise bike, three medicine balls, hand weights and stretchy bands. Framed posters of
athletes celebrating hard-won triumphs: on their knees, foreheads to the ground, kissing gold medals. There was only one
picture of a tennis player and that was the only picture where
the athlete wasn't celebrating. It was a black and white shot of

Martina Navratilova stretching for a backhand at Wimbledon, her face contorted, mullet hair flying around her headband. It would have looked strange if Brooke didn't have a tennis player, like she was making a point, and her parents would have noticed when they came to see the clinic.

'Good old Martina,' said her dad fondly when he saw the picture, as if he and Martina went way back.

'And what if the boyfriend turns up at their house?' said Amy. 'And things get out of hand?'

'I've lost you,' said Brooke. Her mind had wandered. She seemed to have missed a vital part of the conversation.

'What if he has a *weapon*?'

'What if who has a weapon?'

'The *abusive boyfriend*!'

She said, 'Amy, I have no idea what you're talking about.'

There was silence. Brooke sat down at the reception desk and powered up her computer.

'Really?' said Amy. 'You don't know? I thought for sure you'd know.'

The computer buzzed to life.

'Know what?' she prompted. 'I've got an appointment soon.' She looked at the notes on her computer screen. 'Forty-eight years old. Thinks she might have tennis elbow. Remember when Logan thought he had tennis elbow and Dad . . .' She stopped. Sometimes when she pulled out a funny memory from their shared childhood it turned out to be not so funny after all.

'Brooke, I'm talking about Mum and Dad and their weird . . . house guest.'

Brooke took out a clipboard and a new patient questionnaire from the top drawer.

'So they've got someone staying with them? In your old room? Is that the problem?'

Amy moved back into the family home at intervals, whenever the new job or new course or new boyfriend didn't work out.

'I think she probably *is* staying in my room,' said Amy slowly.

There was an aggrieved, faintly aggressive note in her voice. 'But that's fine. I've got my own place, Brooke. I've been living here for nearly six months.'

'I know that,' said Brooke. A share house?

'And I'm employed. Last week I worked over forty hours.'

'Wow,' said Brooke, and she tried not to sound condescending. Amy had actually worked a full working week. Give the girl a trophy. 'Sorry. I've just been distracted with the clinic.' *And my 'trial' separation.*

Where was Amy working again? Was it a supermarket? Or wait, a cinema? No. She was a *food taster*, wasn't she? That's right. They'd heard all about the job interview. 'It was like an exam,' Amy said. 'Very stressful.' She'd had to arrange ten cups of liquid in order of saltiness, and then another ten cups in order of sweetness. She was given tiny jars containing balls of cottonwool and she had to identify their smells. She got the basil and mint right, but not the parsley. Who knew that parsley had a fragrance? Her final task was to write a paragraph describing an apple to someone who had never eaten one.

'I don't think I could describe an apple,' Brooke had said idly, and her mother had said, happily, 'Well, I guess you wouldn't have got the job then, Brooke!'

And Brooke, who had done a four-year degree and two years of clinical practice to become a physiotherapist, suddenly found herself feeling inadequate because *she couldn't describe an apple*.

Amy said, 'Have you honestly not heard anything about this girl staying with Mum and Dad?'

'Nope,' said Brooke. 'Who is she?' She could hear the pompous school principal in her voice, because for God's sake, the *drama*. Why was a house guest such a big deal? Her parents knew a wide circle of people. It would be a former student. So many of them kept in touch. As children the Delaneys had complicated feelings about the tennis students. They were their parents' other children, with better manners, better backhands, better attitudes. But they were too old for that now. Now they laughed about it, teased their parents and each other about it. It was typical that Amy would suddenly make a fuss.

'Her name is *Savannah*,' said Amy darkly.

'Right,' said Brooke distractedly. 'Is Savannah on the circuit?'

'She's no-one, Brooke! She's just some stray girl who turned up on their doorstep.'

Brooke let her hands fall flat on the keyboard. 'They don't know her?'

'She's a *stranger*.'

Brooke swivelled her chair away from her computer. The memory of the weekend's migraine blossomed across her forehead.

'I don't understand.'

'Late last Tuesday night a strange woman knocked on our parents' door.'

'Late? How late? Were Mum and Dad in bed?' She thought of her parents waking, reaching for their glasses from their bedside tables. Her mother in that oversized pyjama top with the sleeves so long they hung past her wrists. Her father in his boxers and clean white t-shirt, with his big barrel chest and leathery legs. He acted like he was thirty but his arthritic reconstructed knees were in a terrible state.

'We're still winning tournaments, darling,' her mother said, patting her hand whenever Brooke expressed concern.

It was true. Her parents were still winning, in spite of the fact that after his last knee operation the surgeon had said to her dad, 'Only run if you're running for your life.'

'Got it,' said Stan. 'No running.' He gave the surgeon a thumbs-up. Brooke saw him do it. Three months later her idiotic, incredible father was back on the court. Serving like a warrior. Running for his life.

'I don't know if they were in bed,' said Amy. 'They stay up late these days. All I know is that she knocked on their door and they let her in and then they let her stay the night.'

'But what . . . *why* would they do that?' Brooke stood up from her desk.

'Well, I think because she had some kind of injury. Mum needed to bandage her up. Her boyfriend did it. Mum keeps referring to her as a "domestic violence victim", in this breathless, excited way.' Amy paused. When she spoke again her mouth was clearly full. 'I can't believe you don't know about this yet.'

Brooke couldn't believe it either. Her mother phoned often, always on the flimsiest of excuses. Early last week she'd called three times in one day: once to tell her something she'd heard on a podcast about migraines, once to correct herself (because she'd found the piece of paper where she'd written it down) and once to tell her that the cyclamen plant Brooke had given her for Mother's Day had bloomed. (Amy had given her the cyclamen but Brooke didn't correct her mother when she gave her credit for it.)

'What are you *eating*?' she said tetchily.

'Breakfast. Orange and poppy seed muffin. Citrusy. Not enough poppy seeds.'

Brooke sat back down and tried to work it out. Her parents were smart people. They wouldn't have let anyone shady or dangerous into the house. They were only on the very outer edge of old age, they were not yet dealing with dementia or confusion, just bad knees and indigestion, some insomnia, apparently. They both seemed a bit bewildered and lost now that they'd sold the tennis school. 'The days are so long,' her mother had sighed to Brooke. 'They used to be so short. Anyway! Shall we meet for coffee? My shout!' But Brooke's days were still short, and she didn't have time for coffee.

'Well, I guess Mum and Dad are pretty good judges of character,' she began.

'Are you *kidding*?' said Amy. 'Good judges of character? Shall I name every cheating, lying little brat who hoodwinked them? Starting right at the top with Harry fucking Haddad, who broke Dad's poor fragile heart?'

'Okay, okay,' said Brooke hurriedly. 'So did they take her to the police?'

'She doesn't want to report it,' said Amy. Her mouth was full again. 'And she has nowhere else to go, so they're letting her stay there until she "finds her feet".'

'But can't she go to a . . . I don't know, a women's shelter or something?' Brooke picked up a pen and chewed on it. 'I know that sounds bad but she's not their problem. There are places she can go for help.'

'I think Mum and Dad just want to help.' Amy sounded airy and philanthropic now. Brooke could sense her deftly switching positions. She'd always had the best footwork in the family. Now that Amy had handed over responsibility, Brooke could be the worried, uptight one and Amy could be the help-the-homeless bleeding heart, a role which suited her far more.

'Did you say she turned up on Tuesday night?' said Brooke. 'This girl has been staying with them for nearly a *week*?'

'Yep,' said Amy.

'I'll call Mum now.' Maybe Amy had misinterpreted everything.

'She won't answer,' said Amy. 'She's taking Savannah to Narelle.'

'Narelle?'

'Mum's hairdresser of thirty years, Brooke. Keep up. Narelle with the identical twins, and the allergy that turned out to be cancer, or the cancer that turned out to be an allergy, I can't remember, but she's fine now. Narelle has opinions about all of us. She thinks Logan and Indira should have a baby. She thinks you should advertise in the local paper. She thinks Troy should go on a date with her divorced sister. Oh, and she thinks I'm bipolar. Mum started listening to a podcast called *Living with Bipolar*.'

Amy was speaking too fast now, in that weird manic voice she sometimes put on that made Brooke wonder if she actually was bipolar. She did it on purpose. She *liked* people to think she was crazy because it made them nervous. It was an intimidation tactic.

'Of course, Narelle. Anyway. I'll call Dad.'

'He's out too. He's looking at cars. For Savannah.'

'Dad is buying this girl a *car*?'

'I'm not one hundred per cent sure,' said Amy. 'But you know how he loves it when someone needs a new car.'

'Jeez,' said Brooke. The end of the pen slipped free and into her mouth. She spat it into the palm of her hand. 'Do the boys know?'

'I don't think so,' said Amy.

'Didn't you call Troy?'

Amy and Troy were the closest out of the four of them. Brooke knew she would have called him first.

'I texted him,' said Amy. 'But he didn't answer. You know he's flying back from New York today.'

Brooke couldn't keep up with Troy's glamorous, international life. 'I guess I did.'

'And Logan never answers his phone. I think he has a phobia about it. Or he does when it comes to us. He talks to his friends.'

Brooke pulled the pen from her mouth. Without realising it she'd begun sucking it again and now her mouth was filled with the bitter taste of ink.

She was the last one Amy had called.

'Anyway, I've gotta go,' said Amy abruptly, as if Brooke had been the one to interrupt her busy schedule, as if she were about to go run a corporation and not sit on a beach eating a muffin. 'Call me later.'

This last instruction was given in her eldest sister do-as-I-say voice. It meant: *Call me to confirm you've fixed this.*

Brooke looked at herself in the mirrored wall and saw that her frown line was deeper than ever and her lips were stained a murky shade of Deep Ocean Blue.

chapter nine

Now

'So have *you* seen these scratches?'

The Uber driver, who was an electrical engineering student, looked in his rear-vision mirror, assuming his passenger (her name was *Amy*; he'd taken against the name ever since he'd briefly dated an evil bitch of an Amy) was talking to him and there were marks on his seats (like, whatever, *Amy*), but he saw she was on the phone and not talking to him at all. She'd obviously launched into conversation without bothering to say hello.

'The scratches on Dad's face,' she said. 'He says he got them climbing through the lilly pilly hedge to rescue a tennis ball.'

Pause.

The Uber driver listened idly, his mind on tomorrow's exam and tonight's Tinder date.

'It's just that Troy says the police will assume they're *defensive wounds*.'

So this was possibly interesting. Her destination was the local police station.

'Meanwhile Brooke is suddenly adamant that we should hold off making a missing persons report at all.'

Pause.

'Because *Dad* told her it's not necessary to report her missing. You know Brooke. Daddy's girl.'

The Uber driver saw his passenger smile faintly. She had supermodel legs in shorts, ratty dyed hair, multiple ear piercings and somehow simultaneously gave off a beachy vibe and an inner-city vibe. She was old, maybe even late thirties, but he'd go there.

'Yes, I think we ignore Dad and still report her missing, just in case. It's been over a week now, so it's . . . probably time. I've got a nice photo of Mum. I printed it out. It's one from when she and Dad went to the beach that day, remember, when they were trying to be happy retirees frolicking in the sun? Anyway, listen, obviously we tell them about Savannah, right? I mean, maybe not every single detail.'

Pause.

'Ah, yes, I will be normal because I *am* normal.'

Pause.

'Nope. Not offended, Logan, never offended. I'll see you there.'

She hung up and met his eyes in the rear-vision mirror as they stopped at a red light.

'My mother is missing,' she said brightly.

'That's scary,' said the Uber driver.

'Oh, I'm sure she's fine,' said the passenger. She turned her face to the window and spoke quietly, almost to herself. 'She's perfectly fine.'

chapter ten

'Joy Delaney. Sixty-nine years old. Last contact was nine days ago when she sent a garbled text saying she was going "off-grid". She didn't take her phone with her.'

Detective Senior Constable Christina Khoury read from her notes as Ethan drove them to interview the missing woman's husband. Ethan's full title was Plain Clothes Constable Ethan Lim but there was nothing plain about his clothes. Today's shirt appeared to be mulberry silk. (Could it truly be silk?) His shoes had the lustre of a grand piano. Christina tucked her own shoes back out of sight. They could do with a polish.

She said, 'The phone was found by the cleaning lady under the bed.'

'I guess if you're going off-grid you leave your phone behind?' She heard him try to suppress the question mark.

She'd been Ethan's designated detective for only a few weeks, and she was still trying to find the right rhythm for their working relationship. He seemed nervous around her, and she didn't know whether to embrace that – keep the kid on his toes! – or try to help him relax.

She wasn't great at relaxing people. She'd been told all her life that she didn't smile enough, and she hated small talk. Her fiancée, Nico, now handled all the small-talk requirements of their relationship, chatting to chatty cab drivers and chatty aunts with ease. Christina sometimes fretted she wasn't bringing enough to the table. 'A relationship isn't a bill you split down the middle,' Nico always told her. He was wrong. It was exactly like that. She'd keep an eye on it.

When she'd been in Ethan's position, her designated detective had taken a kind of avuncular approach that left no-one in any doubt as to where they stood. 'Remember your ABC?' he'd ask, so often it got irritating.

'Accept nothing. Believe nothing. Check everything,' Christina would answer.

But she couldn't pull off avuncular. (Was there even a female version of the word?) 'Just be yourself,' Nico told her. He said, 'The guy wants to learn from you.' Nico never had any trouble being anyone else but Nico.

'Two of Joy's adult children reported her missing yesterday,' she continued. 'A general duties police officer went to interview the missing woman's husband and observed scratch marks on his face.'

Ethan winced.

'The husband is cooperating but not saying much. He did confirm to the officer that he and his wife had argued the last time they spoke. So.' She sighed. Her throat felt itchy. 'Obviously a lot of red flags.'

She could not get sick right now. In addition to this potentially suspicious missing person job, she was handling one street assault, two domestic assaults, a service station armed robbery, a wannabe schoolboy arsonist, a break and enter and a bridesmaid dress fitting.

The bridesmaid dress fitting was after work today and the way her four cousins were arguing over waistlines and necklines, a third domestic assault was possible. Her wedding was still six months away but apparently that was no time, according to her cousins, who specialised in weddings. Christina had thought she handled stress well until she had to organise a wedding. 'Just keep it small and casual,' said her friends who did not belong to big Lebanese-Australian families and therefore did not understand the implausibility of this.

'Need a throat lozenge?' asked Ethan.

'No,' said Christina. She cleared her throat. 'No, thank you.'

She pulled a tiny speck of lint off her suit jacket and discreetly checked that the buttons on her shirt weren't gaping. Her cup size didn't suit either her personality or profession but she was descended from a long line of short, acerbic, busty women, and so this was her lot. If the police force hadn't abolished height requirements in the late nineties, little Chrissie Khoury, the shortest kid in every single class photo throughout her school years, would never have got this job.

No lint on Ethan's suit, of course. It looked bespoke. He came from old money, apparently. Private school boy. Christina tried not to hold it against him. She didn't come from old money or new money but from never-quite-enough money.

They pulled up at a traffic light behind an SUV with three children's bikes tied to the back, the number plate responsibly visible. These shady, leafy streets with their manicured lawns had little in common with the neighbourhood out west where she'd grown up, except for the dead bat hanging from the powerline above them. Still, she was happy not to be working in her old neighbourhood like when she first started out and was forced to lock up people she knew. The very first person she ever arrested used to sit next to her in biology. 'Little Chrissie Khoury is arresting me!' he'd cried with drunken delight as she cuffed him.

'Did she take anything with her?' asked Ethan.

'She took her wallet, house keys and nothing else. No luggage. No clothes. No sign of activity on her bank accounts or social media.'

Christina pulled out the colour photo of Joy Delaney provided by the family. She looked like a sweet, tiny lady, younger than sixty-nine, smiling on a beach, one hand on her head to stop a straw hat from flying away in the wind. A photo of someone wearing a hat wasn't great for identification purposes. She would ask the family to provide another one. At least two or three. In this one Joy wore a t-shirt over a swimming costume. The t-shirt was white with three flowers in a row across the chest: red, yellow and orange. The flowers were gerberas. Christina had only recently become aware of the names of flowers. The bridal bouquet was next on her list. She'd honestly rather solve a murder than choose a bridal bouquet.

'Looks like a nice lady,' she said to Ethan, flicking the photo against her knee.

'Any history of domestic violence?' he asked.

'Nope,' said Christina.

They pulled into the driveway of a large, well-tended family home. Silver Volvo in the driveway. Pink, purple and white flowers (which she could now identify as hydrangeas) spilled from garden beds. A tiny grey cat streaked across the front lawn and through a fence. The white edge of a letter poked out from a wrought-iron letterbox with the house number, the word 'POST' and an engraving of two birds, beak to beak, as if they were kissing. This was a neighbourhood of family pets and garden sprinklers, paid-off mortgages and nicely modulated voices.

She said, 'But just because it wasn't reported –'

'Doesn't mean it didn't happen,' finished Ethan.

He listened. Rare for a private school boy.

'Remember your ABC?' she said suddenly, on impulse, as Ethan turned off the car ignition.

He didn't hesitate. 'Accept nothing. Believe nothing. Check everything.'

Her mood elevated. Maybe they had their rhythm.

She gave him an avuncular thumbs-up, opened the car door, got out, straightened her jacket and tugged hard on her shirt.

Somewhere in the distance an ice-cream truck played its familiar tinkling chords.

★

Two hours later the house no longer looked quite so benign. Blue and white checked police tape hung from the letterbox and ended at the side fence.

Christina had put in a request for a crime scene warrant and sealed the house immediately following her interview with Mr Stanley Delaney.

The interview had told her both nothing new and everything she needed to know. This evening's bridesmaid dress fitting was going to have to go ahead without the bride. Her phone was aquiver with outraged texts from outraged cousins.

Christina didn't care. She was reserving her outrage for Mrs Joy Delaney, because her husband was a liar.

chapter eleven

Last September

It was mid-morning when Logan Delaney drove down his parents' street a little over the speed limit, his head ducked low so as to avoid eye contact with friendly neighbours out washing their cars or walking their dogs.

If the Volvo was in the driveway he might circle the cul-de-sac and keep going, because he wasn't in the mood for solo conversations with the parents. He preferred to have his siblings around to take some of the heat. Being an only child must be hell.

The Volvo wasn't in the driveway so he pulled in. He got out and shielded his eyes as he looked up at the house gutters clogged with leaves from the liquidambars.

He checked the vintage-style letterbox – a present from Troy, naturally – in case there was any mail to bring in.

He wore paint-stained track pants, an old t-shirt and runners. He hadn't shaved and he was a man who looked like a criminal when he didn't shave. His hair stuck up in tufts. His mother would say he looked like a hobo. He was a big, solid guy and he knew he should dress more respectably because women sometimes crossed to the other side of the street if they saw him walking behind them at night. He always wanted to shout out his apologies. 'Oh, that's exactly what you should do, Logan, in fact you should *run* after them shouting, "I mean you no harm, fair lady!"' his sister Amy said once, and then she'd laughed so much at her own joke he'd been morally obliged to throw her in the pool. Troy's rooftop pool: it had an *infinity edge*.

His mother had asked him to do the gutters in that way she had of asking without really asking.

'Oh, gosh, Logan, you should see the leaves in this wind! What's going on? Climate change? They're just *rocketing* down,' she'd said on the phone last week.

'You want me to do the gutters?' Logan had said. *Climate change.* His mother threw certain phrases around at random to make sure they knew she was up to date with current affairs and listened to podcasts.

'Your dad says he's perfectly fine doing them.'

'I'll swing by next week,' he'd said.

After Logan's dad celebrated his seventieth birthday with a torn ligament and a complicated knee reconstruction, the family had begun playing with the idea that Stan was 'elderly'. It was a nurse who first used the word. 'Elderly people can suffer confusion and short-term memory loss after anaesthetic,' she'd said as she checked their sleeping father's blood pressure, and Logan saw all of his siblings jerk their heads in a mutual shocked shift of perspective.

'It's like seeing Thor in a hospital gown,' Amy had whispered. Their dad had never been sick, apart from his bad knees, and seeing him diminished and acquiescent in that hospital bed had been distressing, even though their father suddenly opened his eyes and said very clearly to the poor nurse in his startlingly deep voice, 'Nothing wrong with my memory, sweetheart.'

He had fully recovered and was once again winning tournaments with their mother, but the 'elderly' idea had persisted. *Dad shouldn't climb ladders. Dad needs to know his limitations. Dad needs to watch what he eats.* Logan wasn't sure if they were all jumping the gun. Maybe they enjoyed it. Maybe it made them all feel like they were finally grown-ups, worrying about an elderly parent who didn't really need their concern yet. Maybe there was even satisfaction in it: Thor toppled at last. Although Logan wouldn't be surprised if his father could still beat him in an arm wrestle, and he had no doubt at all that he could still beat him on the court. His father knew his strengths, his weaknesses, his strategies. Logan was powerless against all that knowledge. Ten years old again: hands sweaty, heart thumping. Jesus, he'd wanted to beat his dad so badly.

It had been two years since they'd been on the court together. 'Go have a hit with your father,' his mother would invariably suggest when he visited, and Logan would make up an excuse. The subversive idea had begun to creep up that he might just *never play again*. It felt like treason and yet who would care, who would even notice?

Their mother would notice.

Since his father's operation, Logan had begun doing odd jobs around the family home, whenever he thought he could get away with it without his father getting angry. He slid in and out like a ninja. Change a light bulb here and there. Get up with a chainsaw and cut back the overgrown branches around the tennis court.

He couldn't work out how his father felt about it. 'You don't need to do that, mate,' he'd said last time he'd caught Logan changing one of the court lights. He clapped him on the shoulder. 'I'm not dead yet.'

That day Logan had a hangover and his father actually did look to be in far better health than him, ruddy-cheeked and clear-eyed, yet another doubles trophy on the sideboard.

Later that same day his father had asked about how his 'career plans were progressing' and Logan, who had no particular career plan except to stay employed, had felt himself squirm like a kid. His father seemed to always be observing Logan's life the way he used to observe his tennis. Logan could sense Stan's desire to call him to the net, to point out his weaknesses, to explain exactly where he was going wrong and where he could improve, but he never did criticise Logan's life choices, he just asked questions and looked disappointed with the answers.

The slam of his car door sounded loud on the quiet street. He could hear the twitter of magpies and the sarcastic caw of crows from the bushland reserve that backed onto his parents' tennis court. It reminded him of the rhythms of his parents in conversation. His mother chattering, his father's occasional deadpan response.

Logan didn't go inside. He walked straight down the side of the house to collect the ladder from the shed, past the drainpipe where they all had to stand to practise their ball tosses. A hundred times in a row, day after day, until they all had ball tosses as straight and reliable as a ruler's edge.

He wondered where his parents were, how long he had before they returned, and if his father would be angry or relieved to see this particular job done.

Troy wanted to pay people to help out their parents. A gardener. A cleaner. A housekeeper.

'What . . . like a team of *servants*?' said Amy. 'Will Mum and Dad ring a bell like the lord and lady of the manor?'

'I can cover it,' said Troy, with that very particular look he got on his face when he talked about money: secretive, ashamed and proud. None of them really understood what Troy did but it was clear he'd landed on a level of impossible wealth that you were only meant to land on by working really hard at your tennis. Somehow Troy had gone ahead and found another way to drive the fancy car and live the fancy life, and now he played tennis *socially*, with bankers and barristers, and without, it seemed, any hang-ups, as if he were one of the private school kids who got private lessons at Delaneys not because they had talent or a love of the sport but because it was a 'good life skill'.

Their father never once asked Troy about his *career plans*.

Logan opened the shed and found the bucket, gloves, scraper and ladder. Everything was in its place. His friend Hien said the first heartbreaking sign of his own father's Alzheimer's was when he stopped putting his tools back in the right place, but Logan's dad's shed looked as pristine as an operating theatre.

Even the glass of the shed's small window sparkled, revealing the Japanese maple at the side of the tennis court that was just beginning to leaf up for spring. In autumn the leaves turned red-gold. Logan saw himself as a kid searching through a soft crunchy carpet of leaves for a rogue tennis ball, because tennis balls cost money. He saw himself storming past that tree the day he first lost against Troy, the same day his father told him to watch Harry Haddad demonstrate the kick serve that Logan hadn't yet mastered, and maybe part of him already knew he never would master: he simply didn't have that instinctive understanding of where the ball needed to be. He was so worked up that day he threw his racquet as he walked towards the house, almost hitting some poor kid waiting for her lesson, who had to jump aside with a little squeak of fear.

That was the day Logan understood that his younger brother might be better than him and also, more importantly, that Harry Haddad was a prodigy, and had something essential and wonderful that all the Delaney children lacked.

He turned resolutely away from his memories and back to his father's immaculate workbench.

Troy was a fool to think they could *pay* someone to come and do jobs around the house that their father had always done himself. Stan would find that demeaning, extravagant, unmanly. Logan had been in the car with his father once when they'd driven past a man in a suit standing on the side of the road casually scrolling through his phone while a roadside assistance guy was on his knees changing the tyre on the man's Mercedes. Stan had been so offended by the sight he opened the window and roared, '*Change your own tyre, ya big fucken' pussy!*' Then he'd closed the window, grinned sheepishly, and said, 'Don't tell your mother.'

Logan wouldn't let another man change a tyre for him but

Troy sure as hell would, and he'd enjoy it too. He'd amiably chat to the guy while he did it. The last time they all got together, for Amy's birthday, someone asked Troy what he'd done that day, and he said, without shame or embarrassment, 'I had a pedicure.' It turned out, to everyone's amazement, that *the bloke got regular pedicures.* 'Oh darling, *I* could have done your nails for free, saved you the money!' their mother had said, as if Troy needed to save money, and then everyone briefly and unfairly lost their minds at the thought of their mother on her knees trimming Troy's toenails, as if Troy had actually asked her to do it.

Troy was the only Delaney to have ever experienced a pedicure. Their father would rather have pins stuck in his eyes, Joy had ticklish feet, Amy thought pedicures were elitist and Brooke said they caused bacterial infections.

Troy didn't care. Troy was his own man.

No-one would ever call Troy 'passive', even though he was the one passively getting his toenails done like a fucking emperor.

'You didn't even try to stop me,' Indira had said when she called from the airport.

'I thought this was what you wanted,' Logan said. She'd said 'she couldn't go on like this'. Like what? It was never made clear.

'But what do *you* want, Logan? You're so bloody . . . *passive!*' She was crying as she spoke, crying so hard, and he was so confused, he didn't understand what was going on. She was the one leaving the relationship, not him.

Then she'd hung up, so the word 'passive' was the last word she'd said to him, and it kept echoing in his head until he'd become obsessed with it, examining the word and its implications from every angle. He'd even looked up the dictionary definition and now knew it by heart, occasionally muttering it to himself: *Accepting or allowing what happens or what others do, without active response or resistance.*

What exactly was the problem with accepting and allowing what happens, or what others do? Wasn't that a Zen, sensible way to lead your life? Apparently Indira's last boyfriend had been 'domineering'. Logan never domineered. He never stopped Indira from doing anything she wanted to do: even leaving, if that's what she wanted, if that's what made her happy. He wanted her to be happy.

So maybe no-one could make Indira happy. He wasn't going to *demand* she stay.

'You don't want me enough,' she'd said at one point, maybe a week before she left, and he couldn't speak because of the stomping sensation on his chest, and so he'd said nothing, just looked at her, until she sighed and walked away.

'You don't want it enough, mate,' his father had said to him once on the way home in the car after Logan first lost a match to Harry fucking Haddad. Logan remembered sitting silently in the passenger seat, not saying a word, but thinking to himself: *You're wrong, Dad, you're wrong, you're wrong.*

There was clearly something wrong with the way he communicated his own desires, which was ironic seeing as he taught communication skills.

I wanted it too much, Dad.

He put the gloves and the scraper in the bucket and hefted the ladder under one arm. He blinked in the sunlight as he left the darkness of the shed.

'Good morning,' said a female voice, and he nearly dropped the ladder. For a moment he thought it was Indira, as if he'd made her materialise just by thinking about her, but of course it wasn't Indira.

A strange woman was sitting on the edge of his parents' back veranda, her hands cupped around a mug of something hot, which she blew on as she looked up at him.

She had smooth, fair hair cut at sharp angles that swung either side of a skinny, ratty face. Her jeans were so long she'd had to fold them almost all the way to her knees. She wore ugg boots that looked a couple of sizes too big for her. They rolled loosely around on her feet like a child wearing grown-up shoes. Her grey hoodie had a pink logo across the front.

'I didn't mean to scare you,' she said. She smoothed her hair back behind her ears and two straight pieces swung free, so the tips of her ears poked out.

'Who are you?' The fright made him as rude and brusque as his father.

'I'm Savannah.' She gave a little circular wave of her hand, as if she were being introduced while sitting at a table of his friends at a pub.

He studied her. A tiny jewel in her nose caught the sunlight. He felt a familiar childish sense of grievance he instantly tried to quash. This was the way it had always been: strangers strutting about his backyard with their racquets and designer shoes as if they owned the place, but you had to be polite and friendly because they paid the bills. Once, Brooke caught a kid going through her schoolbag that she'd dumped on the back veranda and helping herself to a banana that Brooke hadn't eaten at recess.

'Who are *you*?' The girl imitated his tone, her head on one side.

'I'm Logan,' he said. He rested the ladder against his leg. 'This is my parents' house.' He tried not to sound childishly defensive, as if he needed to prove that he had far more right to be here than she did.

'Hi, Logan.'

He waited.

'I'm staying with your parents,' she said finally.

'Were you a student?' asked Logan.

'You mean tennis?' said Savannah. She smiled. 'No. I'm not *sporty*.'

She put on an oddly genteel accent when she said *sporty*, as if she were saying, I don't eat *caviar*.

'So you're . . .'

'Your parents have gone out to pick up new glasses for your dad,' said Savannah. 'Bifocals. They were ready to be picked up yesterday but they ran out of time because the GP ran late for your mum's appointment and then they got stuck in terrible traffic.'

Again, he couldn't interpret the subtext. Why was she giving him all the detail? Was she mocking Logan's mother, who weighed down every conversation with tangential detail? Her children were the only ones allowed to tease her about this.

'Well, nice to meet you,' said Logan. 'I'll get on with it.' If she didn't want to say who she was, he didn't care. He lifted the ladder. 'I'm cleaning out the gutters.'

'Go for it,' said the girl grandly. She tipped her head back to enjoy the sunlight on her face.

Logan turned to walk towards the side of the house. He stopped and looked back at her. 'How long are you staying for?'

'Indefinitely,' she said, without opening her eyes. She grinned.

He felt a jolt of surprise almost like fear. *'Indefinitely?'*

She opened her eyes and regarded him thoughtfully. 'I was joking. I just meant I'd like to stay here forever. It's so peaceful.' She inclined her chin at the tennis court. 'I guess you all grew up to be tennis champions, then?'

'Not really.' Logan cleared his throat.

'You were pretty lucky to have a court in your backyard.'

He assumed her thin harsh undertone related to money. These days only wealthy people had backyard tennis courts.

'Back in the sixties every single house in this street had a court,' he said, and he heard himself parroting his old man except his father's point was that the tragic disappearance of backyard tennis courts to make way for apartment blocks heralded the end of Australia's golden age of tennis. It meant working-class kids like Stan no longer spent their childhoods whacking a tennis ball but hunched over tiny screens.

Logan's point was: *Don't you dare think I grew up rich and privileged just because this bush neighbourhood got gentrified.*

Logan's dad had grown up in this house, and they didn't know much about his childhood, except that it wasn't happy

78

and he spent hours on his own, working on his serve on the tennis court his own father, Logan's grandfather, had built before Logan's grandmother 'kicked him to the kerb'. Whenever she said that, Logan used to visualise a humorous image, like a children's book illustration, of a grandpa in a rocking chair, with a surprised open mouth, hands on his knees, flying through the air, but he assumed it hadn't really been that comical at the time.

Before Logan was born, his grandmother moved in with her older sister to take care of her while she died, which she took an inconveniently long time to do. Apparently Grandma then sold this house to Logan's parents at 'a very cheap price'. It turned out to be an expensive price, though, because Logan's mother then felt permanently beholden to her mother-in-law and she could never convince Logan's dad to tear up the purple floral carpet in the living room because it would offend Grandma. Even after Grandma was long dead.

When the tennis school started making money, pretty good money thanks to Logan's mother's entrepreneurial streak, the house was renovated and extended. The original dingy dark little Federation bungalow became a light-filled family home, but the purple carpet remained, a constant point of contention. Joy looked away when she vacuumed it. The rest of the house was Logan's mother's preferred arts and crafts style. A lot of timber and copper. ('It's like living in a bloody woodchopper's house,' his father once said.)

'We were the only ones on the street who didn't replace our tennis court with a swimming pool,' he told the girl, who saw only the respectable present, not the complicated past.

'Would you have preferred the pool then?' she asked, head on one side.

There were times when they all would have preferred the pool, especially back when it was a clay court and he and Troy had to spend hours maintaining the damned thing, watering it, rolling it.

She said, 'At least your parents could walk out the back door and be at work, right? That must have made life easy.'

It meant that Delaneys Tennis Academy had swallowed up their lives.

'Yes, although when the tennis school really took off they leased four courts and the clubhouse around the corner. The place with the smiley tennis ball sign?'

He interrupted himself. She didn't care about the smiley tennis ball. It seemed clear she wasn't a previous student or a club member. If there wasn't a tennis connection, then who the hell was she? 'I'm sorry, but how do you know my parents?'

She scrunched up her face as if trying to remember the right answer.

'Are you a friend of Amy's?' he guessed. She had to be.

'I'm wearing her clothes!' She lifted up one straight leg to show the too-long jeans. 'She's *much* taller than me.'

'We're a tall family,' said Logan. He felt protective of Amy, as if this girl had made fun of her height. Amy was actually the shortest in the family.

'Except for your mother,' said Savannah. A bit of her hair got stuck in her mouth and she blew it away with an irritated puff. 'Your mum and I are exactly the same height.' She removed an elastic band from her wrist and pulled her hair back into a pony-tail with one practised movement. 'This hair is driving me crazy. I got it cut yesterday. It's all smooth and slippery. Your mum got me an appointment with her hairdresser.'

'It looks nice,' said Logan automatically. He was well trained. *Sisters*.

'It cost a lot,' said Savannah. 'Your mother paid, which was really nice of her.'

'Okay,' said Logan. Was she testing out his reaction to this information? He didn't care if his mother wanted to pay for some girl's haircut. He saw now that the hairstyle was very similar to his mother's, as if her hairdresser worked from a template.

'You got the day off from work?' she said.

'I work odd hours,' he said.

'Drug dealer?'

He smiled tolerantly. 'I teach at a community college.'

'What do you teach?'

'Business communications.' He waited for the inevitable reaction.

She raised her eyebrows. 'I would have guessed you taught . . . I don't know, some kind of trade, like house painting.'

He looked down at his pants. The yellow splashes were from when he and Indira had repainted their kitchen a sunny yellow that neither of them ended up liking. The blue splashes were from when he helped paint Brooke's clinic. He couldn't remember where the green flecks were from.

He'd actually done house painting for a couple of years after giving up tennis. Followed by plastering. Then roof tiling. 'What about *building* as a career?' his dad had said hopefully, trying to parlay all these different jobs into something more substantial. He wouldn't have minded if Logan had stuck with house painting but he couldn't stand the fact that Logan kept working for other people. Self-employment was the way to impress his father.

'What about a degree, darling?' his mother had said. Neither of his parents had degrees. His mother said the word 'degree' with such respect and humility it broke his heart.

When Logan was seventeen he had turned down a tennis scholarship to an American university. He often wondered what his thinking had been. Was it because he knew his father didn't see an American scholarship as a valid path to success in tennis? 'If you want to make a career of tennis, then focus on your *tennis*, not study.' Or was it fear? A bit of social anxiety? He'd been an awkward teenager. He remembered thinking he wasn't enthusiastic enough for America. He spoke too slowly. He was too Australian. Too much like his dad.

He did do a part-time communications degree eventually. God knows why he did that. But that degree was enough to get him this job teaching business communication skills and it suited him. He had no special interest in the subject itself, but he enjoyed teaching. It was fine. A steady job with good hours. He actually thought he might do it forever.

'Do you enjoy your chosen profession?' asked Savannah. Was she laughing at him? Also, was she deliberately avoiding answering his question about how she knew his parents or had she just got distracted? He wouldn't give her the satisfaction of asking again.

'Sure,' he said. 'Anyway. Better get on with it.'

'Do you want some help?' She slammed the mug down on the porcelain tiles next to her and he winced because the mug was his mother's favourite, the one that said, *There's no place like home: except Grandma's!*

'Careful with that mug,' he said. 'It's my mother's favourite.'

Savannah picked up the mug with exaggerated care, got to her feet and placed it on the table where Logan's father sat to do the crossword on Saturday mornings.

'Sorry,' she said. 'I just grabbed it from the dishwasher.' She picked it up again and studied it. '*No place like Grandma's.* Except your mother isn't a grandma, is she?'

'It belonged to my grandmother,' said Logan. Troy had bought it for their mother's mother as a Christmas gift, and she'd loved it. Of course she had. Troy was famous for buying the best gifts. Her love of the mug had been inexplicable because their mother's mother had never been especially grandmotherly. Whenever they visited she was always keen for a departure time to be specified upfront.

The girl stepped off the veranda onto the grass and walked over to him. She stood a little too close, and Logan took a step back. Amy called people who did that 'Space Invaders'. The Delaneys were not touchy-feely people. Except for their mother. She was a hugger, an arm-patter, a back-rubber, but Joy had always been the exception to the Delaney rule.

Savannah looked up at him with too much interest. Her eyelashes were long and white, like a small native animal's. She had a pointed, freckled nose, thin, chapped lips and a flesh-coloured Band-Aid above one eyebrow. Logan was taller and bigger than most people, but this girl was so small and fragile-looking she made him feel enormous and foolish, as though he were dressed up as a football mascot.

'Do you want to have children?' She looked at him intensely. Was there something a little wrong with her?

'Maybe one day,' he said. He took another step back. 'What happened there?' He indicated the Band-Aid.

'My boyfriend hit me,' she said, without inflection.

He thought her answer was going to be something mundane – in fact, he had no interest in the answer, he was just deflecting attention – and consequently, in his shock, he responded without thinking.

'Why?' The word was out of his mouth before he could drag it back. *Why?* It was like asking, *What did you do to deserve that?* His sisters would tear strips off him. Victim-blaming! 'Sorry. That's a stupid thing to ask.'

'It's okay. So, he came home from work, when was it? Last Tuesday night.' She stuck her hands in the pockets of Amy's jeans and circled the toe of her boot in the grass. 'He was actually in a pretty good mood that day.'

'You don't need to tell me,' said Logan. He held up a hand to try to stop her. He didn't want details, for Christ's sake.

'It's okay, I'm quite happy to tell you,' she said, and he'd asked the stupid question, so his punishment was to endure the painful answer.

'We were watching TV, just chilling out, and then this news story came on about domestic violence, right? I thought, Oh great, here we go. Those stories . . .' She shook her head. 'I don't know why they have to keep putting those stories on TV. It doesn't *help*. It makes it *worse*!' Her voice skidded up.

Logan squinted, trying to make sense of what she was saying. Was she saying a story about violence against women inspired it?

'Those stories always put him in the filthiest of moods. Maybe they made him feel guilty, I don't know. He'd say, "Oh, it's always the man's fault, isn't it? Never the chick's fault! Always his fault."' She put on a deep, jock-like voice to imitate the boyfriend. Logan could almost see the guy. He knew the type.

'So anyway, I changed the channel as fast as I could, I was like, "Oh, I want to watch *Survivor*!" and he didn't say anything, and then I could feel it, he was just waiting for me to do something wrong, and the minutes went by, and I started to relax, and I thought, Oh it's fine, and then, like an *idiot*, like a *fool*, I asked if he'd paid the car registration.' She shook her head at her own stupidity. 'I wasn't trying to make a point. I honestly wasn't.' She looked up at Logan through her sandy eyelashes as if she were trying to convince him of her innocence. 'I just said, "Did you remember to pay it?"'

'Sounds like a valid question to me,' said Logan. He'd never experienced physical violence in a relationship, but he knew how a question could be misinterpreted, how a simple request for information could be flung back in your face.

'Well, it infuriated him,' said Savannah. 'Apparently I was being passive aggressive.' She shrugged and put her fingertips to the Band-Aid over her eye. 'So it all sort of spiralled from there, the way it always did, and next thing you know, he's yelling, I'm crying . . . just pathetic, really. Embarrassing.' She looked off to the side, her hands on her hips. She smelled of cheap perfume, hairspray and cigarettes, like the girls he used to kiss on summer holidays, behind the amenities block at the Central Coast caravan park. The smell triggered a surge of feeling that Logan hoped was nostalgia for that time, not desire for this girl. It was inappropriate to think about kissing this small fragile abused girl. It made him feel complicit with the arsehole boyfriend.

'Anyway . . . whatever . . . so that's what happened.' Savannah hitched up Amy's jeans around her waist. 'He's history. I left, hailed a cab, and I'm never going back.'

'Good,' said Logan, and then a series of thoughts clicked into place.

He said, 'Does your boyfriend know you're here?' He imagined his mother flinging open the front door, in that way she did, always so pleased for company, a smile on her face, to be greeted by some yobbo with a vendetta. He didn't wait for an answer. 'How do you know my parents anyway?'

'I don't,' said Savannah. 'I knocked on their door at random.'

'You what?'

'Logan!' His mother slid back the glass door leading onto the back veranda and put her hands to her cheeks, as if she couldn't believe it was him, as if she hadn't seen his car in the driveway and would therefore already have had plenty of warning that he was here. Her voice had that marginally posher accent she reserved for non-family members. Actually, it was worse than usual. She sounded almost drunk with excitement. 'What are *you* doing here?'

'I'm doing the gutters, Mum,' said Logan. 'Like I said.'

'Oh, you don't need to do that,' said his mother. 'Your father has it under control.' She came over to them and put her hand on Savannah's back as she spoke. 'I see you've met Savannah.' She looked at Savannah and then back at Logan. Her eyes sparkled. 'She's staying with us for a while. She's staying with us for *as long as she wants.*' She patted Savannah gently on the back in rhythm with her words.

She stopped patting and said, 'How's Indira?' with a penetrating look, as if she suspected something about the break-up, but how could she possibly know?

Logan said, 'She's fine. Oh, she wanted me to give you this.'

He pulled the tiny, now rather ratty-looking gift from his pocket. Indira had asked him to give it to his mother weeks ago and he kept forgetting.

'Oh, Logan!' His mother put a hand to her chest. She looked absolutely thrilled.

'It's not anything –'

'She didn't want to be here?' said Joy. She looked around her as if expecting Indira to pop out from behind a hedge. 'To see me open it?'

'It's just a little –'

'Logan's partner is a very special girl,' Joy told Savannah. 'Very special. I wish she were here!' She patted her hair, once again looked suspiciously around the backyard before she ripped off the paper. 'Oh!' Her face fell. 'It's a . . . fridge magnet.'

She turned the magnet back and forth, examining it as if for a secret message. It had a yellow flower on it. Logan had no idea why Indira had bought it for his mother or why it had caused that momentary expression of anguish. What had she expected it to be?

'It's so pretty,' she told Logan. Her eyes were bright. 'Indira knows I love yellow gerberas and that stupid magnet we got in London keeps falling off the fridge! That's why she got it. She's so thoughtful. Please thank her. Well, I'll be seeing her on Sunday, so I can thank her myself!'

You won't be seeing her on Sunday, thought Logan, but obviously he wasn't going to tell his mother about the break-up in front of this strange girl. He changed the subject fast. 'So I was just hearing how . . . Savannah knocked on your door?' He cleared his throat. 'At random? That's . . .' Did *Brooke* know about this yet? Brooke was the youngest in the family, but the most sensible and certain.

'She said she had a good feeling about this house,' said Joy. She smiled guilelessly up at Logan. 'She said it felt safe. Isn't that a lovely thing to say?'

'Yeah, it is, so I was just asking Savannah if her ex-boyfriend knew where she was staying.' Logan met his mother's eyes. Joy liked to put on her dippy act but she wasn't stupid.

'He doesn't know where she is,' said Joy. 'And he's got no way of finding out.'

'Don't worry,' said Savannah. 'He can't track me down. I didn't even bring my phone when I left.'

'Yes, and we're going to find a time to go over to her apartment to pick up Savannah's things when he's at work,' said Joy. She spoke as if she were planning a lunch.

'You're not going there, Mum,' said Logan.

'Oh, yes, I'll probably stay in the car. Your dad will go inside with Savannah. Just to be on the safe side.' His mother looked up at him, brightly, craftily, and Logan felt himself slide inevitably forward on the course of action his mother had already set for him.

'I don't think Dad should go either,' said Logan. He sighed. There was no way out. He looked at Savannah and tried to make himself sound gracious, not sulky. '*I'll* take you.'

'I don't need anyone to come with me,' said Savannah. 'I really don't.'

'Your brother can go too,' said Joy to Logan. 'Safety in numbers. That's a good idea.' She said it in a warm congratulatory manner as if it were Logan's good idea. 'You and Troy can help Savannah scoop everything up and get out of there quick smart and that will be the end of that!'

Would it be the end of that? 'Isn't Troy in America?' asked Logan.

'He flew back this morning,' said his mother. 'You can all three go over to Savannah's place tomorrow once he's over his jet lag.'

Troy would be appalled. Logan's mood lifted fractionally at the thought.

'You should go around eleven, I think. Avoid peak hour. You'll have time before you teach your two pm class.'

Logan wanted to say, *Maybe I'm doing something else tomorrow morning, Mum*, but then his mother would demand details.

'No. That's okay. I appreciate the offer but I'll go on my own,' said Savannah, and Logan wanted to laugh because she had no idea how pointless it was to resist once his mother had decided something was going to happen. 'Once your mother has momentum no-one can beat her,' Stan always said, and he was talking about tennis but every single thing Logan's dad said about tennis could also be applied to life.

'I'll go on my own,' said Savannah.

'No you will not, darling,' said Joy. Steel in her voice.

Game to Mum, thought Logan.

chapter twelve

Now

'How would you describe your parents' marriage?'

Detective Senior Constable Christina Khoury flipped the page in her notebook and studied the man opposite her: Logan Delaney. The second of Joy Delaney's four grown-up children. Thirty-seven years old. The slouched posture and relaxed drawl of a surfer dude, but the watchful eyes of someone with an agenda. Looked like a gardener but apparently taught business studies. She and Ethan were interviewing him in the lobby of the community college where he worked. He said his next class started in twenty minutes.

They sat across from Logan in low vinyl tub chairs with a small round table in between them. A noticeboard behind Logan's head advertised evening courses: *So you want to do your own soft furnishings? So you want to write a memoir? So you want to master small talk? So you want to get married?* Some people actually did a *course* to get married? She must remember to tell Nico about that. Or maybe not. He might want to do the course. He had random bursts of enthusiasm for bizarre activities.

'I'd describe their marriage as normal,' answered Logan.

'Good.' He rotated his right shoulder forward and then backward. 'They've been married nearly fifty years.'

'Shoulder trouble?' Christina pretended to care. She cared about finding out what had happened to this man's mother.

'It's fine.' He stilled his shoulder and sat up straighter.

'So, they've been married nearly fifty years. That's a long time.'

'It is.'

'Obviously every marriage has its ups and downs, its conflicts,' she said, and waited.

A beat.

Another beat.

He raised a single eyebrow. Still he didn't speak. He was very much like his father. He didn't rush to fill the gaps.

'Are you married yourself, Logan?'

He looked at his left hand as if to check. 'No. I'm not. Never married.'

'In a relationship?'

He smiled wearily. 'It's complicated.'

'Would you say your parents have a complicated relationship?'

'No,' he said. 'They have an excellent relationship. They're doubles champions. You have to be good communicators to play doubles successfully.'

'What about *off* the court?'

'They ran a very successful business together for thirty years.'

'So their marriage hasn't been . . .' She looked down at her notes. 'Rocky at times?'

'Every marriage is rocky at times.' He peered over as if he were trying to see what she had written down. 'Did someone actually *say* that to you?'

'I believe your sister told the police officers that things had been – what was the word she used? – a little "tumultuous" lately.'

'Which sister?' He lifted his hand to stop her answering. 'I know which sister.' He seemed to come to a sudden decision.

'Look. Can I get one thing straight? Are you guys treating my father as a suspect?'

Of course I am, mate. You know I am.

She assumed Logan had seen the healing scratch marks on his father's face. Stan Delaney said they came from climbing through a hedge to retrieve a tennis ball. They looked to Christina like classic defence wounds.

Yesterday's search of Joy and Stan Delaney's home had revealed little of interest. The house was clean and tidy. It was notably clean and tidy. No signs that remotely indicated a struggle, except for one thing: a faint crack that snaked across the glass of a framed photo in the hallway. The photo was of a child holding a tennis trophy.

'What happened here?' Christina had asked Stan Delaney, and he said, 'No idea.'

It was a lie. Just like the story about searching through the hedge for a tennis ball was a lie. They'd seized the framed picture in the faint hope that it might contain blood or hair.

Stan Delaney had answered all of her questions yesterday with little to no detail. He said yes, he and his wife had argued, but he refused to say what the argument was about. He said yes, it was out of character for his wife to go away like this. He said yes, it was strange that she had not taken her toothbrush, or any clothes as far as he could tell. He was obviously a smart man. He knew he didn't have to be polite and that he couldn't be compelled to say anything he didn't want to say. He was good. He was bloody good. But Christina was better.

'Your mother is missing and I'm hearing that's out of character,' she said to Logan. 'So all we're doing at this stage is collecting information.'

'Dad is worried sick. He's not sleeping or eating. He's not coping well.'

Christina tapped her pen against the notepad. 'May I say, *you* don't seem that worried about your mother, Logan.'

He raised his eyebrows. Waited for the question.

'Yet it was you and your sister who filed the missing persons report.'

Again, he waited for the question.

'As you know, we're holding a press conference later this afternoon. We're putting a lot of time and effort into finding your mother.'

She saw his good manners kick in. 'Thank you. We're grateful. We're worried she might have had an accident. Or that she might have had some sort of . . . episode, or something.'

'Episode?' Christina pounced. 'Do you mean a mental health kind of episode?'

'I guess so.' He shifted in his seat.

'Has she been showing signs of depression?'

'Not really,' he said. He winced and then said carefully, 'Maybe a little bit.'

'Can you tell me more about that?' said Christina.

'She's been not quite herself.' He looked past Christina's head. 'She may have been feeling a bit . . . down.'

'What about?'

'Well,' he said, and she saw him consider and then discard the truthful answer. 'I'm not exactly sure.'

'So she sent a text to each of her children saying she was going away, but she left no message for your father. Did you find that strange?'

He shrugged. 'They'd argued. You know that.'

She sure did know that.

'My dad doesn't have a mobile phone so she obviously couldn't text him.'

'She could have called him on the landline, she could have left a note, she could have found some other way to communicate with him, surely?' pointed out Christina. *The simplest answer is most often correct.*

'I understand how this looks to an outsider,' said Logan. 'But you're wrong.'

No-one wants to believe their parents are capable of

murdering each other, no matter what they've witnessed.

Christina pushed the point. 'Your mother's text message didn't say, *Please let your father know I'm going away.*'

'Her text message made no sense,' Logan reminded her.

Christina said nothing. She waited. Sometimes her job was all about waiting.

Logan banged a closed knuckle on the edge of his chair as if knocking impatiently on a closed door. He said, 'You can't really be thinking that my seventy-year-old father murdered my mother, disposed of the body, and sent us all a garbled text from her phone to throw us off the scent. Jesus Christ. It's fantastical. It's just . . . not possible.'

'Our records show your father never once tried to call your mother's mobile phone,' said Christina.

Her first murder case involved a man making authentically frantic-sounding calls to over twenty friends and family members, but not a single call to his supposedly missing wife. Why would he call her? He knew she wouldn't answer.

'You'll have to ask him about that,' said Logan.

'So where do you think your mother is, Logan? What do you think is going on here?'

Logan continued his previous line of thought, as if trying to work it out himself. 'So he sends the fake text, and then he hides the phone *under their bed*? Of all places? Wouldn't he destroy it? If he's capable of murdering someone, don't you think he's smart enough to destroy a phone?'

Christina said, 'Perhaps he wasn't thinking clearly.'

'I don't know where she is, and you're wrong, I am worried, because you're right, it is strange, and it is out of character.' Logan shifted about in his seat and gave a distracted wave to someone who had walked out of a classroom. 'But at the same time, I feel like maybe she needed to get away for a while, or maybe she's making a point.'

Christina said, 'Why would your mother need to make a point?'

He lifted his hands.

'What point would she be making?'

He shook his head. He looked at a spot on the wall and blew air out of his mouth as if it were a long thin stream of cigarette smoke.

She allowed a hint of aggression to come into her voice. The obfuscation was starting to annoy her. 'That doesn't make sense. You say your parents had a perfect relationship and now you're saying maybe your mother has disappeared to make a point.'

'I never said it was a *perfect* relationship. There were issues. Like every relationship. Like you said.'

'Can you be more specific about those issues, please?'

'Not really.' He sighed. 'How well could you analyse your parents' marriage?'

'My parents are divorced,' said Christina shortly.

She could be very specific about the issues. They divorced over a plate. After he retired, her dad got into the habit of making himself a hummus and tomato sandwich every day at eleven am. Christina's mother suggested he rinse the plate and put it in the dishwasher. He refused. It somehow went against his principles. This went on for years until one day Christina's mother picked up the plate from the sink, threw it like a frisbee at her dad's head and said, 'I want a divorce.' Her father was baffled and wounded. (Not physically wounded. He ducked.) He finally concluded that Christina's mother was 'deranged' and remarried within the year. Meanwhile Christina's mother got into hot yoga and *The Handmaid's Tale*. 'Under his eye,' she said darkly, each time Christina rang her to talk about her wedding arrangements. She said she was very happy for Christina's dad's second wife to be at the wedding just as long as she was 'never within her line of sight'.

'What about housework?' she asked Logan. 'Any issues there?'

'*Housework?*' Logan blinked the way that men tended to blink when women brought up frivolous domestic issues in serious settings. *It was just a plate*, her father kept saying to Christina.

He never understood what that plate represented: Disrespect. Disregard. Contempt.

'My mother did the housework,' said Logan. 'That was never an issue between them. It was a traditional marriage in that way. She's . . . of that generation.'

'But didn't she help run the tennis school as well?'

Logan looked impatient. 'I'm not saying it was *fair.*'

She waited.

He said, 'I'm telling you I never once saw them argue about housework.' Was that an unconscious curl of his lip on the word 'housework'? Did his eyes just flick over to Ethan for masculine support? *Can you believe this chick?* Or was she projecting her own unconscious biases? She never saw her parents argue about housework either, and yet that plate in the sink ended their marriage. *He just ignores me, Christina. I ask so nicely and he just ignores me.* No-one was too old or well mannered for the sudden snap of rage.

'So what did they argue about, then?'

He looked away. 'My dad wasn't always an easy man. He's different now.'

And now we're getting somewhere. 'Was he ever violent towards your mother?'

'Jesus. No. *Never.*' He looked back up at her, seemingly appalled. 'You're getting the wrong impression.'

Yet she saw a flicker of something: a question, a thought, a memory. It was gone before she could grab it.

'Never?' she probed.

'Never,' he said. 'I'm sorry if I've made you think that, because that is so wrong. Dad could just be . . . moody. That's all I meant. He shut down when he was upset. Like a lot of men of his age. But he adored my mother.' He muttered something inaudible.

'Sorry, I didn't catch that.'

He smiled uneasily. 'I said, he *adores* my mother. He still does adore my mother.'

In a moment he was going to shut down himself.

Christina changed direction. 'What can you tell me about this woman who lived with your parents for a while, last year, was it? Both your sisters mentioned her.'

'Savannah,' he said heavily. 'Yeah, well, speaking of complicated. That got complicated for a while there.'

'In what way?'

'In every way.'

chapter thirteen

Last September

'So it's just until she finds somewhere to live,' said Joy to Brooke, the walkabout phone cradled between her ear and her shoulder as she dusted the living room with a green 'microfibre dusting cloth' she'd bought at one of those unbearable parties where she'd had to endure various 'product demonstrations' by a very nice woman whose three children Joy and Stan had privately coached for many years without improvement, and therefore Joy had felt obligated to buy three dusting cloths, one for each kid.

Joy had a rule that whenever one of her children telephoned, she dusted (even if it was Logan calling, whose calls lasted an average of thirty seconds).

She was in a good mood today. Last night she and Stan had sex. Surprisingly excellent sex. If she could still get pregnant, last night would have got her pregnant. (She always used to say that Stan only had to look at her to get her pregnant, which had caused a very embarrassing misunderstanding with Brooke when she was six and one day accused dear little Philip Ngu of trying to get her pregnant at recess.)

It had been the first time in months. Joy had actually been wondering if they were done with it, and she hadn't even been upset about it, which was upsetting in itself. She suspected it was somehow related to Savannah. Maybe it was as simple as the fact that they were closing the bedroom door again, which used to be the signal for sex, or maybe Stan's libido was helped by the sight of a pretty young girl flitting about the place?

Joy honestly didn't care if that was the case. She had on occasion found excuses to wander around her own front yard while Caro's grown-up son Jacob did the gardening with his shirt off. She'd known that boy since he was a child, but he'd grown up to look like a young Robert Redford and Joy was not dead yet.

It really had been very good sex for people of their age, Joy thought. She had to suppress the urge to tell Brooke about how well her parents had performed in the bedroom last night, as if they'd won a particularly tough match.

'Why are you laughing, Mum?' asked Brooke.

'I'm not,' said Joy. 'I'm dusting. It's tickling my nose.'

Brooke had left *two* voicemail messages today. She'd learned about Savannah firstly from her sister, and then apparently Logan had called the moment he left the house this morning, so she was now in a fine state. Joy knew that not calling Brooke earlier was an error of judgement. Brooke expected to be the first to find out about significant family developments. The truth was that Joy had put off calling her, because she knew Brooke would react to the news of their house guest with incredulity, disapproval and anxiety, and this was proving to be correct.

'Logan said he and Troy are helping this girl move out of her apartment tomorrow.' Brooke was talking on the speaker phone as she drove home from work. It was irritating. Her voice kept fading in and out.

'Yes, Logan insisted on it,' said Joy. 'He didn't want your father doing it on his own. He and Troy are going to drive Savannah to her apartment tomorrow and move her out. Then she'll never have anything to do with that vile man again.'

She moved into the living room, holding her cloth aloft, and started on the tennis ball collection. Stan owned forty-three signed tennis balls contained in small glass boxes, and it was amazing how the glass containers collected a thin layer of dust in such a short amount of time. When he died the signed balls would be the first thing to go. Some of them were probably fake. She'd read somewhere once that sports memorabilia fraud was booming.

'What if the boyfriend turns up?' asked Brooke.

'It will be two against one,' said Joy. 'Your brothers can take care of it.'

'What if he has a . . . I don't know, a knife?'

Joy paused. Surely he wouldn't have a knife! 'Should they take knives too?'

'Oh my *God*, Mum!' Brooke exploded. Her excessive reaction calmed Joy. She wasn't sending the boys into an active war zone. Savannah was quite positive that the boyfriend wouldn't be there, and even if he was, Troy and Logan were very big, strong, intimidating men. Everyone said so. They'd be fine. She wouldn't let them take knives. To be honest, part of her still didn't trust the boys with knives, as if they were still little kids who might cut themselves or each other. She knew there was a very significant contradiction in her thinking right now.

'He's not going to be there,' said Joy. 'He's a graphic designer, apparently. Like Indira. I wonder if Indira knows him? I guess that's unlikely. Indira gave me a lovely new fridge magnet, did I tell you?'

She kept telling people about how much she loved the magnet to hide the fact that she couldn't stand to look at it, because she'd been so crushed when she opened it. She'd been idiotically convinced it was an ultrasound picture and that Indira was hiding somewhere in the garden, watching her reaction. Mortifying.

'No, Mum, you didn't mention that Indira gave you a lovely fridge magnet,' said Brooke. Joy recognised the tone. She used to speak to her own mother with the same forbearance.

'Anyway, the boys will be fine,' said Joy.

'I can't believe we need to get involved with these kinds of people,' fretted Brooke.

'*These kinds of people?*' repeated Joy. 'What do you mean, *these kinds of people*?'

Brooke had never, ever been snooty. Joy hadn't brought her children up like that. Troy liked to strut about like a peacock, flicking his shiny black credit card onto the table at restaurants; 'I'll take care of this,' he'd say, but it was *funny* when he did it.

'Oh, you know what I mean, Mum,' said Brooke.

'No, I don't know what you mean. You didn't grow up in Downton Abbey, darling.'

'It's nothing to do with money or class. I just mean people where there might be a, I don't know, a kind of, what's the word, criminal element?'

'We've got plenty of criminal elements in our family! Your own brother was a drug dealer!'

'Troy just sold weed to the private school kids. You make him sound like a drug lord. He just, you know . . . saw a gap in the market.'

'I can assure you that Savannah is a nice girl in a difficult situation,' said Joy crisply.

'I'm sure she is a nice girl, and it's awful what happened to her, but she's a stranger, and she's not your responsibility. You've got enough on your plates!' There was that new condescending tone that had begun to creep into Brooke's voice ever since Stan had his knee operation, as if she were just *weighed down* with the onerous responsibility of taking care of her aging parents. It was sweet but also mildly aggravating.

'What are you talking about? We've got nothing on our plates. Not a thing. Our plates are empty, darling.'

Joy hadn't fully understood how bored she and Stan had been until Savannah arrived on their doorstep. Savannah gave Joy and Stan something interesting and new to talk about, and she was so sweet and grateful and pretty.

'And Savannah isn't a stranger anymore.' Joy peered at Agassi's scratchy ballpoint signature on the ball as she polished. 'Every person you meet starts out as a stranger. Your father was a stranger when I first met him. *You* were a little stranger, when I first met you.' She saw Brooke's outraged little red face as the doctor held her up like an animal he'd rescued from a trap. Amazing to think that angry helpless baby was now this opinionated young woman.

'You didn't let Dad move in to your house the moment you met him,' said Brooke.

'No, but I let you move in!' said Joy, which she thought was rather witty, but Brooke's laugh sounded hollow.

'Anyway, she hasn't "moved in",' Joy reassured her. She picked up the Navratilova ball. 'This is temporary. Obviously.' She spoke in the brisk, business-like voice she used with the accountants. 'It's just until she gets back on her feet. There's really nothing to worry about. You'll like her when you meet her. Logan liked her today! I could tell. You know what she's doing right now?'

'Going through your jewellery?' said Brooke. 'Stealing your identities?'

Sometimes she sounded so much like her father.

'I don't own any jewellery worth stealing,' said Joy. 'She's welcome to it. No. She's *cooking dinner.* Pasta.' The scents of garlic and onion wafted from the kitchen. 'This is the third time she's cooked! She keeps insisting! She says she loves to cook! Do you know how wonderful it is to have someone else cooking for you? Well, you do, because Grant cooks.'

There was a moment's silence, and then Brooke said plaintively, 'I've cooked dinner for you, Mum.'

'Of course you have,' soothed Joy. 'Many times.' Brooke was a perfectly competent cook, like Joy herself, but, also like Joy, she took no obvious pleasure in cooking, grimly plunking down plates with a put-upon sigh.

Joy's family had been, and still were, big eaters. Keeping her family fed had been a never-ending, arduous task and now that it was just Joy and Stan, she had to force herself into the kitchen each night, with the thought: *This again?* Savannah, on the other hand, cooked as if it was a lovely pastime, not a chore to endure, humming and cleaning as she went.

Brooke didn't answer, and Joy heard the traffic in the background, the angry toot of someone's horn, and she imagined her daughter behind the wheel, frowning, worrying about that damned new clinic that Joy wished she hadn't so bravely started, worrying about her parents who didn't yet require her concern. *The time will come, my darling, we'll get frail and sick and stubborn and your stomach will twist with love and terror each time we call, but plenty of time, don't get ahead of yourself, we're not there yet.*

'The thing is, I *hate* cooking,' said Joy. The words rushed out of her mouth: traitorously, venomously. 'You've no idea how much I *hate* cooking, and it just never ends, the cooking, night after night after bloody night. Each night at five o'clock, like clockwork, your father says, "What's for dinner?" and I grit my teeth so hard I can feel it in my jaw.'

She stopped, embarrassed.

'Gosh, Mum,' said Brooke. She sounded shocked. 'We should get one of those meal services for you, if you really hate cooking that much. I had no idea you felt like that! All those years. You should have made us help more when we were growing up but you never let us in the kitchen! I feel terrible –'

'No, no, no,' interrupted Joy. She felt ridiculous. It was true she hadn't let her children help in the kitchen. They were too messy and loud and she didn't have the time or patience to be the sort of mother to smile lovingly while a floury-faced child cracked eggs onto the floor.

(She *would* be that sort of grandmother. Grandchildren would be her second chance to get it right. Now she had the time and the eggs to spare, and she would be present with her grandchildren. When she looked at photos of her children when they were little, she sometimes thought, Did I notice how beautiful they were? Was I actually *there*? Did I just skim the surface of my entire damned life?)

'I was being silly, I don't really hate cooking. I just like it when someone else puts a meal in front of me, as if I'm the lady of the manor! And it's no big deal at all now, when it's just for your father and me, it's easy! Now . . . how are you, how was your weekend?'

'It was nice,' said Brooke. 'Quiet.'

A sudden instinct, something about the tension in Brooke's voice and the memory that Brooke had said she might drop by over the weekend but then never had, and Joy had been so busy with Savannah that she only just remembered now, made Joy say, 'Did you have a migraine over the weekend, Brooke?'

'So what else has this Savannah been doing all day?' said Brooke at the same time. 'Apart from cooking?'

'She's been resting,' said Joy. 'She needed a rest. I think she's been through quite a stressful time.'

For the first couple of days Savannah had slept for long stretches, as though she were recuperating from a serious illness, and Joy and Stan had tiptoed about the house, giving each other quizzical shrugs. Initially Savannah hadn't spoken at all, just gratefully eaten whatever food was put in front of her. It was gratifying to see the colour come back into her cheeks. As the days went by she became chattier, and she seemed so interested in Joy and Stan's lives, and to truly enjoy hearing their stories and looking at family photos. She asked them all about the tennis school: How did they come to start it? What was it like in those early days? Was it hard to find students? Did they still play? Did none of their children want to take over the business? It was Stan who answered all those questions, who seemed to want to answer her questions; he kept getting in first – it was so unlike him! – as if he needed to do this, as if her interest was fulfilling some sort of thera-peutic need, giving him 'closure', perhaps? Savannah nodded along, and never seemed to get impatient when Stan spent ten minutes trying to work out if a particular tournament had taken place in 1981 or 1982.

'And what does *Dad* think about all this?' asked Brooke. Without waiting for an answer she said, suddenly suspicious, 'Has he got her on the court yet? Does she play?'

She was so transparent. Always a Daddy's girl. It was Stan's approval she so desperately craved, as if it were withheld from her, and yet she'd always had it, from the moment he first held her. Brooke was Stan's favourite. Everyone knew it except for Brooke.

'Savannah doesn't play,' said Joy. 'She says she's not sporty. But your dad likes her.' It was actually surprising how well Stan and Savannah got on. 'She and your father have bonded over some television series they both enjoy. They talk about the characters as if they're real people.'

'Which series?' asked Brooke urgently, as if that mattered.

'Oh, gosh, I wouldn't know,' said Joy. She'd never been a big fan of television, and the older she got the less patience she had for it – her lower back played up if she sat still for too long – whereas Stan had gone in the other direction and would sit in that recliner for hours watching rubbish.

'Right,' said Brooke.

'How's Grant?' asked Joy. 'And how's work? I gave your card to someone the other day, now who was it? Someone who said they were having back pain, just like me, and I said, "Well, you must see my daughter," and he said –'

'Amy said something about Dad buying her a car?' Brooke's voice was sharp.

'Who, Savannah? He's not buying her a car, we were just talking about how we'd need to get her set up with a car at some point, and your dad was asking her if she'd consider the new Golf, so they went and test-drove one. You know how your dad loves test-driving cars, even if he has no intention of buying one.'

'How is she going to afford a car? Does she even have a job?' asked Brooke.

'I think I already told you that she and her boyfriend had only just moved here from Queensland,' said Joy.

'So why doesn't she just move *back* to –'

'Jo-oy! Dinner!'

'I've got to go, that's Savannah calling to say dinner is ready.' She walked towards the kitchen, the phone to her ear.

'How did Dad react to the news about Harry's comeback?' asked Brooke.

'Oh, well, Savannah has been a good distraction,' said Joy, lowering her voice, knowing Stan was already in the kitchen sorting out their drinks. She could see Savannah through the doorway with three plates balanced on her forearms like a waitress. Her haircut looked lovely.

'It will be interesting to see what he says about Dad in his autobiography,' said Brooke. 'Do you think Dad will read it? Or will it upset him too much?'

'Autobiography?' Joy stopped. She spun around so she was facing away from the kitchen.

'Supposedly he's writing one,' said Brooke. 'Or he's probably paying a ghost writer to write it for him.'

Would they ever be free of that boy? 'I didn't know that.'

She should have predicted it. All the big names in tennis wrote their stories eventually. Everyone loved a success story. Their 'So You Want to Write a Memoir' teacher had said 'rags to riches' and 'overcoming the odds' were the most popular themes for memoirs.

There was something demeaning about Joy doing Caro's silly memoir-writing course, while Harry, a kid whose bloodied skinny-boy knees she'd once bandaged, wrote a *proper* memoir that people would actually want to read. It made Joy's entire life feel silly. A *lady's* life.

'Will *you* read it?' asked Brooke.

'I don't know,' said Joy slowly. 'Probably.' She heard the low timbre of Stan's voice as he spoke to Savannah in the kitchen.

She walked to the couch, sat down and picked up a cushion.

She caressed its soft tasselled fringe while she monitored her reaction to this revelation. Her heart had quickened but it was certainly not *racing*. There was really no need for concern here. After all, she and Stan represented only one chapter in Harry's illustrious career. Harry would simply trot out a more detailed version of the by now well-worn raffle ticket story: how Harry's father, Elias, won the private lesson at Delaneys, gave the lesson to his son, first time the kid ever held a racquet, blah, blah, blah.

There would be no further revelations. Harry knew nothing. He'd been a kid, his eyes firmly fixed on his future. His readers wanted to hear what it was like to win Wimbledon. They wanted *Harry's* secrets. Not his father's secrets. Not Joy's secrets.

She saw Elias Haddad's handsome face: that slow, sensual wink. It used to make her blood run cold. She'd see him at an interstate tournament and think, *Don't you dare wink at me again, Elias.* But sure enough he'd wink at her over the heads of their oblivious children. As if it were all just a joke. Well. She refused to be worried. She would put it out of her mind. It was all so long ago.

'No need to dwell on things,' her mother used to say. Everyone did far too much dwelling these days.

'I must let you go, darling,' she said briskly to Brooke. 'I know you're busy.' She could smell her dinner waiting for her. She replaced the cushion in the corner of the couch. 'We'll see you on Sunday, for Father's Day. You can meet Savannah then.'

'She'll still be there?' There was a crack of genuine distress in Brooke's voice. 'On Father's Day?'

Joy lowered her voice and her head to the phone once more.

'Darling,' she said. There was a myth in Joy's family, one that Brooke liked to perpetuate, and the myth was that even though Brooke was the youngest, and the one with the debilitating health condition, she was the most robust of the Delaney children, the least sensitive, the one who had her professional and personal life sorted, and that Amy, the oldest, who should therefore have been the most responsible, was the flaky, fragile one who was always getting her feelings hurt, but Joy knew better.

She knew exactly what lay behind the façades her children presented to the world. Yes, Amy had her mental health challenges but she was as tough as nails at her core; Logan pretended not to care about anything but cared about everything; Troy acted so superior because he felt so inferior; and Brooke liked to present herself as the most grown-up of them all, but sometimes Joy caught the fleeting expression of a frightened child crossing her face. Those were the times Joy wanted to gather her six-foot-one daughter in her arms and say, *My baby girl*.

'Savannah won't find somewhere to live by the weekend,' she told Brooke.

'No. Of course not,' said Brooke. She sounded flat and distant now. 'That's fine, Mum. This is a really kind thing you're doing and I'm glad you're getting a break from cooking. I'll see you Sunday. Love you.'

'Love you too,' said Joy, but Brooke had already hung up.

Joy went into the kitchen, where Stan had put three wine-glasses in a row on the island bench: white for Savannah, red for Stan, a spritzer for Joy.

Savannah put a big green salad in the centre of the table and angled the good shiny silver salad servers just so. Someone had given Joy those salad servers years ago and she'd never used them, as if no occasion was ever good enough, not even Christmas, but Savannah automatically used all the nicest things in Joy's kitchen on a daily basis: the good placemats, the good glasses, the good cutlery, and consequently dinner each night felt festive and delightful. She had a knack for setting the table. Joy's mother used to have that knack, and Joy had not inherited it. Tonight Savannah had even picked a little sprig of cherry blossom and put it in a tiny vase she'd found in the back of a cupboard.

'Music?' Joy held up her phone, head on one side. Asking this made her feel like she was maybe in her thirties, living in a share house like Amy. (She had never in her life lived in a share house.)

Logan had helped her set up her Spotify account ages ago, but, like the salad servers, Joy hadn't found the right occasion to use it until Savannah came to stay.

'Yes, please.' Savannah moved deftly behind her to pick up the salt and pepper grinders from the sideboard.

'This pasta looks delicious, Savannah,' said Stan. He would never have said, 'This looks delicious, Joy' about something Joy had cooked, although occasionally he might grunt, 'Looks good' as he picked up his fork. Stan's formality was just like the good crockery and cutlery. It added a nice sheen to the night.

He winked at Joy – just a loving, husbandly wink without subtext – and she thought about his hands on her body last night, his voice low in her ear, and as the first notes of Neil Diamond's 'Sweet Caroline' filled the kitchen, Joy let any thoughts about Harry's memoir and her worry about Brooke fade away as a deep sense of contentment spread throughout her body, as blissful as a fast-acting paracetamol.

chapter fourteen

Now

'Did you kill your wife, Mr Delaney?'

'Eh?' The old man, huge and hunch-shouldered, with reddish thumbprints under his eyes, lifted his bald head, seemingly bewildered by the question. 'What's that?'

The baby-faced journalist in a natty suit and tie shoved a chunky microphone towards his mouth. 'Did you have anything to do with your wife's disappearance, Mr Delaney?'

The old man stood on the front lawn of his suburban house, shoulder to shoulder with his four adult children, surrounded by a semicircle of journalists and camera operators. The journalists were all young, in smart-casual brightly coloured clothes, no patterns, solid colours, sharp shoulders, their faces smooth and opaque with make-up. The camera operators were older, all men, with ordinary, impassive faces and weekend hardware shopping clothes: jeans and polo shirts.

'Mr Delaney?'

'That is *defamatory*. Get *away* from him, you parasite!' It was one of the old man's daughters who spoke. She slapped the microphone. A swift, smooth backhand. She was a tennis player, apparently. They all were.

One of her brothers stepped forward, a protective arm in front of his father's face.

But the other two siblings said and did nothing; they appeared instead to take tiny steps away from their father, and the internet saw.

Minds were made up. *Two of his children think he did it.*

chapter fifteen

Concerns are growing for a Sydney woman who has not been seen for ten days. Police have today launched an appeal for information on the whereabouts of retired tennis coach Joy Delaney.

The 69-year-old was reported missing by her adult children, and officers have been unable to locate her. Family members say they received a text message on Valentine's Day described as 'out of character'. It is believed that she may have been riding a green bicycle with a white wicker basket.

A search of local bushland and bike tracks involving more than one hundred volunteers from the local community has found no sign of her. Police are requesting that anyone with CCTV or dashcam footage in the local area please come forward.

A silver Volvo has been seized as part of the investigation and will be tested forensically over the next few days.

Investigators are keen to talk with a former visitor to the family home, Savannah Pagonis, who may have important information. Police have stressed that Ms Pagonis is not a suspect or a person of interest. 'Any piece of information, no matter how small or seemingly trivial, could prove crucial at this point,' said Detective Senior Constable Christina Khoury.

The missing woman's husband, Stanley Delaney, is helping police with their investigations.

'Helping police with their investigations,' murmured Teresa Geer as she carefully cut out the article from that day's paper with the big kitchen scissors, as was her habit, even though her children teased her for it. It was strange how everyday habits like clipping newspaper articles had suddenly become antiquated.

She couldn't decide if she would show this clipping to her daughter when she got back home from her appointment. Obviously Claire would have already heard that her ex-husband's mother had gone missing.

It would be worrying and confusing for her. There was nothing worse than having to feel sorry for people who had wronged you. You don't want lottery wins for your enemies but you don't want tragedies for them either. Then they got the upper hand.

Damn those Delaneys. Teresa had once been fond of the Delaney family, but that had all changed in an instant five years ago. She would never forget her daughter's shattered face when Claire told her what Troy had done.

Not only had he broken her heart, but it was all Troy's fault that Claire was now married to an American – a nice American, but an American who lived in *America*.

When Troy and Claire had been married they had lived one of those hybrid lives where they continually travelled back and forth between the US and Australia, as if New York and Sydney were merely a bus ride apart. That's how Claire became friends with a Texan girl in New York called Sarah, who eventually invited her to her wedding, a year after Troy and Claire had split up, which is where Claire met Sarah's divorced brother, Geoff, and there was nothing wrong with Geoff, except for his address. Austin was a very fun and friendly city, but so was Sydney! Her new son-in-law just smiled when she pointed that out. He wasn't quite as interested in her as Troy had been. Troy had been kind of flirtatious with her. Teresa had enjoyed his flirtatiousness. It upset her now to remember that. They'd all been hoodwinked. Geoff was no Troy. He hated flying. He didn't want a hybrid life. He wanted a life where Claire saw her Australian family maybe once a year. Claire was back in Sydney now, staying in the spare room, which was wonderful, but once she got back on that plane, Teresa might not see her only daughter for *months*.

So thank you for nothing, Troy Delaney.

She pushed the point of her scissors against the headline of the newspaper article: CONCERNS GROW FOR MISSING WOMAN.

His damned mother would choose to disappear right now, of all times.

She had liked Troy's parents. They were just an ordinary, down-to-earth couple, like her and Hans. She had imagined them all being grandparents together. Surely she would have noticed if there had been cracks in their marriage that could have led to . . . something catastrophic. But that was five years ago, and maybe every marriage had secret cracks that could turn into chasms.

She laid down the scissors and crumpled up the carefully clipped newspaper article into a ball. She wasn't going to say a word to Claire about her former mother-in-law unless she mentioned her first, and then she'd tell her that yes, it was upsetting, but she must try her hardest not to be upset. The Delaneys were nothing to do with them anymore.

If only that were true.

Damn that Troy Delaney.

chapter sixteen

Last September

Troy Delaney watched the streets of his childhood glide by from the passenger seat of Logan's car: lush lawns, sharp-edged hedges, ivy-covered brick walls. A postman on a motorbike slid a single letter into an ornate green letterbox, a magpie swooped violently towards a cyclist's helmeted head, a dog-walker trotted after three little designer dogs, a young mother pushed a double stroller. There was nothing wrong with any of it. There was nothing to complain about (except for the magpie, he hated magpies). It was all perfectly nice. It was just that the unrelenting niceness made him feel like he was being lovingly suffocated with a duvet.

He closed his eyes and tried to recall the cacophony of noise and canyon-like streets of New York, where he'd been twenty-four hours earlier, but it was like Sydney suburbia cancelled out New York's existence. Now there could be nothing else but this: this soft, bland reality, his older brother driving, a tiny, smug grin on his unshaven face, because Logan knew Troy didn't want to be here.

'Love the scarf, mate,' he'd said, predictably, when he saw Troy, who'd worn it just to annoy him. 'You look really intimidating.'

'Pure cashmere,' Troy had answered.

'This is really very kind of you guys,' said a low female voice from the back seat.

'It's not a problem.' Troy turned and smiled at the girl sitting composedly behind them in his brother's shitbox of a car.

Savannah. His parents' bizarre little charity project. She sat upright, her hair pulled back in a schoolgirl ponytail to reveal slightly protruding, tiny ears, like an elf's. Her pale face was make-up free. She had the kind of thin bony body and hard face that speaks of addiction and the streets. There was a nearly healed cut over one eye with faint purplish bruising, and Troy tried to feel the sympathy she obviously deserved, but his heart was as hard and suspicious as an ex-girlfriend's.

Troy's parents had no idea that being abused didn't automatically make you *good*. Savannah could be a petty thief, a psychopath, or just an opportunist who had seen their big house and soft elderly innocent faces, and thought: *Money.*

He and Logan were 'the muscle' in case the boyfriend showed up. Troy covertly checked out his older brother, who didn't have a gym membership but still looked gallingly buff, although he'd stacked it on around the belly. He wondered what Logan could bench-press if he could ever be convinced to bench-press.

How would they handle it if this guy did make an appearance? When Troy was in his 'angry young man' stage he would have relished the opportunity to hit someone with justice on his side, to defend a wronged woman, to blow off all that angry energy, but he no longer walked around with his teeth clenched as tight as his fists, looking for someone to blame. That stupid angry kid no longer existed. Now the thought of being involved in a physical altercation seemed grotesque.

He gripped his fist, watching his knuckles. Did he still know how to hit someone? What if everything went pear-shaped and he got charged with assault? He imagined a twenty-year-old cop handcuffing him and leading him away, hand firm on the back of his neck. To lose control of his life would be unbearable.

If he got arrested he'd no longer be able to travel back and forth between Sydney and New York. He knew how lucky he was that he didn't have a youth criminal record to cause difficulties at the borders, which he sailed through with such ease and regularity. It was all thanks to his mother that he'd been let off with a caution when he'd got caught with cannabis during his 'entrepreneurial days'. She'd arrived like the cavalry, following a phone call from Troy's girlfriend at the time, and launched a full-on Joy Delaney charm offensive that had taken down the older of the two police officers.

Troy had just ten minutes earlier made a profitable sale to the school captain of an 'elite' school, which meant he had a lot of cash on him but only a small amount of drugs: small enough that he could argue it was for personal use. Troy could tell the younger officer badly wanted to charge him, that he represented something that guy couldn't stand. 'Your luck won't last forever, mate,' he'd said to Troy, hatred in his eyes.

'Don't talk to me, don't even look at me,' his mother had said, rippling with fury, on the drive home.

His mother was also the one who'd somehow magically convinced Harry Haddad's father not to call the police when Troy punched the kid in the face for cheating.

'If I'd been there I would have called the police on you myself,' Troy's dad had said.

'Your dad would *never* have done that,' Joy had told him in private. 'He's just upset.'

But his dad had said those words and never taken them back.

Apparently Harry Haddad was going to release an autobiography next year. Troy wondered if he'd include the story of how his first coach's son jumped the net and nearly broke his nose for cheating. Presumably not. Didn't fit with his wholesome *brand*. Troy wouldn't be reading the fucker's book anyway. He hated Harry for dumping his father even more than he hated him for cheating.

Troy shifted in his seat, kicked at an old Subway wrapper

caught on the tip of his shoe from the floor of Logan's car, and *for no reason at all* found himself considering what had happened in New York, even though he had not given his brain permission to consider it – in fact he had expressly forbidden himself to think of it again for another twenty-four hours.

His ex-wife had met him for a drink and presented him with an ethical dilemma so excruciating he thought it might have given him an instant stomach ulcer. Did people still get stomach ulcers? Nobody seemed to talk about them anymore. The word 'ulcerate' seemed appropriate for the sensation he experienced at that moment: like a tiny cyst had burst and flooded his stomach with corrosive acid.

'This is not about evening the score,' Claire had said with a tremulous smile, after she'd taken a sip of an overpriced, over-accessorised cocktail. She'd flown in from Austin just to talk to him.

Logan turned onto the highway and stopped at the first traffic light. A dead bat hung from the powerline. Whenever Troy left his parents' place he got a red light here, and thought, *I always get a red light here*, and then he looked up and thought, *Isn't that dead bat always there?* He got trapped in a permanent loop of pointless thoughts.

Further down the road a bus had stopped and a handful of people disembarked. Troy saw an ancient old lady totter towards the bus stop, face desperate, arm raised. She reminded him of his long-dead grandmother, who'd drunk too much and was spiteful to his mother, but Troy had adored her. She had a scar from when her husband, the grandfather Troy had never met, threw her across the room. She wore the scar with pride, like a tattoo she'd chosen for herself. 'I threw that bastard out of my house,' she told her grandchildren. 'I said, "I never want to see your face again." And I never did.'

The last passenger emerged from the bus. The old lady picked up the pace.

Troy reached across Logan and banged his fist hard on the

horn to get the driver's attention. Too late. The doors slammed shut. The bus took off. For fuck's sake.

Logan looked at him sideways. 'She'll get the next one.'

Troy kicked again at the Subway wrapper. 'Eeuuuuw. Christ almighty. It's stuck on my shoe. Oh God, that yellow fake cheese will stain.'

'Looks like you're due for some new shoes anyway,' said Logan.

'They're brand new Armani suede loafers!' protested Troy.

Logan smirked.

Troy reached down and grabbed the Subway wrapper, scrunched it into a ball and shoved it in the side pocket of the car door, which was filled with coins, a pair of service station sunglasses missing a lens, and a CD without a cover. 'When did you last clean your car? Sometime back in the nineties?'

'Troy would rather not be seen in my car.' Logan looked at Savannah in the rear-vision mirror. Wait, did he just wink at her? He wouldn't be flirting, because he was in a long-term relationship with Indira. Indira was *way* out of Logan's league, as far as Troy was concerned. It was a mystery what these women saw in him.

The only skill Logan had was recognising the good ones. Sometimes, Logan saw something in a woman that Troy didn't see straight away. When they were in their late teens they'd both dated girls called Tracey, and Troy developed a secret, shameful crush on Logan's Tracey. She was the superior Tracey! The worst part was, Troy had met Logan's Tracey first, so he *could* have made a move, but he didn't see her appeal until Logan saw it.

'You've got a fancy car, Troy,' said Savannah. 'What type is it?'

They'd taken Logan's car because he had a bigger boot for Savannah's stuff. Troy was happy not to park his car outside Savannah's flat, which he assumed was in some crummy low-rent area where it would get keyed within five minutes.

'It's a McLaren 600LT.' Troy tried to say it in a neutral tone and ignored Logan's inevitable faux awed whistle.

'How much does a car like that cost?' asked Savannah. 'Is that rude to ask?'

'Are you kidding?' said Logan. 'He's always looking for an excuse to bring his net worth into the conversation.'

'Fuck off,' said Troy, because as a matter of fact the very last thing he wanted discussed in front of this potential con artist was his net worth.

'What do you do, Savannah?' He turned around to look at her again. 'For a living? Is *that* rude to ask?'

Savannah turned her head and spoke to the car window. 'Bit of this, bit of that.' Her nose piercing glinted. 'Mostly retail. Hospitality.'

So she'd worked as a check-out chick and a waitress.

She turned away from the window and looked at him deliberately, her chin lifted. 'We'd only just moved here to Sydney, so I hadn't lined up any work yet. Obviously, I *will*, once this is . . .' She gestured at her forehead. 'I'm not intending to sponge off your parents forever, if that's what you're thinking.'

'I didn't mean that,' said Troy, embarrassed and wrong-footed, and irritated that he'd been made to feel that way. He turned back around to face the front and shifted in his seat as he tried to straighten his legs. He thought of the lavish leg room on his Emirates flight from JFK, the stunning flight attendant leaning down to refill his wineglass, bringing with her a cloud of seductive perfume (Baccarat Rouge 540: he knew he had it right, but had checked to be sure), and now here he was, in a car that smelled of bacon.

He shifted position in his seat. Shifted again. He sensed Logan noticing and made a decision not to move for the next minute. He counted it in his head. *One elephant, two elephant, three elephant.* He made it to thirty seconds and then he had to move. He was eleven years old, the Delaney kid incapable of sitting still.

'SIT STILL, TROY DELANEY!' his teachers used to roar, and sometimes, if he liked the teacher, he would try to sit still, he would try *so* hard, truly, but his body just moved of its own accord, as if he were a puppet with a malicious master tugging strings to jerk his limbs.

He gave up trying and let his legs jiggle and his fingers drum against his thighs.

'And what do *you* do, Troy?' said Savannah. 'For a living?'

'I'm a trader,' said Troy.

'What do you trade?' she asked.

He knew she'd lose interest in a moment. Everyone did. 'Anything that moves.'

'I don't know what that means,' said Savannah humbly.

'Nobody does,' said Logan.

Troy didn't look at him. 'It means anything with volatility: interest rates, equities, currencies, commodities – that's my bread and butter.'

'You're a risk-taker, then,' said Savannah, and he looked at her in the rear-vision mirror again and saw that she had her head bowed and was examining her fingernails.

'A calculated risk-taker,' said Troy. His family thought he played blackjack all day long.

Logan said something under his breath.

'What?' Troy looked at him.

Logan lifted a shoulder. 'Didn't say anything.'

How could he have that smug grin while driving a car filled with Subway wrappers?

'Do you have a . . . partner?' asked Savannah.

'He's straight,' said Logan. 'Just likes to act camp.'

'Do you?' said Savannah to Troy. She'd lifted her head, interested. 'Like to act camp?'

'Apparently so,' said Troy.

He didn't care when people thought he was gay. He kind of liked it. Kept everyone on their toes. He didn't do it on purpose. Or maybe he did. To differentiate himself from Logan, who was a 'man's man'. Logan thought there was only one way to be a man: their father's way.

Silence filled the car as they drove down the highway, every traffic light inevitably turning red as they approached, causing Troy to just about lose his mind. Logan hummed under his breath, elbow halfway out the car window, head back against the headrest, as if he were a layabout teenager off to the beach with his friends. He probably still went to the beach with his friends. They probably had barbeques and played beach cricket. Logan was still in touch with his entire circle of high school friends, which made Troy feel both contemptuous – how parochial, how very Sydney – and envious.

Troy liked the idea of old friends, just not the reality. When old friends tried to get in touch with him, he always shuddered. It was like they were trying to take something away from him, to peel off an outer layer and show everyone the uncouth, unsophisticated kid he used to be. He was always kind of surprised old friends still *existed*.

Logan continued to whistle. The guy needed a haircut, a shave, probably a shower, for fuck's sake.

It was the same toneless, two-note tune Logan used to hum on long car journeys to tournaments when they were kids, the tune that would malevolently worm its way into Troy's consciousness until he had no choice but to resort to violence, because come *on*, now, how many times did he have to ask him to stop?

'Don't.' He touched Logan's shoulder. 'Please don't.'

Logan stopped humming abruptly. He glanced once at Troy, switched on the radio and changed lanes unnecessarily.

Troy closed his eyes so he didn't have to see the next traffic light turn red, and it occurred to him that maybe Logan's humming was a nervous tic, and in the way that a random thought about your childhood can suddenly offer a startling new adult clarity, he saw in a flash that this was true: *Logan hummed when he was nervous*. He had hummed on the way to tournaments because he was nervous and Troy couldn't stand the sound of it because *he* himself had been suffering pre-game nerves.

So Logan was nervous right now.

It wouldn't be the threat to his own safety worrying him, but the possibility of being involved in a disagreement. Logan had a severe conflict allergy. He'd pick up his cutlery and eat rather than tell a waitress, 'That's not what I ordered.' Even if it was *vegetarian*. When he used to play the most notorious cheats on the circuit, he never questioned their calls. It was his brother's most significant and, for Troy, most mystifying flaw.

Of course, Logan's conflict allergy hadn't applied to Troy. The two of them used to fight to the death. Troy traced his finger down the faint white line on his forearm. Sixteen stitches. He and Logan had smashed through a window onto the front lawn while they were fighting, like a scene from *Die Hard*. Logan had a similar scar on his thigh. It was one of Troy's favourite childhood memories: the two of them looking at each other with shocked, thrilled eyes, bloody limbs, glass fragments shining in their hair, their poor mother screaming her head off.

Now Logan competed against Troy by *not* competing, which was fucking genius. You couldn't win if only one of you was playing.

Savannah spoke up from the back seat. 'When I said that about not sponging off your parents, I hope I didn't come across as . . . ungrateful.'

Troy opened his eyes. 'Not at all.'

He slid the words 'at' and 'all' together to make the one word 'a-tall', a linguistic habit he'd taught himself as a teenager, when he'd heard it used by someone on the radio and decided it sounded sophisticated. It still gave him pleasure. Like a fashion choice.

He saw the harbour and his heart lifted at the sight of apartment blocks, office towers, skyscrapers, the Harbour Bridge: *civilisation*, even if it was only Sydney civilisation, not proper civilisation.

Savannah continued talking. 'Like, I'm really grateful to you both for doing this, and to your parents, your parents are fab.' *Fab.* Odd choice of word. Circa 1990? 'They're, like, one of a kind. Amazing people. Truly.'

Amazing people. Troy looked at Logan. They'd heard a lot of that growing up: *Your parents are so cool. Your parents aren't like other parents with boring office jobs. We wish we had parents like yours.*

'It's all good,' said Troy. 'No problem a-tall.' He twisted around to smile his most dazzling smile at her. She smiled back. A girl had once told Troy that he had a 'devastating' smile. He secretly treasured that compliment. *Devastating.*

'So we take a left here, right?' said Logan.

Troy jerked his head. He had not bothered to ask the location of Savannah's unit, but had assumed they were heading over the bridge to some suburb he'd never heard of, way out in the boondocks, right under a flight path or two. Instead he saw they were driving through a hip harbourside neighbourhood where he himself had lived in his twenties. He'd had after-work drinks at that pub on the corner. He'd taken dates to that little Thai restaurant. This was an area for IT guys in hoodies, junior execs in high heels and law graduates in new suits. People here were too young and happy, attractive and cashed-up to hit their girlfriends.

'Go straight at the roundabout,' said Savannah. 'And then it's the big apartment block right there. That's it. There's heaps of visitors' parking.'

Troy craned his neck. 'You must have good views?' He realised he was now feeling more sympathy towards her, as if someone who lived in this suburb *really* didn't deserve a violent boyfriend. His neck turned red with shame.

'Our unit doesn't face the harbour,' said Savannah. 'It's just a one-bedroom. They reduced the rent because it's got a really crappy kitchen and bathroom. It's the only un-renovated apartment in the building.' It was like she was explaining how they could afford to live here, like she'd seen his neck and read his thoughts.

Logan parked and he and Troy got out of the car, unwinding their bodies with relief, the way men of their height did when released from cars and aeroplanes.

Logan removed from the boot a couple of supermarket card-board boxes that their mother had given them for Savannah's belongings, while Troy stuck his hands in his pockets and kicked his heels against the pavement. He looked about for any nefarious types but the place was deserted. Everyone would be at work right now. This wasn't an area for young families.

'Um . . . is she getting out?' Troy said to Logan after a moment.

Logan shrugged. He ducked down to look. 'She's just sitting there.'

'Should we give her a second?' said Troy.

Logan shrugged again. It was like his default gesture.

They waited.

'How's Indira?' asked Troy.

'She's fine,' said Logan, his face blank.

'You still living –'

'Yes.' Logan cut him off. So they were still crammed together in that crummy one-bedroom townhouse Logan had bought decades ago. Troy's mother had mentioned that Indira wanted to move a few years back but that had obviously gone nowhere.

'How was New York?' Logan asked, without discernible interest.

'Great,' said Troy.

As far as Troy knew, Logan had never been to New York. Imagine never having been to New York and acting like it didn't matter. Did Logan even have a passport right now? The thought of not having a valid passport made Troy hyperventilate but Logan seemed to live his life within the confines of a tiny radius encompassing his workplace, their parents' house, and the homes of his married-with-children high school friends. Today's exciting adventure to Savannah's apartment might be the furthest Logan had travelled in years.

It wasn't like he hadn't had the opportunities: Logan was offered a tennis scholarship to the University of Chicago, two years before Troy was offered one at Stanford, but he'd turned it down. He'd said, *No thanks, I'm good,* without apparent regret.

In fact, all four of the Delaney children had been offered tennis scholarships to prestigious American universities. Troy was the only one with the brains to take the offer, the only one capable of seeing what a chance like that could mean to a Sydney public school kid. It still infuriated him. His brother and sisters could have changed the direction of their lives. They thought it was a decision about *tennis.*

They didn't get that tennis was merely the key that unlocked the door to a bigger, shinier world. Tennis didn't just get Troy into Stanford, it kick-started his career. His family enjoyed that story. Once he'd even overheard Logan recounting it: how Troy was in New York doing a summer internship competing against a group of terrifyingly slick young graduates for a coveted permanent position, when one day a grey-haired guy came into the office and said, with quiet menace, 'Which one of you kids is the tennis player?' Troy raised his hand and the guy said, 'I'll pick you up after work. Full whites please.' Troy had to run into Macy's in Times Square (it wasn't Times Square, it was Herald Square but he'd given up correcting his family, his mother said Times Square sounded better) in his fifteen-minute lunch break and buy the first white clothes he could find, no time to try them on. A shiny black car took them out to a pompous tennis club where they played doubles against two guys – one old, one young – who they decisively beat: 6–0, 6–0. Turned out the scary grey-haired guy was the big enchilada and he hated the other old guy, for a reason never explained. There were a lot of hard-eyed smiles that day.

Guess who got the permanent position?

Yes, his family loved that story. They loved any story where a Delaney won a match, or won anything. But it was almost like he needed each of his siblings to say: *I should have taken the scholarship like you, Troy, then I'd have a life like yours,* when in fact all three of them seemed to view Troy and his life's choices not with envy but with a kind of amused, detached superiority, as if money and success were shiny, childish toys, comical and absurd.

It was true that Brooke's migraines gave her hell when she was a teenager, so she had no choice but to quit tennis altogether and stay in Sydney to study. Amy was Amy. She couldn't cope with the stress of competitive tennis. He never got his older sister until the day she explained it: 'Think of your worst pre-match nerves. Except there's no match. It's just Tuesday morning. That's how it feels to be me.' But *Logan* should have said yes to Chicago! He'd been smarter than Troy at school, and he had that incredible forehand. Did he ever do anything with that brain or that forehand?

Troy tried to imagine his brother in a classroom teaching. Who exactly took these classes? And what exactly did he teach in 'business communications'? How to format a business letter? How would Logan know? Had he ever sent one in his life? People emailed these days. He imagined Logan wearing a cheap Kmart tie, one their mother had probably given him for Christmas, standing at an old-fashioned blackboard scribbling in chalk: *To whom it may concern, Yours faithfully, Dear Sir/Madam*. And then shrugging whenever a student asked a question.

To be fair, he was probably a good teacher. He'd been the best out of all four of them at coaching, and the only one who seemed to actually like it. He got that same fixed, focused look on his face as their dad did when he watched a kid play. Any kid. Even the useless ones. Logan was probably only fourteen when Troy heard him say, 'You look away from the ball at the last second' to a little kid who Troy would have written off as having no hand–eye coordination.

But that was tennis. Logan couldn't feel passionate about spending his days teaching business communication skills to help little wannabe businesspeople enter a world Logan had no interest in entering himself. It was just . . . wrong. Logan was leading the wrong life and didn't care, and for fuck's sake, *why did Troy care that he didn't care?*

When he was a kid all he'd wanted to do was beat his older

brother, in anything and everything. It was the point of his entire existence. Winning his first match against Logan had felt like a cocaine high, except, just like cocaine, it also made him feel sick. He always remembered, with resentment and mystification, how nausea had tainted the edge of his win, how he'd gone to have a shower to cool off and thought he was fine, but then he lost his temper with a tennis kid who had wandered through the back door into their house. (He *hated* it so much when kids thought their kitchen was a clubhouse facility.)

It was almost like he'd felt guilty for beating his brother, as if being two years older gave Logan a lifelong right to win against Troy.

These days their father seemed to be equally impressed – or equally unimpressed – by the careers both his sons had chosen. Brooke was the only one who impressed their dad, because she was his favourite and she was 'starting her own business'. Stan didn't seem to notice that Troy had also been his own boss for years.

This was what happened whenever Troy saw his family. He regressed. His emotions started to gallop all over the place. He wanted to beat Logan when Logan wasn't even playing. He got jealous of the attention his dad showed his baby sister for her little physiotherapy practice. For fuck's sake, you would think he was *Amy*. It was humiliating.

'You were in New York for work, right?' said Logan.

'And pleasure,' said Troy.

There was no point talking about the work part. Whenever Troy tried to explain what he did for a living, his family would get the same expressions of focused yet vacant concentration as they might if they were trying to tune in to an out-of-area radio programme and were only hearing every twentieth word through the static. His mother, bless her heart, had even subscribed to a podcast, *Chat with Traders*, and took notes while she bravely listened to it, but to date she was still none the wiser.

'So . . . been on the court lately?' Troy gave Logan a speculative look. It had been years since they'd played each other.

Logan gave an irritated exhalation, as if Troy had asked this same question multiple times before, which he was pretty sure he had *not*. 'Nope. Not for a while now.'

'Why not?' asked Troy, genuinely interested. 'Not even with Mum and Dad?'

'No time.' Logan fiddled with his left wrist as if to indicate an invisible watch.

'No *time*,' repeated Troy. 'What a crock of shit. You've got time to burn.'

Logan shrugged. Then he said suddenly, as if he couldn't help himself, 'I don't get how you play *socially*.'

He said 'socially' like the word smelled.

'I enjoy it,' said Troy truthfully. He had friends he played with on a semi-regular basis both in Sydney and New York. They were all former competitive players like him. He won maybe seventy per cent of the time. 'Keeps me fit. It doesn't matter anymore.'

'You're saying you don't care if you win or lose?'

'Obviously I play to win,' said Troy. 'But it's not life or death.'

They contemplated each other. They were exactly the same height, although Troy preferred to think he had just a fraction on his older brother. It was probably just his hair. He used mousse.

Logan said, 'I don't mind having a hit, but the moment we're scoring, I start to care if I win or lose, and then I just . . .' He paused. 'I can't stand it.'

He looked warily at Troy as though waiting for him to throw this revelation back in his face.

After a moment Troy said, 'But you still follow the tennis, right?'

'Sure,' said Logan.

'I don't follow it. Don't even watch the finals,' admitted Troy. 'If it's on TV, I switch it off. I can't stand watching it.'

There were still a couple of guys playing in satellite tournaments who he and Logan knew. Guys they'd beaten. Logan gave a half-smile, half-grimace to show he got it. Troy understood why Logan couldn't play. Logan understood why Troy couldn't watch.

Tennis was complicated. For all of them.

'What about the girls?' asked Troy, suddenly curious. He should know this but Logan was more involved with family life than him.

'Brooke plays with Dad fairly often,' said Logan. 'I don't know about Amy. The last I heard of her having a hit was that time she grifted that beach volleyball player.'

They both grinned with identical derision. *Beach volleyball.* Every now and then Amy dated a loser who didn't believe it was possible for a woman to beat a man in any sporting endeavour, even if tennis wasn't his sport. She generally capitalised on their sexism with a cash wager.

They stood for a moment in uncharacteristically companionable, brotherly silence and Troy considered telling Logan what was really filling his mind right now. Something of zero consequence and yet mind-bending significance, depending on how he chose to shift the prism of his perspective.

I saw Claire in New York, he could begin. Logan would raise an eyebrow. He'd liked Claire. Claire had liked him. He would listen, with interest and without judgement. Logan couldn't be bothered to judge.

But no. Troy wasn't ready to talk about it yet, and anyway, at any moment Savannah would get out of the car and interrupt them.

He shoved his hands in his pockets. Was the chick going to sit there forever?

Logan began his toneless whistle and Troy felt his mind break free: *Fuck this.*

He marched around to the side of the car where Savannah was sitting, opened the back door and bent down to look at her. She still hadn't even undone her seatbelt. She sat with her hands pushed hard into the centre of her stomach, as if she'd just that moment stabbed herself.

His impatience dissipated. 'Savannah,' he said gently.

She looked up at him with unshed tears in her eyes. She blinked blonde eyelashes. The tears spilled.

Troy couldn't stand to see a woman cry.

'You're safe,' he said. He hunkered down next to the car so they were face-to-face. 'You've got us.'

'I know,' she said.

She wiped her cheeks and fiddled with the tarnished silver antique skeleton key that hung on a cheap chain around her neck.

'I like your necklace,' he said. He'd learned this from Amy's meltdowns: redirect her focus.

'Thanks.' She dropped the key.

'Does the vine symbolise something?' He pointed at the tattoo on her forearm. Green tendrils curled around her purple-veined, stick-thin arm. He had no problem with tattoos – Amy had a few – but this one, though in itself innocuous, seemed a desecration of her childlike arm. 'Or did you just like the look of it?'

'It's Jack's beanstalk,' she said.

'Huh,' he said. He tried to remember the fairy tale. Jack climbs the beanstalk and steals the giant's gold? 'So . . . it's about achieving your dreams?' She didn't look like the type for self-help books and vision boards.

'It symbolises escape,' she said.

'Right,' he said. 'So, speaking of which, let's get in and out of this place as fast as we can.' He went to offer his hand, but then thought better of it. Too domineering. He dropped his hand by his side, took a step back and waved his hand in a courtly, over-the-top, 'this way, madam' gesture. Give her space. Don't rush her. Try to understand.

She undid her seatbelt, swivelled and slid from the car, smiling tremulously up at him as she put her thumbs in the loops of her jeans and hitched them up around her waist.

'Sorry,' she said. 'I know you haven't got all day.'

'Yes I do,' said Troy. 'It's fine.' He hoped the boyfriend *was* here and gave him an excuse to grab him by his shirt and slam him up against a wall like a cop in a movie.

'Before we go up, perhaps we should check for his car.' She delicately touched her nostrils and sniffed.

'Good idea,' said Troy. Logan didn't speak. Troy bounced lightly on the balls of his feet. He was suddenly, unexpectedly jubilant.

They followed Savannah to the undercover parking area. She stopped and her shoulders sagged.

'It's fine. He's not here.' She pointed at an empty space in the far corner.

'Okay, so that's good,' said Logan. 'Great.'

Troy felt himself deflate. Now this was back to being a boring errand to endure. He looked at his watch. He actually did *not* have all day.

'There's something wrong with you,' his mother once said to him as she drove him home from school after another suspension. 'There's something very, very wrong with you.'

I know, he'd thought at the time, pleased.

The three of them went up in the lift to the third floor. Troy looked at the mirrored walls and saw a hundred reflections of himself and Logan, getting tinier and tinier, but always towering over Savannah.

She led them down a carpeted hallway with the familiar lemon air-freshener smell of this kind of well-kept, mid-level apartment block, and unlocked a door.

'Please come in,' she said shyly, as if this were a social visit.

The first thing Troy saw was unframed art leaning against the walls: proper art. Abstracts with violent strokes of paint so thick and textured they still looked wet. He had not been expecting *art*.

'He's an artist.' Savannah followed Troy's eye. 'Amateur artist.'

There wasn't much furniture: a battered double-seater leather couch faced a television leaning against the wall. A tacky-looking glass coffee table contained half-empty takeaway containers, chopsticks shoved upright into the fried rice, an open newspaper stained with blotches of soy sauce, a half-drunk bottle of Corona with a piece of lime floating in the remaining beer. A stack of unopened removalist's boxes sat in the corner of the room. This was a man who unpacked his art before he put up his television. A man who carefully cut up a piece of lime to put in his Corona but left his half-eaten takeaway dinner on the coffee table. A man who hit his girlfriend.

Savannah shook her head at the food on the coffee table and made a move towards it as if she were thinking about cleaning it up, then stopped.

'So these two boxes are obviously yours?' said Logan. He nodded his head at two of the removalist's boxes, one of which was labelled SAVANNAH – CLOTHES and the other SAVANNAH – RECIPE BOOKS.

'Yes,' said Savannah. 'Yes, thank you. Much appreciated.'

Much appreciated. The cadences and colloquialisms of her speech slipped back and forth: one moment twenty years old, the next eighty.

'Let's get everything out of here and in the hallway,' said Logan.

He and Troy carried out the boxes. Troy got the box of books, which made him stagger.

'You right, mate?' asked Logan, straight-faced.

They came back in to find Savannah squatting on the floor in the tiny kitchen, all the cupboard doors open, as she filled a box with saucepans, frypans and a blender.

'I like to cook,' she said to Troy, as if explaining herself.

'So I've heard,' said Troy. 'Mum and Dad might keep you permanently.'

'What else?' asked Logan.

'In the bedroom,' said Savannah. She looked up at them. 'The glory box at the end of the bed. It was my grandmother's.' She winced. 'It's rather heavy.'

They went into the musty-smelling bedroom, the bed a

tangle of sheets and blankets and pillows, clothes strewn over the floor.

'This must be it,' said Logan. He experimentally lifted one corner of the mahogany chest at the end of the bed.

'*What the hell?*' A bare-chested man sat upright from the tangle of sheets.

Troy's heart leaped. He grabbed the nearest thing he could find from a bookshelf and held it up like a weapon. '*Don't fucking move!*'

Logan dropped the chest with a bang. 'Stop right there, mate,' he said, his demeanour as calm and controlled as a country cop, his voice as deep and slow as their father's. People often said Troy and Logan sounded like their father, but this was the first time Troy had realised just how much Logan sounded and even looked like their dad.

The man scuttled backward up the bed until he was sitting with his back against the wall, his hands clutching the bedsheets. He was scrawny, pasty-white with lots of black chest hair and he wore a pair of faded checked boxers with ripped elastic. Troy felt a revulsion so visceral it made him shudder.

'I've about a hundred in cash,' the man said. He reached over for a wallet on his bedside table and held it up. 'T'at's all.' He had an Irish accent. Troy's first girlfriend once said there was nothing sexier than a man with an Irish accent and Troy had been personally offended by the existence of Ireland ever since.

'We don't want your *money*,' said Troy, disgusted.

'What the . . .?' Savannah appeared in the doorway.

'Savannah?' The man picked up a pair of glasses on his bedside table and put them on. Now he looked like Harry bloody Potter. How dare he look like Harry bloody Potter? Harry Potter would never hit a woman.

'Where have you been?' he said to Savannah, as if Logan and Troy weren't in the room. 'I've been out of my mind.'

'Why aren't you at work?' said Savannah. Her eyes darted

about the room. She looked terrified, and her terror ignited a flame of red-hot fury in Troy's chest.

'I'm as sick as a dog,' said Harry Potter. He put his hand to his stomach and a queasy expression crossed his face. 'Dodgy sweet and sour.'

'Your car isn't there,' said Savannah.

'It broke down on the motorway. In the rain. Everything has gone to shit.' His face twisted with remorse. 'I'm so sorry, Savannah, my love. For that night. That was unforgivable, I know, but I wasn't myself, I was upset about . . . But that's no excuse, I know it's no excuse . . .' He suddenly seemed to remember the presence of Logan and Troy. 'Who are these guys?'

'They're friends,' said Savannah coldly. 'They're helping me pick up my stuff.'

'Is there much else?' Logan asked her.

'Friends from *where*?' asked Harry Potter.

'It doesn't matter where we're from,' said Troy. 'We're just getting her stuff and getting out of here.'

Savannah grabbed a suitcase from the corner of the room, wheeled it over to the open built-in wardrobe and began to fill it with clothes, chucking them in still on their coat-hangers.

'But where are you going?' asked Harry Potter. 'Where are you staying?' He made a move as if to get out of bed.

'Stay right where you are,' said Logan.

The guy looked panicked. '*Savannah?*'

'Don't talk to her. Don't say another fucking word.' Troy walked to the bed and loomed over the little fucker with the full might and power of his fit and healthy six-foot-four body. His nostrils twitched at the faint smells of vomit and sweat. 'She doesn't owe you an explanation.'

Troy was showered and clean and wearing a nine-hundred-dollar shirt and a Louis Moinet watch, and he might have made some bad choices in his life and he might right now be facing an ethical dilemma of monumental proportions because of those unfortunate choices, but he had never hit a woman and he never would, he had inherited not a single one of his villainous grand-father's villainous genes, and he *liked* the fear and confusion on Harry Potter's face. Harry Potter deserved to feel fear and confusion, because *he* was legally, morally and spiritually in the wrong.

It happened so rarely that you knew that you were right and the other guy was wrong; Troy was Spider-Man, the Hulk, Captain America. He was goddamned *Batman*.

He had never felt better.

chapter seventeen

Now

'So she sends her sons over to pick up this girl's stuff. Doesn't know her from a bar of soap but she lets her *move in*!'

It was late afternoon and the packed salon hummed with the roar of multiple hairdryers. Senior stylist Narelle Longford only half-listened to her three pm half-head highlights as she prattled on about Joy Delaney. Nearly every one of her clients had been prattling on about Joy Delaney over the last week. Joy was well known in the local community.

'It has to be connected, don't you think? This strange girl and Joy's disappearance?'

'I don't know.' Narelle removed the towel turban from the woman's head. Isabel Norris was known to be difficult about her colour.

'Wait. Don't you normally do Joy's hair?' Isabel spun her head to look at her. 'You probably know more than me! Have the police talked to you?'

'No.' Narelle plugged in the hairdryer. 'Smooth with a bit of volume?'

'Did she tell *you* she was planning on going away?'

'She didn't,' said Narelle.

'I heard that Joy and Stan were having issues. They were barely speaking.'

'I don't know anything about that,' said Narelle, who knew all about that.

'Did she ever mention that girl to you?'

'Savannah?' said Narelle.

'Wait, did you *meet* her?'

She met Isabel's eyes in the mirror. 'I did. I cut her hair.'

'*Did* you?' Isabel looked animated. 'I heard she was a little, you know . . .' She mouthed the word. '*Slutty.*'

'She seemed nice,' said Narelle.

'It's all tied up somehow,' said Isabel. 'Too much of a coincidence. Strange young girl moves in and then the wife vanishes. Don't be surprised if the next thing we hear is that Stan just *happens* to be in a relationship with this girl now he's got Joy out of the way – *ow*, that's a bit hot on my ear.'

'Sorry,' said Narelle unapologetically.

She was Joy's confidante and confessor, as bound by secrecy as a priest or lawyer, but if Joy missed her next appointment Narelle would go to the police and hand over thirty years of secrets. She'd tell them about the betrayals. The ones referred to obliquely and the ones discussed in frank detail. She'd give the police everything they needed to convict her husband. She would say, Here is one possible motive and here is another, because any marriage of that many years has multiple motives for murder. Every police officer and hairdresser knows that.

chapter eighteen

Last September

It was close to midnight and Amy Delaney, oldest daughter of Stan and Joy Delaney, part-time taste tester, part-time normal person, part-time not so normal person, sat cross-legged on her unmade bed, naked, her hair in a perky cheerleader's high ponytail, looking at the poem she'd just written in her journal. Her bedroom was at the very top of the inner-city terrace she shared with three flat-mates. Red and blue neon light from the sign above the miniature golf course next door flickered across the page as she read:

A Strange Girl

There is
A Strange Girl
In the house where I grew up
Sleeping in my discarded
Bed
Wearing my discarded
Clothes
Making lasagne for my
Discarded

Mother
And my mother had to go
In the middle of my call
(I still had things to say)
Because the Strange Girl
Called out her name
In two syllables
As if she had the right
My mother's name is Joy
And when she answered
The Strange Girl
Her voice was full of
Joy

Amy languidly drew thick rectangles over various words in her poem as if she were a wartime censor, tore out the page, crumpled it up, and ate it.

She didn't specifically remember eating paper before but she must have because the taste and texture was familiar. She chewed carefully, swallowed. If she was rating it at work, she would have said it was 'pasty, bland, difficult to swallow, with a chemical aftertaste'.

Apparently Steffi, her parents' dog, had developed a fetish for paper. There was a name for it. Her mother had told her all about it.

Ever since she'd retired, Amy's mother brimmed with facts. She listened to podcasts, clicked on BuzzFeed articles and Googled. Then she called up her children and passed on all the new facts that she'd learned. It was interesting to observe her mother's personality changing after retirement. She'd always been the busiest person Amy knew, impatient and distracted, and now she'd become so uncharacteristically reflective, willing to engage in very long meandering conversations about topics she would have once deemed frivolous.

'Mum needs to do some kind of course to occupy her mind,' Brooke had said, sniffily.

'She's doing a course. She's learning how to write a memoir,' Amy told her. 'Except she says she's never going to write one.'

'Thank God,' said Brooke.

'I'd read it,' Amy had said.

Amy had always been interested in who her parents were before they became her parents: Joy Becker before she became Mum, Stan Delaney before he became Dad. Both Amy's parents were only children with beautiful, complicated mothers: mothers who should never have become mothers. Her father's mother had a scar that trailed down her wrinkled right cheek from where she'd been thrown across the room by Amy's grandfather. Supposedly that was the first and only time Amy's grandfather had hurt his wife, and Amy's grandmother 'immediately chucked him out' and 'that was that' but Amy thought there had to be more to the story. She'd given her father a book about a man who finally speaks about his troubled childhood to his oldest daughter in the hope that her dad might speak about his troubled childhood to his oldest daughter (her), but so far he 'couldn't make head or tail of it'.

'I don't know why you thought *Dad* would suddenly start reading *novels*,' Brooke had said, pleased that Amy's plan hadn't worked, because she believed that Dad belonged to her. 'Did you think he'd join a book club when he retired?'

Then they had both got the giggles imagining their huge taciturn father in a book club, chatting about character development over chardonnay.

'He watches TV now,' Amy had pointed out. 'He never used to watch TV.'

'I know,' said Brooke. 'He told me this long, complicated story the other day about a family where the youngest son had died in a car accident. It turned out he was telling me the entire plot of a movie. I thought it was *real*.'

That was a few months ago now. Brooke was too busy to talk much these days because she was starting her own physiotherapy practice, which was a big step, and knowing Brooke it would turn out to be a proper, grown-up success and Amy was proud of her little sister, although also mystified. Like, *why do that to yourself*? Had Brooke never noticed how the Delaney family business had controlled their lives? The paperwork, the stress, the requirement for all four children to 'help out'.

Once, when Amy was a teenager and in the middle of studying for a history exam, an exam she was destined to fail because this was the first time she'd even cracked open the textbook, a kid had come into the house and imperiously demanded Amy make her a sandwich as if Amy were her servant, and Amy had very nearly got up and made the sandwich before she came to her senses and told the kid to get lost.

They could never escape it. When they were growing up there was a family they knew who had packed up their three kids and gone travelling around Australia for a year in a caravan. Amy had been temporarily obsessed with that family. She thought it sounded like a dream. 'He'll never catch up,' her father had said. He was speaking about the middle kid in that family, the only one who was any good at tennis and therefore the only one who existed. But her dad was wrong, the kid came back, he kept playing, he didn't do that badly, ranked in the top two hundred at one point. 'We should go travelling around Australia,' Amy had said to her mother, and her mother had burst out laughing as if she'd made a clever joke.

Now Brooke was doing exactly the same as their parents: filling her pockets with rocks before she waded out into life. Brooke was meant to avoid stress because of her migraines, not chase it, but she'd always been a martyr. Amy remembered Brooke as a little girl, high pigtails and reflective sunglasses.

'She's got a headache,' Amy would say to her mother, watching her.

'What? No she doesn't, she hasn't said a word.'

But Amy could tell. There was something about the way Brooke walked when she had a headache, as if her head was in danger of rolling off and she had to keep it balanced on her neck, and Amy wanted to cry for the poor little kid walking out there with the weight of everyone's expectations on her shoulders, as if she already knew she would end up as the last hopeless hope for the Delaneys. Amy's parents could read their children's games with perfect accuracy, they could predict their every shot, exploit their every weakness, but in other ways they were clueless, blinded by their love of the greatest sport ever invented.

Maybe it was the migraines that made Brooke so serious.

Amy wished she could take them away from her. She remembered Brooke when she was a baby, dark curly hair in a topknot, only two chipmunk teeth. She never crawled, she bum-shuffled. It was hilarious to watch. Now look at her: so serious, so married, her shoes so sensible, her bra-strap so beige, you'd think she was fifty, not *twenty-nine*. Had Brooke ever danced all night? Had a one-night stand? Brooke would say these were not examples of a life well lived, and maybe she was right, but Amy blamed those cruel migraines for aging her sister beyond her years.

Amy threw her journal on the floor and lay back down in the cold flood of air from her open window. Her three flatmates were all out. She'd moved here six months ago and she'd thought that with three flatmates she'd rarely have the place to herself, but, in fact, she often seemed to be the only one at home. It was cheap rent because the neon light from the sign lit up her room like a disco.

For the last year she'd been keeping herself afloat with a cobbled-together series of part-time jobs. She'd finally accepted that regular full-time work was not for her. It wasn't a matter of finally settling on the right career path. The right job didn't exist. Full-time work caused a kind of claustrophobic terror to build and build within her chest until one day there was a humiliating emotional spillage that resulted in her termination or resignation and her parents looking distressed when she said the new job hadn't turned out to be so wonderful after all.

Now her most regular work was three three-hour shifts a week as a taste tester or a 'sensory evaluator' if she ever wanted to sound more impressive, which she never did. She joined a group of university students, young mothers and retirees to taste and discuss food with immense seriousness. She wore no lipstick or perfume or hairspray. She drank no coffee nor chewed gum beforehand. She sat at a laptop, logged in, spun around on her chair and waited for the kitchen staff, dressed in black, to bring out trays of labelled food. There was no right or wrong, there was no winning or losing. It was very important but also of no consequence whatsoever. No-one got upset, except for the occasional roll of the eyes if someone went on and on making their impassioned point about lemongrass to the panel leader. There was also that one time an executive stormed out because none of the taste testers liked the bolognaise sauce he'd spent a year developing, but that had been exciting.

In between taste-testing shifts she did market research and product-testing work. Today, for example, she'd spent an hour as part of a focus group discussing toilet paper. It was cash in hand, the sandwiches were excellent: that was lunch sorted. Everyone was extremely nice and polite when you did focus group work. She didn't care that it was fake; it was soothing. She got to walk into a lovely plush office in the city like she was part of corporate Sydney and then walk right out again and go to the beach.

This afternoon she'd filled in a long questionnaire about her thoughts on deodorant and in return she'd received a department store voucher that she'd used to buy two bras on special.

It felt like she was getting away with something, like she was living by her wits picking pockets in Dickensian England.

She also had a theory that this sort of work was good for her mental health because it forced her to make multiple choices (*Do you prefer spray or roll-on, with or without perfume?*) and when she was sick she found choices impossible. She could stand in a grocery store staring at a shelf, paralysed with indecision. She hadn't yet found a therapist who fully endorsed this theory.

She would be forty next April.

She wasn't sure how that had happened. She could remember when her mother turned forty, and it had seemed ancient. Amy had assumed there would be flying cars by the time she turned forty.

Forty was too old to be eating bad poetry for dinner, to be living in a share house with twenty-somethings, to have no savings or furniture or boyfriend. She and Brooke should swap lives, except that if Amy was married to a man as deeply enamoured of his own supposed intellect and supposed wit as Grant Willis, she would have to answer 'yes' to that ubiquitous question: 'Have you been experiencing suicidal thoughts?'

She reminded herself to get herself a new boyfriend soon, so she wouldn't wake up alone on her fortieth birthday.

Would this strange girl, this *Savannah*, still be living in Amy's old bedroom by her fortieth birthday?

She listened to the panicked scuttle of a possum's paws as it ran across the roof tiles above her head. Her heart raced within the cavity of her chest and her thoughts scuttled as fast and as foolish as a hundred panicked possums.

It's your fight-or-flight response, explained each new therapist, kindly and patronisingly, as if this were a brand new concept for her. Often they spent precious expensive minutes of the session explaining how cavemen needed the fight-or-flight response, because of the sabre-toothed tiger, but now there was no sabre-toothed tiger, but still we responded as if there was one (they were always so excited by the tiger!) and Amy would drift off, thinking about how there could be occasions in the modern world where you *could* actually face a tiger, like if you were on safari, for example, or if one escaped from a zoo, or how a rapist could represent the tiger, and you needed to race off down the alley, and how she was fast, she was a fast runner, faster than most, she would get away from any rapist or tiger, but she could never get the fuck away from her thoughts, her crazy, stupid thoughts and next thing, time was up, and that will be three squillion and fifty-six dollars, thank you, and our next available appointment is in three years' time, shall we book you in?

She did the four–seven–eight breathing technique.

Breathe in for four. Hold for seven. Out for eight.

In for four. Hold for seven. Out for eight.

Her heart rate slowed from full-blown panic to an acceptable level of high alert, as if she were no longer running from the tiger but she'd climbed a tree and was watching it circle and snarl below. She hadn't climbed a tree in a while but she used to be good at it.

She yawned hugely. *Don't fall asleep in the tree, Amy!*

Tomorrow was Father's Day. She needed to sleep. She had to be up early to make chocolate brownies. Her dad loved her chocolate brownies. If she stayed awake all night, which was a real possibility, she'd have dark circles under her eyes and her mother would notice and worry, or perhaps she wouldn't because she would be so busy noticing and worrying about Savannah, who had proper problems, like homelessness and abusive boyfriends.

She considered her options to make herself sleep:

Sleeping pill.

Hot bath.

Hot milk.

Guided meditation.

Orgasm.

Really boring book.

One of her flatmates read giant, hardback biographies of important men and they were so boring they made Amy want to weep.

Her dad said he played imaginary tennis in his head when he couldn't get to sleep. Amy said, 'Doesn't that wake you up?' Her mother suggested doing the ironing.

Amy couldn't think of anything less restful than playing imaginary tennis and she never ironed. 'That's evident,' her mother said.

Amy rolled onto her side, adjusted her pillow.

She might love this girl who was trying to steal her parents. This Savannah from the savanna where the sabre-toothed tiger roamed.

When she asked Troy about Savannah he said she was 'fine', which was the word he used when a waiter asked, 'How was your meal?' and Troy thought it wasn't that great, but it wasn't bad enough to get all Gordon Ramsay about it.

Logan said he had no opinion on Savannah. She could *hear* his shrug.

Brooke would be meeting Savannah for the first time tomorrow too, but when Amy last spoke to her, she said that she'd spoken to Mum and she wasn't worried and Amy shouldn't worry either, and that their parents were doing something nice for a domestic violence victim and they should all feel proud.

Amy had never had a boyfriend hit her, although she'd had a couple who fucked her when she was too out of it to consent, but that was before consent got fashionable. Those kinds of incidents used to be considered 'funny'. Even 'hilarious'. The worse you felt, the louder you laughed. The laughter was necessary because it put you back in charge. You didn't remember, so you created a memory you hoped was the truth. Sometimes she kept dating a boy, temporarily convinced herself she loved him, just to keep the correct narrative on track. Well. No need to go all the way back *there*. Her mind was filled with catacombs it was important to keep sealed shut, like the sealed-up fireplace in her parents' living room. The brick hearth where her grandmother had smashed her face was long gone.

She thought of her grandfather, her father's father, who nobody talked about because of what he'd done. She would have liked to have at least seen a photo of him. 'Why would you want to see *his* photo?' her younger siblings said, disgusted with her because their grandmother made extraordinary apple crumble and palmed five-dollar notes into their sticky little hands, as if she were tipping them.

He just interested her. Did he regret what he'd done? Did he ever do it to another woman? She assumed her interest in her dead abusive grandfather indicated a pathological attraction to bad men.

Sleep, Amy, sleep.

She heard a door slam downstairs, so that meant one of her flatmates had come home, which was good, no need to imagine robbers in black balaclavas wandering through the place and getting frustrated when they couldn't find anything to steal except forty-dollar biographies.

Breathe in for four.

Hold for seven.

Out for eight.

Supposedly people in the military used the four–seven–eight breathing technique and got to sleep in under a minute.

'Let's start with sleep,' her latest therapist had said. His name was Roger, and she wasn't too sure about his qualifications. He probably read about the breathing technique on the internet. She liked the fact that there was something a bit dodgy about him. She felt more comfortable in his slightly dingy office than she did in the softly lit, plush-carpeted offices of the expensive psychiatrists and psychologists, who she felt were judging her hair and clothes.

She didn't actually expect Roger to 'cure' her. It was just so that when people said to her, as they inevitably did, 'I think you need to get *help*, Amy, *professional* help,' she could answer, 'Sure. I'm getting help.'

She moved through therapists like she moved through boyfriends. She dumped both boyfriends and therapists when they offended her, enraged her, bored her.

The boyfriends said she was a head case, a nut case, a drama queen, a psycho. The therapists said she had ADHD or OCD, depression or anxiety or most likely both, a nervous disorder, a mood disorder, a personality disorder, maybe even a bipolar affective disorder. The word 'disorder' was a popular one.

There was one guy who announced there was nothing at all wrong with her, she just needed stress relief, and then he texted her the following week and asked her out for a drink, which he said would be fine now he was no longer treating her. The fact that she said yes to the unethical sleazebag probably demonstrated that there actually was something very wrong with her.

'Medical diagnosis isn't in my scope of practice,' the new guy, Roger, said anxiously when Amy asked, mildly interested, which particular diagnosis took his fancy. 'I'm a counsellor. I work alongside the medical profession, and I work alongside *you*.' Then he smiled and leaned towards her, confidentially, as if he were sharing a secret, no longer anxious, 'You know, sometimes labels are a distraction. You're not a label. You're Amy.'

Hokey but sweet. It actually did feel like he was sitting shoulder to shoulder with her, on the same team, rather than simply observing her with the cool, professional eyes of some of his colleagues.

She liked him. For now, at least.

She only sometimes took the tablets the good psychiatrists prescribed and she only sometimes took the pills the bad boyfriends offered.

Every now and then she pulled out the hopeful, obligatory 'mental health plan' she and her GP had worked on together, and she did her best to keep up 'strategies' and 'techniques' that made her appear semi-normal to the world: Poetry. Journalling. Exercise. Mindfulness. Nature. Meditation. Breathing. Berries. Vitamins. Superfoods. Probiotics. Gratitude. Baths. Conversation. Sleep.

Sometimes they worked and sometimes they didn't.

'It's just that your feelings are too big,' her dad's mother told her when she was a kid and cried for so long her parents lost their tempers. 'You'll grow into them. My feelings used to be too big too. Have a lemonade, sweetie.'

Apparently her grandmother didn't so much grow into her feelings as flatten them with alcohol, but alcohol and lemonade only amplified Amy's oversized feelings.

'Oh, Amy is just *nervy*,' she once overheard her other grandmother, her mother's mother, say. 'Like Auntie Edna. No need to get your knickers in a knot, Joy, she's fine. Gee, those nervy types do get on your nerves, though. Should we ask her to cry somewhere else?'

Auntie Edna spent the last days of her sad nervy life *tied to a chair*, but no need to get your knickers in a knot.

'We won't let you be tied to a chair, darling,' Amy's mother used to say. 'Anyway, I actually think you're more like Auntie Mary and *she* didn't end up tied to a chair.'

Auntie Mary was killed after she stepped in front of a tram in the city, but she absolutely didn't step out in front of that tram on purpose, no matter what some people implied. The truth, according to Amy's mother, was that Auntie Mary got distracted trying to save a little girl's panama hat when a southerly buster blew it straight from her head one summer afternoon a week before Christmas, which, according to Amy's mother, was exactly the sort of reckless thing Amy would do, and if she did, Joy would never forgive her. Look both ways. Especially when Christmas is coming up. Make *that* one of your funny little rituals. Looking both ways.

Amy didn't have any funny little rituals at the moment. Or none that people would notice. Anyway, they *all* had their rituals and superstitions, their strange little habits. Troy had to tap his nose three times before he served. Logan had to wear his lucky red socks whenever he competed, even when his feet grew too big for them. Brooke *still* had trouble getting out of the car whenever she arrived somewhere. Brooke thought no-one knew that. Amy knew.

'There's nothing wrong with you, sweetheart,' her father said. 'It's all in your head.'

All in your head. Her dad was so cute and clueless.

She lay still and breathed while she chatted with the spirits of Auntie Edna and Auntie Mary. She had never met either of her mad great-aunts but she felt like they would have got along.

I've kind of got a bad feeling about this girl staying with my parents.

Me too, said Auntie Edna.

Me too, said Auntie Mary.

Get rid of her, said Auntie Edna, who was bossy.

The bad feeling intensified, took hold of her stomach, twisted. A car alarm started up down the street. Someone knocked on her bedroom door.

Amy grabbed at the sheets and pulled them up, covering her nakedness.

'Who is it?' she called out.

'Sorry!' said a deep hoarse male voice. 'It's just me.' He paused. 'Simon.' He cleared his throat. 'Simon Barrington.' As if there were several Simons living in the house.

She looked at the ceiling. She'd kind of known this might happen, and she'd told herself that under no circumstances should she let it happen.

'Are you awake?' he said through the door.

'No,' she called back. 'I'm not awake, Simon Barrington.' *Just lying here chatting to the spirits of my crazy dead aunts, Simon Barrington.*

She wouldn't say anything else. It was a mistake to sleep with your flatmates. Especially when they were still in their twenties, and you were on the cusp of leaving your thirties. Simon's long-term girlfriend had recently dumped him while they were out at yum cha. He'd been going out with her since high school and they were meant to be getting married next year, and he didn't see it coming and he *loved* yum cha, which his girlfriend knew, so that added an extra layer of tragedy.

Now he was broken-hearted and drunk and he'd come home and remembered his single flatmate on the top floor, like remembering some leftover takeaway in the fridge, and he'd thought, *Huh.* He was a nice enough guy, sweet and polite and scrupulous about housework, but he read those boring biographies all the way through to the end, and he was an ex–rugby player, with a rugby player's top-heavy body (she liked tall, lean, inscrutable men; there was nothing inscrutable about Simon Barrington) and he had a boring job she could never remember, something to do with telecommunications or property or possibly he was an accountant, and he was younger than her, and shorter than her, and men always said they didn't care about the height thing, but they did, they surely did, and that repressed fury always came to the surface eventually.

So it would be once, and it wouldn't be good sex, and then there would be awkwardness between them for the next seven months of her rental agreement and then she'd have to find somewhere else to live, and she liked it here, she liked the neon light from the miniature golf course, she liked the possum with a panic disorder.

'Sorry!' Simon called through the door. 'So sorry! I'll go.'

She waited.

There was silence. Had he gone? She should let him go.

She got out of bed, put on a t-shirt and opened the door. He was walking towards the top of the stairs.

'Simon?' she said. 'Simon Barrington?'

He turned. His shirt was pulled loose from the waistband of his jeans, his glasses were askew, his eyes were bloodshot and he was in need of a shave.

She lifted her finger. Beckoned.

Impulse-control disorder. That was another one.

chapter nineteen

Now

A phone rang. A printer whirred. A keyboard clacked. A man laughed and said, 'You're kidding me?' A woman sneezed and said, 'Bless me!' It could have been any open-plan corporate office on a weekday morning, with its grey nylon carpet tiles and beige walls, except that the people working here routinely dealt with the worst of humanity. It was no wonder the most senior of them spoke in similar brittle impatient tones that made their partners sigh, 'Why are you always so cynical?'

Christina sat at her desk, drinking a full-cream double-shot piccolo from the café next to the station, thinking about Nico, this morning, sighing, 'Why are you always so cynical, Christina?' when she questioned why his friend-of-a-friend wedding photographer was demanding payment upfront.

Joy Delaney had been out of contact for thirteen days following an argument with her husband. This was a woman whose children couldn't recall her going away for *one night* without her husband.

Why are you always so cynical, Christina?

Because nice ordinary people lie and steal and cheat and murder, Nico.

They'd paid the photographer upfront.

She drank the last of her piccolo, opened the file in front of her and read a printout from Joy's Word documents on her desktop computer:

So You Want to Write a Memoir

Writing a memoir is an enriching experience. Think of this exercise as a warm-up to get those creative juices flowing. Let's start with your 'elevator pitch' – tell us your life story in just a few paragraphs below!

My given name is Joy Margaret Becker. No relation to the famous tennis player Boris Becker, in case you're wondering! (But I am a tennis player.) My mother's name was Pearl, and she was a 'beauty', which is why she never quite recovered from the shock of my father walking out on us when I was four years old. He said he was going to meet a friend, but he didn't mention the friend lived over two thousand kilometres away in the Northern Territory!

My father died in a 'fist fight' three years after he left us. He had a quick temper. I have a quick temper myself, or so I've been told, but I've never been in a fist fight! I was always told that my father adored me but that sure was a funny way to show it.

My mother moved back in with her parents, my grandparents, who were more like parents to me and brought me up. I was especially close to my grandfather, who was the chattiest man I have ever known. He could talk the hind legs off a donkey. I still think of things I'd like to tell my grandpa. My mother was quite a critical, unhappy person. It wasn't her fault. She was born in the wrong time. I think if she was born now she might have been the CEO of a big corporation. Or she might have been a weather girl. She was certainly pretty enough and always very interested in the weather.

My grandfather loved tennis and one day when I was a toddler, I picked up his big wooden square-headed tennis racquet. It would have been so heavy for a three-year-old. My grandfather, just for fun, threw me a ball and I hit it straight back. He said he nearly fell off his chair. I hit ten balls in a row before I missed one. My grandmother said it was only five. My mother said she didn't believe a word of it. Who knows! All I do know is that tennis was all I wanted to do when I was a little girl. I just loved hitting that ball. Hard flat shots from the baseline. That's my favourite. (Too much spin these days. It's the fancy new racquets.) I loved the sound. Clop. Clop. Clop. Like horse's hooves. The smell of new tennis balls is one of my favourite smells. I have never taken drugs (apart from paracetamol, I do quite enjoy paracetamol) but I sometimes feel like tennis is my drug. When the match is over it's like waking up from a beautiful dream.

I started entering tournaments when I was ten. When I was eleven, I played against a thirteen-year-old girl and she cried when I beat her. I didn't feel sorry for her at all. I remember that very clearly. My prize for winning that tournament was an umbrella. (See-through with a red trim.) That was the same day I overheard a man tell my grandfather that I had the potential to be a world champion. That stuck in my mind. My grandfather and I had a plan. First I would win the local junior championships, then the state titles, then the Australian women's singles, then I'd go overseas (I'd never been on a plane!) and win the French and US titles, and finally Wimbledon.

By the time I was twelve my grandfather had to build a new shelf for all my trophies.

I was quite young when I married a tall (very tall!), dark and handsome young tennis player called Stan Delaney. We planned tennis careers. We drove all over the country playing in tournaments while still trying to support ourselves. It was hard but fun. I did a secretarial course after school. My mother wanted me to have a 'back-up' in case 'tennis didn't work out'. Her hope was that I would marry a 'businessman'. She thought tennis was a fairy tale and perhaps she was right because my husband had a very bad injury when he was only twenty-two. He tore his Achilles playing the third set of the Manly Seaside Tournament quarterfinals. He would have

won the match if not for that injury. So that was his Achilles heel!
(But it was his Achilles tendon.) So we left the circuit and a few
years later we started Delaneys Tennis Academy, which went on to
become one of the most successful tennis schools in the state, if not
the country, if I do say so myself! (I told my mother that I ended up
becoming a 'businesswoman' myself but she thought I was trying to
be funny.)

We had four children, two boys and two girls. Even Stevens! All
four were very talented players. We have no grandchildren as yet.

We recently sold the tennis school and now we have the time
to tick things off our bucket list! If only we had a bucket list! Oh
well.

'Christina?'

She looked up to see Ethan, in a turquoise shirt today, at her cubicle entrance, gleaming with health and optimism. 'These young guys are like fucking Energizer Bunnies,' one of the other detectives had sighed to Christina, and he was fifteen years older than her, but she knew what he meant.

'Joy Delaney's internet search history for the day she disappeared,' said Ethan, handing her a sheet of paper. He'd highlighted relevant lines in yellow.

Joy had Googled the following questions:

How do you know when it's time to divorce?
Divorcing after sixty
How does a divorce affect adult children?
Does marriage counselling work?
Does whiskey go off?

'So much for that wonderful marriage of theirs,' said Christina.

'I know,' said Ethan sadly, and he momentarily bowed his head as if to honour a loss, but then he immediately lifted it again, and said brightly, 'I've also got her phone records. One hour before she sent that text –'

'*If* she sent that text,' said Christina.

'One hour before that text was sent,' Ethan corrected himself, 'there was a forty-minute telephone conversation with a Dr Henry Edgeworth. He's a forty-nine-year-old plastic surgeon, married with two children. He's currently overseas and not returning our calls.'

'A plastic surgeon?' Christina frowned. 'How does that fit?'

It didn't fit.

'Booking in for plastic surgery so she could change her identity?' suggested Ethan.

'Yeah. Because she got mixed up with the Mafia,' said Christina.

'Should I look at potential connections with organised crime?' asked Ethan enthusiastically.

She looked up to see if he was joking. She couldn't tell.

She said evenly, 'We need to look at all potential connections.'

Ethan nodded. He looked down at his notes. 'There was that huge hailstorm two days after Valentine's Day.'

'So you're thinking she got hit by a hailstone and now she's got amnesia?'

He looked up at her. Now he couldn't tell if she was joking.

She said, 'How are we going with that house guest of theirs?'

'I'm closing in on her.'

'Good,' said Christina. 'Because I reckon all roads lead to her.'

chapter twenty

Father's Day

On Father's Day morning, Joy woke late and well rested. She was sprawled facedown right in the middle of the bed like a child. There was a little circle of saliva where she'd dribbled onto the sheet. Stan wasn't there. Spring sunshine poured through the window, warm on the skin of her legs, which were bare beneath her t-shirt. She could smell jasmine from the garden and bacon from the kitchen. Savannah must be cooking breakfast.

She was getting far too used to having someone cook and clean for her. This was what it must be like to be a celebrity. No wonder they were so charismatic and cheerful on talk shows. Joy could feel herself becoming more charismatic and cheerful by the day.

In fact, Savannah seemed to treat her and Stan as if they were talk show guests and she the host, fascinated by the intricacies of their celebrity lives. She wanted to hear everything about them: their tennis, the tennis school, the club, the children. She asked questions Joy was sure her own children had never bothered to ask: *When did you know you were right for each other?*

'The first time I saw her,' said Stan. He was sitting when he said this, and Joy was standing, and he grabbed her by the waist and pulled her to him so that she landed on his lap.

Joy saw their marriage through Savannah's young, interested eyes: solid and valuable, like an antique, burnished with age and wisdom. Savannah probably coveted a relationship like theirs. A relationship that produced children and a beautiful house and a successful business and shelves full of framed photos of birthday parties, Easter lunches and Christmas mornings.

Joy stood under the shower, tilting her face up to the spray, and thought about the shameful moments that were never photographed:

her own face ugly with rage, spit flying from her contorted mouth,

the back of Stan's head as he walked away,

sitting in a car on the side of the road, four children silent with shock in the back, while her heart thudded in rapid time with the *click-click* of the indicator.

She shuddered and got shampoo in her eye. Of course, they wouldn't share the nasty secrets with Savannah. There were limits to their honesty, no matter what was going on with their elderly frontal lobes.

The shampoo stung like hell. She blinked furiously and massaged in the expensive volumising conditioner her hair-dresser, Narelle, had told her to use every third day. Narelle's recommended haircare regime was complex, but Joy got a lot of compliments for her hair and she loved Narelle like a sister, or the way that sisters should love each other. Her own daughters absolutely loved each other but one was generally offended or incensed or bewildered by the other one at any given time.

The price tag for the shampoo was still stuck on the back of the bottle. Stan would say, 'What's it made of? Gold dust?' Joy peeled it off with her fingernail, rolled it between her fingers, let it fall and nudged it with her toe down the drain.

Yes, Savannah certainly did not need to know how many

times Joy and Stan had fallen in and out of love over the last fifty years, how there were times when Joy hated Stan so passionately it made her sick to the stomach, how when the older three were very little they'd talked seriously and matter-of-factly, almost pleasantly, about separating, how Joy had believed it was definitely going to happen, how Brooke was a surprise baby conceived during their surprise reconciliation, how it had truly felt like a brand new relationship, how getting so close to losing each other had made them settle into something deeper and richer, but then, yet again, they'd lost their way, and all that love and happiness drained slowly, imperceptibly away, as if there was an invisible tiny leak.

Amy once told Joy that she had *no idea* how lonely it felt to be single. Joy had wanted to tell her that you could still be lonely when you were married, that there had been times when she had woken up day after day crushed with loneliness, and still made breakfast for four children.

She didn't say that to Amy. She said, 'Yes, darling, you're right. It must be so hard.'

You couldn't share the truth of your marriage with your adult children. They didn't really want to know, even if they thought they did.

There was one year, the really bad year, when both her mother and Stan's mother were sick, and then both of them died within three months of each other. As only children, Joy and Stan had to grieve alone. That was when Joy made a secret plan to leave. Her idea had been to wait until Brooke finished high school, at which point her mothering duties would be discharged. It had given her pleasure to plan it all out, even to imagine the pain of it, like a sadomasochistic fantasy.

But then: Brooke finished high school and they were good again. Maybe even better than they'd ever been. They got back into doubles and won tournament after tournament. Winning seemed to permeate everything: their sex life, the business. Joy focused on squeezing money from the tennis school. She opened the café and the pro shop, she introduced the holiday camps. That's what happened. You had a long streak where you felt like you couldn't lose a point, until you did.

Now here they were. She couldn't exactly say if Savannah had caught them on an upswing or a downswing, or if they'd finally found an equilibrium that would last them until death did them part. Sometimes it felt like their relationship ebbed and flowed over a day, or even a conversation. She could feel affection followed by resentment in the space of ten minutes.

She went to rinse off her expensive conditioner and then remembered Narelle had told her to leave it on for at least three minutes. She decided to spend the three minutes doing ankle dips with her eyes closed, which was what Brooke had told her to do every day, to improve 'ankle mobility'. She wasn't nearly as obedient with her daughter as she was with her hairdresser and she wanted to be able to truthfully tell Brooke today that she'd been doing her exercises. She bobbed up and down on one leg, eyes shut, hands outspread just in case she needed to save herself. (Brooke might not approve of her doing these exercises in the shower.) If Stan came in and caught her doing her wobbly naked bobbing, he would laugh and laugh.

Would today be okay? She felt strangely nervous about it.

Of course, the boys had already met Savannah when they helped her pick up her things, and that had all gone fine, although it turned out the ex-boyfriend had been there, but he hadn't given them any trouble and everyone's limbs were intact.

Perhaps Savannah and the girls would become friends? Probably not Brooke. She was so busy with the clinic and she could be stand-offish. On the other hand, Amy collected new friends of all ages, wherever she went. She once made such good friends with her Uber driver that the driver parked her car and joined Amy and her other friends on their night out, and it was all thanks to this nice Uber girl that Amy had found her current share house!

Maybe Savannah could move into Amy's share house if another room became available?

Although, frankly, Joy was in no hurry to have her move out.

Joy stopped bobbing, rinsed off the conditioner and gave herself a final blast of freezing cold water, which supposedly caused her stem cells to form brown fat instead of white fat, and brown fat was good, apparently.

She would ask Brooke about brown fat today, and Brooke would probably laugh at her and say she'd got it all wrong. Joy tried to make Brooke feel clever and medically qualified as often as possible. Brooke *was* clever and medically qualified, just desperately in need of approval, and desperately trying to hide the desire so naked on her darling frowny face. If only she'd wear a little lipstick.

Joy dried herself briskly. Goodness, she really did feel nervous.

Was she worried the children would notice the misalignment between the good-humoured, loving selves she and Stan were portraying to Savannah, and their true selves? The ones they'd grown up with? But come on now, they *were* happily married, for the most part, and they *were* good-humoured and loving, or Joy was, anyway.

All four of her children each fervently believed in separate versions of their childhoods that often didn't match up with Joy's memories, or each other's, for that matter. Sometimes one of them would tell a story about an incident that Joy was positive never happened, or at least not in the way they described it, because she had biographical facts at her disposal: 'But we weren't even living in the Fairmont Street house then!' 'But your grandmother wasn't alive when you turned thirteen!' And sometimes they'd argue about which of them was the villain or the victim, the martyr or the hero. 'That wasn't you that got stung by the bee, helping Grandma after she fainted at Troy's party, it was *me*!' And Joy would think, It was Logan's party, not Troy's, and there was no bee, it was a wasp, and no-one got stung, Amy just thought she did, and none of you helped, and Grandma didn't faint, she passed out drunk.

Her children refused to be corrected. That's what they remembered, therefore that was what happened, and when their memories didn't match up with each other's, they held on tight to their versions of the stories, as stubborn as their damned father.

Although sometimes one of them would get a far-off look, and you'd see something click into place, and they'd re-examine a childhood event with grown-up eyes and say: 'Wait a minute, maybe Grandma was drunk that day?'

Joy put on her dressing-gown to go into the kitchen. For the first few days Savannah was staying Joy had made sure she was fully dressed before she left her room each morning, but it was funny how quickly she'd begun to feel relaxed around her. Most house guests, no matter how pleasant, gave you a sense of something being out of place, so that you only relaxed fully when they were gone, but Savannah had slotted into their home so seamlessly.

Joy noticed that Savannah never closed her bedroom door at night. Not even a little bit. She went to bed with the door wide open, so that if Joy went to bed later than Savannah it was like walking by the bedroom of a small sleeping child. 'Good night!' she'd call out, if Savannah had the bedside lamp on. 'Good night, Joy!' Savannah would call back cheerfully. 'Sleep tight!'

It came to Joy with sick clarity that the poor child had probably learned the art of fitting in when she was growing up. She hadn't said all that much about her childhood but she had told Joy that she'd grown up in the foster system. She said some of her foster homes were great, fantastic! But some were not so great. She'd been moved many times because there were relatives who agreed to take her on but then it didn't work out, or they changed their mind. She said that to be honest, those were the living situations that were not so great. Savannah didn't know anything about her biological parents, although she vaguely remembered some supervised visits with her biological mother, but those had stopped when she was very young, and now she had no idea, and not much interest, as to the woman's whereabouts.

Joy combed her wet hair. She'd blow-dry it after breakfast. She was starving. She looked at herself in the mirror. Did Savannah cook for Joy and Stan to make them like her? The awful thing was it *did* make them like her.

Was that another hair on her chin? For goodness sake. Where were the tweezers? She put on her glasses, leaned in close, and removed it with one tiny violent tug that brought tears to her eyes.

It would be terrible if Savannah was cooking to buy their affection. They weren't *fostering* Savannah, she was a grown woman, but still, Joy needed to be mindful of her background.

She readjusted the tie of her gown. A day like today would be so hard for Savannah. She would have to see Joy's children celebrating their father with gifts and jokes, when she had never had a father herself. Joy had never had a father either, but she had grown up in the one home, with a mother who loved her (albeit in her own peculiar, not especially loving way) but most important of all, Joy had had beloved grandparents who'd more than filled the missing father gap. Poor Savannah had grown up with no *stability*.

Joy walked into the kitchen to find Savannah breaking an egg into the frypan with one hand.

'Good morning, Stability!' cried Joy emotionally. She blushed. 'I mean Hannah, I mean *Savannah*!' Good heavens.

Stan, who was sitting at the table eating bacon and eggs and doing the crossword, looked at her over the top of his reading glasses. 'Are you having a stroke?'

'Morning, Joy!' Savannah lifted another egg from the carton between her fingertips. 'One or two eggs today?'

'Oh, well, just one would be lovely, but you know you really don't have to make us breakfast every day! Especially when you're making lunch!' Joy hovered uncertainly by the stove. It didn't feel like her stove anymore. It had never respected her the way it respected Savannah.

The kitchen smelled of baking. She could see something cooling on a cake tray under a sheet of aluminium foil.

She glared at Stan. 'I'm not having a stroke. If I was having a stroke you should ask me to raise my right arm.'

'Raise your right arm,' said Stan.

'But I love to cook,' said Savannah earnestly. 'It's a privilege to cook in a kitchen like this. Please let me cook.' Her eyes, with those rabbit-like white eyelashes, held Joy's. Sometimes Joy found her direct eye contact almost unnerving. She had to look away first.

'Oh, well, of course you can cook. I love that you cook! Thank you!'

'One of your eyes is bloodshot,' said Stan to Joy. 'Is that a sign of a stroke?'

'I got shampoo in my eye,' said Joy irritably. 'Happy Father's Day.'

'Thank you,' said Stan. He finished his last mouthful, put down his knife and fork and fastidiously patted his lips with the cloth napkin Savannah had laid out for him, as if he were the king of bloody England. 'Best Father's Day breakfast I've had in my whole life.'

'Gosh, that's high praise.' High praise your grown-up children probably don't need to hear. Joy had a flash of memory of Brooke on tippy-toes by the stove, her tongue stuck out the side of her mouth, as she attempted to flip the side of an omelette she was making Stan for Father's Day.

'What's this?' Joy lifted the corner of the sheet of aluminium foil. The smell was heavy, sweet and familiar.

'Chocolate brownies,' said Savannah, and it was so silly and melodramatic how Joy's stomach lurched, as if Savannah had said, 'Snake!' or 'Fire!' not 'brownies'.

'Lovely,' she said. She avoided looking at Stan. 'How lovely.'

She distracted herself by opening the refrigerator door too fast, which sent that damned souvenir magnet rocketing towards the floor, taking with it a recycling notice from the local council that Stan had busily laminated so they could keep it forever (instead of *recycling* it). She caught the magnet just before it fell. The magnet was a souvenir from the London Eye, and it showed a photo of Joy and Stan, arms around each other on the Eye, pretending to be smiling retirees on the trip of a lifetime (when in fact Stan couldn't stop complaining about the cost of the tickets).

When they'd bought that magnet, Stan said it was too heavy for a fridge magnet. 'It's not fit for purpose,' he'd said, dismissively, infuriatingly, because Joy wanted so badly to take it back to Sydney, to put it on their fridge as photographic evidence of the kind of holiday they didn't really have, and it worked, because she'd overheard Savannah asking Stan about it, and he'd gone on about the magical views of London. He'd actually used that word: 'magical'.

The views *had* been magical. What was the harm in it? Why not rewrite the memory and remember it as a perfect day? What was the actual benefit of accuracy when it came to memories? What would her dear sweet little memoir-writing teacher have to say about *that*?

She replaced the fridge magnet and council notice and thought about how she should really throw away the London Eye magnet and use *Indira's* lovely flower magnet, but she was holding an unreasonable grudge against that magnet for not being the ultrasound picture she'd expected. She'd hidden it in a drawer so it wouldn't hurt her feelings every time she looked at it. She planned to tell Indira the magnet was far too pretty for the fridge and that she had it sitting on her dressing table. Joy was an excellent liar when feelings were at stake. Indira would never check.

She opened the fridge once more and stared without recognition at its contents. Everything was unfamiliar because Savannah had gone to the shops yesterday afternoon and done all the grocery shopping for today. Joy had been feeling a little off, and it had been such a relief when Savannah suggested it, although she said she wasn't comfortable taking Joy's credit card, but Joy knew she could trust her, and just to be very sure, she'd already had a quick look at her balance online and Savannah had not bought herself tickets to France.

She closed the refrigerator and pivoted to face Savannah. 'Actually, we might have quite an abundance of chocolate brownies today, because Amy always brings brownies for Stan. They're his favourite . . . and they're kind of Amy's signature dish.'

'Oh no!' Savannah's face fell. 'Her signature dish?' She lifted the sheet of aluminium foil and considered her brownies. They were neat little rectangles. Amy's brownies were always misshapen and lumpy, and were actually a bit too sweet for Joy's taste, although she joined in the family chorus of approval.

'That's okay. I'll freeze them,' said Savannah decisively. 'No problem! Keep them for a rainy day.'

'That might be best. I feel terrible after all that work,' said Joy. 'But –'

'Absolutely not,' said Stan.

They both turned to look at him.

'You can never have too many brownies,' said Stan.

You most certainly can, thought Joy.

'We'll have a taste test – see which ones are best.' He grinned. He was in an excellent mood. 'Isn't that Amy's chosen profession? Taste testing? We'll have a bake-off!'

'You are kidding,' said Joy.

Stan gave a one-shoulder shrug that reminded her of Logan. 'Why not?' he said.

'Because we're talking about Amy.'

'I don't want to rock the boat.' Savannah wiped her hands on her clean apron.

Oh, she was so mature. So much more mature than Joy's own daughter, who was older than Savannah, who had grown up with all the privileges.

'You won't rock the boat,' said Stan.

'Well,' said Joy.

'Amy is thirty-eight years old,' said Stan. 'Not eight years old.'

'She's thirty-nine,' Joy corrected him.

Stan ignored her. 'So two people made chocolate brownies. This is not a crisis.'

Joy wavered. Maybe it *was* silly to make Savannah hide her freshly baked brownies. Amy would understand. She might even laugh at Joy for worrying about it.

'We can't pander to Amy's moods,' said Stan. He spoke lightly, but Joy had spent fifty years forecasting his moods. She knew *his* patterns. She could see the tight clench of his teeth in the line of his jaw. He'd decided he wanted to make a point of this, as if he were still a young father and this was a parenting decision he'd made, and as the man, the father, the head of the household, his word was law, as if there was still a possibility of shaping their children's behaviour like they'd shaped their tennis, with the correct combination of rewards and punishments, and appropriate bedtimes, when in fact Joy had long ago come to the realisation that all her children's personalities were pretty much set at birth.

Stan had always fought so hard against Amy's mental health issues. He thought he could just make her *stop* and *be normal* through sheer force of will. 'I just want her to be happy,' he'd say, as if Joy didn't want the same. 'We don't tell Brooke to just *stop* having a headache,' she said to him once, but he didn't get it.

She remembered how Stan used to admonish Amy to 'Wrap it up!' when she was a little girl and took too long to get to the point of a rambling senseless story, or 'Slow it down!' when she became so deliriously excited her words ran together. Amy's face would fall, her mood would crash and she'd abruptly stop talking, like a tap had been turned off.

'She sounded like a crazy person, I couldn't understand a word she said,' Stan would say afterwards, defensively, guiltily. Joy hadn't understood a word either, but she didn't care, she didn't try to make sense of it, she just enjoyed watching Amy's animated face as she talked her nonsense and enjoyed the fact that she was happy for a change.

But Amy was doing well right now. There hadn't been any 'troubles' for a long time. She was 'in a good place', as people said. Joy liked the sound of this new counsellor. *Roger.* Joy had been to school with a nice boy called Roger.

Anyway, the truth was that Joy could never accurately predict what would upset Amy. Joy had often got herself tied up in knots over some issue she thought might set off Amy, and been completely wrong. The trick with Amy was to go along for the ride with her. Let her talk crazy-fast when she was happy. Let her be sad when she was sad, and resist the urge to list all the reasons why she should not be sad.

'It will be fine, Savannah,' said Joy. 'The more brownies the better!'

The risk of upsetting Stan outweighed the risk of upsetting Amy. The risk of upsetting Stan had always outweighed the risk of upsetting any of the children.

Nearly always.

A hot sour feeling blossomed across her chest like heartburn or a heart attack; at her age either was always a possibility, but she ignored it and sat down at the table to wait for her breakfast to be put in front of her. She resolutely turned her head away from her mother-in-law's china cats. Sometimes they seemed to watch her, the way her mother-in-law had once watched her, with pure malice.

She placed her hand lightly on Stan's forearm and said, 'Maybe change into that blue shirt, darling. The one Amy gave you for Christmas.'

'It's too tight across the back,' said Stan.

'I know,' said Joy. 'But wear it anyway.'

chapter twenty-one

Now

'Chocolate brownie?' asked Joy Delaney's oldest daughter, with such anxious, fervent hope as she held out the plate that Christina and Ethan each took one.

'They're straight out of the oven,' said Amy Delaney.

Christina and Ethan sat side by side on a couch in the front room of Amy's inner-city terrace, which she apparently shared with three flatmates. Amy sat opposite them, on the very edge of an armchair so ripped it looked like someone had taken to it with a knife. It seemed like a fairly typical share house. The room they were in was filled with mismatched furniture and smelled faintly of cannabis and garlic. Amy was a head taller than both Christina and Ethan, and she wore flowing harem pants that looked like pyjamas and a white singlet top inscribed with the words *This is how I roll.* She'd tied back her blue-dyed hair for the press conference, but this morning it was dripping wet as if she'd just got out of the shower.

You wouldn't think she'd grown up in that nice family home with the flowerbeds and garden gnomes, except for the fussy way she hosted them, insisting that she make them cups of tea and bringing out brownies and side plates and napkins.

Christina bit down on the brownie, which was sweet and nutty and gave her an instant sugar rush. She was highly susceptible to sugar highs. Also sugar lows. Nico used it to his advantage. When he proposed he gave her a diamond ring and a Caramello Koala.

The coffee table was too far away to reach the cups of tea that Amy had made them.

'Oh, sorry!' said Amy, noticing, and she got on her knees and tried to shove the coffee table closer to them. The tea sloshed onto the table.

Amy swore under her breath, and looked close to tears.

'It's okay, I've got it,' said Ethan soothingly, and he got to his feet and tugged the table closer in one smooth move.

'Thank you!' Amy fidgeted with the fabric of her pants. 'This room isn't very well set up for guests. Anyway. Thank you for coming to me. That was nice of you. I don't know if I can give you any more information than I already have. I mean, I'm not really that worried. I'm sure Mum is fine. She *told* us she was going off-grid. When she comes home she'll be so cross with us for wasting your time like this! She'll be so embarrassed. *I* feel kind of embarrassed, to be honest.'

Her words said one thing but her body language said something else entirely.

'I'm curious. If you're so sure your mother is fine,' Christina asked the same question she'd asked Amy's brother, 'then why report her missing?'

'Well, I guess *just in case* she isn't fine.' Amy's gaze slid all over the place. She clutched her hands together as if to stop them escaping. Christina ran a practised eye over her for signs of drug use and didn't find any physical signs except for her skittishness and the shadows under her eyes, which could easily be attributed to her concern for her mother.

Amy said, 'Expect the best but prepare for the worst. I thought you'd check out the hospitals, put out an alert, that sort of thing.'

'We're doing all that,' said Christina. 'You were obviously there at the press conference.'

'Yes, I know I was there! That was a great press conference, thank you! It was really . . . professional!' She looked around wildly for inspiration. 'But, um, I guess what I'm saying is, I really didn't expect you guys to treat my parents' house like an actual *crime scene.*'

Christina said nothing. She waited.

'Those scratches on my dad's face are from the hedge out the back of our house. I can show you the hedge! They're not from *my mother's fingernails.*'

Yes, they are, thought Christina. I'd put a million bucks on it.

Amy shuddered so convulsively at the thought of her mother's fingernails that for a moment Christina thought she was having an actual seizure.

Ethan glanced uneasily at Christina as Amy closed her eyes, breathed deeply and grimaced like a weightlifter, as though she were physically taking control of her mental state.

She opened her eyes and when she spoke again her voice was steady. 'Here's the thing. You don't know my father. He's a stranger to you. All you see is a grumpy old man. He suppresses his emotions. That's what men of his age do. That's probably why he looks guilty to you.'

Actually, Stan Delaney was not behaving like a guilty person. Guilty people overexplained. They talked too much and gave unnecessary detail. They were too polite and tried too hard to hold eye contact for too long. Stan answered their questions with terse impatience, as if he had somewhere else to be.

Amy said, 'I mean, you haven't found anything at the house, have you? Like, you haven't found any actual . . . evidence?'

There was a tiny flinch on the word 'evidence', as if she'd burned her tongue.

Christina ignored the question. Instead she threw out a piece of information like a fishing line.

'Amy, were you aware that your father had his car washed and detailed the day after your mother went missing?' she asked. 'He took it to a car wash café he'd never visited before and he got the most expensive service they had to offer. Their "premium" treatment. Normally only people with luxury cars choose that option. It cost him four hundred dollars.'

'Four hundred dollars?' The colour left Amy's face. 'You're saying my dad spent *four hundred dollars* getting his car washed? Are you sure?'

Christina said jovially, 'Would you say that was out of character?'

She didn't need to hear the answer.

From a forensics point of view the car told Christina nothing. The car detailers had done an excellent job. No-one at the car café remembered anything unusual about the car. They did proudly confirm the use of oxidising cleaners, which would have removed all evidence of blood stains.

But a man who gets his car cleaned the day after his wife goes missing has something to hide.

'Do you know a Dr Henry Edgeworth?' she asked Amy.

'Doctor who?' said Amy.

'Edgeworth,' said Christina. 'Henry Edgeworth. Your mother had a long telephone conversation with him on the day she disappeared.'

'Really?' said Amy. She brightened. 'We should call him!'

It was like she honestly thought they hadn't considered this idea.

'We've been trying to contact him,' said Christina. 'But he's out of the country. At a conference.'

'Wait, do you think my mother could be with him?'

'We can't find any record of your mother having left the country,' said Christina. 'We also know she hasn't got her passport with her.'

'Unless she travelled with a fake passport?' said Amy.

Christina couldn't tell if she was serious.

'Does that seem likely?' Ethan spoke up. 'That your mother would have a fake passport?'

'No,' admitted Amy. 'But I guess it's possible she could have a secret life that I know nothing about, right? I mean, your parents can surprise you, can't they?'

'Is it possible your mother was having an affair?' asked Christina.

Amy's mouth dropped. 'Absolutely *not*.'

'You did just say it was possible that she had a secret life.' Christina finished the brownie and licked her fingers.

Amy scratched an insect bite on her arm so hard she drew blood. She pressed her thumb against the spot of blood and said, 'I did just say that, didn't I? Do you really think that's possible? That's she's having an affair with this doctor? I guess stranger things have happened, right? You probably see lots of strange things in your line of work. It's just that my parents, my parents –' She dropped her thumb from her arm and looked back at them, her face open and earnest. 'My parents were the only parents holding hands at school events. They kiss, in public, all the time! They worked together, they played doubles together. Their marriage isn't perfect, I'm not saying that, but it's a good marriage, I know that for a fact. Their marriage is *my benchmark*.'

There was something almost childlike about her view of her parents' marriage. Christina thought of her mother's Google search: *How does a divorce affect adult children?* No wonder Joy Delaney was worried.

'When you first reported your mother missing you mentioned that things had been "a little tumultuous" lately between your parents,' Christina reminded her.

'Did I?' said Amy vaguely, and, it seemed to Christina, regretfully. 'Well, you know that Mum and Dad argued before she left. Dad isn't *hiding* that from us. He told us that straight away.'

'Right,' said Christina. 'But what did you mean when you said things had been a little tumultuous lately?'

There was a pause. Amy fidgeted. 'Just that they'd been kind of snappy.'

'So no hand-holding then,' said Christina dryly, and she saw Amy flinch again, as if she'd hurt her feelings.

'Not so much recently,' admitted Amy, and she avoided eye contact.

'Well, obviously we'll keep trying to get in touch with this Dr Edgeworth. We're also trying to track down the woman who stayed with your parents last year,' said Christina. 'She seems to be a woman of mystery.'

'Savannah,' said Amy heavily. 'I had a number for her but it's disconnected.'

'I'm trying to understand what went on with her.'

'What do you mean?' said Amy evasively.

'Your brother said she caused some dramas in the family.'

'Did he?' said Amy. 'Is that all he said?' She looked at Christina warily.

'Is there more to say?'

'No. I don't know.' She curled a long strand of blue-dyed hair around her finger as she considered her next words. 'I don't think it's relevant, though. To you. I mean to . . . this.'

It was relevant alright. Christina could taste the relevance, as sweet as sugar.

She waited. Ethan quietly cleared his throat.

'Do you remember when you first met her?' asked Christina.

'It was Father's Day last year,' said Amy. 'I made brownies.' She paused. 'So did she.'

chapter twenty-two

Father's Day

Brooke Delaney parked outside her parents' place and sat with her hands on the steering wheel, willing herself to move, to open the car door, to get out, go inside and be introduced to this girl, this *Savannah*, to whom she would try to be kind and welcoming. She didn't want to make conversation with a stranger on Father's Day, especially this particular Father's Day, her first family event since the separation.

She considered putting on lipstick, just to please her mother. Brooke didn't like to wear *any* make-up. She'd always found the whole concept peculiar. Why paint your face like a clown?

She found the lipstick that had been rolling about in the console of her car ever since her mother had pressed it upon her at least two years ago. She put it on, smacked her lips together, and looked at herself. Yep. Clown.

She felt hollowed out, *scooped* out, empty, and not only that, there was a sharp, digging-like sensation at the centre of her chest, like inflammation of the costal cartilage, as if she'd been doing too many plyo push-ups, except she hadn't been doing plyo push-ups, she'd been looking at social media.

That's where she'd seen a photo of her husband, sitting next to a woman she didn't recognise.

There was nothing to say there was anything significant about this woman – and so what if there was, it's a *separation*, Brooke.

Right now the word 'separation' felt as violent and irreversible as an amputation.

Just something about the tilt of her husband's head. The angle of it.

The woman had a heap of long hair tumbling about her shoulders and she wore a lot of make-up. Like, a lot. Grant always said he didn't want a 'high-maintenance' girl. He wanted a girl who camped, who hiked, and who didn't need to blow-dry her hair each morning. Brooke 'ticked a lot of boxes', he said, on their second date.

Three months after she and Grant started dating, they climbed to the summit of Mount Kilimanjaro. Grant's previous girlfriend could never have done that climb because she wasn't 'outdoorsy' and she had a bad knee. The pain went away when she took the weight off her leg. Cartilage issues, presumably. Brooke didn't know why she was still diagnosing her husband's ex-girlfriend's knee. Maybe it was because Lana's knee had been so present in the early days of their relationship. Brooke had *liked* hearing about how much more athletic and easygoing and better in bed she was than Lana. She was a Delaney, she liked winning. Was it possible that this competitive rush had propelled the momentum of her entire ten-year relationship? But how had Grant managed to establish *himself* as the prize?

Would the next woman in Grant's life hear about Brooke's inconvenient migraines, in the same way that Brooke had heard all about Lana's inconvenient knee?

Grant's responses to Brooke's migraines had been exemplary. He helped her into bed in a darkened room. He brought her medication and homemade soup. She couldn't be offended when he joked to friends, his arm lovingly about her shoulder, 'She's just a *little* defective.' That wasn't nasty. It was *witty*. It was funny!

It was her cue to say how supportive Grant was when she had a migraine. She'd never missed her cue.

She imagined him chatting to that woman with the bright red lips and long fake eyelashes. He'd be upfront and honest. He made an excellent first impression. 'I'm very recently separated,' he'd say. No lies. He'd be respectful when he spoke about Brooke. He'd say that although he supported Brooke's career aspirations, a healthy work–life balance was important to him. 'I just think there's more to life than work,' he'd say, and the tumbling-haired girl would agree that there was so much more to life than work, and their eyes would meet for just long enough.

'It sounds risky,' Grant said, when Brooke first said she wanted to go into practice on her own, but he didn't try to stop her. He never said, 'I told you so' when she fretted about cash flow. When she said she couldn't go riding with him on Saturday mornings anymore, because she'd volunteered to be on-site at the local sporting grounds in case of injuries, in *hope* of injuries, that might lead to patients and raise her profile, he never complained, he just looked faintly bored.

She was no longer ticking quite as many boxes.

There had been no counselling, no tears, no shouting. It was an amicable, grown-up separation. 'We should feel proud about that,' Grant had said. It was strange how he'd always made her feel like they were winning as a couple, even when they were breaking up.

'Do you want me to give up the clinic?' she'd asked him.

'Of *course* not,' he'd answered. 'I just think maybe our paths have diverged and we need some time apart to think.'

To think about what? She didn't have time to think.

When her family asked her about Grant today she planned to tell them he was sick at home with a cold. She wasn't going to announce the separation on Father's Day, not with a strange girl at the table. This was going to be a shock for both family and friends. She and Grant had not been a couple who ever fought in public, or even snapped at each other. They were affectionate, without being over the top about it. (There was something suspect about people who were too lovey-dovey.) They socialised and exercised together. They had mutual friends and peaceful dinner parties. She thought people would probably have described their marriage as 'solid'.

It was not in her nature to shock people with developments in her personal life. That was for Amy. Brooke preferred to go under the radar. She realised she felt ashamed, as if by separating from her husband she'd done something slightly distasteful and seedy, which was ridiculous. This was not Regency England. It was the twenty-first century. Her own brother was divorced. Her friend Ines was divorced.

She undid her seatbelt.

Where's Grant? He's at home. He has a bad cold.

She was the worst liar in her family. She used to think it was because she was the youngest, and therefore everyone could see right through her feeble attempts at deceit thanks to their superior knowledge of how the world worked.

She still sometimes caught herself watching for circumspect glances between her older siblings, listening for the nuances of the conversation, as if they might still be keeping secrets from her about sex and Santa, death and Grandma. (Her brothers and sister once convinced Brooke she was adopted because she was the only left-handed member of the family. Brooke believed it. For months! 'Have you not looked in the mirror, you foolish child?' Joy said when Brooke finally tearfully asked if she could please meet her real parents. 'You're all identical!')

If she got through the questions about Grant, the next question from her family would be about the clinic, and she'd have to lie about that too. Over the last few days she'd had four no-shows and three last-minute cancellations. It was unbelievable. It felt like a concerted attack. What was wrong with people? She had a carefully worded cancellation policy on her website but it was difficult to charge patients who she'd never even seen for an initial consultation. If she told her parents, they would be so enthusiastically sympathetic. They would remind her of the ladies who used to book private tennis lessons and then cancel five minutes before. It was selfish of her not to give her parents the opportunity to pleasurably reminisce about the early days of Delaneys but Brooke couldn't bear to hear their helpful tips, to see their furrowed brows as they brainstormed strategies. The added weight of their hopes for her success was too much to bear.

She opened her car door a fraction, put one foot on the ground, breathed in the scented spring air and wondered if she should text Grant to remind him about his hay fever medication. Was that the way one behaved during an 'amicable' separation?

Logan's car was already parked in the driveway. The others would be arriving any minute. The Delaneys were extraordinarily punctual, even Amy, who might arrive hungover or depressed or in some other way incapacitated, but right on time. A good tennis player was punctual. Don't leave the other competitors sitting around waiting for you.

As she watched, Logan came out the front door. He smiled, lifted a hand and walked towards her car. He looked kind of old today. His grey sideburns glistened in the sunlight as he ducked down to see her.

'Have you been sent out on an errand already?' she asked.

'Mum wants me to buy two bottles of mineral water.' Logan opened her car door the full way and stood back. 'You need me to take anything inside for you?'

'We don't need mineral water,' said Brooke. She picked up the green salad she'd made that no-one would eat from the passenger seat, together with her Father's Day gift: a travel-sized massage ball her dad would say was what he'd always wanted, but that her mother would probably re-gift back to Brooke one day. 'We can just drink tap water.'

'Mum says she's noticed that people always expect sparkling water these days,' said Logan as she got out, the salad bowl under her arm, the gift balanced on top of the clingwrap.

'There are no *people* coming. It's just us.'

'Just us.' Logan paused. 'And Savannah. Our new friend.' He looked back at the car. 'Where's Grant?'

He's got a bad cold. He's sick with a cold. He's very sick with a very bad cold.

'We're having a trial separation.' She really needed to work on strengthening her lying muscles.

Logan blanched. 'Oh, wow, I'm sorry.' He took a step towards her as if he was going to hug her, but they weren't a hugging family so he didn't know how to complete the move. 'That's terrible news. That's quite a shock.' He ran his palm along the side of his jaw. 'Are you okay?'

'Well,' Brooke shifted the salad bowl onto her hip, 'he hasn't died.'

'Still. It's a shock.' He seemed genuinely, properly upset. 'I didn't see that coming.'

'I didn't either.' An understatement.

'Mum loves him,' said Logan. She could sense him trying not to sound accusatory but it was as if Brooke had broken one of their mother's favourite belongings and he didn't want her to feel bad about it, but he felt bad for their mother.

It was true that Joy and her only son-in-law seemed to have a special connection, and that Grant made a point of being especially charming with Joy, and Joy went along with it, but Brooke had always wondered how much her mother was truly falling for Grant's charm offensive. Her mother, unlike Brooke, was a fine actress. She'd had all those years dealing with the parents of the tennis students, making them feel like their children were all remarkable.

Brooke put the salad and gift down on the bonnet of her car so she could irritably scratch her nose. 'It's only a trial separation. We might get back together, so I'm not telling anyone yet. I don't want to upset Mum and Dad unnecessarily.'

'Good idea.' Logan shoved his hands in the pockets of his jeans and rocked back and forth on the balls of his feet, chewing on the inside of his mouth, like he used to do before a match.

'How's Indira?' asked Brooke.

'Yeah, that's the thing,' said Logan uneasily.

'What do you mean, "that's the thing"?'

She squinted at him. Then it hit her. They all should have seen it coming. Five years was about right. Long enough for the family to forget Logan's track record of serial monogamy, long enough for the girl to become part of the family, and his girlfriends were always so lovely.

This was why he was so upset about her and Grant. He didn't want their mother to have to deal with simultaneous break-ups. *All* her children would be single. All possible grandchildren swept off the table in one fell swoop. It would knock her for six, as their father would say. He hated cricket, but liked that particular sporting colloquialism.

'Oh, Logan,' she said. 'For God's *sake.*'

'Well, you can't talk,' said Logan.

'I can so talk, I've been with Grant for ten years. We got *married.*'

'Exactly,' said Logan. 'So that makes it worse. You made a proper commitment.'

'And you didn't,' said Brooke. 'Is that what Indira wanted? Was she waiting for you to propose?'

'I don't think so,' said Logan. 'I asked her once if she wanted me to propose and she just laughed.'

'You're not meant to propose to propose, you should just *propose.*'

'She's a feminist.'

'So *what*? Did she want babies?'

'I don't know. I don't think so.'

'You don't *think* so?' Brooke threw up her arms. 'I bet she wanted something you weren't giving her.'

Logan gave his infuriating right-shouldered shrug.

You could never argue properly with Logan because he didn't care. The angrier you got the calmer he'd become. His laid-back philosophy probably charmed his partners for the first five years and then one day they lost their minds.

Brooke's eyes filled with stupid tears. 'She did all that beautiful graphic design work for me and didn't let me pay a cent.' She should have insisted she pay her.

'She was happy to do it,' said Logan. The shrug. Again.

'That's not the point, *Logan*.' She surprised herself by suddenly shoving him, quite hard, in the centre of his chest with the heel of her hand, like she was a little kid again. He didn't budge. His core strength was excellent, even though he never worked out. Maybe he'd known it was coming, even if she hadn't.

'That all you got?' he said. It seemed to have cheered him up.

'I'm sad,' she said. 'I'm really sad about Indira.'

'Yeah, well, I'm sad about Indira too, and I'm sad about Grant. But life goes on. We live to play another day.'

That's what their father used to say when they lost. Nobody found it especially motivational.

Logan lifted his keys to go and then stopped as he remembered something. 'So, guess what Savannah baked for today.'

'What?'

'Chocolate brownies.'

'Oh my word,' said Brooke. Now she was using one of their mother's favourite phrases.

'It's not funny,' said Logan. 'Mum just hissed at me, "Logan, this is not funny."' He looked over her shoulder. 'Here's Troy. Watch him park me in.'

As predicted, Troy parked his gorgeous shiny McLaren with a slick one-handed spin of the wheel directly behind Logan's car. He saw his siblings and smiled that radiant smile that could buy him anything: women, refunds, forgiveness.

Brooke smiled back helplessly as Troy leaped from the car with the glittery confidence of a movie star arriving at the premiere of his own movie. He carried a bottle of wine and a small beautifully store-wrapped gift.

'Love the new car,' she said. She didn't envy much about Troy's life except for the luxury cars, which were replaced with the same regularity as the luxury girlfriends. She shot her dowdy old Ford Focus a resentful glance. It had a persistent problem with the air-conditioning and had recently begun to emanate a deep pained groan each time she turned the steering wheel, but there was no way in the world she could justify a new car right now.

Troy jerked his chin at Logan and gently cuffed Brooke on the back of her head. 'How are you, baby Brooke? You look great. Are you wearing lipstick? Mum will be thrilled. It's maybe just a little smudged there.' He pointed at her lip.

She swore, licked her thumb and wiped it away.

'How's the physiotherapy business?' asked Troy.

She rocked her palm in a so-so motion. 'Why do you look so good?' she asked. 'You're glowing. It's annoying.'

'Just healthy living, Brooke,' said Troy. 'Spot of microdermabrasion. Bit of tennis to keep me active. You should try it. Great sport.' He looked at Logan's keys. 'You going somewhere?'

'Mum says I need to get mineral water,' said Logan. 'Probably for you, now I think about it.'

'Great. Could you make it Voss?' said Troy. 'That's my preferred sparkling.'

Logan didn't even bother to fully roll his eyes. 'I can't get out now anyway. You've blocked me in. You go get your preferred sparkling yourself.'

'How's the newest member of the family doing?' Troy looked towards the house. 'Have you met her yet, Brooke? Savann*ah*.' He said it as if it were an exotic foreign word.

'*Guess* what she baked today.' Brooke stole the moment from Logan. She so rarely had the chance to be wicked with her brothers. It was normally Amy and Troy sitting in a corner, making snarky comments and obscure pop-culture references.

Troy considered the question. His face changed. 'Not brownies.'

'Speaking of which,' said Logan. They all watched as an unfamiliar car slowly circled the cul-de-sac with Amy in the front seat talking animatedly to the car's driver, a young man who was laughing uproariously and not really keeping his eye on the road.

'Has she got another new boyfriend?' asked Brooke.

'It's an Uber.' Logan pointed at the sign on the back window.

'He might be a new boyfriend by now. Didn't she meet the last one when he served her at JB Hi-Fi?' said Troy. 'The one who fixed Mum's computer? I liked him. He added value.'

The car stopped, the driver hopped out and rushed around to open Amy's door like he was a chauffeur and Amy emerged, tangle-haired and bright-eyed, dressed like she'd just got back from a grotty but glorious music festival. She was laden with objects: an oddly shaped, badly wrapped present, a bunch of sunflowers, a baking tray with a flapping sheet of aluminium foil and a Happy Father's Day helium balloon that fluttered above her head.

'*Hello!*' she called out to her siblings as she hugged the Uber driver goodbye. She didn't hug her siblings, just her Uber drivers. The guy had probably shared something deeply personal with her that he'd never told anyone before. People sensed that Amy offered the possibility of redemption.

'Does she look hungover?' muttered Logan. 'It will be worse if she's hungover.'

'Go help her carry the brownies.' Troy nudged Brooke.

'I'm leaving,' said Logan. 'I don't want to be here when she finds out.' He held out his hand to Troy. 'Give me your keys.'

'I'll drive you,' said Troy. 'I'm scared. She has that fragile look about her.'

'Don't you dare ask if she's off her meds,' said Logan to Troy.

'I haven't said that in years,' said Troy, offended. 'No-one says that anymore.' He winced. 'Do you think she is?'

'Do not leave me,' said Brooke. It wasn't so funny anymore, now that she could see Amy actually carrying her tray of precious brownies. Now it was kind of stressful, and mean, and Brooke felt personally responsible.

She swung back and forth like a pendulum when it came to

Amy. Growing up, she and her brothers had believed Amy to be a drama queen, who felt the same things everyone felt, but chose to make a bigger deal of them. They made fun of her. At times they got angry with her when she held them up or stole their mother's attention. How could you tell what was truly going on in her head? Brooke got depressed, she got anxious, but she still managed to get herself out of bed each day. It was a *choice*, surely? There was no need for Amy to lean into her feelings with such gusto. But then a university friend got diagnosed with depression and described it to Brooke as a kind of half-paralysis, as if all her muscles had atrophied, and Brooke had a sudden memory of Amy eating cereal in slow motion, swaying like seaweed under water, and she realised she was offering this friend more sympathy and understanding than she'd ever given her own sister. These days she tried hard to see Amy with objective, compassionate eyes, but it was hard, because this was still her big sister, her bossy, charismatic sister, who used to call Brooke her 'peasant'.

'What are you all doing milling about out there?' Their mother opened the front door and called out from the front porch. She wore a tea dress with a cardigan, as if she were hosting a garden party, and she was in hectic, pink-cheeked 'we have special guests' mode. 'Come inside, all of you! Forget the mineral water, Logan, Savannah says we don't need it.'

Troy said, 'Oh, well, if *Savannah* says we don't need it.'

'Hurry up!' Joy beckoned impatiently. 'Your father is wondering where you all are! Is Grant coming separately, Brooke? I hope he's on his way. I think Savannah is ready to serve.'

'What don't we need?' trilled Amy.

'Brownies,' said Troy.

Amy's smile vanished. 'I beg your pardon?'

A familiar constellation of flashing dots appeared in Brooke's peripheral vision.

chapter twenty-three

'Well, this has been a very special Father's Day,' said Joy. 'Very special.'

She sat at the head of her beautifully set dining room table, like a woman in a magazine or a television show. Savannah had picked yellow freesias from the garden and put them in a water jug, and they looked perfect.

Joy's head felt a little *swimmy*. She thought maybe she'd drunk more wine than she was used to drinking at lunchtime. Savannah kept refilling everyone's glasses, like a waitress. In fact, Savannah had spent most of the lunch on her feet, no matter how many times people suggested she sit down, or offered to help. Eventually everyone gave up and let Savannah serve them an incredibly delicious lunch: lemon and rosemary roast chicken, roast potatoes and a green salad with walnuts and goat's cheese. (Poor Brooke's salad looked positively wilted in comparison.) It was quite remarkable that this level of quality had been produced in Joy's kitchen. What must her oven think?

Savannah had served their lunch efficiently, without that whirling, feverish *Oh I nearly forgot the bread rolls*, up-and-down-and-up-again thing that Joy knew she did whenever she hosted, and Joy's greedy family had gobbled everything up and accepted offers of seconds.

Now everyone had a cup of tea or coffee in front of them, along with their glasses of wine, and there were two plates of brownies on the table. Every person at the table had carefully, fairly, taken a brownie from each competing plate.

Even Steffi had been waited upon by Savannah like one of the Queen's corgis. She sat now in the corner of the room curled up on an old cushion that Savannah had set up for her, her head resting on her paws, occasionally licking her lips and thumping her tail with the happy memory of the various morsels and scraps that Savannah had convinced her tasted better than paper.

Stan sat at a strange sideways angle at the other end of the table from Joy, trying to avoid the bobbing Happy Father's Day balloon that Amy had tied to the back of his chair. Every now and then it brushed against his face and he batted it away like a fly, which was normally the sort of thing that would eventually make him lose his temper, but he was still in a remarkably good mood: expansive and chatty. It was either the revival of their sex life or the change in his diet since Savannah had taken over the cooking. If Savannah hadn't turned up he would probably have spent this Father's Day privately obsessing over Harry Haddad's comeback.

Joy's children, on the other hand, were not at their best. Joy wanted to say to Savannah: *They're normally much nicer than this!*

She'd been looking forward to Savannah seeing her children all together, in the same way that she would feel about any new friend meeting her children. But today, nobody had much to say, although they had been polite and complimentary about the food, thank goodness; they all sat in a similar fashion, their shoulders rounded, backs hunched, especially when compared to Savannah, who sat so upright, like a small well-behaved child. Her posture was beautiful.

Joy scanned her children.

Amy was sulking about the brownies and pretending not to, and needed her hair brushed.

Logan seemed to have entered a kind of dissociative state, staring vaguely into the distance. If he behaved like that too often, Indira might get impatient and leave him. Joy wished Indira was here today. *She* was a breath of fresh air, and she would have been polite to Savannah.

Troy, normally the life of the party and the one to cajole Amy out of her moods, seemed preoccupied and not quite as handsome today.

Meanwhile Brooke was dead-white and wearing a shade of badly applied lipstick that did not suit her at all. Joy worried that a migraine loomed, and also, where the heck was Grant? Brooke said he had a cold too, but it seemed like too much of a coincidence that both Indira and Grant would be sick, and as far as Joy could remember that man had never even had as much as a blocked nose. He drank those awful green smoothies.

Brooke was a terrible liar. Could Grant have run off with another woman? Joy had always nursed a secret, never-expressed fear (except to her hairdresser, Narelle) that Grant might have an affair. He wasn't especially good-looking but he was very charming and chatty, and Brooke *would* insist on keeping her hair so short. Narelle agreed that a longer style would soften Brooke's sharpish features.

'Why is today so special, Mum?' asked Brooke.

It was special because Joy hadn't had to do a single thing except hand over her credit card and turn up, but obviously she wasn't going to say that to her children.

'I don't know,' said Joy. She took a bite of Amy's brownie, put it down on her plate and then took an equal-sized bite of Savannah's brownie. Savannah's was better, sad to say. 'It just feels special.'

'Maybe it's the abundance of brownies,' said Troy.

His father chuckled and Troy looked pleased with himself.

'Troy.' Joy put a warning finger to her lips and shot a look at Amy.

'Mum, please. I am *not* upset that Savannah made brownies,' said Amy. 'For God's sake.' She tipped back her head and drained the last drops of her (second) glass of red wine and wiped her hand across her mouth like a small child drinking a glass of milk. She looked around the table. Her words were starting to soften and slur. 'Is that what everyone thinks? That I'm upset about *brownies*?'

'Absolutely, categorically not.' Troy sat upright and looked mock-serious. 'Why would we think you would be upset about brownies?'

'But I am honestly not upset!' cried Amy, looking very upset. 'And by the way, Savannah, your brownies are delicious. The sweetness is just . . . perfecto!' She kissed her fingertips. 'If we were rating this brownie at work it would be what we in the business call a *hero product*.'

'Amy tastes food for a living,' said Joy, hoping to change the subject. She was mystified as to how Amy had managed to trick people into paying her to eat. On 'pasta days at work' Amy didn't eat breakfast or lunch. 'So she knows what she's talking about.'

'I think your brownies are very good,' said Savannah to Amy. She took a tiny bite. She ate like a mouse. That first night, when she'd eaten that huge plate of leftover casserole and two bananas, had been an aberration. 'Much chewier than mine. I left mine in the oven for too long.'

'Thank you, Savannah. But in spite of what my family might lead you to believe, my self-worth doesn't rest on my ability to make brownies,' said Amy. 'It's like you all think I have the maturity of a four-year-old.'

'You were actually very mature when you were four,' said Joy. 'When you started preschool your teacher called you "a remarkable child".'

'Wait, I thought that was me,' said Brooke. 'Wasn't I the remarkable child?'

Joy reflected. Oh dear. 'Well, yes, it may have been you,' she admitted. 'But Amy was also remarkable. You were all remarkable.'

Troy chuckled and rocked back and forth on the rear legs of his chair, which was something they had been trying to get

189

him to stop doing since he was a child. He was a man now. If he wanted to break his neck that was fine with Joy, she wasn't going to look after him!

'Stop *rocking* on your chair, Troy, for goodness sake!' she snapped, because she *would* end up looking after him, no matter how old he was, and he'd be a terrible patient.

Troy stopped. 'Sorry, Mum.'

'Didn't I get expelled from preschool?' said Amy. 'Because I wouldn't stop crying? And all the other kids got sick of the sound of me?'

That was also true. *Separation anxiety* was the very first label Joy heard applied to her oldest child, the first of many labels she'd hear over the years, but Joy had felt no sense of foreboding when she heard that first one. She'd felt foolish pride: my child can't bear to be separated from me! That's how much she loves me. Amy used to cling to her like a koala, her face pressed against Joy's collarbone.

'I was happy to have you home with me,' said Joy. She said to Savannah, 'When Amy was just three years old she used to trot about the court picking up balls while I coached, desperate to join in the lessons.'

'That must have been cute,' said Savannah encouragingly. She was always so interested in Joy's family. It was lovely.

'Remember when she first picked up a racquet?' said Stan to Joy. 'It was bigger than her.'

'She was better than kids twice her age,' said Joy.

'They were all four better than kids twice their age,' said Stan.

'Wow,' said Savannah. 'A lot of talent in one family.'

No-one moved or said a word in response, but Joy felt a change in the mood of the room: like a slump or a sigh. It was as if her children were all inflated toys and they were slowly leaking air. What was wrong with them?

'So I don't know anything about tennis but I assume you all . . . played in, I don't know, tournaments or whatever?' said

Savannah, as she used her fingers to remove another crumb from Amy's brownie and put it on the tip of her tongue.

'They were all in the top five players of the country at some point,' said Stan.

'That's amazing,' said Savannah.

'In the *juniors*,' Brooke quickly corrected her father. 'Top five juniors.'

'Still,' said Savannah.

'But none of us made it any further,' said Amy. 'We *never quite got there.*'

'What do you mean by that?' said Joy. 'You all did extremely well!' She was surprised and disappointed to find an intense wave of irritability sweep over her, washing away the wonderful sense of wellbeing she'd been experiencing since she woke up this morning. She could feel her bad mood like a physical sensation: an actual fever of aggravation heating up her face.

Amy raised a single eyebrow in a condescending manner. 'I mean exactly that, Mum, we never quite got there, we all got close enough to make you think it was going to happen, and then one by one, we crashed and burned.'

This was technically true, in fact, it was distressingly accurate, but there was no need to say it in that hard, bitter tone. Joy and Stan had never revealed their disappointment to their children, only their pride. It was something they hadn't even properly admitted to each other.

Joy remembered their trip to Wimbledon last year. Their first time. Their lifelong dream. They'd been giddy with anticipation. This was the *point* of their big trip: not seeing Buckingham Palace or the Tower of London or riding that overpriced London Eye. The point of the trip was Wimbledon. After all these years, they finally had the time and the money and they were *there*. Their kids and their friends had been texting: *Send us photos!*

She'd seen the moment it hit Stan: the realisation that they should never have come, not like this, not as ordinary fans, as ordinary people, because Stan had never really believed they were ordinary when it came to tennis. If he couldn't play at Wimbledon then he should be there as the coach for one of his kids, and if not one of his kids, then one of his students, and if none of the above, then he should be watching from his armchair at home with his chilli crackers and cream cheese and his dog.

'I don't feel great,' he had whispered, his face pasty-white. It was the men's semifinals. The tickets had cost them six thousand dollars each. She thought: heart attack. Like poor Dennis Christos. He said, 'You stay.'

But, of course, she didn't send him off to have a heart attack on his own.

She'd dreamed of playing at Wimbledon too, and she'd dreamed of seeing one of her children or one of her students play at Wimbledon, and she'd dreamed, far more reasonably and feasibly, of one day being a spectator at Wimbledon, but her dreams didn't have the same ferocious entitlement as Stan's, because she was a woman, and women know that babies and husbands and sick parents can derail your dreams, at any moment they can drag you from your bed, they can forestall your career, they can lift you from your prized seat at Wimbledon from a match later described as 'epic'. She thought she'd need to call an ambulance or take him to a hospital. She was thinking about travel insurance and telling the children, and how would they transport his body home?

But it wasn't a heart attack. He said it was something they ate. She didn't believe it.

Joy watched the match on television, and sent fraudulent texts about how Wimbledon was wonderful, 'like a dream', 'they couldn't believe they were there', while Stan lay curled on his side in their king-sized bed, his eyes closed, forehead creased, so much like Brooke with a migraine that Joy had wondered if she should do the same as she once did with Brooke and press her hand to his forehead, firmly, the way Brooke wanted, *Harder, Mummy, harder*, except it was never hard enough to make it go away.

Stan got up the next day and said, 'I'm so sorry,' and couldn't meet her eye.

She said, 'You don't have to say you're sorry,' because he didn't. If they started saying sorry, where would it begin and where would it end? They went down to the hotel buffet breakfast, silent in the lift, and never spoke of it again.

'We were always so proud of you!' said Joy now to her children. 'You were all incredibly talented and you all did your best . . . and that's all we could ask for!'

Troy snorted. Joy glared at him.

Stan said to Savannah, 'Every single one of my kids was good enough to play on centre court at Wimbledon –'

'Except clearly we weren't,' interrupted Amy.

'You were!' Stan pounded his fist on the table, so hard that the crockery rattled. The Happy Father's Day balloon spun frantically.

Joy looked at her children: Brooke had her elbow on the table, her forehead rested on her hand, Logan lifted his eyes to the ceiling, Troy grinned that inane grin and Amy pulled a strand of blue-dyed hair across her face and sucked it, a childish habit that made Joy want to scream.

Was it because none of them had partners with them today that it felt like she'd hurtled back through time to the dinner table of their childhoods? Or was it the sudden explosive sound of Stan's fist on the table? He had no right. They were grown-ups. Didn't the stupid man realise that he no longer had the power to send anyone to their room? They could stand up and leave whenever they liked. They could move interstate or overseas. They could choose to never visit, to never call, to never have children.

The children had all the power now.

And how inappropriate to behave like this in front of Savannah. Stan's fist on the table might remind her of previous foster placements with abusive fathers. No-one knew what that child might have suffered.

Stan leaned forward on the table, his shoulders huge and muscled in the shirt that Amy had given him, a size too small.

'This one was a *beautiful* player.' Stan pointed at Amy, his eyes on Savannah. 'Impeccable ground strokes. The ball just fizzed off her racquet. It was a pleasure to watch her play.'

Oh, it was true. It *had* been a pleasure to watch Amy play. Joy and Stan used to exchange smiles as their ponytailed daughter glided back and forth across the court, when she was maybe eight or nine, back when she had a 'funny little personality' not 'a possible mental illness'. (Joy never forgave the GP who wrote that particular referral letter.)

'We used to call her the Comeback Queen,' reflected Stan. 'Remember?'

He looked down the table at Joy.

'I do remember,' said Joy carefully, because that was much later, and that wasn't such a good memory. She'd suspected that as Amy got older she began to deliberately lose points or games just so she could claw her way back to a win. Amy loved being the underdog. It was a dangerous, stupid strategy against the better players. The better players gripped that lead between their teeth and ran with it. Amy had lost matches she should have won because she'd mounted her comeback too late.

'Once she lost nine games in a row and still went on to win the match,' reflected Stan. 'Incredible.'

'But?' said Amy airily.

'Does anyone need another tea or coffee?' asked Joy.

'But then she got to fourteen or fifteen, and she started choking,' said Stan. 'Simple as that.'

It had been awful to witness. Amy would *shout* at herself. It wasn't her opponent she was fighting but herself, the voice in her head. *Amy! You stupid idiot!* Sometimes Joy felt like that summed up Amy's whole life: a constant power struggle with a cruel invisible foe.

'Choking?' asked Savannah.

Amy wrapped both hands around her throat, stuck her tongue out and put her head on one side.

'It's a sports term,' Stan explained to Savannah. 'It basically means that your state of mind prevents you from reaching your potential.'

'Stan,' said Joy. It felt like he was undressing in public. Or undressing his family. It felt deeply personal. These were conversations they'd had about their children, in the privacy of their bedroom. Amy did choke. If she was serving for the match you could almost guarantee she'd double-fault.

'Joy,' said Stan.

He couldn't be stopped. It was like standing in front of a semitrailer speeding towards you.

He said, 'Amy lost the match in her own mind before she'd even walked out on that court and her mother and I, we just couldn't work out how to . . .'

'Fix me,' finished Amy.

'No,' said Stan. 'Not fix you. Help you.'

'Move it along, Dad,' said Amy. She bundled her hair up into a messy topknot, put her elbows on the table, and locked her hands together. Joy knew it was only a defence mechanism but Amy's mocking, glamorous smile reminded Joy of Stan's mother. Joy hated it when Stan's bloody mother made a guest appearance on her beloved children's faces. 'Let's hear why the others failed.'

'No-one *failed*.' Joy's stomach cramped. 'And I'm sure Savannah isn't interested in this.'

'Oh, no, it's very interesting,' said Savannah brightly, as if she couldn't sense the tension in the room. It was the first time Joy had ever felt even slightly annoyed with her.

Stan jerked his head at Logan. 'This one was an *athlete*. Jesus, he was an athlete. Doesn't look like it now, of course.'

'Gee, thanks, Dad.' Logan lifted his wineglass in a mocking toast.

'He had one of the most powerful forehands I've ever seen. Extraordinary.'

'Powerful, yes, but would we call it accurate?' asked Troy with a sidelong look at his older brother, and Logan gave him the rude finger, as if they were both little boys.

'Logan was so fit.' Stan ignored Troy. He was into his stride now. It had been years since he'd had the chance to talk to someone with no previous knowledge and such apparent interest in the topic of his children's tennis.

'He could play for hours and look like he'd just walked onto the court. I remember one match when Logan was up against this kid who was meant to be the next big thing.' Stan's eyes shone with the memory of that long-ago January day. 'Logan wore that kid out. Every game was deuce, ad, deuce, ad, deuce, ad. Every rally was a marathon. We're talking ten, fifteen shot rallies. One hour in, that was it, this other kid, this supposed star, he was *done*.' Stan sliced his palms sideways. 'Meanwhile this one –' He pointed his thumb at Logan. 'Fresh as a daisy. Barely broke a sweat.'

Joy hadn't been at that match, but she must have heard the story a hundred times, and each time Stan told it with such delight, his head unconsciously going back and forth like a tennis spectator as he chanted: 'Deuce, ad, deuce, ad.'

'But,' Logan took another two brownies, one from each plate, 'my turn for the "but".'

'Logan never truly committed to the sport. He just didn't want it enough. He never had that burning desire, it was like he could take it or leave it, he was too –'

'Passive?' said Logan, with a strange expression on his face. 'Is that the word you're looking for, Dad?'

'I was going to say you were just too nice,' said Stan. 'I sometimes wondered if you even liked winning. You hated seeing the other kid lose.'

'I liked winning,' muttered Logan. He aggressively massaged the back of his neck. 'Bloody hell, Dad, how much of my childhood did I spend on the court if I didn't commit to the sport? How much more committed did I need to be?'

'Yeah, but, mate, like I said, you just didn't have that *desire*.' Stan discarded poor Logan and turned his gaze to Troy. 'Now Troy had the desire, because all he cared about was beating you and Amy. Younger siblings always end up the better players. Look at Venus and Serena. But see, the thing with Troy –' Stan shook his head and clicked his tongue. 'Troy was a show pony.'

'Still is,' said Logan.

Troy whinnied. Brooke giggled. Savannah smiled uncertainly.

'He was all about the show reel,' said Stan. 'He'd go for shots that Federer wouldn't go for. *Show-off* shots, and sometimes he'd get those shots, but I'd say to him –'

'*Spectacular doesn't win the match*,' filled in Troy. He picked up his glass. 'Could someone pass me the wine?'

'Exactly.' Stan twitched as the Father's Day balloon brushed against his face. 'Spectacular doesn't win the match. You have to have *substance*.' He pushed the balloon gently away as if it were a small child trying to look over his shoulder.

If Joy and Stan were having this conversation alone she would have told him it was nothing to do with bloody substance. It was focus. Troy could keep his concentration for only so long and then it was gone. *That* was the kid's fatal flaw. He'd be a set and a half up and Joy would see him staring dreamily at the sky or checking out some attractive young girl in the stands. He did the show-off shots to keep himself interested.

'Behold, a man without substance.' Troy made jazz hands.

'And then there was the altercation with Harry,' said Stan.

Shut up, thought Joy. *Shut up, shut up, shut up, you stupid man.*

'Isn't it my turn yet?' asked Brooke quickly.

'You never really came back from that,' said Stan to Troy.

'I did get a tennis scholarship to Stanford,' Troy told Savannah. 'But that meant nothing to my parents.'

'It certainly did not mean nothing!' said Joy. *It meant you went to the other side of the world and returned an entirely different person.* After America, it was like he'd been shellacked. You could tap your fingertip against that shiny hard cheerful surface.

'Troy couldn't control his temper,' said Stan. 'Inherited his hot temper from his mother.' He chuckled, as if he could turn one of the most distressing events of their family history into a funny anecdote suitable for sharing with new friends. 'He was a racquet thrower. We had to tie his racquet to his wrist.'

'Not we,' said Joy. 'You. I thought it would ruin his grip.'

'But it didn't, did it?' said Stan. 'His grip wasn't the problem.'

'I know it's your day, Dad,' said Amy. 'But could we change the subject?'

'Don't worry about it, Amy,' said Troy as Brooke silently passed him the wine. 'I don't care.'

'Anyhow, I thought we had the temper under control. He was thirteen when it happened,' said Stan to Savannah. 'He got banned for six months. Fair enough too.'

He was fourteen, thought Joy. He'd turned fourteen the day before.

'Playing against a Delaneys student. Harry Haddad.' Stan paused, allowing space for Savannah to give a little gasp of recognition, but Savannah just looked blankly back at him.

'Famous Australian player. Former number one? Won Wimbledon twice? Won the US Open a few years back?' It was beyond Stan's comprehension that she wouldn't recognise the name.

'Oh! Yes! Of course. I've heard of him,' said Savannah, clearly pretending. Joy thought how refreshing it was to have someone in the house with so little interest in tennis she hadn't even heard of Harry Haddad.

'He was a former student of mine,' said Stan. He glanced at Joy, corrected himself. 'Former student of *ours*. He's been in the news because he's in training now to make a comeback. Anyhow, so back to the story. Troy was playing against him and not doing so well –'

'Dad,' said Amy. 'Please. Let's not talk about Harry Haddad. It's not good for my mental health. I feel like it's not good for your mental health.'

'Another thing to mention is that Harry Haddad was a snivelling little *cheat*.' Troy studied his wineglass.

'Never saw it happen,' said Stan, calmly, but with that edge: the edge still sharp enough to make his children bleed.

He still didn't get it, even after all these years. He never saw how he betrayed Troy every time he made that statement.

'Doesn't mean it didn't happen,' said Troy evenly.

'How can you cheat?' asked Savannah. 'Isn't there like a . . . ref?'

'There are no chair umpires at the lower levels,' said Brooke. 'The players make their own line calls. It's hard for some kids to be . . . ethical.'

'It's hard for some grown-ups,' said Joy. She'd seen plenty of players at the club make questionable line calls. 'Sometimes umpires can be biased too.'

She thought of the first time she played in the Under 13s grass court championships at White City. Her grandfather was busy that day and so her mother took her. Her mother, bored out of her mind, flipped through *Vogue* while Joy played. Joy couldn't understand why the umpire kept calling her shots out and her opponent's shots in. She later discovered the umpire was her opponent's mother. 'Well, you're much prettier than her,' her mother said on the way home, as if that was what counted. (It did help a little bit.)

'Look at his talent, Troy. Look at where he got. He didn't *need* to cheat.' Stan was still stuck on the topic of Harry. He would forever be stuck on the topic of Harry. He grabbed the string of the balloon and snapped it free from the chair, so that it floated up to the ceiling.

'Oh,' said Amy sadly, watching it go.

'Good to see you're still so loyal to him, Dad,' said Troy. 'Considering how loyal he was to you.'

Brooke sucked in air through her teeth as if she'd stubbed her toe.

Stan pulled at the fabric of his too-tight shirt with such

ferocity Joy was reminded of the Incredible Hulk bursting free of his ordinary clothes when he lost his temper. Troy used to adore that show. Perhaps because of his own unstoppable temper.

'It was Harry's father's decision to drop me.' Stan spoke calmly. He wasn't going to explode into the Hulk. 'To drop us.'

He directed his attention to Savannah. 'Harry's father decided to change coaches.' He shrugged. A big fake shrug. 'It happens. Tennis parents are a unique breed. They get some success and they start looking for something bigger and better. That's life in the coaching game.'

Maybe it wasn't a fake shrug. His insouciance seemed almost believable. Did he truly feel that now? Was he over it?

'But I guess you must still feel really proud that you discovered him?' said Savannah.

'We do feel proud,' said Stan. 'Sure.'

He looked uncertainly around the table. 'Where was I?' His eyes caught on Brooke and his face softened. 'The little one.'

'The little one who is a whole inch taller than me,' commented Amy, her gaze still on the balloon.

'Brooke was the smartest of our kids,' said Stan.

'Thanks, Dad.' Troy tipped his finger to his forehead.

'On the court,' said Stan. 'She was the smartest and most strategic one on the court. She had to be, because she was playing you lot and you were all so much bigger and faster than her. She was analysing her competitor's weaknesses at an age when most kids were just thinking about getting the ball over the net.'

It was true that Brooke was clever on the court, but Joy had never really enjoyed watching her play as much as the others, because Brooke herself seemed to take no pleasure in the game. That permanent frown made its first appearance when Brooke was about eight. Even before the headaches.

'But Brooke gets migraines,' said Stan. 'It was a terrible, terrible shame.'

He shook his head with such regret and sadness you would

think he was describing Brooke's early death, not her early retirement.

Joy remembered the day Stan and Brooke came home hours early from a tournament.

'What are you doing here?' Joy had asked. She was rushing out the door on her way to fill in for one of the coaches who had called in sick. She was in a permanent rush in those days.

'She's done,' said Stan. 'She's finished.'

'What happened?' Joy asked as Brooke walked past her and went straight to her room without saying a word, but the look she shot at Joy seemed so accusatory, and when she looked at Stan she saw the same accusation in his eyes: *You failed*. Because the children's medical care was her responsibility and she couldn't fix Brooke's headaches.

'That doctor you take her to has no fucking clue,' Stan had said, and what Joy should have done was tell Stan to take her class for her, and she should have gone and comforted Brooke, but she was so angry with Stan for swearing at her, for blaming her, that she didn't even think of it, she just left, slamming the door behind her.

'If we'd got the right medical advice things might have been different,' said Stan now, and Joy felt that long-ago frustration rise within her as if it were yesterday.

Savannah lifted up Amy's plate of brownies. 'Would anyone –'

'I took her to doctor after doctor after doctor!' said Joy.

'No-one is blaming you, Mum,' said Brooke as the dog began to whine.

'Well, it certainly *sounds* –'

'Indira left me,' said Logan, and the room fell instantly silent.

chapter twenty-four

Logan sat upright and stoic after his announcement, his forearms on his armrests as if he were strapped to the electric chair. Even the dog seemed shocked and gazed steadfastly at the wall as if to point out this awful business was nothing to do with her.

'Eh? What's that?' said Stan confusedly.

'Now just seemed like as good a time as any to mention it,' said Logan.

'Oh, *Logan.*' Amy looked back down from the balloon. 'We *love* her.'

When Logan had arrived today and said that Indira was at home sick, Joy had a thought, a deliriously hopeful thought: Maybe she's feeling sick because she's pregnant.

That cryptic look on Indira's face the last time Joy saw her had not been the indication of a special secret announcement she was waiting for the safe twelve-week mark to make. She'd been getting ready to leave. The flower magnet Joy had so hoped was an ultrasound picture had been a *farewell* gift.

'I loved her too,' said Logan.

'Did she know that?' asked Amy.

'Should have put a ring on it.' Troy shook his head in mock exasperation.

'Says *you,*' said Logan.

'I've been married.'

'You haven't stayed married.'

Brooke opened her mouth as if to say something and then briefly closed her eyes.

'Have you got a migraine coming on, Brooke?' asked Joy. A cramping sensation hit her lower abdomen again. She suppressed a groan. 'You mustn't drive home if you do. You must never drive when you're suffering a migraine.'

'I'll drive her home,' offered Savannah.

'I don't have a migraine!' snapped Brooke. 'We've talked enough about migraines today.'

Joy didn't believe her. She really didn't look well. 'If you do, maybe you should stay here. Grant won't be much use to you if he's sick.'

'GrantandIhavebrokenuptoo.' Brooke spoke so rapidly it took Joy a moment to separate out the words.

'I beg your *pardon*?'

Brooke exhaled, and her shoulders sagged. 'It's a relief to say it.' She looked at her father. 'Sorry to ruin Father's Day.' She looked at Logan. 'Although Logan started it.'

'It's alright, sweetheart,' said Stan with deep sadness. He patted Brooke on the shoulder before slumping back in his chair. 'These things happen.'

Joy said, 'You mean you're getting a *divorce*?'

'It's just a trial separation for now, but . . .' Brooke squinted as if at a sudden bright light. 'It looks that way.'

Joy should have realised this was more than a migraine. The poor girl looked exhausted, pale and haggard, with dark circles under her eyes, and her hair was just so *lank*.

Troy put his arm around his sister.

'How long?' he asked.

'We've been separated for six weeks.'

'Six *weeks*?' Joy didn't mean it to sound like an admonishment, but how could Brooke have been separated for six weeks without saying a single word about it to her parents?

'Was it all the pressure you put on yourself with that *damned* clinic?' Now she was accidentally giving away her hatred of the clinic. She was getting this all wrong. This was becoming one of those pivotal life moments she would wish she could go back and do again so she could say all the right things. She put her fingertips to her hairline. She was sweating. Food poisoning? Savannah's roast chicken had been so wonderfully tender! Was this the price you had to pay for tender chicken? It was too high a price!

'I should have helped out more at the clinic,' she said to Brooke. She *should* have! Grant probably felt neglected. 'I should have insisted.'

'Oh, Mum,' said Brooke wearily.

'I can't believe you never told me,' said Amy.

'Can we not make it about you, Amy?' said Brooke.

Amy's face crumpled. 'I just meant I could have helped you.'

'Okay, well, thank you, I'm fine.' Brooke massaged tiny circles in her forehead with her fingertips. 'I'm sorry. I just wasn't ready to talk about it. I thought we might . . . work it out. Nobody needs to get upset.'

Savannah had folded her napkin into a neat square, concealing her mostly uneaten brownies. What must she think of them all? It was embarrassing to remember how she'd worried that Savannah would be envious of Joy's loving, stable family.

'Well!' Joy said to Savannah. 'I hope this isn't too awkward for you. All these upsetting announcements on Father's Day!'

'Sorry, Dad,' said Logan remorsefully. 'I didn't mean to ruin Father's Day.'

'Neither did I,' said Brooke. 'Sorry, Dad.'

'No-one needs to be sorry,' said Stan. He looked at the balloon floating above his head, grabbed for the end of the string and pulled it down. He clutched the balloon like a child in a stroller being pushed around a fairground.

'What are you *doing*?' Joy asked him.

'Holding my balloon,' said Stan.

'Do you actually need me to give you all some privacy?' asked Savannah. 'I could go to my room –' She corrected herself in a sudden fluster and glanced at Amy. 'Not *my* room.'

'We don't need privacy,' said Stan. 'We're fine. These things happen. It's no-one's fault.'

'Of course it's no-one's fault,' said Joy doubtfully, although she'd quite like to ascertain where the fault did lie in each of these break-ups.

'Does anyone need –' began Savannah.

'We're fine,' Stan cut her off.

There was silence for a moment. Stan kept idiotically clutching his balloon. Joy didn't know if it was fury or nausea rising in her belly. Was she about to vomit or yell, faint or cry? All of them seemed like possibilities.

Troy said, 'Seeing as the curve balls are coming from every direction, I might throw one more.'

'Fabulous,' said Joy through gritted teeth. 'You do that, Troy. Throw us another curve ball. You throw it right at me, darling.'

'Right, well, okay then, Mum,' said Troy. He actually looked nervous. It couldn't be another break-up. He wouldn't bother telling them. He was in and out of relationships all the time. 'I was considering keeping it a secret, but to hell with it. I could do with your advice.' He moved his glass to one side, sloshing red wine onto the white tablecloth. Was he drunk? Was Joy herself drunk? She really did feel very strange indeed.

He said, 'So, you remember Claire?'

'Well, for goodness sake, Troy, yes, we remember *Claire*,' said Joy.

Claire was Troy's ex-wife, once a much-loved member of the family, just like Indira and, to a lesser extent, Grant. It was like a death each time her children broke up with someone, and over the years there had been many, many deaths.

(She would write that in her memoir: *When I look back over the last decade, it's like looking at a battlefield strewn with the corpses of all the perfectly lovely young men and women who have been in unsuccessful relationships with my annoying, ungrateful children.* What would the little innocent teacher think of that? She did say to try to be colourful.)

Troy said, 'So, I saw Claire when I was in the States –'

'Are you getting back together?' Amy's face was full of foolish hope.

'Of course they're not getting back together,' said Joy, to conceal her own foolish hope. Surely not. Hadn't Claire gone off to Texas or somewhere like that – somewhere that made you think of cowboys – and married an American cardiologist? A friend of a friend from when Troy and Claire lived together in the US?

'No, she's happily married, permanently settled in the US,' said Troy. 'She's ready to have a baby.'

'Well, I'm not surprised. She was ready to have a baby with *you* all those years ago,' said Joy bitterly. Claire and Troy had been in the process of going through IVF when their marriage broke up. Apparently Troy had been unfaithful and at the time Joy had been so angry with him she hadn't been able to look him in the eye for a good six months. She shivered violently. It was too hot or too cold in here.

'So, she and her husband have been trying for a long time now and apparently they haven't been having any luck,' said Troy.

'Oh no,' said Brooke. 'Tell me she doesn't want to use –'

'Yes,' said Troy. He looked at his sister, who seemed to have guessed something that Joy couldn't even imagine. 'Yes, she does.'

'Use what?' asked Stan.

'Well, we've kept our embryos on ice all this time. From when we were doing IVF. Claire has been paying the storage costs. Anyway, now she's wondering how I would feel if she . . . tried her luck with one of those.'

Joy felt like she was stumbling about in the dark for a light switch. 'You mean Claire wants to have *your* baby? But I don't understand, why can't she do IVF with her new husband? Make some new . . . embryos?' She tripped over the word 'embryos'. When she was getting pregnant, there had just been babies or no babies.

'She had low ovarian reserve back when she was doing IVF with Troy,' said Brooke, who remembered everyone's medical histories. 'She's probably got no more eggs.'

'But *you'd* be this child's father,' said Joy, and she saw Troy as a baby: the cutest and naughtiest of her babies. He'd wail so loudly each time he woke you'd think he was dying, and Joy would go running, tricked every time, and the instant she picked him up the crying would stop like a switch had been flicked and he'd smile that heart-melting smile, crocodile tears still wet on his fat rosy cheeks.

'She wants her husband to formally adopt the child as soon as it's born,' said Troy, and Joy heard him trip on the word 'husband' in the same way she'd tripped on 'embryo'.

'But *could* you be involved? If you wanted to be involved?' asked Amy.

Troy shrugged. 'She says it's up to me, but what would be the point of me turning up every few months and taking the kid out to McDonald's like some sad divorced dad? Better if it just thinks the cardiologist is its father, don't you think?'

Joy was on a boat being rocked about on a stormy sea.

She met Stan's eye. He looked stunned. She could tell he didn't really get it. The brand new possibilities and dilemmas created by modern technology, modern science and modern thinking were beyond him.

'You *like* this idea?' asked Logan.

'No, I don't like the idea at all,' said Troy, and there it was: a flash of anguish. 'To be frank, I hate the idea.'

'Well, then, mate, you're not obliged –'

'But it could be Claire's only chance to have her own biological child.' Troy lifted his hands in a hopeless gesture of surrender. 'Her only chance. Ever. How can I take that away from her? When those embryos are just sitting there? It would be so cruel.' His voice dropped and he moved his wineglass around in circles on the red wine stain on the tablecloth, as if he could rub it away, which he couldn't. That stain would be there forever.

Troy added in a small remorseful voice, 'Especially after what I did to her.'

Oh, for goodness sake.

This was exactly how Joy used to feel when Troy got in trouble as a kid, and he'd sit there in front of her and Stan, head hanging, hands dangling between his knees, looking so sad, remorseful and bewildered, as if the actions he'd taken hadn't been his choice, not really, but he was once again stuck with their consequences.

'I think I have to say yes, don't I?' He looked up the table at Joy. 'Don't I, Mum?'

Joy sighed. She put a hand once again to her burning cheek and shuddered. She was freezing.

'Don't you think, Mum?' said Troy. 'I have to say yes?'

He needed an answer. He'd always looked to her, not his father, for answers to the moral quandaries in which he found himself.

I stole this CD, Mum, and now I feel bad about it. Should I just take it back to the shop and tell them? But I kind of scratched it.

'Oh, Troy.'

Joy thought of Claire's parents. She and Stan had met them only a handful of times but they'd liked them. Uncomplicated and kind people. They'd even played doubles against them. The mother, Teresa, had a nice double-handed backhand. Joy had been mortified when her son had broken Teresa's daughter's heart like that. She'd phoned her and told her she was so sorry and she was ashamed of Troy, and Teresa had been kind and gracious. If the situations had been reversed Joy would have been well mannered too, but cool and snippy. Now that nice woman would get Joy's grandchild, and Joy wouldn't be allowed to see it, to hold it or know it. What if the baby had Troy's smile? And

Claire's beautiful red hair? Joy would have especially loved a red-headed grandchild!

'Yes,' she said to Troy. 'You're right. You have to say yes. It's the right thing to do.'

'Well, I don't know,' began Stan uneasily.

'It's *the right thing to do*,' Joy hissed at him.

He shut up.

Yes, this was the right thing to do, but it was also the wrong thing.

What if this child, this dear little red-headed child who she already loved but might never meet, turned out to be Joy's *only* grandchild?

She said suddenly, 'Maybe you should all go home now.'

Everyone stared at her.

'I'm not feeling the best,' she said. 'I feel like I'm coming down with something.'

All of a sudden she recognised the combination of symptoms she'd been experiencing for the last few days. What a foolish old woman she was. She had a damned UTI, just like the one she had on her honeymoon, because of the recent unusual sexual activity.

Now she was furious with Stan, sitting there like a silent, stupid monolith at the end of the table with his balloon, contributing nothing except a UTI! At her age! She picked up her glass and took a long drink of water, although that ship had clearly sailed. She needed antibiotics, and it was Sunday, so she couldn't go to her lovely GP, Susan, she'd have to go to a medical centre, and she'd have to tell a kid straight out of medical school about her sex life.

'Dammit to hell,' she said to Stan.

'Eh?' said Stan. 'Why are you looking at me? What did *I* do?'

'Well, for one thing, you killed Dennis Christos!!' she said, and it was so strange because she hadn't even been *thinking* about poor Dennis, what with everything that was going on, but the accusation had been sitting there these past six months, ready and waiting in her subconscious for just the perfect moment.

'Dennis Christos died of a heart attack!' Stan responded instantly, without any confusion at all, conclusive proof of his guilt.

'You made him think he was going to break your serve and his poor heart couldn't handle it!'

'He could not really have believed he was going to break my serve,' scoffed Stan.

'You let the game get to love–forty!' cried Joy.

'Well, I'm sorry,' said Stan, sounding not at all sorry.

'Don't apologise to me! Apologise to poor grieving Debbie Christos!'

'Never admit liability, Dad,' said Troy. 'That's my tip.'

'I bet it is,' said Logan.

'Dennis Christos once made a very inappropriate remark to me,' commented Amy. 'If that makes you feel any better, Mum. *Very* inappropriate.'

'Should we give Dad our gifts before we go?' asked Brooke anxiously.

'What have I done *wrong*?' The words exploded from Joy without her permission.

Everyone looked at her like stunned bloody mullets.

'You haven't done anything wrong, Mum,' said Amy soothingly.

'Then how is it that not a single one of you can maintain a long-term relationship? Did your father and I not set a good example to you? Of a good marriage?'

Her children all dropped their heads as if she'd called for volunteers for an unpleasant task.

'So your dad and I weren't perfect,' she said. 'But, well, we weren't *that* bad, were we? Are you *punishing* us for something? For what? For making you play tennis? We did not make you play tennis! Never! You loved tennis! You were all so talented!'

'We're not punishing you,' said Troy. 'That's crazy talk, Mum.'

'It's just bad luck,' said Brooke. 'Bad timing.' She shot Logan a steely look. 'I couldn't believe it when I heard that Logan and Indira had broken up *too*.'

'Mum,' said Amy. 'You will get to be a grandmother. I mean – obviously *I* won't have kids, but someone will.' She indicated her sister and brothers. 'One of them will! In the normal way. Not like what Troy is doing. Which is obviously weird and upsetting. But you *will* get a proper grandchild. I promise you.'

'How can you promise me that, Amy? I don't see your brothers and sister rushing to agree with you! And what do you mean, you *obviously* won't have children? Why not? Anyway, why are you talking about grandchildren? Have I mentioned grandchildren? Ever? Not once!' Joy's whole body burned and shook with the injustice of it. 'Never once! Did I? Well, did I?'

If she wasn't to be rewarded for her forbearance, it should at least be recognised.

'You never did, Mum,' said Brooke, and she sounded so sad, as if she might cry, and also frightened, as if Joy were drunk or mad or sick.

'Just like you never said how much you wanted us to win,' said Troy, quietly.

Joy stood. Her legs were wobbly. The only person whose eyes met hers was her damned husband.

She could see what he wanted to do right now. She could see it settle over him: a deadly stillness, or silence, like everything was shutting down. It had been twenty years since he'd done it but she still recognised the signs. She always used to know when it was coming. She'd see it before the children did, and if she acted fast she could intercept, she could avert the crisis. The feeling had been like running to catch something before it shattered, except you weren't allowed to run. Maybe it was how bomb disposal people felt.

But she was no longer in the business of bomb disposal. She was too old for it and she could not believe she had ever put up with it in the first place.

'Don't . . . you . . . dare.' She pointed a shaky finger at him. *'Don't you even think about it.'*

She swayed on her feet. The ache of grief and humiliation spread not just across her stomach but all the way up her left side.

It was Savannah who got to her first, and supported her with a surprisingly strong grip.

'Make them all go,' Joy said to her. 'Make them all go home.'

chapter twenty-five

Now

It was now fifteen days since Joy Delaney had been seen by her family.

'My mother got very sick on Father's Day,' said Brooke Delaney. 'She collapsed. It turned out she had a kidney infection. We had to call an ambulance.'

'That must have given you all a fright,' said Christina.

Christina and Ethan were interviewing Joy Delaney's youngest daughter at her physiotherapy practice, surrounded by exercise equipment. There were only two chairs. Ethan had accepted Brooke's offer to sit on the balance ball, which he did with great aplomb, diligently taking notes. Christina would have fallen off.

They had met Brooke at the press conference, but it had taken a few days for this interview to be scheduled. Christina couldn't be sure if Brooke had been deliberately delaying. Right now she seemed keen to be cooperative, or at least to give that impression.

'Well, yes, it did give us a fright,' said Brooke. 'We didn't know what was going on at first. Mum was behaving so oddly. We thought it was because she was upset, not sick.'

'What was she upset about?'

'I felt especially bad,' reflected Brooke. 'Because I'm the one with medical training. She had a fever. I should have realised.'

'She was upset about something?' pushed Christina.

'Just family stuff,' said Brooke. 'My brother and I had both broken up with our partners. Oh, and Dad decided it would be a good day to do a comprehensive analysis of our failed tennis careers.' She gave a faint smile.

'So what was your impression of Savannah?' asked Christina. She burned her tongue sipping the too-hot cup of tea that Brooke had made for her.

'She was just a sweet, quiet girl. She'd cooked all this food for us but then she was kind of *serving* us, in our parents' house. It was odd and uncomfortable. It was like she was Cinderella, barely eating anything herself, and both my parents had become strangely . . . enamoured of her. Dependent on her. It was like she'd turned up and solved a problem we didn't realise needed solving.'

'What problem was that?'

Brooke considered the question. 'I guess, maybe, the problem of cooking? Or the problem of retirement? My parents aren't the sort of people who dreamed of retirement. They loved to work.'

'Has your mother shown signs of depression recently?'

'Absolutely not,' said Brooke. She blinked. 'Things haven't been great recently, but Mum is not the sort of person to get depressed.'

'What about your father, then? Is *he* the sort of person to get depressed?'

'He can get grumpy,' said Brooke carefully. 'But never violent. If that's what you're implying.'

'I don't want to imply anything,' said Christina. 'I'm just gathering information about your parents' states of mind.'

'I wish you could see my father coaching a child,' said Brooke. 'Even a child with no talent. *Especially* a child with no talent. He was so gentle and patient, so passionate about tennis, he just always wanted everyone to love tennis as much as he did.'

This told Christina nothing. Gentle people snapped. People who were patient and kind in some circumstances were cruel and vicious in others.

'But he's not coaching anymore, right? Your parents are retired and you said they loved to work. So I take it they haven't been enjoying retirement?'

'They've been floundering a bit,' said Brooke. 'They tried travelling, but they didn't know how to holiday. We didn't really do holidays in our family.'

'You never went on a holiday?'

'Well, we did. Every summer we went for a week to a caravan park on the Central Coast,' admitted Brooke. 'Which was kind of fun.' She frowned. 'Kind of not.' She sighed. 'But there was never time for many holidays because we all played competitive tennis. We were either travelling to a tournament or training for one, and my parents were trying to run a coaching school at the same time.'

'Was it a happy childhood?' asked Christina. She hadn't got a handle yet on this family. On the surface they seemed loving and cheerful but she could sense dysfunction bubbling ominously beneath their sporty, matter-of-fact demeanours.

'I don't know,' said Brooke. She picked up a ballpoint pen, chewed on it, and then seemed to catch herself, removed it from her mouth and put it back on the desk in front of her and pushed it away. 'I mean, yes, it was happy. It was very busy. It was dominated by tennis. Tennis hijacks your childhood. There's no time for anything else.'

'Did you resent having your childhood hijacked?'

'Not at all. I loved tennis. We all loved tennis.'

'You still play?' Christina looked at the framed print of a tennis player on the wall.

Brooke's nostrils flared. 'Not competitively. I play with my dad every now and then. For fun.'

'So growing up, did your parents put a lot of pressure on you to win?'

'We put pressure on ourselves,' said Brooke. 'We all wanted to win.' She followed Christina's eyes to the picture of the tennis player, who was stretching for a backhand as if a life depended on it. 'It's hard to want something so badly and give it your all and then not get it. There's this idea that all you need to do is believe in yourself, but the truth is, we all can't be Martina.'

'Martina?' Christina checked her notes. Was that the older sister?

'Navratilova,' said Ethan. He pointed at the poster.

'Oh, of course,' said Christina. The only tennis player she knew was the angry one from the eighties. McEnroe. She had an uncle who used to put on an American accent to imitate his tantrums: 'You can*not* be *serious.*'

Ethan said to Brooke, 'When you said "things haven't been great recently", is that because there was some fallout following that Father's Day lunch?'

Astute question. Christina watched Brooke's body language as she answered. Her shoulders went up and she stretched her neck in a turtle-like manner to make them drop.

'There was no fallout,' she said definitively. 'There were just a few things said out loud that day that had never been said out loud before, that's all. Then Mum was sick in hospital, and we all focused on that.'

Was that the truth? Or was that when things began to fray?

'Okay then, so why do you think things "haven't been so great" lately?' asked Christina.

Brooke went very still. 'I don't know,' she said, and she didn't blink.

There was the lie. Right there. Christina could point at it like a doctor points out a fracture on an X-ray.

She did so know.

Christina waited.

'Are you sure?' she said gently. 'Are you sure you don't know?'

Two spots of colour rose on Brooke's cheeks. 'Yes, I'm sure.'

'So back to your parents' house guest,' said Christina. 'She was alone with your father? While your mother was in hospital?'

'Yes,' said Brooke. 'It was only two nights.'

'Right,' said Christina. That was long enough. She waited. Brooke didn't flinch.

'Then your mother came home from hospital and Savannah stayed on.'

'Yes,' said Brooke. 'We were grateful because she was doing all the cooking.'

'I believe it's around this time that your brother Logan discovered something unwelcome about Savannah.'

This time Brooke definitely did flinch. Had she not expected this information to be passed on? If not, why not?

Brooke recovered fast, although she had to work too hard to maintain eye contact.

'Did Logan tell you that?'

'He did,' said Christina. Logan had mentioned it in a sudden rush, just before he had to hurry off to teach a class. 'Can you tell me more?'

'Well,' said Brooke, and she spoke gingerly, as if she were tiptoeing her way through broken glass. 'Logan was just sitting at home one day when he discovered something about Savannah that made us all feel a bit . . .' She broke eye contact to try to find the right word.

Ethan wobbled on his balance ball.

'Nervous,' finished Brooke.

chapter twenty-six

Last October

It was the middle of the day, the middle of the week, the middle of his life. Logan had taught an early-morning class and now he was back home, on his green leather couch, in his half-empty townhouse, on a clear, sunlit day filled with birdsong, lawnmowers and leaf blowers, and the sound of his next-door neighbour learning the cello. She'd left a pre-emptive note: *Thank you for your patience while I learn the cello!*

Logan channel-surfed, drank warm beer and ate cold leftover pizza for his lunch, and tried to stop his eyes continually leaving the television and returning to all the blank spaces in the apartment left by Indira.

There was a blank space in front of him where Indira should have been standing right now, hands on her hips: *Do you realise the sun is shining out there?*

She thought it was illegal to watch television when the sun was shining. It was because she and her family had emigrated from the UK when she was twelve and she still appreciated Australian sunshine in a way that Logan, who grew up with the sun in his eyes, never could. He saw sunlight as a peril, an obstacle to overcome on the court, like the wind. She saw it as a daily miracle.

She'd left behind literal blank spots too, like the faded rectangle on the wall where she'd hung that god-awful abstract painting she'd bought from an artist at the markets in Hobart, and the flattened carpet by the front door where her pointless vintage hat rack used to stand, except apparently it hadn't been pointless because Logan kept going to chuck things on it, like his hoodie, and it kept right on not being there, its absence so surprisingly consistent, like the balls of dirty grey fluff that still floated disconsolately around the space in the laundry where Indira's bamboo laundry hamper once stood.

She'd left behind her washing machine. It glared at him each time he attempted to use it. It was a small, fiddly front-loader with too many cycle options. Indira had done all their laundry. She loved laundry. She'd sometimes peeled socks off his feet just to wash them.

At least the fridge still liked him. He'd had it for years. It stayed, solemn and stolid, humming softly to itself through each relationship break-up as the tubs of Greek yoghurt and punnets of strawberries vanished, to be replaced once again by pizza boxes and multiple six-packs of beer.

Faithful old fridge.

For Christ's sake, he was turning into his mother: personifying his appliances.

He stared at the blank rectangle on the wall, as if it were a bricked-up window and he was uselessly looking for a view that was long gone, for an explanation that was not forthcoming.

'It's beautiful,' she used to say, about the god-awful painting. 'It makes me feel alive.'

'It's god-awful,' he would say, and he'd heard the echo of his parents in their banter, or he thought that's what he heard. Maybe Indira heard something else. Her parents had an unhappy marriage. She might have heard the echoes of something entirely different. He thought he was being funny and flirty, but maybe she thought he was being nasty. Maybe she hated doing the laundry. Maybe they'd been living side by side in entirely different realities.

It *was* an awful painting, but he missed it, just like he missed her questions, her perfume, her insistence he eat bananas (for the potassium, she was obsessed with potassium), her runners by the front door, her high-pitched sneezes, the unfathomable pleasure she took in capturing the Pokémon that apparently loitered invisibly throughout their apartment (were they still here? Waiting hopefully for her to capture them on her phone?), her butterfly kisses on the back of his neck early on a Sunday morning, her – Jesus.

Enough.

He picked up his phone and called his friend Hien, because Logan was not fucking *passive*. He was keeping a daily inventory of his non-passive actions. He was the only one in his circle of old school friends who ever picked up the phone and all his friends' wives noticed this and told their husbands, 'You're all so lucky you've got Logan.'

'You thought about it yet?' asked Hien as soon as he answered.

'Eh?' Logan hadn't thought about anything. 'Thought about what?'

But then he remembered that Hien believed his six-year-old son was the next Nadal, and he wanted Logan to coach him, and he didn't care that Logan hadn't coached since he was a teenager helping out at Delaneys. Logan had preferred coaching to all the other jobs they had to do but he didn't need to do it now.

'I told you already, I don't coach,' said Logan. 'I gave you a list of names.'

'Just see him play,' said Hien. 'Just once. I used to come to all your matches.'

'You did not.'

'I came to one,' said Hien. 'You were *good*.'

'No shit, Sherlock,' said Logan. 'I ranked –'

'Yeah, whatever, mate, I don't care what you ranked, your time is done, but my kid is the future and he could be your future. You'll see. You and Indira come for lunch, and then we'll head down to the local courts and see what you think.'

'Hien,' said Logan.

'I want you to coach him. No-one else. Not even your dad. I'm doing you a favour. You think about it. Gotta go.'

Logan tossed the phone aside on the couch and laughed a little. Even hard-nosed Hien had turned into a typical tennis parent, blinded by love for his kid.

Hien's wife and Indira were good friends. But Indira must not have told her yet about the break-up.

His friends would react in the same way as his family had on Father's Day. People liked Indira more than him. He'd always known this and this was the first time he'd cared. He felt unfairly maligned. Even bloody *Troy* had looked at him like he was a fool for letting her go.

He remembered his mother's words just before her dramatic collapse: *Did your father and I not set a good example to you? Of a good marriage?*

He'd never considered his parents' marriage something that could be rated. In his mind it didn't exist relative to anything else. It just was. He guessed that he had an unconscious, childish belief that his parents were not really two individuals but one unit. They had been together for half a century, after all, and they worked together, played tennis together. He rarely saw them apart. *Had* they set a good example of a good marriage? For the first time he truly considered the question.

He liked the way his parents teased each other. It was like watching them play a game, and when he and his siblings were little they hadn't understood the rules but they'd known it was a fun game. He obviously preferred to know nothing about their sex life but he liked that they'd always touched and hugged and kissed: more than other people's parents. His father was so large and his mother so small, he could lift her up under her armpits and put her down somewhere else when he chose, and even as a child Logan could tell his mother liked it when he did that, even when she pretended to resist, which was part of the game.

Logan would never attempt to do that to Indira. She was violently ticklish. She would probably have head-butted him if he ever tried to pick her up. She also believed herself to be too heavy for him to lift. She had issues with her body. He loved her body but he had to be meticulously careful about what he said. Indira preferred to pretend she didn't have a body at all. In the beginning he used to compliment her, and she'd turn on him: *You're lying, you're just saying that, how could you say that, I know you don't mean that, my legs are revolting, my arms are disgusting.* Suddenly he would find himself in the position of defending her body against a cruel attacker, and he didn't know how long or how vigorously he was meant to fight back when she was the attacker, so eventually he surrendered. He stopped saying anything at all. Every relationship has its quixotic rules. You just had to follow them. Only his hands could talk, and he tried to let his hands say everything he wasn't allowed to say out loud. Theirs was a relationship with a lot of touching, not just in the bedroom: they held hands in the street, they lay side by side on this couch when they watched TV. He'd thought all that touching meant that everything that needed to be said was being said.

If he'd thought about it, and now he was thinking about it, he might have realised that growing up he hadn't liked certain aspects of his parents' marriage. He'd hated it when his mother made faces behind his father's back and muttered bitter remarks, so low that only her children could hear: *Well, I TOLD him that was going to happen and did he listen? No, he did not listen.*

He hadn't liked it when his father used to get the final word in an argument not by yelling, but by leaving.

I hated it when my father left.

He felt a rush of memory as if he'd smelled a long-forgotten scent from his childhood. There was a dropping-away sensation in his stomach like tripping in a dream. He hadn't thought about that in years. Maybe he'd never really thought about it. At some point his father had stopped doing it, and the memory had vanished, the way old clothes vanished and you forgot they had ever existed until an old photo reminded you: I loved that t-shirt.

One day his father came back and never did it again, and years and years piled on top of those particular memories, obliterating them from view. His mother no longer pulled faces or made bitter asides and his father no longer left.

His phone rang and he jumped. He picked it up, saw it was Indira. He studied her name, considered putting his thumb on 'Decline'.

Indira was determined to 'stay friends'. She had this new way of talking to him now, without a trace of emotion. She sounded like a friendly customer service representative. She was a nearly perfect clone of his Indira, except that something essential and beautiful was missing.

He muted the television, answered.

'*Hi,* Logan,' she said in her friendly telemarketer voice. 'How are you?'

'I'm well, Indira. How are *you?*' He didn't quite imitate her tone, but close.

She paused and in a slightly less friendly but more normal tone said, 'I thought I'd just call to check if your mum has been discharged from hospital.'

She could have texted: *How's your mum?* That's what he would have done. Or she could have just disappeared from his life like other ex-girlfriends, but she was staying in touch, remaining dutifully apprised of family news. He wanted to tell her this wasn't necessary. If he wasn't getting her warm body next to him in bed, he didn't want her cold friendly voice in his ear.

'She's back home,' he said. 'They only kept her two nights.'

'Oh, good. That's good. And is that girl still staying with them?'

'Yeah,' said Logan. 'She is. She cooks for them. Mum loves it. It's . . .' It's strange. It's nice. It's comforting. It's kind of frightening. He didn't know what to say or feel about Savannah. She seemed to make both his parents happy. How could he complain about that? He looked at the blank spot above the television. 'How are you?'

Indira was in Perth, where her parents had relocated a year ago. She did not get on with her parents. Yet she was prepared to stay with them on the other side of the country. That's how badly she no longer wanted to be in a relationship with Logan.

'This morning my parents yelled at each other for ten minutes about a water glass,' she said, and she forgot to use her clone voice. 'They don't even seem to be aware they're yelling. That's just their default position.'

'I'm sorry,' he said. *Why did you leave me?*

'Anyway, I'm checking out a place this afternoon that looks promising.' Back to her friendly clone voice.

'We never yelled at each other,' said Logan, and he held his breath because talking about their relationship was against their unspoken rules of engagement. *Come home. Please put your god-awful painting back up on the wall.*

There was a long pause.

'We never really argued,' said Logan. 'Did we?' *Why did you leave? Can you come home now please?*

'There's no point talking about this now,' said Indira. 'I've got to –'

Logan spoke fast. 'On Father's Day, just before Mum collapsed, she was getting really upset about you and me breaking up, and Brooke and Grant breaking up –'

'Brooke is well rid of *him*,' said Indira, who had taken against Grant in a way that Logan had never really understood.

Logan barrelled on. 'And anyway, she asked if she and Dad had not set a good example to us. Of a good marriage.'

'Your mum and dad have a great relationship,' said Indira. 'They're so cute together. I'll call your mum today.' He could hear pain in her voice. She loved Logan's parents. She'd probably talked more to them in the past five years than Logan had. Talking to his parents was like a domestic duty he'd handed over to her because she was so good at it, like she'd handed over bathroom cleaning to him because he was so good at streak-free shower screens.

'They do have a great relationship,' agreed Logan. 'Although, it's funny, when you called I was thinking about how my dad used to . . .' He couldn't find the right word for what his dad used to do and he wasn't sure if he really wanted to talk about it anyway.

'How your dad used to what?' said Indira, as if she wanted to know, and if this was a way to keep her on the phone and hear her normal voice, then he would take it.

'He used to do this thing when we were kids . . . maybe three or four times a year. Not that often. It wasn't a big deal.' Except that it was kind of a big deal. 'I'm sure I told you,' he said.

'You never told me,' said Indira. Her voice sounded a little louder in his ear, as if she'd just sat up, and so he sat up straighter too.

'Oh,' said Logan. 'Well. If my dad got angry enough about something, he'd just . . . walk away.'

'You mean he avoided conflict,' said Indira. There were certain syllables where he could hear the trace of her long-lost English accent. Just on the 'con' in conflict.

'I guess that's what he was doing,' said Logan. 'It didn't feel like he was avoiding conflict, it felt like a punishment. Because you never knew how long it would be before he came back.'

'But – I don't quite get it. Where did he go?'

'We never knew.' What would happen if he asked now? Where did you go, Dad? What was that all about?

'So he didn't just leave the *room*. He left the house?'

'Yeah,' said Logan. 'Once Troy and I were fighting in the back of the car on the way to a tournament, and Dad stopped the car on a six-lane highway, got out, walked off, and we didn't see him again until the following night.'

'The following night!' screeched Indira.

It did sound quite strange now that he said it out loud.

He remembered how they had all sat in the car watching their father walk away: his pace unhurried, as if he were right on time for an important appointment. The car had felt hot and stuffy and airless, the only sound the whoosh of passing traffic and the monotonous *tick, tick, tick* of the indicator that their father had left on when he pulled over.

That was the day Brooke got her first migraine, or the first one that Logan remembered anyway, the day their mother said, flatly, after twenty minutes, 'He's not coming back,' and got out of the car and went around to the driver's seat and drove them to the tournament, where Logan lost 6–2, 6–1 against that troll of a kid from the Central Coast with no technique. He didn't remember how the others went in their matches.

Dad must have hitched a ride, Logan thought now, for the first time. Obviously that's what he did. There was no Uber to call back then. No mobile phones. Not that his dad had a mobile phone now.

He must have stuck out his thumb, hitched a ride, and spent the night in a cheap hotel. No great mystery. It had all seemed so terrifyingly mysterious when they were children, like he'd vanished into thin air.

He thought about ringing up his dad now and saying, 'So what? You stayed at a Travelodge? Good on you, big man. Big *deal*, Dad.'

'The longest time he was away was five nights,' said Logan. He'd counted the nights. It was after Troy jumped the net and beat-up Harry Haddad, so the whole family was angry with Troy.

'Five nights! But your mother must have been in a state!' said Indira. 'Didn't she call the police?'

'I don't think she ever did,' said Logan. He didn't know if she ever called the police or not. He assumed not. 'Because he always came back. She knew he'd come back.'

He remembered Brooke crying into her spaghetti bolognaise while their mother soothed her, as if this were no more serious than running out of parmesan cheese. *Daddy is coming back, silly girl, stop making such a fuss! He just needs to clear his head.*

There were no bitter asides from their mother about their

father when he was gone, just reassurances that he would be back, not to worry, he'd be back 'any minute' and they could forget all about it. You just had to be patient.

'You never asked where he went?' asked Indira.

'You weren't allowed to ask. You had to pretend nothing happened. That was like . . . the rule.'

'I can't believe your mother put up with this,' said Indira. She paused. 'Surely *Amy* asked where your dad went.'

Logan had a sudden distressing flash of memory: Amy running down the hall and launching herself against their father when he came back one time, pummelling his chest with small fists, screaming, 'Where did you go, stupid bad naughty Daddy, where did you *go*?' and their mother pelting along behind her, unpeeling her from Stan, who stood as unresponsive and expressionless as a tree.

Was that the time his dad turned around and left again? Or was that another time?

'He did it at my ninth birthday party,' said Logan. 'Before we sang "Happy Birthday".'

'That's awful,' said Indira. 'That's really awful. *Stan!* Lovely Stan. I thought he was just a big old bear.'

'Oh, well,' said Logan. 'It's not the worst thing a man can do, and he wasn't gone for that long that day. He was back in time to put me to bed.'

That time his dad had bought him a Crunchie bar. He remembered the gold shimmer of the wrapping as his dad put it under the covers next to him. It was the closest he ever got to an apology. And the taste of the illicit chocolate in bed, shared with no sibling, *after* he'd cleaned his teeth. He knew objectively that his father had behaved badly that day, even cruelly, but still the memory of the Crunchie bar shimmered gold in his memory, evidence of his father's love.

'At some point he stopped doing it,' said Logan. 'I don't remember exactly when. Sometime in my teens, I guess. And we all just forgot about it.'

'Still, that would have been pretty formative,' said Indira. 'For you.'

'No,' said Logan.

He was suddenly profoundly irritated. Indira's parents were both psychologists, and he hated it when she attempted to apply this kind of simplistic cause and effect psychology to him, because she was a graphic designer, so what did she know, and surely her parents were not *good* psychologists, because if so you'd think they might have analysed themselves and diagnosed themselves as awful, and maybe they might have noticed that their gorgeous daughter hated her gorgeous body.

'It wasn't formative. It was just a weird habit my dad had, and he grew out of it. It didn't *form* me. Did I ever do that to you? Did I ever disappear on you?'

Indira didn't answer.

'Indira. You know I didn't. I never did.' Something was building in him.

'You never physically left,' said Indira slowly. 'But whenever we had any kind of disagreement, you definitely . . . checked out.'

'I checked out,' said Logan. 'What the hell does that mean?'

Now, he could hear the echo of his mother, except that his mother would say: *What the heck does that mean?*

He didn't wait for an answer. What did it matter now? *Indira* was the one who had left, who had 'checked out' without an explanation.

'I've gotta go,' he said.

'Yeah,' said Indira coolly. 'I expect you do.'

Now, what the hell did *that* mean? He didn't wait to find out. He hung up and slammed down his phone on the wooden arm of the couch. He sat for a moment, his heart beating fast. He remembered times throughout his relationship with Indira when he'd actually felt the desire to do exactly as his father had done, to stand up and leave the room, to go for a drive around the block to calm himself down over a disagreement, an accusation, an *issue* that seemed to be upsetting her, and he never once had.

It had taken all his self-control to force himself to remain, and as often as not, *Indira* had been the one to suddenly throw her hands up, to walk away, to slam the door behind her, and now she was acting as if that demonstrated some sort of character flaw. He hadn't yelled like his mother. He hadn't left like his father. He certainly hadn't done anything unforgivable like his grandfather, whose violent actions hung like a shameful pall over their family. As a child, Logan had once found a tiny black and white photo of a man in a fedora and trouser suspenders in the back of a drawer, and when his father caught him studying it he'd snatched it from his hands as if it were porn. Stan didn't need to say that the man in the fedora was his father. Logan had felt his father's hot shame and he shared it, he accepted it as part of his heritage, like his height and hair.

Whenever there was conflict in his relationships he took immense care not to repeat the mistakes of the past. He clenched his body tight and waited for those potentially catastrophic feelings to pass, which they eventually did. But there was no recognition or praise or approval for what had cost him so dearly.

It doesn't matter how hard you try, you won't ever be good enough.

It was true about tennis. It was true about everything. He would always be average. Smack-bang in the middle of the bell curve on every scale. Good enough to get a girl like Indira, not good enough to keep her.

His heartbeat slowed. He was done. He saw it very clearly. He was done with relationships. The relief and absolute correctness of his decision reminded him of when he made the decision to give up competitive tennis. No more striving. No more failing. The absolute bliss of thinking, *I will never lose again.*

He would be a bachelor. His refrigerator would never see another tub of yoghurt. He would have no pictures on his walls, no hat stand, no throw cushions on his bed.

He would be fine. He would be better than fine.

His phone rang again.

He picked it up and saw that the screen had a spider web of cracks across it as though it had been shot with a miniature bullet. If it was Indira calling back, he would ignore her, but he saw it was the head of his department, so he answered in his professional voice.

'Logan, mate,' said Don Travis. He had a deep slow voice like Logan's dad, but he was a relaxed Queenslander, and the one word that could never be applied to either of Logan's parents was 'relaxed'.

'Mate, just wondering if you've got any problems with . . . ah, ex-girlfriends at the moment?'

'Ex-girlfriends?' Logan's head snapped back so fast he hurt his neck. 'What do you mean? Why?'

He looked wildly around his apartment. Was he being bugged? How could Don possibly know about Indira? Logan kept his personal life completely separate from his work. There were no office parties or drinks. There was an annual Christmas party that Logan had never attended.

'We got an anonymous telephone complaint about you.'

'What kind of complaint?' Logan was well liked by his students. He never got complaints. He got thankyou letters.

'Well, she was *kind* of implying sexual harassment, although it wasn't really clear exactly what she was implying.'

'What the −?' Logan got to his feet.

'I know, Logan, I know. Your record is impeccable. That's why I wondered if you might have been through a relationship break-up recently.'

'I have just broken up with someone,' said Logan. 'But she would never. Never in a million years.'

'You sure, mate? Because sometimes people lose their minds after a break-up.'

'I'm one hundred per cent sure.' He would bet his life on it.

'Well, we explained the process and what she needs to do if she wants to make an official complaint, but she hung up,' said

Don. 'It was a week ago now, and seeing as she didn't give a name, or even say which class she'd taken, we're not going to take it any further. I just wanted to give you a heads-up that there might be someone out there with some kind of vendetta.' He cleared his throat. 'No need to be embarrassed. I had an ex who gave me a whole world of trouble once, so I sympathise. Or maybe it was just a random crazy. It happens.'

Logan thanked him, and hung up.

He thought about the ex-girlfriends before Indira.

No. No. No.

All the way back to Tracey, when Troy was also dating a Tracey. *Troy's* Tracey might have done something like that, but not Logan's Tracey.

Logan picked good girlfriends. He always got invited to their weddings. (Would he one day get a cheerful invitation to Indira's wedding? The thought of watching Indira marry someone else was like imagining the death of a loved one.)

It must have been a 'random crazy' as Don had suggested. But still, it was unsettling. This whole day was feeling very unsettling.

He picked up his beer and the remote, unmuted the television and flicked through channels: an episode of *Friends*, an episode of *Seinfeld*, an episode of *Antiques Roadshow*. Everything at this time of day was a re-run.

He stopped on a pretty woman with brown curly hair talking to an interviewer.

The camera was close on her face as she said, pleadingly, 'I don't know why they put those shows on television, they don't help. It makes it *worse*!'

He must have seen it before. He didn't recognise her, but there was something so familiar about the way her voice skidded up on the word 'worse'.

She continued on. 'Those stories always put him in a filthy mood! I think they made him feel guilty. He'd be like, "It's always the man's fault, never the chick's fault."'

Logan was standing in his parents' backyard and Savannah was telling the story of her boyfriend hitting her. He was almost positive that some of the words were identical to the words Savannah had used: *It's always the man's fault, never the chick's fault.*

He put down his beer, turned up the volume.

The girl said, 'So I changed the channel super-fast, I was like, "Oh, I want to watch *The Bachelor!*"'

Not exactly the same story. Didn't Savannah say she changed the channel to some other show? Was it *Survivor*?

It must be a weird coincidence.

'I started to relax,' said the curly haired girl. The camera zoomed in on eyes swimming with tears. 'And then I thought, Oh it's fine, and then, like a stupid *idiot*, I asked if he'd paid the car registration.'

She'd asked if he'd paid the car registration. That's what Savannah had said too. He was absolutely certain that's what she'd said. It had to be more than a coincidence. Surely? That two domestic violence incidents could be precipitated by a question about car registration?

'I wasn't trying to make a point. Apparently I was being passive aggressive. And then it all just spiralled from there. He broke my jaw. Three ribs. I was in hospital for longer than he was in jail.'

An old photo of the woman filled the screen. It made Logan wince and look away. The girl's face was unrecognisable: like swollen black-bruised fruit.

Had Savannah helped herself to someone else's painful story?

Something had happened to Savannah. Her injury was real, even if it was minor, and hardly compared to the atrocious injuries this poor woman had suffered.

He looked back at the television. Another woman in a white coat with a stethoscope around her neck sat behind a desk, talking with despairing expertise about the scourge of domestic violence she had personally witnessed.

Logan remembered Savannah's ex-boyfriend sitting up in

bed, grabbing for his glasses. Something had felt off. The guy had just seemed so confused. But Logan had sternly chastised himself. His instincts were wrong and evil. How dare he question a woman's story of being abused, just because the man didn't look like 'the type'?

Logan picked up his phone, scrolled through his contacts and considered who to call. He didn't want to disturb Brooke at work, and she had enough to worry about at the moment with her separation. He could call Troy but Troy's first instinct would be to throw money at the problem. Would he offer money to Savannah to make her go away? Maybe it wasn't a bad idea. Except that she seemingly made their parents so happy.

He would call Amy. He realised he'd always been going to call Amy, because in spite of everything, she was still in charge. She was their mad queen, to whom they still all swore their lifelong allegiance.

'What's on your mind?' answered Amy, in her big sister voice.

'Savannah,' said Logan.

'Oh, me too,' said Amy happily. 'I don't like her at *all*.'

chapter twenty-seven

Now

'Apparently the husband had a habit of walking out the door and disappearing when family life got too much for him,' said Christina to her boss.

She was in his office giving him an update on the Joy Delaney investigation.

'Smart man,' said her boss, Detective Sergeant Vince Oates. He had four children under the age of five. He drank Red Bull like it was water.

'Some of the family think this is payback,' said Christina. 'It's the wife's turn to walk out.'

'What do you reckon?'

'She's been gone sixteen days now. The longest the husband ever left was five nights and that was over twenty years ago.'

'The last thing we need this year is another no-body homicide case,' said Vince morosely. He rattled his empty can of Red Bull.

'I know,' said Christina. They'd just had a high-profile case fall apart. Too much media. No result. Dispiriting for all involved. 'I really want a body.' She paused. 'I mean, obviously I *don't* want a body.'

'If she's dead you do.'

'If she's dead I do,' agreed Christina.

If she were a betting woman, she would have put a hundred to one on Joy Delaney being dead.

chapter twenty-eight

Last October

As soon as Amy got off the phone from Logan she went downstairs wearing nothing but a t-shirt and bumped straight into Simon Barrington, who should have been at work at this time. The house was meant to be hers during business hours. Her young flatmates all had sensible young person corporate jobs, which was the way she liked it.

'Sorry!' Simon flattened himself dramatically against the wall and averted his eyes, as if they hadn't had sex last weekend. This was the problem with sleeping with your flatmates. It put everything out of rhythm, and with everything going on with her family right now, she wanted things to remain in rhythm.

'We had sex last weekend,' she reminded him, to put him at ease. The sex had been vigorous and wholesome, as sweet and delicious as apple crumble. She didn't think she'd ever slept with such a *clean* man. Even when dishevelled and drunk he'd smelled of soap and clean laundry.

This didn't seem to put him at ease at all. He blushed. He actually blushed. He was a darling.

'Yeah, I'm sorry about that,' he said. He paused. 'I mean I'm not actually sorry about it.' He cleared his throat. 'Should I be sorry about it?'

Amy sighed. 'Why aren't you at work right now, Simon Barrington?'

'I resigned,' he said. 'I'm making some big life changes.'

'So you're not going to be an accountant anymore?'

He looked taken aback at the thought. 'Oh, no, I'll still be an *accountant*. Just not for that particular practice. I'm going to take a few months off. Clear my head. Maybe travel.'

A shadow of a frown crossed his face.

'Do you like to travel?' she asked.

'Not much,' he said. 'Anyway.' He took a deep breath and clapped his hands together in an adorably geeky way. 'What are you up to?'

'I'm getting my jeans out of the dryer and then I'm going to visit my parents. There's a strange woman living with them right now. My brother thinks she's up to something.'

'What, you think she's a scammer?' said Simon.

'Well, so far all she's done is cook really excellent food for them,' admitted Amy.

'But you're trying to work out her end game,' said Simon.

'Exactly,' said Amy. 'My parents are extremely innocent.'

'All parents are innocent,' said Simon. 'My parents nearly fell for that latest Tax Office scam, if you can believe it.'

'Oh no,' said Amy, who had nearly fallen for it herself. Thankfully she'd called Troy when she was on the way to the bank to withdraw money to pay her apparently unpaid taxes. *It's a scam, you idiot*, he'd shouted from America.

'I can give you a lift over to your parents' place if you like,' offered Simon. 'You don't drive, do you?'

He said this with interest rather than implied criticism. Some people couldn't get over her lack of a driver's licence. It was like her dad's refusal to own a mobile phone. People took it personally.

'I've never been behind the wheel of a car,' said Amy. 'I'm

pretty sure I died in a car accident in a previous life. Possibly involving a bridge.'

She really did think this. She had fragmented memories of a crash. Water. Glass. Screaming. It may well have been from a movie.

'Were you driving?'

'What?'

'In your previous life,' said Simon. 'Were you behind the wheel?'

'Oh,' said Amy. 'I think so.'

'So you have been behind the wheel of a car,' said Simon. 'Just not in this life.'

'That's right,' said Amy. 'You're very . . . *accurate*, aren't you?'

He had actually been very accurate, even when drunk.

'I have good attention to detail,' said Simon. 'I'm thorough.'

'You are,' said Amy, straight-faced. 'Your attention to detail is *scrupulous*.'

He held her eyes for just long enough to show he got it, and then he said, 'I could give you my accurate opinion on this potential scammer.'

'Your accurate accountant's opinion?' said Amy.

'That's right,' said Simon. 'I don't have anything else to do right now and one of my goals for the next few weeks is to improve my spontaneity.'

'Why?' asked Amy, interested. She had always been advised to pull back on her spontaneity.

'You know I was meant to be getting married this April? When my fiancée was explaining why she'd decided to end the relationship she had a list of . . . you know, things about me that didn't work for her. And one of them was my lack of spontaneity.'

'She wrote a list of things that didn't work for her?' asked Amy.

'She liked lists,' said Simon. 'It was something we had in common.'

'She sounds just lovely,' said Amy.

'You sound like my sister,' said Simon.

Amy looked at him. He radiated good health, as if he'd just stepped out of a bracing cold shower after a run. His t-shirt was crisp and clean.

'Do you iron your jeans?' she asked. He was so *exotic*.

'Of course,' he said.

'Okay,' she said.

'It's okay that I iron my jeans?'

'No, that is definitely not okay. I mean, okay, you can come with me to meet the scammer. The possible scammer. She may also be a nice girl who is down on her luck. It's up to us to make that call.'

'I'll keep an open mind.' He looked pleased.

'I'll just go put my unironed jeans on,' she said.

'No problem.' He courteously waved his hand to let her pass him on the stairs.

She was a head taller than him, so now that she was on the step below him they were eye to eye. He had bushy old man eyebrows and good honest tax-paying eyes.

'Before I do that,' said Amy. She moved a fraction closer.

'Before you do that,' repeated Simon, and there was a catch in his voice.

It was like the satisfaction of striking a match first go. She saw the understanding spark and shine in his eyes.

'We could work on your spontaneity,' she said.

'We could,' said Simon.

'Just very quickly,' said Amy.

So they did that.

★

An hour later, Amy stood at her parents' front door and rang the doorbell that didn't work, just in case it had been fixed, and then, without waiting, because she knew it would never be fixed, knocked hard with her knuckles.

She looked at her clean, delicious flatmate, standing next to her in his white t-shirt matching his white teeth, with his buzz cut and broad shoulders and glasses, like a door-to-door missionary or the nerdy best friend from a teen vampire movie. Her mother would ask Simon lots of probing questions, and Simon would be the type to answer them in polite comprehensive detail, and her mother would remember that comprehensive detail for years after Amy had forgotten Simon Barrington's very existence.

He was a distraction from the visit's main purpose, which was to subtly collect as much biographical data about Savannah as possible, particularly as it related to the *alleged assault*.

You brought your flatmate? Why? She could just hear her sister and brothers, that careful patient tone they sometimes used, as if she were an explosive device that could detonate at any moment.

'Is this where you grew up?' Simon asked, looking about him.

'Yes,' she said.

'Happy childhood?' asked Simon. He looked at the big pots of flowers, the shiny clean terracotta tiles and the stone figurines in the carefully tended garden beds. 'It looks like the setting for a happy childhood.' He touched the tip of his runner to the base of the statue by the front door. It was a blank-eyed little girl in a bonnet holding an empty basket.

'What happened to her eyes?'

'The crows took them,' said Amy.

'She looks like a demon child,' commented Simon.

'I *know*,' said Amy. 'I always think that!' Maybe she and the accountant were actually soulmates.

The door opened the tiniest crack.

A low, husky voice said, 'Can I help you?'

For a second Amy wondered if she'd somehow come to the wrong house, anything was possible, but then the door swung open just to the length of the security chain, and Savannah stood there, wearing not Amy's old clothes but a long-sleeved paisley shirt tucked into three-quarter-length black pants that Amy was pretty sure belonged to her mother. It was worse seeing Savannah in her mother's cast-offs than in her own.

'Oh, hi, Amy,' she said. 'How are you? Your mum is asleep at the moment.'

When Joy collapsed on Father's Day, it had been Savannah who caught her and carefully laid her on the floor. Joy's head had ended up resting on Savannah's lap, and one could hardly say, *Get out of the way, strange girl, that's my mother, her head should be resting on my lap.*

'That's okay.' Amy had talked to her mother a few times on the phone since she'd got out of hospital and she knew she'd been napping. 'I won't wake her. What's Dad doing?' She waited for Savannah to hurry up and release the security chain.

'He fell asleep in front of the television,' said Savannah, and she stuck out her lower lip to convey *Aww, isn't that adorable?* 'I think he got a real fright when your mother was in hospital last week, so they both have some catching up to do.'

'Oh,' said Amy. Her father was a veteran snoozer. He always dozed in front of the television. He'd be awake any minute. 'Well. I'll still come in and –'

'Now is not such a good time,' said Savannah.

Now is not such a good time? Did she really just say that?

Amy felt many emotions on a given day: desire for inappropriate men, nostalgia for long-ago days that never actually happened, great rolling waves of happiness and sadness, bouts of high-level panic and low-level anxiety, but rage was an emotion with which she was not familiar, so it took her a moment to identify the feeling whooshing through her veins.

Was this girl really going to block her from entering her own childhood home?

'Hi there.' Simon leaned in front of Amy. 'I'm Amy's boyfriend. Sorry to be a pain but could I come in and use the bathroom? I'll be very quiet if everyone is asleep.'

He didn't really think he was her boyfriend just because they'd slept together twice, did he? She gave him a look. He winked.

There was a beat. Of course Savannah knew Amy was single. She knew everything about Amy's family although they knew virtually nothing about her. Savannah tapped a fingertip against her lower lip, almost as if in parody of Joy, who did the same thing to indicate scepticism.

If Savannah denied Amy's 'boyfriend' this valid, ordinary request, she would kick down the door.

'Come in.' Savannah opened the security chain with an upward flick of her finger, opened the door and stood back, *as if she lived there*, which technically she did, but temporarily. Supposedly.

There was just nothing guest-like in her behaviour.

Steffi, the traitorous hound, sat at Savannah's feet as though she were *Savannah's* beloved pet, and politely cocked her head at Amy like they were meeting for the first time.

Once again, Amy registered how the house felt perceptibly, but pleasantly, different, as it had on Father's Day. It was like it had been styled by a clever real estate agent for inspection by potential buyers. There were flowers on the sideboard in a vase that Amy had never seen before. All the family photos on the wall were the same but they'd been straightened, or dusted, or polished so that all those familiar shots of their childhood were suddenly thrown into sharp relief.

Simon held out his hand to Savannah.

'Hi there. I'm Simon Barrington,' he said in a loud, showy voice, completely unlike his own. 'So pleased to meet you.'

She took his hand. 'Hi. I'm Savannah.'

'Savannah . . .?' He kept holding her hand, waiting for her surname, like someone's embarrassing uncle.

'The bathroom is this way,' said Savannah.

'*I'll* show him the bathroom,' said Amy, and she knew she sounded thirteen. Then she said, 'Well, but you know, what actually *is* your last name, Savannah?'

Because how were they going to secretly investigate her if they didn't even know her last name? Did their parents even know it? They may never have even asked and had probably never bothered to Google her, just blithely believing every word she had to say.

'It's Pagonis,' said Savannah. 'Savannah Pagonis.'

The cut above her eye had completely healed, and she was wearing just a touch of make-up, and there was a kind of creamy, settled confidence to her, as if she were wearing her own clothes in her own home and Amy and Simon were unwelcome guests who she would soon be sending on their way. Amy's mother's clothes didn't look wrong on her. They looked exactly right. She was a younger version of Joy. She could be Joy's daughter. Joy had probably dreamed of a pretty feminine little daughter like this. Amy and Brooke had talked about this over the years: how their mother sometimes made them feel *huge*, like big lolloping orangutans.

'Oh, that's unusual. How do you spell that, Savannah?' asked Simon. It was like watching an accountant perform in an amateur community production. He was *terrible*, but so adorably committed.

'P-a-g-o-n-i-s,' answered Savannah, eyebrows arched.

'Huh,' said Simon. 'Is that, let me guess, Greek?'

'Apparently,' said Savannah shortly.

'Savannah Pagonis,' repeated Simon. 'I bet people never spell it correctly. I hope your middle name is something simple. Like Anne? Marie?'

Amy looked at him admiringly. His delivery remained forced and theatrical, but the strategy couldn't be faulted.

'You guessed it, it's Marie,' said Savannah. 'Do you want me to spell that too?'

Could he really have guessed it that fast? Or was Savannah just going along with it to shut him up?

'It's my mother's name,' said Simon. 'Marie is very popular as a middle name.' He opened his mouth to ask another question and Amy took him by the arm. Next he'd be asking for her date of birth and tax file number. If Savannah did have evil plans, Amy didn't want her feeling compelled to fast-track them.

'The bathroom is this way,' she said.

'Wait, is this you?' asked Simon in his natural voice. He'd stopped in front of a photo of Amy triumphantly holding up a tiny trophy with both hands, racquet resting against her thigh, big Wimbledon-winning smile, even though it was just the Under 9s regionals.

'Yes, that's me,' said Amy.

'You were so cute,' said Simon. He kept standing there, examining the photo. 'I didn't know you played tennis!'

'Yep,' she said.

'I play a bit of social tennis,' said Simon. 'We should have a game sometime. You'd probably beat me.'

'I would definitely beat you,' said Amy. She pointed down the hallway. 'Second door on the left.'

Simon looked at her blankly, forgetting his ruse to get inside.

'Bathroom?' Amy reminded him.

'Ah yes! Thank you, Amy!' He returned to his loud, overly enunciated tone.

When he left, Amy and Savannah looked at each other. It was the oddest feeling. Amy was in the home where she grew up, with photos either side of her attesting to this, and yet she still felt like Savannah was the host. She couldn't seem to find the right balance between two indisputable facts: Savannah should feel grateful to Amy because her family had given her shelter in her time of need. Amy should feel grateful to Savannah because she was taking care of her parents, and doing a better job than any of the Delaney children ever would or could.

'I'll just pop my head in the door and see if Mum is still asleep,' said Amy.

A complicated expression crossed Savannah's face. 'Sure. I'll get back to the kitchen. I'm in the middle of making minestrone. Sing out if Joy needs anything.'

Sing out if Joy needs anything.

Because I am the one who can provide your mother with everything she needs.

244

'Sing out' was a Joy phrase. This girl was a mini Joy.

The besotted dog pattered off on Savannah's heels.

Amy resolutely turned her head the other way as she walked past her old bedroom where Savannah now slept. *Selfish! Childish! No-one else in the family still considers any room in this house 'their bedroom'!* She heard the toilet flush as Simon completed his fake bathroom visit.

She pushed open the door of her parents' bedroom. It smelled as it always had: a comforting mix of her mother's perfume, her father's deodorant, and the old-fashioned furniture polish still used by Good Old Barb and Amy's mother when they cleaned together.

Her mother lay on her side facing away from the door, the covers pulled right up over her shoulders. Her hair – which brought her so many compliments – was mussed against the pillow. Amy tiptoed to the end of the bed. Her mother was asleep, breathing steadily, one hand curled up near her lips so that she seemed to be kissing her knuckles. She had told her children this was because she had sucked her thumb as a child, and it still gave her comfort to have her banned thumb close to her mouth.

The lines on Joy's face looked like crevices. Amy breathed fast as that old familiar terror gripped her. All children feared their parents dying. Except Amy had once been so consumed by her fear that she hyperventilated, and had to breathe into a paper bag, and the babysitter had to call Joy and Stan to come home fast because this kid was *weird*.

She wondered what would have happened if her mother *had* died when Amy was a child. How could the reality of grief be worse than her imagining of it, when she had imagined it so very, very hard? How would she cope now, when her parents inevitably did die, as parents inevitably did, and you had to be so grown-up and mature about it? How did people *cope* with ordinary predictable tragedy? It was impossible, insurmountable . . .

'Amy?'

Her mother opened her eyes and sat up. She put on her glasses from her bedside table, smoothed down her hair and smiled. 'Amy? You've caught me napping.'

'It's good that you're napping, Mum.' Amy breathed slowly in and out. Her mother wasn't going to die for decades. 'You've been in hospital. You should be resting.'

Joy waved her hand dismissively. 'I took my last antibiotic this morning. I'm fine now. I just get tired in the middle of the day. Come here.' She patted the side of the bed. 'Give me a hug.'

Amy went and sat next to her, and her mother hugged her fiercely.

'You look especially beautiful today, darling. I wasn't so keen on the blue hair at first but now I think it really makes your eyes *pop*.'

'Thanks, Mum, although I guess they'd pop more if my eyes were blue. You should dye *yours* blue.'

'Narelle is in charge of my hair, and I don't think she's keen on blue.' Her mother stifled a yawn. 'Why are you here, anyway? Where's Savannah? Where's your dad?'

Savannah before Dad.

'Savannah is making you soup, and Dad is asleep in front of the television.'

'He has this idea in his head that he never naps,' said her mother. 'He just "briefly closes his eyes". Will you please pass me my hairbrush?'

Amy got up and passed her the heavy silver embossed hairbrush that had always sat on her mother's dressing table since Amy was a child. Her mother had received it when she won a district tournament as a teenager, back when 'brush and comb' sets were common prizes for female competitors, while the men got cigarette cases. Amy still coveted that brush. It looked like something a princess would use.

'You visited the hospital. You didn't need to come again.' Her mother used swift movements to brush her hair back into its smooth white bob, so that the frail old lady vanished, to be replaced by Amy's trim, senior citizen mother, wearing a long-sleeved cherry-coloured jersey. She threw back the covers to reveal her vulnerable little legs in tracksuit pants. 'Have you seen Brooke? How do you think she's coping with this separation? I couldn't tell when she visited. Do you think Grant left her for another woman?'

'No,' said Amy. 'But I think he'll move on to someone new with lightning speed.'

'Do you remember when Brooke was a little girl?' said her mother. 'And every year she fell in love with a new boy in her class?'

'I do,' said Amy. 'She was very cute.' Brooke used to write love letters to boys. It was hard to imagine now.

'I was just thinking about that,' said Joy. 'For some reason. She used to be so *passionate* and then it felt like growing up just . . . flattened her. Those damned migraines.' She frowned and put a hand to the side of her mouth and whispered, 'I feel like Grant kind of flattened her too.'

Amy put a hand to the side of her own mouth and whispered, 'Me too, Mum.'

'We might get her back,' whispered Joy.

'We might,' whispered Amy.

Joy's eyes danced and she spoke again at her normal volume. 'Anyway. Thank you for coming. I know how busy you are but you don't need to worry about me because I've got Savannah!'

'Yes, you do,' said Amy, deflating.

'She's doing everything! I don't need to lift a finger. I'm treating her to a shopping day tomorrow to thank her.'

'A shopping day.' Amy shuddered at the thought. 'That's nice of you.'

'It's not nice of me! It's the least I can do for her. Do you know – I can't remember the last time I cooked a meal?'

She said this as if it were something to be marvelled over.

Amy couldn't remember the last time she herself had cooked a meal either, unless heating up leftover Uber Eats in the microwave counted. Brooke had mentioned that their mother was obsessed with the fact that she didn't have to cook anymore.

'It's like she's had this secret loathing of cooking all these years,' Brooke had said. 'Once Savannah moves out we'll have to do something about getting her help.' She'd paused. '*If* Savannah ever moves out.'

'How much longer do you think Savannah will be staying for?' Amy asked her mother.

'Oh, gosh, we're not even thinking about that right now. I need her,' said her mother. 'For example, *who* would have cooked for your father when I was in hospital?'

As if that – her father's dietary requirements – was the most significant thing about her hospital stay.

Amy said, 'Well, I guess we would have. Or he could have got takeaway, or he might even have cooked for himself.'

'Very funny,' said Joy. 'Anyway, I'm sure she will want to be on her way soon. I don't want to take advantage of her. She's doing so much now that I feel like we should actually pay her some sort of a wage.'

'Like a live-in housekeeper?' said Amy.

'Imagine that,' said her mother dreamily.

'The thing is, if you *were* employing a live-in housekeeper, you would get references, so I'm just thinking –'

'Well, obviously I'd never get a real live-in housekeeper!' said Joy.

'I'm just saying that we don't really know that much about Savannah,' said Amy, and she lowered her voice and looked towards the door.

'I actually know lots about her,' said Joy. 'We've had some long chats while I've been recuperating. Do you know – and I find this just so interesting, so fascinating!' Joy's face lit up. 'Savannah has something called *highly superior autobiographical memory*.' She ticked off each word on her fingers as she said it. 'She can remember whole days in her life with a degree of detail that you and I, ordinary people, would find impossible.'

'Really?' said Amy sceptically. She bristled at the way she had been lumped into the category of ease 'ordinary people'. She herself felt she could remember events from her life in quite significant detail, thank you very much. 'She's actually received a diagnosis of that?'

'Well, I don't know, I don't know if you get diagnosed with it, I don't think it's an *illness*, as such, although she did say it's both a blessing and a curse, because while it's nice to remember the good events, she said she also remembers the bad ones, and, as we know, she has not had a normal happy life – poor girl.'

'Huh,' said Amy.

She took the hairbrush that her mother had left sitting on the bed in front of her and replaced it carefully on the dressing table, then she went and quietly closed the door and sat back down again.

'What is it?' Her mother sat up straight and propped a pillow behind her back. 'What's happened? Has something bad happened?' Panic flooded her face. 'Dammit, I thought that new counsellor was helping? I thought you were *good* at the moment!'

'I'm fine, Mum,' said Amy testily. Why did her mother always assume there must be some crisis or other in Amy's life? She registered the irritated 'dammit' that accompanied her mother's panic. Her mother would never shout, 'Stop being so ridiculous, Amy, pull yourself together!' like she had done when Amy was a kid – she now knew all the correct supportive modern things to say about mental health – but Amy knew that there was an unconscious part of her that still wondered if Amy did indeed need to just stop being so ridiculous and pull herself together. Amy was like a defective household appliance that would never be replaced but that everyone knew could break down at the most inconvenient of times.

'So what is it?'

'Logan called me today. He saw a re-run of a documentary on television, and it was about domestic violence, and the girl on it told almost the exact same story that Savannah told him about her boyfriend – he said it was virtually word for word.'

Her mother knitted her brow, baffled. 'So, what are you saying? I don't –'

'It just seems like too much of a coincidence,' said Amy.

'But I still don't understand. Are you saying this girl on the television knows Savannah?'

'What? No! I'm saying maybe Savannah saw that show herself and thought, That would make a good story, and if she really does have this "superior memory" thing, I guess that's why she could remember it so well.'

'There was no "story", Amy,' said Joy, coldly, furiously, totally unlike the helpless sleeping old lady of moments ago, more like the mother of Amy's youth who had 'had it up to here with you lot' and 'was at the end of her tether'. 'I bandaged up that injury myself.'

'I'm not saying her injury wasn't real, but maybe the *cause* of the injury –'

'You're accusing a woman of lying about domestic violence.' Amy's mother's eyes were bright. 'That's outrageous. You're a feminist! Have you heard of the *I believe her* movement?'

Oh God, she was simultaneously so with it, and so naïve.

Amy said, 'Mum, it just seems like a *really* big coincidence –'

'That poor girl is in my kitchen right now making my favourite soup,' said Joy. 'Do you know how much effort goes into minestrone? How much *chopping*? It's extremely laborious! Let me tell you, Amy, *I believe her.*'

She was ready to march the streets, a placard held high. Somehow their positions had reversed. Amy was the middle-aged cynic, her mother the zealous idealistic teenager.

The bedroom door swung open and her father was there, holding a mug of something steaming.

'Hi, sweetheart,' he said to Amy. 'Does the young bloke sitting in the kitchen belong to you?'

chapter twenty-nine

Now

'Did you ever meet the mother?' Liz Barrington asked her younger brother as he sat at her kitchen table doing her tax return for her.

Simon didn't look up from the pile of receipts.

'The missing mother,' clarified Liz.

He frowned at a faded receipt. 'I can't read this.'

'Your flatmate's missing mother,' said Liz. 'Amy's missing mother.'

It was all thanks to Liz that Amy had moved into Simon's share house in the first place. Liz had been Amy's Uber driver. (Now she had given up Uber driving because she had her own, much more fulfilling mobile spray-tan business: Tan-at-Home-with-Liz.)

The night Liz picked up Amy, they got chatting and Amy convinced her to park the car and join her for a drink with her friends, which had been okay, but Amy's friends were so random. One of them was, like, *sixty* years old, *literally* sixty years old, and if Liz wanted to talk with sixty-year-olds she'd go visit her mother, thanks very much.

That night Amy mentioned that she needed somewhere new to live and Liz told her that her brother's flatmate had just moved out. So that was how her brother and her Uber passenger ended up living together.

'Her name is Joy. I have met her,' said Simon. 'I met the father too.'

Liz was thrilled. 'So what do you think? Do you think he's guilty? Everyone seems to think the father did it.'

'I don't know,' said Simon.

'Have you got to know Amy very well?' asked Liz. 'She must be upset. Imagine if *our* mother went missing and everyone was accusing Dad. I mean, I can't even imagine it.' She reflected on this for a moment. 'I could totally imagine the reverse. Mum would do a really good job cleaning up the evidence, wouldn't she? She's always deleting her search history, which is actually quite suspicious.'

Simon said nothing.

'How well do you know her? Amy?'

'I know her pretty well,' said Simon. He squinted at the next receipt. 'Did you really think *eyelash extensions* were tax deductible?'

Liz shrugged. 'I need eyelashes for my work.'

'No you don't.'

'Well, we'll have to agree to disagree on that.'

He picked up the next receipt.

'So you've, like, hung out with her?' asked Liz.

He bent his head to her receipts again.

'Oh my God, Simon,' she said. She felt a rush of love for her clueless little brother. First his cow of a fiancée breaks his heart, then his weird older flatmate gets her claws into him. You had to watch those cougar types who dressed like twenty-somethings. Boys couldn't see the Botox. Although Liz was pretty sure Amy wouldn't have had Botox, she was too hippie and new-age, but she definitely dressed and acted younger than her wrinkles.

'Amy must be, what? Fifteen years older than you?'

'Twelve years older,' he said. 'Twelve years, three months and twenty-four days.'

chapter thirty

Last October

'I'll try the apple crumble,' said Joy to the waitress at the David Jones cafeteria, where she sat opposite Savannah, surrounded by a triumphant array of stiff, shiny, string-handled shopping bags at their feet.

'With ice-cream or cream?' asked the waitress.

'With both,' said Joy firmly.

It was a family tradition to always try the apple crumble whenever it was on the menu, in the forlorn hope that they might one day find an apple crumble as good as the one Stan's mother used to bake. It was her signature dish, like Amy's brownies. Everyone apart from Joy got misty-eyed when they ate apple crumble and said, 'Not as good as Grandma's,' while Joy thought to herself, *Trust the old bag to never share her secret recipe.* One day someone would work out the missing single ingredient and then she'd be properly dead.

'Please may I have the apple crumble too?' said Savannah in that funny, almost childlike well-mannered way she had. 'Also with ice-cream and cream.'

'Same as your mum, then.' The waitress flicked her notepad closed. It was the second time that day they'd been mistaken for mother and daughter as they'd shopped, trying on clothes in adjacent change rooms. 'Do you want to see what your daughter thinks?' a shop assistant had said to Joy as she tried on a long-sleeved floaty floral dress in a colour she would never normally wear.

Savannah had convinced Joy to buy the dress. 'You look really beautiful,' she'd said, eyes narrowed. 'And it's twenty per cent off. It looks well made.' She'd dropped to her knees on the floor beside Joy and folded back the hem of the dress to show her. 'Look at the stitching on the lining. That's real good quality.'

That's real good quality.

The phrase had snagged in Joy's consciousness. It sounded incongruous from a girl of Savannah's age. Like something Ma from *Little House on the Prairie* would say. And yet it was one of those moments where Joy felt she was seeing the real Savannah, as if her interest in the dress made her forget herself for a moment and a veil was lifted. Savannah was so ready to serve, like a hotel concierge, unfailingly courteous and warmly interested in your plans, that Joy sometimes had to remind herself not to bask in that interest, just like a self-absorbed hotel guest. It was an effort to make Savannah talk about herself but she was chipping away at it. She'd noticed it helped if it was a bit later at night, and just the two of them, especially if Joy suggested a nice little glass of brandy. That was when Savannah had told her about her 'highly superior autobiographical memory'.

They'd been talking about Joy's memoir-writing class and how there were some periods of Joy's life that were just a blur.

'I wish my memories would blur a bit,' Savannah had said, looking into her glass. 'I remember everything. The details never fade.'

Now Joy pushed aside the cutlery on the café table to lean forward, chin resting on her hands, to properly examine Savannah. She definitely looked better than when she'd arrived on her doorstep. Joy wished she could say it was because she'd done such a good job looking after her, when in fact the opposite was true: Savannah had done such a good job looking after *her*.

'Are you feeling tired?' Savannah asked her.

'Not at all,' said Joy, although she was a little. 'Thank you for convincing me to get that dress.'

Savannah smiled. 'I bet Stan will love it.'

'He'll love the discount,' said Joy.

'It's a good dress,' said Savannah.

Joy's mother would have appreciated Savannah getting on her knees to check the dress's lining. She used to do that sort of thing: check the stitching of the seams, tug at the hems. Sniff contemptuously if it wasn't to her liking.

Joy had loved a long lingering day of shopping with her mother. It had been hard when the children were little and their tennis was all-consuming, but once every year she and her mother would have a day just like this. It was so satisfying, so pleasurable, going from shop to shop, hunting out bargains, accessorising an outfit, realising that the blue in that new blouse was a perfect match for the blue in that skirt, and then sitting down for a break at a café like this to rest your aching feet and discuss what else you needed.

Joy's daughters both hated shopping. Amy began to mutter about commercialism and bright lights and 'feeling like a rat trapped in a maze', or some such nonsense, while Brooke was so task-focused, tapping her feet, her hand on the small of Joy's back, hurrying her along: 'Chop, chop, Mum, a fast shop is a good shop.'

Brooke only ever shopped online these days ('You should try it, Mum, click, click and you're done!') and Amy apparently got her clothes by scrounging through charity bins, so Joy had given up suggesting shopping excursions.

But when Joy had suggested she treat Savannah to a day at a fancy shopping mall to thank her for everything she'd done while Joy was in the hospital, Savannah's face had lit up even as she quickly said, 'Oh, that's not necessary.'

'It would be *my* pleasure,' Joy had said, truthfully, because today had been like rediscovering a forgotten part of herself, the part that perhaps only existed when she was with her mother, who had no interest in Joy's tennis, or even, to be honest, Joy's children, but did have passionate opinions about the right colours and necklines to flatter Joy's body. Joy had assumed her daughters would at least have a passing interest in fashion, but they both found it frivolous and irrelevant, almost contemptible, like playing with dolls, which neither of them had done either. Joy had spent hours playing with dolls as a child.

'I know exactly the right necklace to go with your shift dress,' said Joy to Savannah. 'A long kind of heavy chunky pendant that sits right here.' She pointed at her collarbone. 'Although I've noticed you nearly always wear that key necklace, don't you? Is it sentimental?'

Savannah's young face became momentarily rigid and jaded, as if she were thirty years older. 'A friend gave it to me for my twenty-first birthday.' She lifted the key from her neck and tapped it against her chin. 'She said it symbolised "doors opening for a brighter future".' She smiled cynically at Joy. 'I'm still waiting for those doors to open.'

'I'm sure lots of doors are about to open for you!' said Joy. She recognised the rousing tone she used to employ to little avail when Amy got 'the bad feeling'.

'Well, you opened your door to me.' Savannah's face softened. 'So that's a start! Maybe I could get a green pendant.' She bent towards the shopping bags, pulled out a corner of the dress and pointed at the fabric. 'To pick out the green colour of those little squares? What do you think?'

'Perfect,' said Joy, and her eyes filled with unexpected tears as she felt a thin, sharp, strangely pleasurable piercing of grief for her mother, who would have loved this day so much, who might have found it so much easier to bond with a granddaughter like this. Her mother had died over twenty years ago, and Joy's grief at the time had been so complicated and strange. Her mother hadn't been an especially good mother, and she was an even worse grandmother: she found her grandchildren too loud and too large, and so excessive in number. 'Why would you want *more*?' she'd said to Joy when she told her she was pregnant with Brooke.

When she died, just three months after Stan's mother had died, Joy kept spinning in the opposite direction when faced with her grief, which was hers and hers alone, because she had no siblings, and her children much preferred their other grandmother, because of the secret cash hand-outs and that damned apple crumble.

It was perfectly possible to avoid grief when you have four children who all play competitive tennis, and nearly one hundred more tennis students requiring your attention, and one husband grieving his own mother and dealing with his own mid-bloody-life crisis, and when your relationship with your mother had always been entangled in disappointment and love, so Joy spun and she spun until one day her grief caught her, in the laundry, as she pulled a ruined blouse out of the washing machine, a blouse that her mother had told her to only ever wash by hand in cold water.

It was as though Joy's subconscious had only just that moment caught up with what she rationally understood: that she truly wouldn't see her mother again. Her mother would never again phone at an inconvenient time with an unreasonable request. She would never again tell Joy that she hated February. Or that she hated August. Or that she hated November. (She only liked April.) Pearl Becker never would find the happiness that had continually eluded her and their relationship would remain a puzzle forever unsolved. That day Joy had lowered herself to the floor with her back against the washing machine, the sodden ball of her ruined blouse dripping all over her skirt, and sobbed, violently and shockingly, and then, shamefully, she'd shouted at a tennis kid who unexpectedly opened the laundry door and caught her there. (It was a wonder she hadn't got a complaint from that kid's mother.)

But this sadness she was feeling now felt natural, wholesome and uncomplicated, as if finally, after all these years, she was grieving the way normal daughters grieved for their mothers: the way she'd like her own daughters to grieve for her one day, not coldly stuffing their mother's clothes into a big black garbage bag, the way Joy had done, the day after her mother's funeral, without a single tear, or even a tender thought, but also not crying on the laundry floor weeks later in that strange paroxysm of grief that would have so mortified her mother. ('Get up!' Pearl would have cried, yanking Joy up by the elbow. 'Someone might see you!')

'Thank you.' Joy leaned back as the waitress delivered their apple crumble. She said to Savannah, 'I know just the shop for that necklace. We'll go there straight after this.'

'Well, only if . . . if that's okay,' said Savannah, suddenly looking uncomfortable. 'You've already spent quite a lot on me. Your children might not approve.'

'Darling, I should be paying you a *salary*,' said Joy. 'You are like a full-time chef! And housekeeper! This is the least I can do.'

'Well, but don't forget I'm getting free rent,' said Savannah.

'I'm the one getting the bargain here,' said Joy stoutly. She thought of Brooke, on the phone this morning: 'Mum, if you actually want to employ this girl as a housekeeper or whatever you want to call it, you need to do it properly.'

Of course Joy couldn't employ Savannah as a full-time chef or housekeeper. She didn't know anyone with a *housekeeper*. That was for movie stars and Americans. Possibly people from the eastern suburbs. Not for ordinary people like her and Stan. However, it had occurred to her last night that perhaps they could let Savannah stay as a kind of *lodger*. Why not? Savannah could get a job, somewhere local, and stay in Amy's room, and pay nominal rent, or no rent at all if she kept on doing the cooking.

But Stan wasn't at all keen. He said, when they were in bed last night, the door shut, that it had been over six weeks now and it was probably time for Savannah to think about finding her own place.

'But why the rush?' Joy had said, taken aback. She thought he enjoyed Savannah's company as much as she did, but since she'd come back from the hospital, he'd become more reserved around Savannah. All that chattiness had stopped. He found excuses not to join them at mealtimes. He and Savannah didn't seem to be watching that television series together anymore. It was such a pity.

'Did something happen while I was in hospital?' Joy had asked him.

'Like what?' said Stan, his jaw clenched.

'I don't know,' she said. 'You just don't seem as happy about Savannah as you were in the beginning.'

'She's been here long enough,' said Stan. 'That's all I'm saying.'

It had been so odd.

After a moment she'd said, 'Have you been talking to the children?' The children were being such *children* about Savannah. She could not believe that Amy had accused Savannah of making up the story about her boyfriend, based on some documentary Logan had supposedly seen with a similar story, as if there couldn't be similarities in people's experiences.

Stan had said nothing and she refused to give him the satisfaction of innocently, idiotically repeating the question, a little louder, the way she would have when she was twenty, or yelling, 'Answer me!' like she would have when she was forty.

She was sure she was right: the children had got to him and that's what accounted for his sudden coolness towards Savannah. He was more influenced by their opinions than he liked to pretend. He would argue vehemently with one of them about a particular issue and then, just a month or so later, spout the very same argument presented by one of the children as if it were his own, and categorically deny that he had ever said or thought otherwise.

It was all very well for *Stan* to say that Savannah had been there long enough. He wasn't the one who would be back in the kitchen at five pm every day, staring with despair and boredom at the refrigerator's contents, sliding the vegetable crisper open and closed, open and closed, hoping for inspiration.

This hatred of cooking must represent something else, because why get so worked up about it now, after all these years? Once upon a time Joy was up at five am every day, she'd coach class after class, deal with the laundry, the dog, the accountant, the homework, her mother, her mother-in-law, and *then* she'd cook dinner for a family of six (at a *minimum*, there were always extra people at the table), and she'd done it without conscious resentment or complaint.

Now that it was only ever her and Stan at home, cooking should feel like a breeze. She had whole days at her disposal to plan and prepare, to pore over recipe books if she chose, the way Savannah pored over her beloved recipe books (so many for a girl so young!) with such focus and pleasure, her mouth hanging slightly open as if she were reading a romance novel. Joy had time to wander about specialty supermarkets looking for unusual ingredients, except she wanted to cry with boredom at the thought. What was wrong with her? She thought of Brooke's brisk, surprised suggestion that they try some sort of meal delivery service, or, if she wanted a housekeeper, hire one! According to her children, anything could be fixed online. They were always reaching for answers on their phones, they couldn't go more than five minutes without looking something up. *I'll look it up, Mum. I've got it. I've booked it. I've ordered it.* They tap-tap-tapped with their thumbs and it was done. There was no need for her elderly fuss.

'I've been meaning to thank you for taking care of Stan while I was in hospital,' said Joy now to Savannah. 'I hope he wasn't too grumpy? He can be grumpy.'

'It was no trouble,' said Savannah. Joy couldn't read her face. Had he been grumpy with her? Or just odd? He could be strange, and young people weren't patient with strangeness, they wanted clear-cut explanations for everything, including exactly why people behaved the way they did. They hadn't yet learned that sometimes there were no answers.

'My daughters would say that he shouldn't need anyone to take care of him,' said Joy. 'But he's from a different generation. No help in the kitchen at all.' She paused, reflected. 'He's good at opening jars.'

She wondered how Debbie Christos was going without Dennis there to open jars. Debbie had dainty wrists. Joy should tell her to call Stan anytime she wanted a jar opened. *Any* time.

'How is the apple crumble?' asked Savannah, because she knew about the family's quest to replicate Grandma's apple crumble.

'It's a good one,' said Joy. 'But still missing something.' She licked her spoon. 'Actually, it's not even close, to be honest. I don't know *why* she could make such a good crumble. She couldn't bake anything else. She was a nasty old drunk.'

Yet for some reason her apple crumble tasted of love. It was a mystery.

'Maybe the secret ingredient is some kind of alcohol,' said Savannah. 'Whiskey?'

Joy pointed her spoon at her. 'Now that would make sense. Clever.'

'I'm going to try it this weekend,' said Savannah, and Joy could see that she'd pleased her by calling her clever. 'I'm going to crack the Delaney family apple crumble mystery.'

Joy watched Savannah touch her spoon with the tip of her tongue and put it down again. She didn't really eat. All she did was cook. She was too thin. Joy wanted to tell her she was too thin but she'd learned that you had to be careful what you said. Amy and Brooke had once overheard Joy saying, 'My daughters have enormous feet,' and she'd never heard the end of it. She hadn't meant anything bad by it! They did have enormous feet.

'You don't eat much, do you?' she said to Savannah. Surely that wasn't offensive. 'For someone who loves to cook so much, I mean.'

'I used to have a big appetite when I was a kid.' Savannah dug her spoon into her apple crumble and swirled it around. Did she think Joy couldn't tell that she wasn't actually eating? 'I was always hungry.'

She looked at Joy with a fixed, almost belligerent expression, and Joy backed down. Perhaps she'd accidentally 'body-shamed'. There were a lot of new rules for life and she hadn't caught up on all of them. Her children, who had come into the world completely uncivilised and learned all their good manners from her, sometimes cried, '*Mum!* You can't say *that!*' She always laughed as if she didn't give two hoots, but in truth these inadvertent transgressions upset and embarrassed her.

'How long had you been going out with that boy?' she asked Savannah. 'The one who –' She touched her own eyebrow where Savannah's injury had been.

'About a year.' Savannah's face was impassive. She scraped a spoonful of froth from her cappuccino.

'Had he ever hurt you before?'

She wasn't checking up on her story. Absolutely not. She was just asking questions, trying to understand her.

Savannah put down her spoon and said, 'Can I ask you a question? About your . . . marriage?'

Joy had that odd feeling again that here was the real Savannah, relaxing for a moment, being her true self, taking off her mask.

'Go right ahead,' she said expansively.

'Was there ever any . . . infidelity?'

'Oh!' said Joy. She wiped her mouth with her napkin and sat back.

'It's a very personal question, I know,' said Savannah.

It *was* a personal question, but Joy had just been asking Savannah personal questions about her relationship, so why shouldn't she ask them back?

'No,' she said, and it was no problem at all to bat away that blurry shameful image of another man's lips bending towards hers.

'As far as you know,' said Savannah.

Joy blinked.

'I didn't mean to imply anything by that,' said Savannah.

'Of course you didn't,' said Joy. 'You're right: as far as I know.'

'You were lucky,' said Savannah thoughtfully, 'to meet your soulmate when you were so young.'

'Soulmate,' repeated Joy. 'I don't know about that. He was just a boy. He's not perfect. I'm not perfect. When you're young you get so worked up about things you think you could never forgive, like, I don't know . . .'

'Birthdays?' Savannah lifted a crumb of the apple crumble topping and rubbed it between her fingertips. 'Like forgetting a birthday?'

'That sort of thing, yes,' said Joy, although she'd never cared that much about birthdays or anniversaries. She wanted to say, *Oh, darling, you've no idea.*

She remembered that day they were all driving to the Northumberland Open on the Central Coast and the boys wouldn't stop fighting in the back seat, and she could feel Stan becoming unnaturally still in the driver's seat and her stomach was churning in anticipation, and she turned and hissed at the children, violently, silently contorting her face to try to make them stop. It was during the height of the battles between Logan and Troy, when it seemed like each argument between them was a matter of life and death.

And then Stan put on his indicator. His *flicker.* That's what they used to call the indicator back then. Funny how words disappeared, became quaint and ridiculous, like fashions and opinions you once held dear. He put on his flicker, stopped the car, undid his seatbelt, got out, closed the door, and Joy thought, *You must be joking, Stan. We're on a highway.* But he wasn't joking. He missed that day's matches. The kids all lost their matches. *Bizarre* behaviour.

Husbands could do worse! That's what she'd always told herself. She knew of husbands who hit or shoved or shouted terrible abuse. If Janet Higbee lost a game on a double-fault her husband tweaked her nose and said, 'Stupid goose!' Janet always laughed merrily, but it wasn't funny, anyone could see that it hurt and humiliated her, and poor Janet was annoying but she didn't deserve her nose tweaked just because her ball toss was too low.

Joy remembered another club member from years ago, a pretty girl called Polly Perkins who was an absolute demon on the court, not scared of coming to the net, as aggressive as any man, but had to record every cent she spent in a little notebook for her husband, a hot-shot university professor. Once, Polly told Joy about a terrible argument she and her husband had the previous night because he wouldn't 'give her permission' to buy a new iron. Polly said the old iron kept spitting rust stains onto her clothes. She showed Joy the brown dots on her white tennis skirt. Six months later Polly walked out on her husband and moved back home to New Zealand and Joy often thought of her when she did the ironing and hoped that she'd found happiness and a new iron that didn't spit rust.

A husband could leave, like Stan, but a husband could also never return, like Joy's father. Stan always came back.

The truth was that most of the time Stan was more patient and less prone to anger than Joy. When the kids were little her mood remained set at a permanent low level of simmering irritability.

Did he not think that she too dreamed of walking straight out of her life when she got angry? She regularly fantasised about doing what her father had done all those years ago: walk out the door to 'see a friend' and never come back. Sometimes she abrogated responsibility by fantasising about kidnappers bursting into the house, bundling her into the back of their van and taking her away for a long rest in a nice, cool, quiet dungeon.

But walking out the door was never a real option. She was too necessary. Only she knew the children's schedules, where everything was, the vet's name, the doctor's name, the teacher's name.

But Stan could walk out without a moment's thought.

Sometimes he simply left the room and that was fine. Normal people did that. Sometimes he walked around the block and perhaps normal people did that too. Sometimes he went for a drive and came back an hour later. Two hours later. Three. Four. The longer he went, the less normal it became. The longest time was five days.

'Here's what you do,' Joy's mother said when Joy finally confided in her about her husband's strange, shameful habit. 'Make sure you're wearing lipstick and your nicest dress when he walks back in the door. Don't cry. Don't shout. Don't ask a single question about where he's been. Hold your head up high, and act as if *you didn't even notice* he was gone.'

She'd followed her mother's instructions to the letter. If she gave those same instructions to her daughters they would have *howled*.

She only broke her mother's rule once. It was late at night and she and Stan were in bed, the door shut, both still breathing heavily from sex.

'Why do you do that?' she'd whispered into his chest. 'Disappear? Walk out?'

At first she'd thought he wasn't going to answer, and then he finally spoke.

'I can't talk about it,' he said. 'I'm sorry.'

'It's okay,' she'd said, and it was okay, but it also wasn't okay. There were tiny seeds of bitter resentment at the centre of her heart, like the tiny bitter seeds at the centre of even the sweetest apple.

They never talked of it again. When she said, 'It's okay,' she accepted the deal. He always came back, and it only happened maybe once, twice a year, and as his hair greyed and receded and eventually vanished, and his cartilage crumbled, he did it less and less, until one day she realised it was something from their past, like his long curly black hair, like her PMT.

'You have to make compromises in a relationship,' she said to Savannah. 'You muddle along.' She stopped because she could see Savannah watching a woman and a little girl in a pale pink leotard and tutu who were sitting at the next table. The girl's hair was pulled back in one of those ferociously smooth ballet buns.

'Cute,' she said to Savannah.

'I did classical ballet.' Savannah's eyes were still on the child.

'*Did* you?' said Joy, with interest. In spite of Savannah having said that she had 'highly superior autobiographical memory', she hadn't shared all that many of those memories that she remembered in such superior detail, presumably because they weren't such good memories. It was nice to get a new concrete detail. It made sense too. Savannah had that beautiful straight-backed posture and a kind of grace to her movements.

'My mother would have loved me to do ballet. Did one of your foster carers get you into it?' asked Joy.

Savannah looked at her with unfocused eyes. 'Huh?'

'The ballet?' said Joy. 'How did you get into ballet?'

It didn't seem like a typical pastime for a child shunted between foster homes, particularly 'classical' ballet.

'Oh,' said Savannah. 'I just did a few introductory lessons. That's all.' She looked at the little girl and her lip curled. 'She shouldn't be eating a cupcake if she wants to be a ballerina. So much sugar!' She spat the words out through thin, pursed lips. She sounded once again like someone else. Joy wondered if she were unconsciously imitating some awful authority figure from her life.

Savannah pushed aside her apple crumble with contempt, as if someone had been forcing her to eat it. 'I've had enough of this.'

'Yes. Me too,' said Joy. She sipped her tea and looked again at the little ballet dancer, her tan-stockinged legs kicking as she happily munched on her cupcake.

Joy felt all at once desolate, because she knew that Savannah had just lied to her about ballet, and Joy didn't understand the lie, but if she was lying about that, then perhaps Joy's children were right about Savannah, and she so didn't want her children to be right about Savannah.

'Joy?' said a familiar voice, and Joy quickly rearranged her face into one of warm sympathy for her widowed friend Debbie Christos, who had walked into the café, which was disconcerting because Joy had moments earlier been thinking about her dainty wrists, and also about kissing her dead husband.

chapter thirty-one

Now

'I actually met that girl the police want to talk to,' said Debbie Christos to her friend Sulin Ho. 'I bumped into Joy at the David Jones cafeteria last year. They'd been out shopping. I remember thinking they looked like mother and daughter.'

'I heard about her, of course,' said Sulin. 'But I never met her.'

Sulin was driving Debbie to Monday night tennis, as she had done for the last month.

Losing one's husband, like so many of life's milestones, had turned out to be an interesting test of friendship. Debbie had lost friends, like the one who imperiously told her not to 'wallow in her grief' when she didn't want to go to the theatre, and she'd deepened her friendship with others, like Sulin, who was not a widow yet seemed to intuitively understand the way Debbie felt six months after losing Dennis: so raw and sensitive the very air was harsh against her skin.

Sulin hadn't said, 'Let me know if there's anything I can do for you, Debbie.'

She'd said, 'I'll pick you up at seven.'

When Debbie's son delivered the eulogy at Dennis's funeral,

he said, 'Dad died doing what he loved, just after he'd won the match at Monday night tennis.'

Debbie wished he'd let her fact-check his speech. Dennis had won the point, not the game, and certainly not the match. They were playing against Joy and Stan and no-one beat the Delaneys. About twenty people listening to that eulogy would have thought, *In your dreams, Dennis.*

'What was she like?' asked Sulin. 'The girl?'

'I don't know,' admitted Debbie. 'I didn't take much notice of her. I wish I had. I've been looking back, trying to remember things that Joy said or did, if she seemed unhappy or depressed, but she seemed fine! She was fine with me, anyway.'

'Oh, where *is* Joy?' said Sulin suddenly as they stopped at a traffic light. She turned to look at Debbie. 'It's just not like her, is it?'

'No,' said Debbie. 'It is not like her. Not at all. That's what worries me.'

It was seventeen days now.

Both Debbie and Sulin had been part of an organised search yesterday through bushland near the bike path that circled the St Helens Reserve. The bike path was the closest biking area to the Delaneys, and Joy had received a new bike from her son Troy at Christmas, which she supposedly loved, although not a single person had ever seen her riding it.

The four adult Delaney children had taken part in the search. Stan Delaney had not. Debbie didn't know what to make of that, although a lot of other people knew exactly what to make of it.

'There's something I've been thinking about,' said Sulin now, her eyes fixed on the road ahead. 'It was last October.'

She looked worried, as if she were confessing something.

'I was driving home from book club, about nine o'clock at night, when I saw a man sitting in the gutter on Beaumont Road. I thought it was some drunk teenager, but then the headlights caught his face, and I thought, That's Stan Delaney.'

'Sitting in the gutter?!' Debbie was scandalised. Stan Delaney was not the sort of man to sit in a gutter. He was far too tall.

'I *know*! So I pulled over, and he told me he'd been out walking and tripped and hurt his knee again. It just seemed odd because he was wearing jeans. He certainly wasn't dressed for exercise. It was more like he'd wandered out of the house.'

'Gosh,' said Debbie.

'Yes, and something else,' said Sulin carefully. 'I think . . . I might be wrong, but I'm pretty sure he'd been crying.'

'*Crying*?' said Debbie. She tried to work it out. 'Because of his knee?' Men did get tearier as they got older.

'There was something going on,' said Sulin. 'I know there was, because I helped him into the car and drove him back home and all four children were there at the house. I didn't get the feeling it was a celebration of any sort, that's for sure. It was more like they'd just got terrible news. Something had happened . . . the atmosphere! You know how you just know? You could cut the air with a knife.'

'Was the girl still staying with them then? Savannah?' asked Debbie.

'I didn't see her,' said Sulin. 'I think she must have been gone by then. By the way, I haven't told anyone else that.' She took her eyes off the road and shot Debbie a brief anxious look. 'I don't know if I should.'

'I don't know if you should either,' said Debbie.

She thought of the gossip and rumours swirling about the tennis club. Joy and Stan's marriage had become public property. Everyone had an opinion to give. Some people said they'd never seen a happier partnership, on or off the court. People were in awe of the way the Delaneys silently communicated when they played doubles, switching spots without a word; it was like they had a telepathic connection. You never heard the anguished cries of other married couples: 'Yours!' 'No, yours!' 'I *said* I had it!' When they won, which they invariably bloody did, Stan would lift Joy up like she was a child, spin her around and kiss her smack-bang on the lips.

Others were eager to explain that it was all a front. People were sharing the subtle signs they'd witnessed over the years of marriage difficulties, violence, unhappiness, infidelity and financial trouble. Late last year Joy had begun coming to Monday night tennis on her own. It was supposedly because of Stan's latest knee injury, but *still*, and then Joy herself had stopped coming sometime around Christmas. It felt like an awful invasion of privacy to hear people discussing the Delaney marriage. It was as if people were rummaging through Joy and Stan's bedroom, and in fact, everyone knew how Barb McMahon had found Joy's phone under the marital bed. It made Debbie feel obscurely angry and she knew it had something to do with all the opinions people now had about *her* life and choices. When Dennis was alive she was part of a solid, respectable, unassailable unit: Mr and Mrs Christos. But the moment he died she was untethered. An elderly lady living alone. She was *vulnerable*, said her son. She must be so *lonely*, said her daughter. It all came from a place of love but sometimes she wanted to scream.

Thank God for Sulin, who still treated her like a person.

'We'll play hard tonight,' said Sulin. 'For Joy. Distract ourselves.'

'Yes,' said Debbie. She saw the old folksy Delaneys sign with the smiling tennis ball on the skyline. Everyone still called the courts and clubhouse 'Delaneys' even though Joy and Stan had sold the tennis school over a year ago. It was not as if the Delaneys had ever owned the courts, they leased them from the local council, but it was true that Joy and Stan had been the ones who led the way in lobbying the council to build them in the first place.

Debbie and Dennis had been there at that first meeting with the council. Joy did most of the talking. They were all four founding members of the tennis club. They'd been so young, with no idea of their youth or beauty.

For many years, Stan was president and Dennis was treasurer and Joy and Debbie made sandwiches. This seemed outrageous now. Joy should have been president, and Debbie should have been treasurer (she was a *bookkeeper*!) but they hadn't thought anything of it at the time.

Dennis's death had made those years of their early marriage so much fresher in her mind. Was it just the slideshow her daughter had made for the funeral? There had been a photo of the four of them at a party at the clubhouse, where they all got quite drunk on Joy's homemade Hawaiian punch. It had been so strange sitting in the chilly church, seventy-four years old in stockings, seeing herself up on the screen in her orange mini-skirt. She could literally taste the sickly sweet punch and feel the fabric of that miniskirt against her thighs. It felt like it was all still *there*, that time of their lives, somewhere metaphysical, accessible through some magical means other than memory.

Joy had been smiling sideways at Dennis over her glass of punch in that photo, while Dennis, with a huge handlebar moustache, looked back at her suggestively, and Debbie and Stan smiled unsuspectingly at the camera. Debbie had forgotten what a bombshell Joy used to be. (Wasn't that the word Dennis once used for Joy? The Delaney Bombshell?)

Debbie's daughter hadn't noticed that she'd chosen a photo for her father's memorial slideshow of him flirting with another woman. (She'd been more intrigued by the 1970s refreshments: cheese and pickled onions on toothpicks stuck in oranges so they looked like hedgehogs. 'Oh my God, Mum, what are those things?')

Had Debbie been the only one at that funeral to see that photo flash by and wonder if anything had ever gone on between Dennis and Joy?

It was very possible.

Dennis was no angel. Debbie had been a bit wild herself. They'd both had 'flings' in the early years of their marriage, before the children were born. Nothing important. She wouldn't have used the word 'affairs'. Just a bit of fun. No feelings were hurt, or not that badly hurt. They'd even been to a key party once. 'How did we find the energy?' they marvelled once they reached their fifties. They'd never told their children. Young people today were strangely puritanical about sex even as they pouted their lips and flaunted their bottoms online.

'Whatever happened to topless sunbaking?' Dennis had said gloomily at one of their last trips to the beach. Debbie, trying to be helpful, had pointed to a group of girls in G-string bikinis. 'Nah, they just look silly,' Dennis had said. He was a boob man. Joy had been wearing a low-cut top in that photo. Dennis hadn't been admiring Joy's pretty eyes, that's for sure.

Debbie wouldn't be cross with Joy if she had slept with Dennis. She wouldn't send her a thankyou card. But she wouldn't hold it against her.

It was all such a long time ago. It surely had nothing to do with Joy's disappearance.

Unless it indicated that Joy was a serial cheater?

Had she run off with a *paramour*?

Who could be bothered at their age? Perhaps Joy could be bothered. She'd always been so energetic.

Sulin parked and Debbie's back twanged as she got out of the car, just to remind her that she wasn't actually thirty, no matter the freshness of her memories.

'Steel yourself,' said Sulin as she locked the car. 'Mark Higbee approaches.'

Mark Higbee played the Monday night social comp with immense gravitas, bouncing the ball about four hundred times each time he served and stopping to mop his brow with a towel in between games as if it were the Australian Open. He also had that horrible habit of tweaking his poor wife's nose, which made Debbie want to punch his.

'Ah, this man is a stupid egg,' said Sulin under her breath, and Debbie shot her a surprised look because Sulin never normally had a bad word to say about anyone.

He walked towards them, tall, thin and grey-bearded, a giant racquet bag slung over his shoulder. 'Salutations, ladies!' he said with an amused smile. He saw women as dear little inferior beings. 'You heard the latest about Joy?' His face was bloated with the pleasure of delicious, shocking gossip.

'No,' said Sulin in a chilly tone.

'You do know she's missing?' said Mark.

'For goodness sake, of course we do,' snapped Sulin. '*We* both helped with the search yesterday.'

'It's obvious that Stan is their quote unquote *chief suspect*,' said Mark, oblivious to her snappiness. He caressed his bearded chin with his thumb and index finger, as if he were parodying a professor deep in thought. 'But without a body . . . they're royally screwed.'

'Without a body?' said Debbie. 'You don't mean *Joy's* body?'

'Of course I do,' said Mark, as if he'd never heard anything so stupid. 'Who else's body would I mean, Debbie?'

Debbie thought of Joy's lovely tanned legs. The woman never stood still. She'd brought around a lasagne when Dennis died, in a baking tray, and then instantly confessed that she hadn't baked it, she'd bought it from the Italian deli and tried to transfer it to the dish to make it look homemade. She'd looked so *guilty* it had made Debbie laugh.

'You've got to face facts,' said Mark paternally. 'It's unlikely she's alive. Stan had scratch marks on his face. What does that tell you?'

'There are many ways that could happen,' said Sulin, but her voice faltered with the horror of it.

'The police might be calling it a missing persons investigation,' said Mark, 'but anyone with a brain knows they're treating it as a murder investigation.'

'She texted all her children that she was going away,' said Debbie.

'It's not exactly hard to send a text from someone else's phone,' said Mark. 'The phone was still at the house. Barb McMahon found it hidden under their bed.'

'Stan doesn't know how to text,' said Debbie. 'If that's what you're implying.'

'So he says,' said Mark.

Debbie said, 'Stan is our friend. You shouldn't say things like this.'

'I heard there was an affair,' said Mark. His eyes sparkled. Debbie had never seen the man so cheerful. 'They had an attractive twenty-something girl staying at their house last year, a quote unquote *family friend*, and I'm guessing that when Joy was in hospital the temptation was too much for Stan. You know, when the cat's away, the mice do tend to play!'

'Stop it,' said Debbie. 'Just stop talking. I do not believe a word of it.'

But it was hard now not to put that together with Sulin's story of Stan, sitting in the gutter last year, *crying*.

Mark raised his palms. 'Don't shoot the messenger, Debbie! Keep this to yourselves, but I have a theory about where he's buried the body.'

Sulin said, 'We're not interested in your theory, Mark.'

'Under their court,' said Mark. 'They had it resurfaced. Perfect place to hide a body. I told the police: Guys, you need to dig up that tennis court. I think they probably will. You heard it here first.'

'But, wait, they resurfaced it back in January –' began Debbie.

Mark barrelled on. 'Not only that. I *saw* Stan, covered in dust, bloodshot eyes, buying chocolate milk at the mini-mart down on Hastings Street two days after Joy went missing. I said, Stan, what happened to you? He ignored me. Literally ignored me as if I didn't exist. Told the police about that too.'

'You think he buried her body and then went and bought himself a chocolate milk?' asked Sulin.

'That's exactly what I think,' said Mark. 'Burying a body is thirsty work!'

'That's not funny,' said Debbie.

'It's not funny, Debbie, it's an absolute tragedy,' said Mark cheerfully. 'I also told the police they should look into that son of theirs, the one driving about in the poser cars who supposedly makes all his money doing "online trading". He used to deal drugs. Know that for a fact because he sold them to my son.'

'Troy?' said Debbie. Troy had dated her daughter. She knew Troy had dated a lot of people's daughters but she still had a soft spot for him. 'That was when he was a teenager, Mark, I think we've all moved on.'

'I told the police they needed to look at possible money laundering, maybe an international white collar crime syndicate, who knows how he makes all his money.'

'So, wait, now you're saying you think *Troy* had something to do with his mother's disappearance?' said Sulin.

'Anything is possible, ladies!' Mark shifted the racquet bag on his shoulder and sauntered off. 'See you on the court!'

'Oh, fuck you, Mark Higbee,' said Sulin, and Debbie was fairly confident this was the first time that particular word had ever crossed her friend's lips.

chapter thirty-two

'Do you reckon the husband had an affair?' asked Ethan.

He and Christina were walking from the car down the endless gravel driveway of a stately home to take a statement for their schoolboy arsonist case, but they were discussing, as they usually were these days, the Joy Delaney investigation.

'With this Savannah girl? It's a possibility,' said Christina. 'There's a whole lot that family isn't telling us.'

'Protecting their father?'

'I assume so,' said Christina. 'Or protecting themselves.'

She did a mental line-up of the four Delaney children as potential suspects.

Amy Delaney: Skittish as a small-time criminal.

Logan Delaney: Calm as an experienced one.

Troy Delaney: Smooth as a slippery salesman. (Except Christina didn't know what he was selling and she felt like maybe he didn't know either.)

Brooke Delaney: Circumspect as a spy.

Could one or more of them be responsible for their mother's disappearance? Or was it more likely that one of them aided and abetted their father?

'If my father had an affair with a young girl and then my mother went missing,' mused Ethan as they stepped onto an arched and columned portico fit for a prince or a poor, misunderstood little arsonist, and rang the doorbell, 'I'd throw him straight under the bus.'

'Me too,' said Christina. She bit on the ragged thumbnail she was meant to be leaving alone for her wedding day.

So why, then, were the Delaneys being so cagey?

She said, 'Did their mother let them down in some way?'

'Mothers can do that,' said Ethan, and she was wondering if he meant that in a general or specific sense when the arsonist's mother opened the door, her son's guilt written all over her exquisitely renovated face.

chapter thirty-three

Last October

Troy couldn't make himself care or focus. The market was quiet, but not that quiet. His heart wasn't in it. He'd made only one trade in the last two hours. That was a signal he should stop for the day, according to his own rules, and rule number one was Follow Your Own Rules.

He looked away from his monitors at the floor-to-ceiling windows where a solitary seagull wheeled across a cloudless pale blue sky. The rippling harbour loomed ahead of him like a landing strip. He'd landed a 747 at Salzburg Airport once. It was a flight simulator experience. A gift for his thirtieth birthday from his ex-wife. The instructor said he had excellent instincts. Troy was now confident he could land a plane if the pilot got in trouble and the (beautiful, panicked) flight attendant came running from the cockpit begging any passenger with flying experience to come forward.

Could have been an airline pilot. Could have won Wimbledon. Could have been a married soccer dad in the suburbs, who made his mother a grandmother, like she deserved to be, instead of donating his kid to another man, making the other man the soccer dad, standing there on the sidelines, cheering on Troy's kid, who would be fucking good at soccer, because the Delaneys were good at all sports, not just tennis.

Troy would let his kid play any sport he wanted to play. But not this particular kid, because it wouldn't be his kid.

It was stupid to get sentimental. If he really wanted a kid he could have one. No problem. Claire had been the one with the problem. Troy had a high sperm count and excellent motility. 'That is just so typical,' Claire had said when she read his sperm analysis, back when she still loved him. He'd been relieved. He hadn't slept the night before they got his results, terrified that the test would reveal a secret hidden failing. His father got his mother pregnant just by looking at her. Of course he did.

Handing over the embryos was the generous, kind, altruistic thing to do, except he couldn't pretend to be an altruist because if Claire had cheated on *him*, he would have been vengeful as hell. He would have said, *Let those little suckers thaw, give them to science, chuck them in the bin*.

He was paying an over-inflated price for a not especially satisfying sexual episode with a girl whose name he couldn't remember, although he remembered her job and her perfume: Pharmaceutical Sales Executive and White Linen. He'd never liked that scent but now he detested it. He remembered going home afterwards in a cab, looking out on rain-sodden city streets, opening the cab window in a fruitless attempt to make the stench of her perfume and his regret go away.

No regrets. That was another of his trading rules. Never waste time thinking about what could have been.

He hadn't given Claire his answer yet. He'd been holding out hope for a last-minute reprieve: a reason to refuse her. Right now it was dinnertime in Texas. He imagined her sitting down to dinner with her husband. 'Any word yet, honey?'

They must hate having their future dreams dependent on him.

The Texan cardiologist would never break Claire's heart. The guy was a heart *specialist* after all. He probably treated Claire's heart with all the specialist loving tenderness she deserved. Troy hoped he did treat her heart tenderly, even as he wished he didn't.

He wished he hadn't hurt her. He didn't understand why he'd done it, except that all through his life he'd been at the mercy of a powerful desire: the desire to blow everything up.

What if I put the tip of my finger against that fragile ornament my mother said not to touch, and not only do I touch, I *push*? What if, halfway through a boring Geography lesson, I stand up and walk out without saying a single word? What if I jump off that bridge with the sign that says NO JUMPING? Take that pill? Go for that impossible shot? What if I pick up a girl at a city bar while my wife is going through IVF to have a baby we both supposedly want? It was like an invisible force took hold of him: *Do it, do it, do it.*

The girl meant nothing. She was just a girl sitting next to him at a bar, with giant teeth and a harsh laugh. Claire was smarter, funnier and prettier, her teeth were perfectly sized and her laugh was beautiful.

His actions were inexplicable. It was all kinds of fucked-up.

'You must have wanted an excuse to get out,' Claire had said, her face ashen. And it was true, he must have wanted an excuse to get out of the relationship, although he wasn't consciously aware of wanting to get out, but why else had he done it, and more to the point, why had he instantly confessed the moment he got home, before he'd even taken off his shirt? While Claire looked up from her book in their bed and smiled, and the cells of their potential children multiplied and divided in a Sydney clinic? It was called self-sabotage, according to Amy, who was the only one in his family who kind of understood, because she had a tendency towards it herself, although even she took a long time to forgive him for breaking her beloved sister-in-law's heart.

Enough! Troy slammed both fists on his desk so hard that his three oversized monitors rattled. He did not do this. What was done was done. He walked to the windows of his home office and pressed his forehead against the glass. Every single person in the world who came to his apartment talked about the incredible views, except for his brother. Logan had walked into this room, laughed out loud, clipped Troy on the back of the head and said, 'Jesus, mate.' Maybe that was his way of saying it was incredible, but why couldn't he just say it was incredible? Why was it funny? Just give him credit for the view, for Christ's sake. Even their father had said, 'Bloody good view.' Although Stan followed it up with, 'Hope you can afford it.' Sometimes he wanted to show his dad his bank statements, like a preschooler giving him a finger-painting: *Look what I did, Daddy. I got rich without tennis, Daddy.* Except not as rich as Harry fucking Haddad. Troy kept a permanent eye on the dickhead's net worth.

He went back to his desk, opened his email, typed in Claire's name and wrote the message, fast. *Dear Claire, I've thought about it, it's fine, go ahead, make it happen, I'll sign all the forms you need. Love, Troy.*

He pressed send. He looked at his hands still resting on the keyboard. What had he just done? Those words were now on a computer screen in Texas. It felt inappropriately futuristic. A message of that significance should have been sent in a hand-written letter that took months to cross the ocean. But everything about this moral dilemma had once been impossibly, laughably futuristic. Frozen microscopic babies waiting to be brought to life.

She could be reading it right now. He tried to imagine his ex-wife's face. What would she think of the word 'love'?

He would never have said yes if he didn't still love her.

The thought hit him like a punch in the nose. It wasn't just about redemption, it was about love. Was the email he just sent his first ever act of unconditional love? The most unselfish act of his life? To zero out the most selfish one?

His apartment buzzer rang. He walked to the security monitor in a daze.

'Hello?' he said roughly.

A face loomed in the screen. He took an instant step back, appalled.

282

It was Savannah. What did *she* want? Something must have happened to his parents. Was his mother back in the hospital? Had his father hurt his knee again?

'Oh, hi, Troy, it's . . . ah, Savannah here.' She leaned in even closer to the camera. 'Your . . . mother's friend?' Her voice crackled through the speaker.

Your mother's friend. That was a strange way to put it. He waited.

He pressed the speaker and said, 'Are my parents okay?'

'They're fine. Can I come in?'

He looked around his apartment. He felt an overwhelming, irrational sense of resistance to the idea of Savannah being here, her rabbit-like eyes darting back and forth, evaluating and judging. He had no idea if that judgement would be negative or positive. All he knew was that she would be far too interested in everything she saw.

But he could hardly say no, not when she'd been taking care of his parents, preparing their meals, even doing their laundry, apparently. She'd cooked that extraordinary Father's Day lunch: the best food Troy had ever eaten in his family home. She'd been the one to grab hold of Troy's mother, supporting her safely to the floor when she'd fainted. She'd said, 'Call an ambulance,' while Troy's family all froze, their minds still trying to catch up. Instead of Savannah feeling indebted to them, the family was increasingly feeling indebted to *her*, and that was making everyone feel off-balance. Amy, Logan and Brooke had all recently left messages for Troy saying to call them urgently regarding 'the Savannah issue' and he hadn't yet called back.

But now Savannah was here. At *his* place. Why not his brother's or sisters'? He wanted to say, *You've got the wrong guy. I'm busy. I've got other things going on.*

'Come on up. It's the top floor.' He pressed the buzzer.

He looked around, trying to see his home through her eyes. Troy's apartment was meant to be minimalist yet glamorous, luxurious yet understated, but was it possibly . . . pretentious?

For one terrifying moment a seismic tremor of doubt shook his entire belief system. His heart raced. Jesus. Pull it together. He was turning into his sister. Next thing he'd be in therapy.

He opened the door to his apartment, his most devastating smile locked and loaded.

'Hi,' said Savannah as she emerged from the lift. 'Wow! Have you got this *whole* floor to yourself?'

'Not quite.' His devastating smile faltered. There were two apartments on the top floor of the building, although his faced north so it was the better one. Was she somehow making him feel bad about his multi-million-dollar north-facing harbour view apartment with a *rooftop infinity-edged pool*?

'Come in,' he said. 'This is a nice surprise.'

'Is it?' said Savannah. She looked different. She had a kind of stylish bohemian look going on: yoga teacher with money.

'You look great,' said Troy. He felt an unexpected surge of attraction. She wore a long pendant with a greenish-coloured stone. It somehow complemented the trashy key necklace she always wore. Her hair was tied up in a half-up, half-down way that no longer reminded him so strongly of his mother's style: not quite as voluminous.

'Your mother bought me all this.' Savannah gestured at her outfit. 'Your mother has been very good to me.'

'You've been good to her,' said Troy, carefully, because she seemed to be making a point. 'Can I get you a drink? Tea or coffee?'

'No, I think I'll just get straight to it,' said Savannah.

'Right then,' said Troy. It was like this was a pre-arranged business meeting. He indicated his custom-made white leather couch. Amy had managed to get chocolate on it last time she visited. 'Have a seat.'

She sat at the very edge of the couch, feet together, back straight. She adjusted the pendant between her breasts.

'Extraordinary view.' She swept her arm in a quick graceful arc, as if getting a required formal acknowledgement out of the way. She didn't even look at the view.

'What can I do for you, Savannah?' He sat in the Eames chair opposite her and smiled. She didn't smile back, which was disconcerting. People generally smiled back when Troy smiled.

If he'd had to guess, he would have said she was here to ask him to invest in a crummy small business venture with little hope of turning a profit, like a nail salon or a vegan café. Although she was a good cook, so maybe she *could* turn a profit on a vegan café?

She said, 'While your mother was in hospital, and it was just your father and I alone, he . . .'

She stopped, lowered her eyes and fiddled with the green pendant, turning it this way and that as if she were considering buying it.

'He what?'

She dropped the pendant and looked back at him steadily.

Troy's heart stopped. 'No.'

Her eyes held his, patiently, insistently, gently, like a doctor insisting you must understand that the cancer is incurable. 'I'm sorry, but he did.'

'He didn't actually –'

'He made a very specific request, which I refused.'

'You must have misunderstood,' said Troy.

'There was no doubt,' said Savannah. 'I can give you his exact words if you like.'

Troy recoiled, held up his palm, tried to control his nausea.

'I was really upset,' said Savannah. 'Because your parents seem so . . . happily married, and I really love your mother. I think she's great. Truly. I thought your dad was great too.' She sighed, grimaced. 'I've been at sixes and sevens trying to decide what to do.' She looked at the ceiling. 'On the one hand I think she deserves to know the truth –'

'No,' said Troy. 'I don't think so.'

It was unbearable. He could not bear to imagine his mother's pain, her shock, her shame. She would be so *embarrassed*.

How dare his father do this: his father who had spent Troy's whole life sitting up there on his umpire's chair, judging Troy's every action.

'I don't understand how you could lose control of yourself like that,' Stan had said after Troy jumped the net and attacked Harry for his flagrant cheating, propelled by white-hot rage. It was as though Troy had lost control of his bowels in public. 'I just don't *understand* it.' Troy had seen that same disgust each time he transgressed throughout his life, except there was never again disbelief, just resignation, as if it were to be expected now, as if once again Troy had proven himself to be exactly as disgusting as his father knew him to be.

'You're a fool,' his father had said when Troy cheated on Claire. 'She was too good for you.'

'I know,' Troy had said. *That's why I did it, Dad. Before she noticed.*

His father's betrayal felt like his own betrayal, as if *he* had been the one to make a move on Savannah. Hadn't Troy just moments ago felt a faint flicker of desire for this girl? He might have acted on the very same desire his father had acted upon, as his young house guest, young enough to be his daughter or even his granddaughter, walked past him in Troy's family home. Did his father think Savannah would feel obliged? That he had some power over her because she had nowhere else to go? Because she'd already been knocked around by one guy? Did he forget that he was Stan Delaney, retired tennis coach in old-man slippers, not Harvey Weinstein in a bathrobe? Jesus Christ. *Mum is too good for you, Dad.*

Or did he think, *No harm trying? Worth a shot?* Because he didn't get much these days? Oh, for fuck's sake, now he was thinking about his parents having sex, and his father having sex with Savannah, and it was quite possible that Troy's own sex life would be irretrievably damaged by this single moment.

Or was this just part of an ongoing pattern of behaviour? Had his father cheated before? It had always been a possibility in the back of Troy's mind that the reason for their father's disappearances all those years ago was another woman or even another family.

'But it was always so random,' Amy said, the one and only time they discussed it, when they were both at the right level of drunkenness to bring up their father's former habit. 'So arbitrary.'

'Exactly,' said Troy. 'It seemed arbitrary to us because he needed an excuse to see his girlfriend. We were walking on eggshells trying not to upset him when he'd already decided ahead of time that something stupid and meaningless was about to upset him.'

'That would be too cruel,' Amy had said.

'Well, it *was* cruel,' said Troy, and he'd been surprised and embarrassed by the break in his voice. 'What he did was cruel.'

But all that had happened such a long time ago, when everything was different: their clothes, their hairstyles, their bodies, their personalities. If he saw old footage of himself he couldn't believe he'd ever spoken at such a high pitch, or with such an uncouth flat-vowelled drawl. His parents were no longer those people. Now they were smaller, weaker, less impressive, no longer in charge of anything, not even the tennis school. Once he'd run late meeting them for dinner and when he got there his eyes skimmed right on past the elderly couple in the corner, and he'd kept looking for *his* parents, his huge intimidating father, his energetic tiny mother, and then he saw the elderly couple waving at him, dissolving into his parents, like that optical illusion where you saw either the old hag or the beautiful girl and once you knew the trick you could see both: it became a choice.

He could choose to see a vile old sleaze making a move on a young girl or a pathetic elderly man trying to reclaim his lost youth. He could choose to see the father who had chosen to believe Harry Haddad over him or he could choose to see the father who appeared like magic, huge and hairy in his boxer shorts, there to slay the monster, the moment Troy screamed 'Daddy!' from his bed.

But then he grew out of his nightmares, and it was his mother who kept coming to his rescue after his dad gave up on him because of Harry fucking Haddad. It was his mother who charmed school principals and police officers. She was the one who helped get him back on the track that had led directly to this enviable life he now lived.

He had to ensure his mother never heard about what his father had done. He had to save her, the way his mother had always saved him, and in doing so he would give his father the pardon that he never gave Troy.

'You must not tell my mother,' said Troy.

'Like I said,' Savannah placed her hands on her knees, 'I'm still trying to decide.'

And now he got it. Why she'd come to him and not one of his siblings, and why she was behaving like this was a business transaction.

She was here to make a deal.

chapter thirty-four

'Who can explain the difference between active and passive listening?' Logan asked his Wednesday afternoon class.

Passive listening: that word again. Was that the way he'd listened to Indira? Passively?

A motley mix of students sat at the semicircle of desks surrounding him: teenagers straight out of school, women looking to get back into an unrecognisable workforce after years spent raising children, older men who had worked all their lives in industries that no longer existed.

'Active listening is the way I listen to my husband,' said star student Rani. 'Passive listening is the way he listens to me.'

A few women chuckled. The teenagers glanced up briefly from their phones and then instantly dropped their heads again as if there were magnets on their foreheads.

Rani was only a few years younger than Logan's mother, and she was retraining to get back into the workforce after she and her husband had lost all their money to a charming, fraudulent financial adviser now doing prison time.

'We thought this man was the bee's knees,' Rani had said in her 'about me' presentation at the beginning of the semester. 'We mortgaged our home to invest with him. It was like we were under his spell.'

Rani's sparkly demeanour reminded Logan of his mother and Logan wondered now if Joy might one day describe Savannah as someone they once thought of as 'the bee's knees'. His mother was spellbound by her, or at least by her cooking, but Joy was astute when it came to money. There was no way she'd mortgage the house for Savannah. Or would she? In return for a roast chicken lunch?

As Logan's class brainstormed techniques for active listening (verbal affirmations like 'Yes, I see' and non-verbal affirmations like nodding your head) he thought about how Amy had said their mother was furious when she heard of Logan's doubts about Savannah's story. Logan was kind of furious with Amy. Telling their mother was not the plan.

'You were going to ask Savannah out for a drink,' Logan reminded her.

'I know,' said Amy. 'But she gives me the heebie-jeebies. She didn't want to even let me in the door! It was like she was their *carer*.' Logan had forgotten that you could never rely on Amy to stick to a plan.

'To be fair, she does make excellent minestrone,' Amy had said. 'Simon and I had two bowls each.'

Simon, it transpired, was Amy's flatmate, and for some unexplained reason he had been at their parents' house too. Simon was going to help Amy do a 'deep dive' on Savannah.

'A full-on background check,' Amy told Logan. 'Like the FBI would do.'

'Right,' said Logan.

'Because he's an accountant.'

'How does that help?' said Logan.

'He's very thorough,' Amy said, and then she'd chuckled suggestively and Logan had hung up and called Brooke, who said not to waste any more time with Amy and that she herself had begun preparing a 'dossier' on Savannah weeks ago and she'd come back to Logan with some proper information soon. She said the word 'dossier' with a lot of satisfaction.

Troy hadn't returned anyone's calls and for all anyone knew might have been out of the country, so he was no help. In the meantime, their mother had taken Savannah shopping last week and bought her a whole new wardrobe, which was upsetting for Amy and Brooke, not because they wanted to go shopping with their mother – they couldn't think of anything worse – but what with Savannah's incessant *baking* and her *tiny feet*, the girl was clearly intent upon transforming herself into their mother's 'dream daughter'.

'Let's role-play some active and passive listening,' said Logan to his class. He didn't ask for volunteers. He chose Brian, an Irish automotive worker who had lost his job of thirty years when Holden closed its doors, and Jun, a bright, bubbly hairdresser who wanted her boss's job because her boss was 'a real b-i-t-c-h'.

'Tell Jun a story, Brian,' said Logan. 'About anything. And, Jun, I want you to be a passive listener.'

Brian launched into a story about a grossly unfair parking ticket, which Jun found impossible to listen to passively, because she'd been booked at the exact same intersection near the college (so had Logan). Brian's Irish accent became more pronounced the more excited and upset he became and Logan was reminded of Savannah's similarly Irish-accented boyfriend, sitting up in bed, reaching for his spectacles, the terror on his face.

He stopped dead and banged the whiteboard marker against his palm.

The source of truth. Or at least another version of the truth.

He'd go talk to the little Irish fucker.

★

Later that afternoon Logan stood at the apartment building where Savannah had lived with her boyfriend. He remembered the apartment number because his birthday was on the twenty-fourth so he'd always had a fondness for the number.

'Hello?' said an Irish-accented voice.

'Hello?' Logan panicked. He hadn't thought it through! But the man said instantly, impatiently, 'Come on up. Second floor.'

The security buzzer went and in his relief, Logan pushed the glass door so hard it crashed against the wall with a bang.

When he got to the apartment he saw that the door had been propped open with a battered old sneaker.

Logan tentatively pushed open the door.

'Hello?'

Nothing. He could hear music playing from somewhere inside. Norah Jones. It was like the guy was doing everything possible to make himself look benign.

Savannah had mentioned his name but Logan was struggling to remember it. Something bland and one syllable.

He looked at the abstract painting leaning against the wall. It was god-awful. Indira would love it. He remembered when he and Troy first came here, Savannah had said the boyfriend was the artist. He studied the signature. Did it possibly say David? Was that the bloke's name? Dave? Dave.

'Dave?' he called out.

A voice called over the music, 'Yeah! Thank you! Just leave it anywhere.'

He walked into the dining room. It was like walking onto a building site, albeit one with Norah Jones crooning from a speaker. A giant paint-stained tarpaulin protected the carpet. The unpacked removalist's boxes had been stacked in a corner and the coffee table had been tipped on its side and propped up against the wall. Dave – he assumed his name was Dave – stood in front of a giant easel. He was in the process of squeezing paint from a tube onto a piece of cardboard he was using as a palette. He wore a mechanic's blue boilersuit. There was a blob of paint on his glasses, another on his earlobe. The canvas he was working on featured swirls of queasy yellow similar to the colour of Logan's kitchen. The mood in the apartment was industrious and joyful. This was someone completely lost in something they loved to do, and Logan found himself feeling envious. He'd once lost himself in tennis, and then only sex and television. Now there was only television left.

Indira wanted to paint. Like this, maybe, Logan wasn't sure. She'd told him this about a year ago, as if she were confessing to something deeply personal and private. 'Go for it,' Logan had told her. She said she needed somewhere to paint and that maybe they could think about moving to a bigger place where she could have a studio. 'Just do it right here,' Logan had said, and he'd pushed the coffee table up against the wall. Not passive listening, active listening. Very active listening! It was a heavy coffee table. The woman wants to paint, the man makes space for her to paint. But she'd said, sadly, 'No, that won't work.' And then she stopped talking about it.

If she really wanted to paint, she'd have painted. Look at this guy. This apartment had half their living space.

'Yeah, hi, thanks for that, did you . . . need something?' said Dave. He replaced the lid on his tube of paint.

'I'm Logan.' His mind was still on Indira.

Logan was totally supportive of her desire to paint. He just didn't want to sell the townhouse. *Just in case it didn't work out.* No, absolutely not, that was not the reason. He was committed to the relationship. But sometimes you lost when you were meant to win. The townhouse was in his name. If it didn't work out, nothing needed to change, the girl left, Logan stayed. And see, look what happened: the girl had left. Once again. His strategy was sound.

'Yeah, thanks, Logan,' said Dave, a bit impatiently. 'So the pizza is . . .?' He looked over Logan's shoulder.

'Oh,' said Logan apologetically. 'I'm not delivering pizza. I'm, um – hoping you might talk to me about your girlfriend. Your ex-girlfriend. Savannah. Just quickly.' He remembered his strategy: ask for help, throw himself at his mercy. 'I need your help.'

Dave took a step backward. 'Fuck.' He put down his tube of paint. 'You're one of the angry guys who came with her that day.'

Logan had a sick feeling that the poor guy was urgently scanning the room looking for a weapon with which to defend himself. He was even younger and smaller than Logan remembered.

Logan lifted his palms. 'I come in peace.' *What in the world?* He tried to stoop and round his shoulders to make himself smaller and less intimidating. 'I just want to talk. Savannah is staying with my parents.'

'Your parents?' Dave had picked up a paintbrush, which he clenched in his fist as if he might stab Logan with the pointy end. 'She's staying with your parents? Not you? And she's okay?'

'She's fine,' said Logan. He thought of Savannah gliding about his mother's kitchen with his mother's haircut. 'She's good.'

'How does she know your family?' asked Dave.

'She doesn't.'

'I don't get it.'

'She turned up on their doorstep late one night, bleeding. She said that you hit her.'

'*Hit* her?' Dave's mouth dropped. His face became stupid with shock. 'She really said that? That I hit her?'

'That's why my brother and I came here to help her pick up her stuff. But then the other day I saw something on TV. It was a girl telling the same story as Savannah told me. About you. Almost word for word. It made me think she might have made it up, and well, that's fine if she made it up.'

It wasn't fine if she made it up, but he wanted to be clear that he was an easygoing, accepting kind of guy. All he wanted was information.

'She's living with my parents, and my mother loves her, and I guess we're just trying to understand. We just . . .' He felt suddenly overcome by the peculiarity of this whole situation. He'd walked into a stranger's apartment, just like Savannah had walked into his parents' life. People weren't meant to behave like this. 'We just need to know if we should be worried. We just don't . . . we don't quite *get* her.'

The kid's shoulders dropped. 'Right,' he said. 'Right then.'

He took off his glasses and cleaned off the paint from the lenses with an old rag from his pocket. 'Well, firstly I did not hit her. I've never hit anyone.' He looked up at Logan. 'Man or woman.'

'Okay,' said Logan. 'I believe you.'

'Is that why you two looked like you wanted to kill me that day?' Dave put his glasses back on and peered at Logan. 'Because you believed I'd –'

'We didn't want to kill you,' said Logan uncomfortably.

'Your brother did. It was a nightmare. Like a home invasion.'

'You were apologising to her. You kept saying sorry to Savannah,' remembered Logan. He kind of wanted to find mitigating circumstances. 'You were apologising for *something* you'd done, something pretty bad.'

'Not for *hitting* her!' said Dave. 'I was apologising for forgetting her birthday. I was meant to meet her at a restaurant for her birthday, and I never showed. She was all dressed up, in this fancy restaurant, waiting, waiting, and my phone battery was dead.'

'Wow,' said Logan.

'I know,' said Dave. He shook his head remorsefully. 'I still can't believe I did that.'

'So. This story she told me . . .'

'She probably did repeat it from something she saw on TV. She does that. Like, monologues from movies. Stories that people told her. Or that *I* told her. She's like a parrot. It's her party trick.'

'Okay,' said Logan. Some party trick: pretending you were a victim of domestic violence.

'Supposedly she has this thing called superior memory syndrome, or something like that. She says she can remember every day of her whole life. I never knew if that was true, or if even *that* was something she'd seen on TV.' He looked uneasy. 'She could be kind of . . . loose with the truth.'

'She's a liar,' said Logan. 'That's what you're saying.'

The apartment buzzer rang, and they both jumped.

'That's my pizza,' said Dave. 'I thought you were my pizza.'

'Yeah, I got that,' said Logan.

'You mind if I let him come up?' asked Dave carefully, as if he were being held hostage.

Logan took a step back, held his palms up again, idiotically. 'I won't take up much more of your time.'

Dave buzzed in the pizza guy, and then they both looked at each other, awkwardly, waiting.

'What sort of pizza?' asked Logan.

'My favourite from my local,' said Dave. 'It's called the Saucy Stripper. Chicken strips and sweet chilli sauce. You hungry? I won't eat it all.'

'Starving,' said Logan honestly. 'But that's okay, I won't –'

'Family-sized Saucy Stripper for Dave?' called out a deep voice at the door, and Logan and Dave grinned in mutual involuntary appreciation, which somehow lifted the mood, and that was how Logan found himself sitting on the floor of Savannah's ex-boyfriend's apartment, drinking beer and eating excellent pizza, and strangely enjoying himself.

'My girlfriend wants to paint this sort of . . . stuff . . . art.' Logan gestured at the easel. 'My ex-girlfriend.' He looked about the room. 'I said she could just paint in our living area, like you're doing. She said she needed a studio.'

He wanted Dave to say: *high maintenance*.

'Yeah, well, I'm only doing it here because Savannah moved out,' said Dave. 'Otherwise I'd need my own space. That's the silver lining of her leaving. I've suddenly got my own studio. Your girlfriend couldn't paint with you breathing down her neck.'

'I wouldn't have done that,' said Logan.

'She would have felt embarrassed to paint in front of you.' Dave peeled off a piece of chicken from his pizza and spoke with his mouth full. 'Especially if she's only just getting started. That's the thing about art. It's so visible.'

'Oh,' said Logan. 'She never said. I could have gone out. Left her to it.'

'Sure,' said Dave. 'But she probably got it in her head that a studio was the answer to overcoming her fear. She wants to paint but she's afraid to paint.'

'Why would she be afraid to paint?'

'In case she's no good,' said Dave. 'In case she can't get what's in her head and her heart onto the canvas. Maybe she's afraid of being afraid. That she'll be so paralysed by fear she won't do a thing, she'll just stand there with her paintbrush, feeling like a fraud.'

Logan put down his slice of pizza, suddenly bereft. He'd thought it was just a passing whim, and the truth was Indira became weirdly reticent each time she brought it up, as if she didn't really care all that much. She'd raise it and then she'd instantly back down. She never pushed that hard. Was it possible the reticence was because of fear?

He should have understood that she could have passionate, complicated feelings about art, just like he had passionate, complicated feelings about tennis. Art wasn't a hobby for Indira, like tennis could never be a hobby for him. When she walked through art galleries she felt what Logan felt when he watched the grand slams: pain and pleasure, like unrequited love.

He was a fool. They could have afforded a bigger place. Why did he insist they stay? Because he never felt like changing anything: his job, his address, his bank, his gym. Jesus. It would have been so simple to move to a two-bedroom place with a second room she could have used as a studio. She could have closed the door, faced her fear. She was probably good. Probably better than this guy. She was probably *great*.

'Did she break your heart, then?' asked Dave.

'No,' said Logan. 'It just ran its course.' He changed the subject back to the point of his visit. 'How long had you been with Savannah?'

'It was only early days,' said Dave. 'About three months.'

'You moved in together pretty fast,' commented Logan.

'Probably too fast,' agreed Dave. 'I told her on one of our very first dates that I'd been thinking of moving to Sydney, and she said she'd been planning to do the same, but it was so much more expensive than Adelaide –'

'Wait – she told us you both moved down from the Gold Coast together.'

'Adelaide,' said Dave.

'Why would she say the Gold Coast?'

Did coming from the Gold Coast sound more tragic and dramatic than coming from Adelaide? Maybe it did.

Dave shrugged. 'She did that. It's a habit of hers. She lies about things for no reason, things that don't matter, that are easy to catch her out on, like, I don't know, what she'd had for lunch. I'd say, "But, Savannah, I *know* that's not true," and she'd say, "What does it matter? It's so trivial, who cares what I had for lunch?" And I'd think, yeah, it is trivial, I *don't* care, but it made me feel kind of befuddled.'

'I bet,' said Logan.

Dave helped himself to another slice of pizza and said, 'You know, I did some research. Savannah actually fits the definition of a pathological liar, which is someone who lies *when there is no benefit to lying*. That's exactly what she'd do. Lie for the sake of it.'

Logan tried to channel his mother and show compassion. 'I guess it might have something to do with her growing up in foster care?' He warmed to the subject. 'She maybe got used to saying whatever she thought people wanted to hear and –'

'Yeah, no, mate,' said Dave. 'She didn't grow up in foster care.'

Logan slumped back. 'She didn't?' His compassion vanished.

'No,' said Dave. 'Her father died when she was a baby. I don't think they ever had much money, but she definitely was never in foster care. She'd lived in the same house from when she was seven. She used to do ballet. She says her mother still has all her trophies displayed, like a shrine to her ballet career. I know that part is true. I've seen photos of her performing.'

Logan felt queasy. All these unnecessary lies. Had she stolen the details of her childhood in foster care from some poor contestant describing their 'journey' on a talent show? None of it was necessary to arouse Logan's mother's sympathy. She could have just admitted she was an ordinary girl from Adelaide who had been stood up by her boyfriend on her birthday and Logan's mother *still* would have let her stay the night, although perhaps Logan's father would not have let her stay the second night.

'So that night when you forgot her birthday, is that when she left?' Another thought struck Logan. 'How did she hurt herself, then? She was bleeding when she got to my parents'.'

'So I worked late. I'm the new guy, trying to impress.' He lifted his bottle to his mouth, took a long swig. He was loosening up now that he'd nearly finished his beer, becoming voluble. 'We'd both got new jobs straight away when we moved in, so we were busy. I was working full-time as a graphic designer, and Savannah was working odd hours at two jobs. We were both exhausted.'

Savannah had two jobs? What happened to those two jobs? The last Logan had heard was that Savannah had said 'there wasn't much out there right now'.

'I had in my head that the birthday dinner was another week away. So I got home and my phone was flat and I couldn't find the damned charger. We'd only just moved in. We still had boxes to unpack. I was getting hungry because she does all the cooking.' Dave dolefully considered his slice of pizza. 'She's a great cook.'

'I know,' said Logan, although it felt wrong to admit he'd enjoyed Savannah's cooking, while he was here investigating her.

'And then finally she came home. I thought, Yes, dinner! But then I saw she was all dressed up and I said, "Oh, feck, it's not today, is it?" Like, it was obviously the first time we'd celebrated her birthday together, so it was a real balls-up.'

He clearly still felt bad about it.

'It's strange because she didn't seem that angry at first. She was upset, but not crazy angry. She said it didn't matter, we'd go there again another time. She made pasta! We were watching TV, having a glass of wine, it was all good, and then suddenly, out of nowhere, it was like she lost her mind. She stood up from the couch and said, "I can't take this anymore." She was walking back and forth holding her wine and it was like she was having some kind of *episode*, and we still had boxes and shit everywhere. Next thing she trips over my guitar case. She'd asked me to move it out of the way, and I never did.' He looked at Logan. 'I'm officially the lowlife in this story.'

Logan sucked his teeth sympathetically, which was a good example of a non-verbal affirmation while active listening.

'The wineglass smashed when she fell, and she cut herself.' He put a hand over his own eye as he remembered. 'I thought she'd lost an eye for a moment. All that blood. I was trying to help her, and she wouldn't let me look at it, she was turning in circles, muttering to herself. Next thing she just . . . *left*. Bare feet. It was a cold night. No money, no phone. Gone.'

'Where did you think she'd gone?'

'I had no idea. I said, "Where are you going?" And she said, "*I'm going back there*."'

'Going back where?' said Logan.

'That's what I said, "Going back *where*?" I assumed she meant going back to Adelaide. I said, "You can't get a flight at this time of night!"'

Logan studied him, looking for the holes in the story that his sisters would find. 'You must have been worried.'

'I didn't know whether I should call the police or what. I didn't sleep. But then the next day I went to work – it's a new job, I had to work – and she'd left this weird, whispered message on my voicemail, like she was calling from a library. She said she was staying with old friends, and I thought, What friends? I didn't think we knew anyone here. She said that she "wished me well". I took that to mean we were done.'

Logan winced. 'She wished you well.'

'I know,' said Dave. 'That was the way she talked sometimes. Like an old lady. Or like she was playing a part. I feel like I never even knew her. And you know, since then I've talked to people about it, and I just think, man, that's one of those short relationships where you look back and think, What was *that* all about? Because she was fun and sweet but she was weird. I think maybe I dodged a bullet.'

'Maybe you did,' said Logan. Was that dodged bullet now headed straight for his parents?

'I don't think she's dangerous,' reflected Dave. 'She's just a really strange person. That night, her behaviour was weird; so out of the blue. I remember thinking, Is this actually nothing to do with me missing her birthday? Was it something on TV that upset her? But it couldn't have been. We weren't even really watching it. It was just some random news story about tennis.'

'Tennis?' said Logan sharply. He'd been about to have a mouthful of beer, and the bottle banged against his teeth. 'What about tennis?'

'Savannah has less than zero interest in sport, so it couldn't have been that.'

'But you said there was something on TV about tennis. What about tennis?'

Dave shook his head adamantly, trying to make it clear that Logan had the wrong end of the stick.

'It was nothing,' he said. 'Just something about that player making a comeback. What's his name?' He frowned, snapped his fingers. 'Harry Haddad.'

chapter thirty-five

Now

'I just think if we tell the police everything about Savannah it might distract them from finding Mum,' said the client in the reception area of Marshall and Smith Criminal Defence Lawyers. 'It will make them think Dad has a possible –' She lowered her voice. 'A possible motive.'

The receptionist, who had been at Marshall and Smith for over a decade, was used to overhearing conversations like this of a personal and sometimes salacious nature. It was a perk of the job.

The client, a woman who had very short hair but was a noticeably *long* person – she seemed double the length of an average woman, like someone about to stride out onto a field and win the gold medal for high jump – was here for a first appointment with the senior partner, Chris Marshall. She was speaking quietly into her phone, but the receptionist had excellent hearing, which was not her fault.

'If they work it out themselves, that's fine, I mean, we worked it out ourselves. I'm sure they're more efficient investigators than us. I just don't see why we need to hand it to them on a platter. It's not relevant. It just makes Dad look bad.'

There was a long pause, and then she suddenly said, 'Well, that's up to you, Troy. I can't stop you. But you may as well know that I'm finding Dad a lawyer. Just in case.'

Another pause.

'Yes, I'm standing by him.'

Another pause.

'No, I didn't say I'm standing by him *no matter what.*' Her voice was full of suppressed emotion. 'I'm just trying to do the right thing. Oh, *go to hell!*'

She dropped the phone into her lap and looked straight ahead. The receptionist lowered her eyes to her keyboard. It was awkward to witness another person lose control.

'Brooke Delaney?' Chris Marshall stood at the door of his office, smiling expensively.

'That's me.' The woman leaped to her feet, breathed through her nostrils and lifted her chin as if she were about to set that high jump record, and went striding into his office.

chapter thirty-six

Last October

Do a reverse image search, suggested the internet when Brooke asked how one would go about doing a background search on a suspicious person staying with one's parents. *It's easy!*

Not if I don't have a photo of her, Brooke told the internet. She locked her hands together and raised them high above her head.

She was sitting at her desktop computer in her study at home, except it felt like she was sitting in Grant's study at Grant's computer in Grant's home. It had technically been a shared study, but Brooke had been the one who always worked on her laptop at the dining room table, as if Grant's career was the one that mattered. It had *felt* more important, although she didn't know why Grant's work as a geologist in a government 'geoscience' department should be more important than hers as a physiotherapist.

Why was she thinking this? Grant had never *once* implied that his work was more important than hers. He also had bad posture so he needed the chair with better lumbar support. That was absolutely her choice. She'd insisted on it, in fact.

Her marriage had been an equal modern partnership: nothing like her parents' lopsided, old-fashioned marriage. It had been a shock to hear her mother say she hated cooking. No wonder Joy thought Grant was so wonderful. Grant was a great cook. They had never had a single argument over who did what around the house. It just wasn't an issue for them. Everything was split so fairly.

Brooke was nothing like her mother. *Nothing.*

She readjusted the chair to suit herself. It was a good chair. Grant's lower back probably missed it.

She turned up the volume on Taylor Swift to inspire her. She loved Taylor Swift. Grant said she couldn't possibly love Taylor because she wasn't thirteen, but she did so love her. It was kind of a relief not to have to sit and listen to the latest album from an alternative rock band Grant had discovered. You had to listen to the full album in the correct order because that was what the artist intended. Brooke just liked to listen to her favourite song on repeat.

Brooke had Googled Savannah weeks ago, as soon as she got her full name. Initially her mother said she didn't know it. 'I didn't ask! Why would I ask?' Yes, indeed. Why would you ask for the full name of the person who has moved into your home? And then her mother said her name was Savannah Polanski, 'just like that dreadful film director', and nothing had come up for Savannah Polanski except an obituary, and then, days later, 'Oh, actually I got that wrong, it's not Polanski, it's Pagonis.' Brooke had Googled again, and still nothing turned up except for a three-star review of a sushi restaurant in Byron Bay.

Now she stared with blank frustration at the computer screen. She was used to the internet providing all the answers she needed.

Wait, Brooke *did* have a photo of Savannah.

Her mother had texted her a photo of them on their shopping trip: a selfie of the two of them looking radiantly happy wearing new dresses, tags dangling, in a change room. The photo was in focus so Savannah must have been the one to take it and hold the phone steady. Apparently they'd spent *six hours* at the shopping centre! They stayed so long they would have had to have paid extra for parking if Savannah hadn't discovered some extraordinary loophole regarding parking validation, which saved them seven dollars! They had apple crumble! It wasn't bad!

Brooke had been irritated by the photo and the shopping expedition.

Now she found the photo on her phone, cropped out Savannah's face and did her first reverse image search.

The internet said, *That's not Savannah Pagonis, that's Savannah Smith.*

Two years ago, 'Savannah Smith' had been photographed at the bookstore launch of a celebrity chef's new recipe book. It was definitely Savannah, although her style had changed dramatically. Her hair was longer and curlier then and she wore bright red lipstick and big earrings.

But what did that tell Brooke? That Savannah once had a different surname and hairstyle? A former marriage? It was hardly shocking that Savannah had been at the launch of a recipe book.

Brooke sighed. She shouldn't be disappointed. She didn't *want* to find out that her parents were living with a serial con artist, did she? Maybe she did. Maybe she was hoping for an excuse to drive over there and yell at Savannah, *You stop being so nice to my parents!*

She looked at the time. She kept forgetting that her friend Ines would be turning up soon. Word had recently got out about the separation (not thanks to her, she'd told no-one except her family) and people had begun to message Brooke their condolences, as if Grant had died. Ines's text had been brief. *Just heard. I'll come over tonight.*

Brooke texted back, *I might have plans!*

Ines texted, *No you don't.*

Well. It was true. Her only plan had been to investigate Savannah and write an article, *Ten Tips for Back Pain*, in the hope that she could get it placed on a women's health website. She was trying to 'build her profile'. She also needed to do a new 'engaging' post on Instagram.

She kept Googling 'Savannah Smith', trawling through multiple wrong Savannah Smiths across the world until she stopped on a grainy black and white image from a newspaper article dated fifteen years earlier. The headline read: ELEVEN-YEAR-OLD SAVANNAH DANCES INTO A BRIGHT FUTURE!

It was only a very short one-paragraph story from a local newspaper in Adelaide about how Savannah Smith had won first place in *the biggest ballet competition in the region* and how it was *a great thrill for the quiet, shy, talented little girl* because it was *her dream to one day dance professionally.*

The photo on Brooke's screen showed a little girl in a tutu, up on her toes, arms above her head in that classic ballerina pose. A very skinny, almost skeletal, intense, serious-looking little girl with her hair pulled so tightly back from her head in a bun that it looked painful. Her elf-like ears stuck out. She didn't have the right ears for a ballet dancer.

Years ago there had been similarly hyperbolic newspaper stories about the future tennis careers of Brooke and all three of her siblings. It happened all the time. Talented kids turned into ordinary grown-ups: butterflies became moths.

Apparently her dad had a project underway where he was carefully laminating every single one of their ancient press clippings for posterity, which made Brooke feel melancholy. What a monumental waste of time.

Something about the photo tugged irritably at Brooke's memory. The little girl reminded her of someone or something in the past. Something to do with a migraine, her vision blurring, the smell of fresh-cut grass, someone shouting.

The doorbell rang and she jumped, startled out of her reverie.

Ines arrived with a bottle of champagne and an overloaded recycled shopping bag looped over one shoulder.

'Too heavy!' said Brooke as she swiftly removed it and led Ines to the kitchen, suddenly filled with affection for her old friend. She hadn't *forgotten* her friends but it did strangely feel as though she was just now remembering them.

'Love the overalls,' said Ines, indicating Brooke's blue denim overalls, which she'd pulled out from the back of a drawer on a whim. 'Very retro.'

'They're comfortable,' said Brooke. 'Grant said they made me look like a zookeeper.'

They opened the champagne and Brooke filled her in on everything Savannah. 'She's been doing *all* the cooking for them.'

'What a lowlife.' Ines handed her a fizzing glass of champagne.

Brooke giggled, and then stopped abruptly, because she realised how the sound and feel of that voluptuous giggle was both familiar and unfamiliar, like something she'd thought she'd packed away forever along with her old schoolbooks and uniform. This had been happening more and more as the weeks went by and Grant's presence became fainter. Brooke was discovering old habits, old clothes, old music and now, her old laugh. It was absurd to think she hadn't laughed in ten years. She certainly had laughed because Grant was funny. *So* funny. He was proud of his wit. It was important to him that he be recognised as 'the funny one' in their relationship.

Ines said suddenly, 'It's really nice to see you.'

'I know, I've been so busy with the clinic –'

Ines interrupted, 'I meant it's nice to see you without Grant.'

'What do you mean? You liked Grant, didn't you? Everyone liked Grant!' Brooke looked at the bottle of champagne. 'Wait, is this champagne *celebratory*?'

'I didn't dislike him,' said Ines. 'He's one of those people you feel like you *should* like . . .' She paused. 'It just always felt like you were concentrating.'

'Concentrating?'

'Like you were very aware of *him*.'

'Isn't that just being a good partner? Being aware of the other person?'

'Sure. But it seemed like it only went one way. I never felt like he was concentrating on you. It was like he was the CEO and you were his devoted assistant.'

'*No*,' said Brooke. She was a strong, smart, educated woman who had no problem with flat tyres, spiders, light globes, over-charging mechanics or tough-talking real estate agents. She was deeply offended. 'That's not true. That is *absolutely* not true.'

'I'm sure it's not,' said Ines steadily. 'What would I know?'

They silently drank their champagne.

'I'm sorry,' said Ines. 'That was a stupid thing to say. Look, I'll show you what I bought.' She heaved up the grocery bag onto the counter. 'I got mood-boosting foods. Salmon. Bananas. I seem to remember you were always eating bananas at school.'

'I *did* love bananas,' said Brooke. 'But then one doctor told me to cut them out in case they were triggering my migraines so I stopped eating them.'

She took the bunch of bright yellow bananas from Ines. 'Sugar bananas,' she said vaguely as a memory from childhood materialised, the image becoming slowly clearer, like a developing photo.

She was in her winter school uniform, dropping her schoolbag on the back veranda and running to rescue a tennis ball from the mouth of their extremely naughty black labrador. When she came back to retrieve her bag, a strange kid was on the back veranda, which was nothing new. There were always strange kids in their backyard, stealing their parents' attention, except this one was rifling through Brooke's bag, helping herself to a banana: an unbruised sugar banana Brooke had run out of time to eat at school, but one she still had every intention of eating, and there were flashing lights in Brooke's eyes that she didn't yet understand, but every time she told her mother about them, she was too busy to listen, too busy with other kids like this one, and how *dare* this stupid strange kid go through Brooke's bag and steal her banana? Brooke felt enraged, *violated*, sick to the stomach.

She'd yelled, 'Hey! You! Put it down! That's my bag! That's my banana!'

Brooke had never been a yeller. She was more of a sulker. It had been almost exciting to know she had the ability to yell as loudly as that, with righteous fury. The little girl looked up. Hair pulled back so tightly off her forehead her eyes were pulled into cat's eyes. Elfin ears. Resentful face. She'd dropped the banana. Run away.

That's why Brooke had recognised that little girl's face in the article. She'd met Savannah as a child. It was no coincidence that she'd turned up at her family home: she'd been there before.

chapter thirty-seven

Now

'So the *bananas* sparked this memory,' said Ines Lang to her mother as they waited at the menswear counter to buy her dad a new tie for his birthday. 'It was just after she and Grant – sweet Jesus, speak of the actual *devil*.' Ines couldn't believe it. 'Don't turn around.' She dropped her gaze, but it was too late. He was heading towards them, threading his way past the racks of clothes.

'Ines! I thought it was you.' Brooke's ex-husband, Grant Willis, was an ordinary-looking guy with a receding hairline and large ears, yet he carried himself as if he were a sex symbol, and he almost became as good-looking as he believed himself to be. Women awarded extra points for self-confidence. Men weren't as generous with their marking.

'Hi, Grant,' said Ines. Not rude, but frosty. 'Mum, this is Brooke's ex-husband.'

'Hold your horses, we're not divorced yet,' said Grant.

'But you will be,' said Ines. She said to her mother, 'They will be.'

'We're not focusing on that right now,' said Grant. 'With Brooke's mother missing.' He looked momentarily uncertain. 'I'm really fond of Joy. We were close.'

'Aren't you living in Melbourne now, Grant?' asked Ines. Brooke had told her that he'd accepted an interstate secondment early in the year. Ines and Brooke had agreed this was good news. It was preferable ex-husbands left the state if not the country or the planet. So why was he lurking around Sydney?

'Here for work,' said Grant. He took a step closer towards her. 'Brooke hasn't been returning my calls.'

'She's got a lot on her mind.'

'I know that! It's just . . . I thought the police might have contacted me by now.'

'Why would they contact *you*?' asked Ines.

'I was part of that family for a long time.'

'Sure . . . but that was a while ago now.'

'Not that long!' said Grant. 'I have information.'

'Oh, please.' Ines dropped all politeness in a fit of irritability. 'If you've really got *information*, Grant, that might help the police find Joy, call them with it!'

'I should probably do that,' said Grant. 'I just feel like I have a responsibility to make sure *someone* has told the police that Joy once . . .' He licked his lips. 'Had an indiscretion.'

Ines met her mother's widened eyes. 'An indiscretion?'

'That's right. It was many years ago, but obviously if Stan somehow discovered it, well, that might go to motive.'

Go to motive. The man was a geologist, not a lawyer.

'I'm sure the family have passed on all the information the police need,' began Ines.

'Brooke is the only one in that family who knows about this particular incident, and she's always been a Daddy's girl. I'm guessing *she* won't be telling the police.'

'Right,' said Ines. She felt sick. How dare he?

'I mean, Brooke has her dad's back and I get that,' said Grant. 'But I'm Team Joy, and if Stan hurt her, then I'm going to help put him behind bars.'

chapter thirty-eight

Last October

'Turns out your potential scammer is an actual scammer,' said Simon Barrington to Amy as she sat at the dining room table rating the cheesiness of a new savoury cheese cracker.

Simon took a cracker as he sat down opposite her.

'Cheesy,' he said.

'Overly so?' asked Amy.

'I'd say perfectly cheesy.'

His words penetrated. 'Savannah *is* a scammer? Seriously?'

She noted that although her heart was definitely going over the speed limit, it was doing so in a controlled manner, staying in its lane. Her therapist, Roger, used a lot of car metaphors.

Simon opened a manila folder. 'I did an ASIC search.'

'Clever!' Amy tried to remember what ASIC stood for.

'Australian Securities and Investments Commission. She's on the disqualified director list. Three years ago she was the director of a business that was selling fraudulent tennis memorabilia.'

'Wait. Fraudulent *tennis* memorabilia,' said Amy. 'That seems –'

'Like a big coincidence,' agreed Simon solemnly.

Their eyes met. Amy thought of her father's precious signed

tennis ball collection. She'd always wondered if those players really had sat there and signed them themselves.

'You think she deliberately targeted my parents?' asked Amy.

'I do,' said Simon.

'I think we should go over there.' He held up the file, waved it. 'Confront Savannah with this. See what she says.'

'Well,' said Amy. 'I'm really grateful for this but —'

She wavered. This would be the second time he'd been to her family home. He was acting like a boyfriend: a sweet young boyfriend who deserved an equally sweet young girlfriend. She would break his already broken heart.

'Okay,' she said, because simply looking into his clear brown eyes was as cleansing to her soul and calming to her heart rate as half an Ativan washed down with half a glass of wine.

chapter thirty-nine

Now

'Three years ago, this Savannah Pagonis, who at one point went by the name Savannah Smith and may have other aliases, was selling fraudulent tennis memorabilia on the internet,' said Ethan to Christina.

'Okay then,' said Christina. She sat back in her chair, tapping her pen against her teeth. 'Tennis memorabilia. She clearly didn't pick the house at random the way she said she did.'

'She was trying to scam them?' guessed Ethan. 'Something to do with the tennis school?'

'Maybe,' said Christina. 'And maybe she was successful? Because whenever I hear the name "Savannah" from anyone in that family I get the sense she had some kind of emotional impact.'

'Like they're angry with her?' asked Ethan.

Christina considered his question.

'No,' she said finally. 'More like they're sad and possibly . . . guilty?'

chapter forty

Last October

Joy stood outside Savannah's bedroom and pushed tentatively on the half-opened door.

When Amy was a child and this was her bedroom Joy hadn't hesitated to do some sleuthing when Amy was safely at school, searching for clues that would solve the mystery of her daughter. She never found much: a packet of ordinary cigarettes, one 'funny' cigarette, a bottle of crème de menthe that Amy had stolen from her grandmother's house. (None of these items came close to what she found under *Troy's* bed.)

Joy had been far more distressed by the confusing, rambling diary entries that were so difficult to decipher because Amy had a habit of scribbling over the most important words: *I am really worried about scribble scribble and scribble. I wish I never scribble with scribble.*

But Savannah was her guest and Joy had no parental rights to justify her actions. The only justifications she had were Logan's bizarre accusation about the television documentary he'd seen on TV the other day, and the gently ringing alarm bells in her own head.

Savannah was not at home right now. She'd announced earlier today that she was 'going out'.

'Where are you off to?' Joy had asked. 'Do you need a lift?' Apparently Savannah was having dinner with 'a friend' and she didn't need a lift, she'd walk to the station and catch the train into the city.

Joy had managed to stop herself asking, What time will you be home?

Savannah had suggested that Joy and Stan eat the leftover cottage pie from the night before, and she'd even prepared a pea, fennel and feta salad before she went, leaving the good salad servers resting conveniently on the drum-tight piece of cling film as if Joy and Stan were her children, incapable of finding the right cutlery in their own home. It was very sweet.

It was peculiar without her in the house. For such a small, quietly spoken person, Savannah's absence was strangely notice-able. Joy felt as if a spell had been broken. There was a buzzing sensation in her ears, as if she'd walked out of an intense movie or a loud party.

She didn't really believe that Savannah was out with a friend. She couldn't even imagine her having a friend. What *sort* of friend? That was the problem. She was so very fond of Savannah, but she didn't understand her. She didn't really know her. All she had were these tiny jigsaw pieces of a personality that didn't fit together: a love of cooking and a dislike of eating, classical ballet and foster care, grandmotherly manners and a tattoo of a vine.

Joy wasn't angry or frightened, but she did want the facts, before her children proudly presented her with them, which she suspected they desperately wanted to do. Brooke had made such a big deal about the fact that Joy had initially said Savannah's surname was Polanski rather than Pagonis, which could happen to anyone. She'd acted as if Joy was a dithery old lady. Joy had reminded her that Brooke had believed that carpenters laid carpet until she was sixteen, and Brooke said, 'That was actually a completely logical assumption, *Mum*,' and Joy said, 'So Jesus laid carpet then, did he, *Brooke*?'

Remarkably, they'd both got the giggles at that point. It was nice to hear Brooke laugh. She had a lovely laugh. Grant was very witty, very clever, but he never seemed to make Brooke laugh like that.

She had a lightweight doona folded up under her arm, as an excuse, should Savannah suddenly, impossibly, materialise and catch her snooping. 'The nights are getting warmer,' she'd say. It was also in case Stan caught her. She didn't want him to know that she had any concerns about Savannah. He already seemed to have turned against the girl.

As she stepped into the room, the house phone rang and she gasped as if there had been an explosion. For goodness sake.

'Can you get that?' she called as the phone stopped mid-ring and she heard the deep rumble of Stan's voice. Good. That was him out of the way. It would either be for him or a telemarketer, not Joy. Everyone called her on her mobile, because she was progressive.

Savannah's room was spick and span, in stark contrast to the cyclonic aftermath that appeared when Amy lived here, both as a child and when she intermittently moved back in as an adult. Savannah's bed was made with hospital corners, the covers pulled army-straight, and the windowsills and skirting boards gleamed in a way that neither Joy nor Good Old Barb ever achieved.

Amy's old school desk was clear except for a foolscap-sized hardbound journal, sitting right there in the middle of the desk, with a pen next to it. Well, if it was a diary, Joy certainly would not read it. Absolutely not. That sort of gross invasion of privacy was only appropriate for one's own children. Anyway, hadn't Savannah implied that the problem was that she remembered *too much* about her past? She wouldn't need to record her days if they were permanently recorded in her memory.

Joy looked over her shoulder, walked towards the desk. She would not look. There was no point in looking. It was not a diary. If Savannah had something to hide, she wouldn't leave it there in plain sight.

Who was she kidding? Of course she was going to look.

She flipped open the book. The pages were covered in tiny, rigid handwriting. She put her fingertips to the page. The surface was bumpy. Joy's mother used to write like that, pressing so hard with her pen it left an imprint on the page, as if she were trying to engrave her words forever.

She squinted. She needed her reading glasses. Heavens to bloody Betsy. Leaving the room to retrieve her glasses made the whole process feel too calculated. Perhaps if she got them fast? She darted from the room, ran down the hallway. She could hear Stan on the phone. His voice was raised. She hoped he wasn't telling off some poor telemarketer who was only trying to earn a living.

She retrieved the glasses from the kitchen table, ran back down the hallway. He was properly shouting now. She dithered. Should she go and try to help sort it out?

But the volume of his voice dropped, became conciliatory. That was Stan. The telemarketer might even be making a sale now.

She went back into Savannah's room, put on her glasses and picked up the book. Right, then. She read:

Sunday
Quarter apple
Five sultanas
1 x Toast. No crusts. No butter.
Bolognaise pasta. Eleven spoonfuls.
Half orange

Day after day it went. Detailed listings of tiny portions of food. She flipped to the last page and saw the beginning of that day's entry. All it said was: *Eight spoonfuls of Chia Yoghurt Pudding.* Savannah had made the chia yoghurt pudding last night. It was delicious. Joy must have had at least a hundred spoonfuls.

She closed the book and carefully placed it back in exactly the position she'd found it.

All that time Savannah spent creating beautiful food, and then she came back to her room and recorded every mouthful in bleak, rigid detail. The *pleasure* she'd given Joy and Stan with her cooking. It was almost humiliating how much pleasure Joy had taken in it, especially when contrasted with this disciplined transcription.

She sat on Savannah's perfectly made bed and pressed her palms to the tightly pulled sheets. *Oh, darling. What's going on in that head of yours?*

It wasn't a surprise. Not really. She'd seen the way Savannah swirled the same spoonful of food around her plate, putting it down and picking it up again. Was she suffering from a full-blown eating disorder? Or was it just a strange, compulsive habit to record everything she ate that made her feel in control of her life?

Joy's first instinct was to fix it: to get Savannah in to see a professional. As if that would be the silver bullet. It was exactly the way she'd felt when Amy was growing up. They would wait and wait, sometimes months, to get the next available appointment to see the next person. All those different diagnoses they were offered with varying degrees of confidence. She remembered that nice tired-looking psychologist who, when Joy said, 'You lot keep changing your mind!' replied, 'Ours is not an exact science, Joy. It's not like she has a headache.' Joy had thought, resentfully, *Well, no-one can bloody well fix headaches either!*

'Where are you?' shouted Stan. She could hear his heavy footsteps pounding through the house.

'In Savannah's room!' she called back.

'You mean *Amy's* room,' he said, furiously, in the doorway.

'Amy doesn't live here,' said Joy. She looked up at him. His face was white, his eyes red. He radiated fury.

'What is it?' she asked. 'Who was on the phone?'

'It was Troy. Helpfully letting me know that he has just paid Savannah some exorbitant amount of money not to tell you that I harassed her.'

'You *harassed* her?' Joy looked at him blankly, trying to

understand. Her first confused, irrational thought was that he'd harassed her to do tennis drills, like he'd once harassed the children.

'Sexually harassed her,' said Stan. 'Your idiotic son actually believed it. He genuinely believed it.'

Joy stood. She crossed her arms. 'What happened?'

'Well, I didn't bloody well sexually harass her if that's what you're asking!'

'Oh, of course you didn't,' sighed Joy.

Neither of them had been perfect. There had been parties. It was the seventies. They didn't exactly embrace the free love movement, but there was flirting. She was reasonably sure that Brooke once caught her kissing Dennis Christos at the Delaneys Christmas party in the clubhouse kitchen after too many glasses of punch. Dennis couldn't serve to save his life but the man could kiss. Joy confessed it to Stan years later, and he certainly wasn't thrilled but he didn't make a big deal of it, although poor old Dennis did start to look alarmed at the speed of Stan's serves.

Stan might have strayed. It was reasonable to think that he might have considered it in the bad year when they truly thought they were going to separate. Women found him attractive. Joy had never asked the question because she didn't care to hear the answer. She knew it was possible to be kissed by another man and for it to mean nothing at all except that she'd put too much gin in the punch and Dennis was an outrageous flirt, although she still never doubted his love for Debbie.

There were worse betrayals.

But there was no way in the world Stan would have been inappropriate with Savannah. He had always been hyper-aware of the propriety of his position when it came to children and young girls. Joy had seen the way he interacted with Savannah. He saw her as a daughter or a student.

'Did Savannah misinterpret something you said?' Joy asked him. It could have happened when she wasn't there to smooth things over and explain to Savannah what her clueless husband really meant. 'Did you try to make a joke? Because these days you have to be so careful –'

'For Christ's sake, I didn't *try* to make a joke,' said Stan. 'If you must know, while you were in hospital, she gave *me* certain signals –'

'What?' Joy guffawed. 'Darling, she didn't, she wouldn't. You misunderstood.'

'I don't think so.' He pressed his lips together in the way he did when Joy served tuna casserole, the smell of which supposedly made him feel sick, so she only made it when she wasn't happy with him. 'I don't think I misinterpreted anything. Not now she's done this. Not now she's taken Troy's money.'

Joy looked around the neat room, at the book on Amy's desk full of her tiny inscriptions about food. She had no idea who this person was. Her heart quickened. She'd opened her home to a stranger.

'Tell me.' She cleared her throat. 'Tell me what happened.'

'It was subtle,' said Stan. 'So subtle that at first I thought I *was* imagining it. Just, you know . . . eye contact, and a hand on my arm, and there was one day she came into the kitchen straight from the shower wearing nothing but a towel and she kept talking to me and I didn't know which way to look, and I thought, Well, the girls always used to walk around in towels . . .'

'They're your daughters!'

'Well, I didn't know,' said Stan defensively. 'I got out of the room as fast as I could. I felt very . . . uncomfortable.'

'Why didn't you tell me?' asked Joy.

'I thought you'd laugh at me,' said Stan, and Joy's stomach lurched with love and guilt because he was right, she would have laughed. It would have been inconceivable. It still felt inconceivable. How far would Savannah have taken it if Stan had responded?

'That's why you wanted her to leave,' said Joy.

'I felt sick about it.'

'Oh, Stan,' said Joy. She went and put her arms around him and put her face to his chest.

He stood for a moment and then put his arms around her.

'I can't believe Troy,' said Stan. 'He handed over money before he even asked me if it was true. He thought I'd *thank* him. I said, "Mate, that was borderline moronic."'

Joy stepped back and out of his arms. He never gave Troy the benefit of the doubt. *Borderline moronic.* What a thing to say to his own son who was only trying to help.

She said, 'Stan. He obviously thought he was protecting you. Protecting *me.*'

Troy thought he was giving them a gift. She thought of Troy's hopeful face whenever he watched a family member open one of his thoughtful gifts.

'How much money did he give her?' asked Joy. She sat back down on Savannah's bed.

'He said it wasn't that much,' said Stan. 'It couldn't have been that much. It wasn't like she was covering up a murder.'

'Did he write her a cheque?' asked Joy. 'Can't he cancel it?'

'I don't think he has a chequebook. No-one writes cheques anymore.' Stan sat down next to her on the side of the bed. 'I think he transferred it straight into some kind of account. The height of stupidity. You know what Troy said to me when I finally convinced him he'd been scammed? He said he didn't care. He can *afford* it.'

'He only wants to impress you,' Joy sighed.

'Yeah, well, that didn't impress me. It was dumb. And disrespectful. To you and me. To our marriage. For him to think that I would . . . in our own home . . .'

His voice trembled and her heart softened again. It was always like this with Troy and Stan. She was caught in the middle, her sympathy flying back and forth like a ball.

She put her hand on his thigh and they sat in silence for a moment.

'So . . . what happens now? Where is Savannah?' asked Joy.

'I don't know where Savannah is,' said Stan. 'But I told Troy to call his brother and sisters, and get them over here now, so we can discuss next steps.'

Discuss next steps. He was puffed up with the self-righteousness of a wronged man. A *rarely* wronged man.

'We need to be sure nobody else is handing over their hard-earned cash,' Stan continued. 'We obviously need to get the police involved.'

'Oh, I don't know if *that's* necessary.'

'You need to check our bank accounts. She's probably had plenty of opportunities when you were out of the room to go through your purse and take all your credit card details.'

Joy decided not to mention that not only had Savannah had plenty of opportunities to do exactly that but she'd literally handed her credit card to Savannah on multiple occasions.

'All her things are here.' Joy looked around her at the neat room. 'Surely she won't just leave them.' She picked up Savannah's pillow and hugged it to her. 'I think she might have some sort of eating disorder.'

'*Eating* disorder?' Stan said 'eating disorder' like it was some kind of new fangled fashion choice. 'Who cares if she has an eating disorder? She just blackmailed our son!'

'Oh, well,' said Joy, trying to imagine what in the world they would say to her. She didn't feel angry so much as blindsided. It felt like there had to be another explanation.

'Oh, *well*? Joy, did you seriously just say, *Oh, well*?'

'She's obviously troubled,' said Joy. 'Have a heart.' She could feel herself and Stan slipping into their old parenting roles in response to Savannah's actions. The angrier Stan got with a child, the more likely Joy was to defend them, and the worse the transgression, the calmer Joy's response. She was more inclined to shout about dirty laundry thrown on the floor instead of the basket, than a serious-sounding telephone call from the school principal. If she hadn't witnessed the crime herself, she wanted proof, or at least to hear her child's version of the story first. Stan was always too ready to deliver a damning verdict before they'd heard all the evidence. She needed to talk to Savannah. She needed to talk to Troy. She believed Stan's side of the story but part of her still felt as if this must be some kind of dreadful mix-up only she could sort out.

'Joy, for Christ's sake, do you understand the implications of this? If she went public with this kind of accusation? In this day and age?'

'Well, I'm sure she had no intention of going *public*,' said Joy uneasily. 'And of course this is all very upsetting but –'

'But *what*?'

'Don't you dare call me *borderline moronic*.' Joy threw the pillow away from her and stood. Her eyes fell upon Savannah's glory chest. The boys had struggled to carry it inside that day they'd picked up her things.

She lifted the heavy hinged lid. There wasn't much inside: a stack of hardbound journals like the one on Amy's desk and a handful of old-style battered-looking photo albums. Nobody really did photo albums like that anymore. They got those professional-looking bound books printed.

Joy picked up the first spiral-bound album and flipped through it. It was clearly a child's album. The photos had been stuck in crookedly and some of them were so out of focus only a child would consider them worth keeping. The edges of the photos were peeling away from the sticky backing. She looked at a page of photos of two children sitting under a Christmas tree. It could have been a scene from her own albums: the dated summer pyjamas, tousled hair, strewn wrapping paper.

'Stan,' she said quietly.

'What?'

She sat back next to him on the bed and dumped the open album on his lap.

'What?' he said again.

'Look who it is,' she said.

'It's her,' said Stan. 'Savannah. Obviously. When she was a kid.'

'Yes, but look who the boy is.' Joy slid her finger over to the child sitting next to Savannah: the big eyes, pudgy cheeks and shock of hair.

Stan stiffened. 'That's not . . . it couldn't be, why would it be?'

'It is,' said Joy. 'It's Harry Haddad.'

'But why is Savannah with Harry?' asked Stan.

'She's Harry's sister,' said Joy.

'I don't remember a sister,' said Stan.

'You only met me once,' said a voice and they looked up to see Savannah standing at the bedroom door.

chapter forty-one

For just a moment the man and woman seemed to cower, their lined faces slack-soft with shock, as they looked up at Savannah from where they sat side by side on her bed, in her bedroom, except that it was clearly no longer her bed or her bedroom. This was no longer her room. No longer her home. What did she expect? That she could take a hammer to this delightful life and yet find it still magically intact? It was always meant to be temporary. Everything was always meant to be temporary.

After Troy transferred the money (she would have accepted half as much) she'd considered never coming back, abandoning her possessions, but she'd felt an insane desire to spend one last night here, to be the Savannah that Joy saw, to experience one last time her fierce gratitude when Savannah placed a meal in front of her. Food was never just food for Savannah, and it clearly wasn't just food to Joy.

Joy recovered first, straightened her back.

'You're Harry's little sister,' she said. 'I forgot there was a sister.'

Joy looked at her with wary, searching eyes, as if trying to see her properly, and Savannah felt her personality slip away and she stood on the precipice of that terrible endless void.

She was nothing

no feelings
no thoughts
no name
a plastic mannequin of a girl.

But just before she disappeared into the void, before she dissipated like dry ice, a new personality clicked conveniently into place.

She had thousands of hours of television at her disposal to call upon. Hundreds of characters. Lines of dialogue. Facial expressions and useful gestures. A dozen ways to laugh. A dozen ways to cry.

'Ah, don't feel bad about it,' she said. 'Everyone forgets there was a sister.'

She was a new Savannah. Surname not specified. Dry sardonic cool girl. Could be the heroine or the villain. Could be the one to save the day or rob the bank. The viewer didn't know exactly what she had planned.

Joy said, almost to herself, 'I *knew* I knew you from somewhere! That very first night!' She looked down at the photo album on Stan's lap and then up again. 'We only met the mother a handful of times.' She corrected herself. 'I mean . . . *your* mother.'

Joy's eyes searched her face. 'Your parents divorced, didn't they? You went with her. Harry stayed with his dad.'

Also my dad.

For a moment she was Savannah Haddad, with a mum and a dad and a brother, but the second her brother first held a tennis racquet, everything changed. The Haddad family was sliced cleanly in two as if by a sword.

Joy said, with a perplexed little smile, 'I guess you didn't knock on our door that night because "you had a good feeling about this house"?'

'It was my birthday,' said Savannah.

'Was it?' Joy put a hand to her heart as if she would have ordered a cake if she'd known, and Savannah thought of the sideboard crowded with framed photos of birthday celebrations, as if every birthday was worthy of celebration.

She saw a girl dressed so carefully and idiotically for a birthday dinner in a fancy Sydney restaurant, waiting for her boyfriend who never showed up, who never answered his phone. That girl knew her boyfriend had just forgotten. He got distracted. He loved his art more than her, just as her brother had loved his tennis more than her, and her father loved Harry's tennis more than her, and her mother loved her collection of bitter resentments more than her, and nothing would ever fill her hunger. She would always be hungry. Always.

When she got back to the apartment that day she took off her good clothes and put on the oldest, dirtiest ones she could find, and she made Dave pasta, and she was fine, she forgave him, she said, 'I should have reminded you this morning,' although she'd reminded him the previous night.

She drank her wine and because she had not eaten all day in preparation for the special restaurant meal, it went straight to her head and she floated free of her body like she often did, and thought, *Who is that girl sitting with that boy?*

Then the news story came on the television and the pasta blocked her throat as her brother's face filled the screen.

Harry Haddad was announcing his comeback on her birthday.

Three years earlier he'd been everywhere. She couldn't turn on the television without seeing his face. She would get in the car, switch on the radio and hear his voice. She once saw footage of him signing a tennis ball for a fan and thought, *I GAVE him that signature*. She was the one who worked out how to link the two 'H's in Harry Haddad with a flamboyant curl when they were kids. It was basically *her* signature. She had a right to use it. She'd started a business selling tennis balls, t-shirts and caps signed by Harry Haddad, and she'd done quite well out of it until somehow Harry's 'management team' got word of it and it all came crashing down.

Since his retirement her brother had begun to fade from the public consciousness, from her consciousness. Unless she looked him up, which she had learned not to do, he didn't exist, but if he played professionally again, he would once again be everywhere: on her phone, on her television, on her computer screen. She would slam up against her past, over and over again, like slamming her head against a wall, like kicking a locked door.

You are the failure, he is the success, your father got the good one, your mother got the dud, we are the poor ones, they are the rich ones, we are stuck on the ground, they are flying high.

She had been so stupid to think she could ever be a normal girl who was able to go to a fancy Sydney restaurant on her birthday with her Irish artist boyfriend.

The pain had begun in her stomach and radiated out. All she'd wanted was to escape the pain, and then she'd tripped over that damned guitar case and banged her head and it had really hurt and there was blood in her eye, the pain was everywhere, and the memories were refusing to stay locked up safe and sound, they were flooding like poison through her body and brain, and all she could think was that she had to get out of that apartment, and away from those boxes and the boy, and it occurred to her that she should go back to *where it started*, as if she could travel back through time and stop Harry taking that first lesson, or if not that, at least make sense of it, or if not that, make that family pay for what they'd started.

When she'd got downstairs, there was a cab dropping off a happy, drunkenly swaying couple at the apartment block, and she'd got in and asked the driver to take her to the Delaneys Tennis Academy, which she knew was just up the road from the house where her brother had his private lessons. As soon as she saw the sign with the smiley-faced tennis ball, she'd been able to direct the cab driver to the house without hesitation.

The part about finding cash in the pocket of her jeans was nearly true. It was a credit card. Not one that belonged to her. It was a souvenir from a previous incident. She wasn't sure it would work, but she tapped it against the cab driver's machine and the word 'Approved' appeared like magic.

'I was thinking I might throw a brick through your window,' she told Joy. She'd thought some low-level vandalism might be helpful. Cathartic. It had worked in the past. 'But I couldn't find a brick. I couldn't even find a stone.'

'*What?*' said Joy.

'Well, it was a loose plan,' said Savannah.

Joy looked like she might burst into tears.

'You need to leave,' said Stan. He stood. He was still a big intimidating man. 'You need to leave our home.'

'I never *did* it,' said Savannah. 'I just thought about it, but it was so cold out there, on the street, and I was bleeding, and I felt really dizzy, so then I thought, to hell with it, and I knocked on your door, and I felt quite faint, and then . . . well, then you were both so *nice* to me. So very, very nice. It was strange.'

They were so kind and loving and welcoming. They treated her as if she were a daughter returning home. She was fed and bathed and put to bed, and because they treated her like a girl in need of help, she became a girl in need of help, and another girl's story from a documentary about domestic violence slid into her memory and became the truth.

'But why?' said Joy. 'Why would you want to throw a brick through our window? What did we ever do to you? I don't understand.'

She'd put on a little weight since Savannah had begun feeding her. So had Stan. There had been pleasure in watching their faces smooth out as Savannah increased their calorie intake. She was like the wicked witch in *Hansel and Gretel*, fattening them up before she ate them.

'I just hated this house so much,' said Savannah. 'I hated all of you so much.'

Joy gasped in surprised pain at that, as if she'd burned herself.

'We don't need to hear this,' said Stan.

'Be quiet, Stan, we do so need to hear it,' said Joy fiercely.

331

...was so tiny but she could instantly quell that giant man ...in her quick, snippy remarks. Savannah found her inspirational. She already knew that she would keep some of her speech patterns for future use: *What the heck? Oh my word! Heavens to Betsy!*

'Explain it to me,' Joy said to her. 'Start from the beginning.'

Savannah took a breath. Was it even possible to untangle the multitude of memories that had led to this particular moment in this bedroom?

'I was the one who bought the raffle ticket,' she said. That was the very beginning, if she threaded her way back to the start.

'Raffle ticket?' Joy frowned. 'You mean the ticket for the free private lesson? The one Harry's father, *your* father, won?'

'I gave it to him for Father's Day,' said Savannah. 'I bought it at a shopping centre with my own money. My brother said, "That's a stupid present." You would think when the ticket won my father might have given *me* the private tennis lesson, not my brother. Imagine that. Harry might never have picked up a racquet if I hadn't bought that ticket.'

'Do you blame your parents' divorce on us?' asked Joy. 'Is *that* what you're trying to say?'

'We've heard enough. You need to leave,' said Stan. 'You lied to Troy. About me.'

People made accusations of lying with such triumph: as if pointing out a lie won the game, as if you'd just shatter with the shame of it, as if they'd never lied themselves, as if people didn't lie all the time, to themselves, to everyone.

'Did I?' said Savannah archly. It was always possible to plant doubt. Most men carried the guilt of their gender. You just had to apply a tiny flame to the kindling. She'd seen the terror fly across his face when she walked around the house in nothing but her towel. He felt compromised the moment he looked at her.

'Stop this!' shouted Stan. A woman's lie could terrify but so could a man's shout. It made her want to hunker down and put her hands over her ears.

She pressed on. 'You remember what you *said* to me?'

He'd never said a single inappropriate word, he'd been unfailingly kind, he'd been nearly as fatherly as Joy had been motherly, but Stan's fatherliness was a flimsy façade Savannah could smash with ease, not with a brick but with a lie, which was why she had to do exactly that, to prove it wasn't real. Look how easily she'd flipped him from affection to hatred. Love was never real no matter how authentic it seemed.

She said, 'You remember what you asked me to do?'

(Not him, but another man, not her, but another girl. There was another girl's awful truth at the heart of her awful lie.)

He loomed over her, savage with rage. '*Stop this, stop this, stop this!*'

chapter forty-two

Now

'Stop this, stop this, stop this!'

Stop what? Caro Azinovic was one hundred per cent positive those were the words a man – it had sounded like Stan Delaney – shouted over and over on a coolish night last spring. Caro had been dragging her yellow 'glass and plastics' bin to the kerb, and she'd heard the shouting over the rattle and scrape of her bin and stopped in her tracks, a little shocked.

She didn't know what had suddenly made her think of that night now, all these months later, as she carried a vase of dead tulips from her dining room into her kitchen.

Should she tell the police about that night? When the police interviewed her she'd told them that her neighbours were a nice ordinary happily married couple. This was absolutely true and absolutely not true. There was no such thing as a nice ordinary happily married couple. But obviously the fresh-faced police detectives were far too young to get their heads around that.

It was unusual to hear any noise at all from the Delaneys' house. Of course, years ago, when all those giant children still lived at home, the Delaneys' had been the noisiest house on the street. Once, Caro had phoned Joy because she'd heard a kind

334

of maniacal screaming as if people were being murdered, but it turned out they were just playing a board game that got out of hand. They were very competitive people. When the Delaney children came over to swim in their pool, Caro's own children ended up coming inside and watching television. 'They're scary,' her daughter had said to her.

Caro studied the once bright yellow heads of her tulips, slumped over the side of the vase, as if overcome with despair.

When she'd looked over at the Delaneys' house that night she had been reassured to see the familiar figures of Logan and Brooke under the porchlight at their parents' front door. She'd hurried back inside before they caught sight of her and felt embarrassed about their parents arguing loudly enough for the whole street to hear.

She'd assumed it was just an argument. Caro knew retirement could be stressful. No routine. Just the two of you stuck in your home, stuck in your aging bodies. An argument over a damp towel left on the bed could last for days and then it often turned out that the argument was not about the damp towel at all but about something hurtful that was said thirty years ago and your feelings about your in-laws.

The newspaper articles were full of innuendo. 'There was no history of domestic violence.' *Up until now.* That was the implication.

Had Joy been in need of a friend and Caro hadn't been there for her the way Joy had always been there for Caro?

Caro's son, Jacob, who had come over to mow the lawn, was chatting right now to a young female journalist from the local paper, who was parked outside the Delaneys' house.

'I'll see what I can find out,' he'd promised Caro.

Caro bet that if Joy had been young and beautiful the street would have been crawling with reporters.

Joy *had* been so young and beautiful when Caro moved in across the road from the Delaneys all those years ago. She could remember when she first laid eyes on her neighbours. She was unpacking boxes in her front room when she heard a commotion and pulled back her curtain to see a family milling about, right there on the street. (The Delaneys always treated the cul-de-sac as if it were their own personal property.) A gigantic man, who of course turned out to be Stan, was talking to a young woman wearing very short shorts, her long hair in a ponytail. A fat baby bounced and laughed on her hip, while three older children played tip like it was the Olympics. Caro actually thought Joy was their teenage babysitter until Stan kissed her. Caro could still remember the way he pulled on her ponytail so her head tipped back as he kissed her. It had seemed stunningly erotic to Caro, a man kissing his wife like that right there in the middle of the street, but maybe she'd misread the signs of an abusive relationship. Caro had secretly rather enjoyed *Fifty Shades of Grey*, but her daughter had explained that the book was about an abusive relationship and Caro had felt foolish because her daughter, who had struggled to learn to read, now had a degree in English literature so she was right and Caro was wrong and she should not have enjoyed that book, how embarrassing.

The past could look very different depending on where you stood to look at it. The fat baby bouncing on Joy's hip turned out to be Brooke, who was now treating Caro's sciatica.

'Stop that!' snapped Caro as the cat clawed at her pants leg. Otis stalked off, deeply offended. No doubt he would reappear in a while with a random piece of clothing in his mouth. Apparently cats stole laundry for attention. Caro remembered how she and Joy had laughed when Caro returned the lacy underwire bra Otis had stolen from her clothes line.

'That's a very sexy bra, Joy,' Caro had said, and Joy retorted, 'Well, you know, I'm a very sexy woman, Caro.'

How could Caro live here without Joy across the road? How could she finish their memoir-writing course? How could she cope with the annual neighbourhood street party?

'They've found a body,' said Jacob from behind her.

The vase of tulips slipped straight from Caro's hands and shattered on the kitchen floor.

chapter forty-three

'We have reports that a body has been found in bushland in Sydney's north,' said the radio newsreader.

Sulin Ho slammed on the brakes of her car. A car behind her tooted furiously.

'Police are treating the death as suspicious after a bushwalker made the gruesome discovery late yesterday.'

Sulin raised her hand in apology to the person behind her, pulled over and put on her hazard lights.

'A crime scene has been established and forensic officers are collecting evidence. There is no further information available at this stage.'

'That's very sad news just breaking there,' said the shock jock in the overly ponderous tone he used to indicate he was being serious now, folks, so listen up. 'Obviously we're all wondering and worrying if it's that poor missing grandma, and no-one knows if that's the case, but either way, that's very sad news for some poor family.'

'She's not a grandma, you stupid egg!' Sulin shouted at the radio, and then she burst into tears because if it was Joy's body, she would never get to be one.

chapter forty-four

Last October

Logan was the first to arrive for the 'family meeting' called by their father to discuss Savannah. He could see Brooke's car pulling up behind him in his rear-vision mirror.

'We all need to be on the same page,' Stan had said on the phone, when he called just as Logan was leaving Dave's apartment, full of good pizza and information. His dad had sounded upset, but he was also clearly in resolute crisis mode. The Man of the House was going to fix this. (How did one develop Man of the House confidence? Did it just arrive automatically with fatherhood?)

Logan waited for Brooke to get out of the car, which she did with uncharacteristic haste. 'Savannah didn't just come here randomly,' she said, slamming her door behind her.

'I know,' said Logan. 'I was just at her ex-boyfriend's apartment. She's got some tennis connection.'

'You were? You talked to the boyfriend? What did you find out?' She didn't wait for an answer. She was speaking in a rapid, ragged fashion. She sounded like Amy. 'This is all so strange. When Dad called I'd literally just had this memory, I was looking at these bananas that Ines – but anyway, what about

Troy? He *believed* Dad would make a move on Savannah! That's so disgusting. She's younger than me.'

They walked towards their parents' front door. Logan could hear Caro from across the street pulling her bins out.

'She probably made it sound believable,' said Logan. He wasn't going to bother giving Troy a hard time about falling for Savannah's story.

Brooke knocked on the door while Logan turned back to look over his shoulder. 'Do you think I should go offer to help Caro with her —'

'*Stop this, stop this, stop this!*'

They both startled. It was their father's voice, raised in a kind of terrified fury that Logan wasn't sure he'd heard before.

Brooke had her key out of her bag first. She opened the front door with swift efficiency, shouting to their parents, 'Mum! Dad!'

'In here!' called Joy from Amy's old bedroom.

By the time Logan and Brooke crowded into the bedroom the yelling had stopped and no-one was saying a word.

Logan's father and Savannah stood opposite each other, his mother in the middle of them: her classic position of stopping an argument between two siblings. She had one hand on Stan's chest, the other on Savannah's shoulder. Logan's dad was breathing rapidly and furiously as if he'd just lost a long rally, while their mother had that look of controlled impatience she used to get when her children fought and she didn't have time to properly lose her temper because she had things to do.

Only Savannah looked serene. A mildly amused smile twitched her lips. She stepped away from Joy and ran her hands down her arms, pulling her sleeves smooth.

'Look who's here,' she said. 'Are you all expecting dinner? I think we can stretch it.'

'What's going on?' said Brooke.

'Yes, what *is* going on?' It was Troy, who had sauntered in through the front door they'd left open. He looked like a cocktail party guest, not a scam victim. Maybe Logan would give him a hard time after all.

'She's Harry Haddad's sister,' said Stan.

There was a pause as they all took that in.

'I didn't know there was a sister,' said Logan blankly.

'Wait, *was* there a sister?' asked Brooke.

'It's a lie,' scoffed Troy. 'It's just another lie.'

'We're pretty sure it's true, but you're right, it's hard to see for the lies.' Logan's dad plonked himself down on Amy's old bed.

'Maybe we should all go into the living room and sit down,' said Joy. 'Talk this out.'

Savannah said, 'I could heat up some –'

'Enough!' shouted Joy. Logan's mother was a stick of dynamite with a very long fuse, but then all of a sudden, *kaboom*. 'You can't make these terrible accusations and then suddenly *cook* for us. What's wrong with you? You're lying! You *know* you're lying! And if you hate us so much, why do you keep *feeding* us? I don't understand why you're doing it!' Her arms windmilled. She stamped her foot. Her children all took automatic steps backward. 'Why? We don't even remember you!'

'I remember all of you,' said Savannah. She dropped her chin and fiddled with the heavy green pendant at her neck. 'I only came to this house once. My mother and I were picking up Harry from his lesson. Normally my dad did that. Tennis was his domain.' Logan got the feeling she was unconsciously parroting someone from her past: Tennis was *his* domain.

'But my dad couldn't get his car to start. So Mum and I picked Harry up. Mum stayed in the car. She wanted nothing to do with Harry's tennis. She thought tennis was boring.'

Logan saw both his parents flinch at the casual denigration of the greatest sport in the world.

'I remember everything about that day,' said Savannah. She lifted her head. 'You shouted at me that day too, Joy. Just like you did then.'

Logan's mother recoiled. 'What? Why would I have shouted at you?'

'You were wearing a denim skirt and a paisley shirt with short puffed sleeves and you had earrings like feathers that matched the red in the shirt. You looked very pretty.'

Logan saw his mother's face change. 'Do you mean you were the child who tried to come into the house? Through the laundry?'

'You're the kid who went through my schoolbag,' interrupted Brooke.

'Yes.' Savannah turned to Brooke. 'You shouted at me too. That same day.'

'Well, you were stealing my banana,' said Brooke defensively.

'I was starving,' said Savannah.

'Still, that didn't give you the right to –'

'You don't get it,' said Savannah. 'I was *literally* starving.'

Her tightly clenched tone stilled them all. A space seemed to open up around her.

'What do you mean?' faltered Joy.

'Just that.'

'But I don't understand,' said Joy. 'You couldn't have been starving. I know for a fact your brother ate well. He had to, to play at that level.'

'My brother lived with my father,' said Savannah. 'I lived with my mother. Harry ate rib eye steak and potatoes every day. If he was going to play at Wimbledon, then I was going to perform with the Royal Ballet. That's what my mother said. My brother needed to be strong, I needed to be *ethereal*.'

Her lip lifted on the word 'ethereal'.

'But . . . what about your father?' asked Joy. 'Didn't you tell him you were . . . hungry?'

'I tried,' said Savannah. 'I tried to tell my brother, too. But my mother told them I was making it up. Being dramatic. I only went to my father's place one night a week. It had to be a week-night because on the weekend Harry had his *tennis commitments*.'

She said 'tennis commitments' the way someone gives the name of their ex's new partner.

'I used to *stuff* myself on that one night a week at my father's house. That's where I perfected my binge-eating skills.' She gave a ghoulish kind of grin. 'Anyhoo.'

'Oh, Savannah.' Joy dragged her fingertips down her cheeks. All that red-hot anger seemed to have left her as suddenly as it arrived. She looked sad and exhausted and old, and Logan remembered the feeling of disbelief, as though he were witnessing a natural disaster, when his mother's legs gave way on Father's Day. He moved closer. This time he'd be ready.

Joy said, 'All I remember is that you and your mother lived in South Australia.'

'We moved there a year after Harry's first lesson with you,' said Savannah. A chatty dinner party guest quickly summing up her life story. 'I didn't see my dad and brother anymore. It was like they forgot I existed. Dad sent money. I was just an annoying bill he had to pay. Like the electricity.'

'I'm so sorry.' Joy's hands fluttered helplessly.

'Oh, no, it's *fine*,' said Savannah, as if Joy had apologised for cutting in front of her in a queue. 'I mean, there *were* some really bad years in Adelaide . . .' She stopped. No longer the chatty guest.

She breathed deeply, widened her shoulders, pushed them down and back, as if waiting for the music to begin.

She said, 'But then I gave up ballet. Best in the neighbourhood, one of the best in the state, but I was never an *extraordinary* dancer, the way Harry was an extraordinary tennis player. When my mother finally realised I'd never be as good at ballet as Harry was at tennis, she lost interest. So no more food deprivation – hooray!'

Logan and Brooke exchanged glances. He could see his own doubt reflected on her face. Was any of this bizarre story even true?

Logan knew that Savannah had taken the story she'd told him

from that documentary. He knew that she'd lied to Troy about his father. So wasn't it possible she'd also taken this story of a starving child in their midst from somewhere else? Did it even matter now? The facts kept slithering from his grasp. Trying to see Savannah was like trying to catch a true reflection in a funhouse maze of mirrors. The cadences of her voice, her gestures, her stance: he saw now how constantly she merged and morphed into different kinds of people. One moment she was a genteel middle-aged lady and the next she was a rough, tough-talking teen.

Logan tried to take control with the facts he'd gathered, the facts he knew to be true. 'Savannah, I went to see your boyfriend. Dave. That story you told about him hitting you. It never happened.'

Savannah lifted her chin. 'Well, he would say that, wouldn't he?'

'You lied to us,' insisted Logan. He needed her to confirm the truth of this so he could find his footing and they could move forward. 'I *know* it's a lie.'

'No, you don't,' said Savannah pleasantly.

'Nah, mate, it was out,' Savannah's brother used to say, so innocently and convincingly, so *calmly*, when questioned on one of his calls. Harry Haddad was a natural on the court, and also a natural cheat. His flagrant cheating had enraged Troy to the point of lunacy whereas it baffled and unbalanced Logan. He saw the ball go in, yet Harry said it was out. That called everything into question: right and wrong, the laws of physics.

Lying clearly ran in the family.

Stan met Logan's eyes and lifted his hands hopelessly. Logan didn't think he'd ever seen his father so defenceless, even when he'd been in the hospital for his knee.

'You were there that day too, Logan.' Savannah looked at him coolly and his heart lurched.

'I never met you,' said Logan. He was one hundred per cent confident of this.

'You threw your racquet at me,' said Savannah. 'Like I was a stray dog.'

'I did not,' said Logan. 'Why would I do that?'

Troy was the racquet-thrower. Yet another lie.

'I would never —'

He stopped. He saw himself walking off the court the day he first lost against Troy, the same day his father told him to watch Harry's kick serve, the day he understood that if he could lose against his younger brother, and if there were players in the world like Harry, there was probably not much point in continuing, although he did, for another five years.

'Wait a minute, I wasn't throwing it *at* you,' he told her weakly. He'd lost the advantage. He'd always felt bad about that little girl jumping clear of his racquet.

'So you do remember me,' said Savannah sweetly.

She had her brother's ability to play offensively, pushing his opponent further and further back.

She turned her attention to Troy. 'What about you, Troy? Do *you* remember me?'

'I don't care if I did meet you,' said Troy flatly.

'Someone left the back sliding door open,' said Savannah dreamily.

It would have been Logan. He was forever in trouble for not closing that sliding door properly because it jammed.

'I walked in through your back door and went into the kitchen,' said Savannah. 'I thought maybe just . . . if I could just get a glass of milk. Anything. I was so hungry. I hadn't eaten anything for twenty-four hours. I was only nine. I felt so sick and dizzy. All I could think about was food. I was obsessed with food, and there was food everywhere, there were people *eating*, everywhere, all around me, walking down the street eating ice-creams, sitting at a bus stop eating pies, stuffing food into their mouths, but I had no money. *I couldn't get any food.*'

Logan's mother put a hand over her mouth. 'Oh my goodness, Savannah.'

Please let this be someone else's story, thought Logan, because his family were not bad people. They would have fed a hungry child. They sponsored hungry children on the other side of the world. 'Think of the poor starving children in Africa,' their mother used to say if they didn't like their vegetables, and then Amy would become completely inconsolable, sobbing for the poor starving children in Africa, unable to eat, and Logan's dad would sigh and reach over to stab at her broccoli with his fork.

Savannah said to Troy, 'You chased me out of the kitchen like I was a beggar. You'd just got out of the shower. You were all wet, you had a blue bath towel around your waist. You called me a *vulture*.' Her lip lifted again on the word 'vulture'.

'If I said that, I was right, because that's exactly what you are, a vulture,' said Troy. He'd never been a defensive player. When attacked he attacked back, twice as hard. 'You just stole a lot of money from me.'

'I didn't steal anything,' said Savannah. 'You gave me that money of your own free will.'

'Under false pretences!'

'What'd I do, Savannah?' said Logan's father. 'What's my role?'

'Nothing,' said Savannah. 'You looked right through me. All you saw was Harry. I didn't even exist to you because I didn't play tennis.'

'So this is about revenge, then?' said Troy. 'Because our father made your brother a tennis star? Because none of us would give you food? But why didn't you just, I don't know, *ask*?'

'She did ask,' said Amy from the doorway. 'She came into the dining room and asked me to make her a sandwich.'

Then she did the strangest thing, the thing that only Amy would do, would even think to do.

She walked directly to Savannah and threw her arms around her.

'I'm sorry,' she said. 'I'm so sorry we were all so awful to you that day. I'm sorry we didn't help that hungry little girl. We should have helped you.'

Savannah stood stiffly for a moment, her arms by her side,

and then she rested her forehead against Amy's chest, like a child being comforted by her mother.

'It was a pretty bad day,' she said, her voice muffled.

'Oh my goodness, that is awful, that is really awful.' Joy pressed her fingertips together in a steeple over her nose. Brooke turned away, her hand to her forehead. Troy looked at the ceiling and their father looked at the floor. A strange young man in a very white t-shirt cleared his throat by the door. He met Logan's eye and held out his hand.

He said quietly, 'Simon Barrington. Amy's new boyfriend.'

'He is not,' said Amy over Savannah's head, but Logan saw the ghost of a smile.

Their father stood, his arms hanging heavily by his sides. 'I want her out of my home.' He gestured with his chin at Savannah. 'Now.'

'Dad,' said Amy. 'We were awful to her.'

Savannah took a step away from Amy. 'It's fine.'

'I really don't *care* if we didn't make you a frigging *sandwich* one very bad day in your very bad childhood,' said Stan. He jabbed his finger in her face. 'Lots of people have bad childhoods. They get on with it.'

'*Dad*,' said Amy. 'Don't talk like that! Stop it!'

Stan ignored her. 'If you're so jealous of your brother's success, go scam *him*, go tell lies about him, go throw rocks through *his* window. We didn't make any money out of him! Your family did nothing for us. Your father dumped us the moment Harry —'

'But it wasn't my father's decision for Harry to leave Delaneys,' interrupted Savannah. Logan caught sight of his mother's face, haggard with fear.

His stomach lurched.

Savannah stood, as if beneath a spotlight, her heels together, her toes splayed.

All this time she'd had a grenade in her pocket. Finally she threw it.

'That was your wife's decision.'

chapter forty-five

Now

'Guess what I finally got us,' said Christina. She slapped her phone triumphantly back down on her thigh.

She and Ethan were driving towards the bushland trail where the body had been found. A ten-minute drive at most from where Joy and Stan Delaney lived. All the pieces were falling and slotting into place.

'What?' asked Ethan.

'The motive.'

chapter forty-six

Last October

Stan didn't gasp or swear at Savannah's revelation. He didn't ask for clarification or proof, or call her a liar. He seemed to know instantly that this time Savannah was telling the truth. Perhaps he'd always suspected, although he had never once asked or accused Joy.

He said, 'Excuse me,' to Amy's besotted young man, who had been hovering in the doorway of her old bedroom, watching these dramas unfold, and who obediently stepped aside to allow Stan to make his silent, stately departure.

They heard the front door shut.

It was strange how very familiar it felt to Joy after all these decades; the wheel of time spun smoothly back and her children were still her children, still looking to her to explain their father's actions, to make them normal and acceptable. She could feel all those old phrases springing automatically to her lips. *Don't worry. He'll be back. You know how he is. When your dad gets angry and upset he needs to get away and clear his head. It's nothing to get upset about. Let's go have ice-cream!*

'Is it true, Mum?' Logan spoke first. 'Did you tell them to leave?'

'Oh,' said Joy distractedly. She was thinking about Stan. It was all very well when he was thirty and forty and even fifty but he was too old to walk dramatically off into the night now he was seventy. He had medication to take. 'Yes, well, that part actually is true. Don't worry, he'll get over it, but did any of you park in the driveway? Your father won't be able to get his car out.' It was a cool night. He wasn't dressed warmly enough. He was wearing jeans and slippers.

'Why would you do that to Dad?' Brooke asked Joy. Her eyes burned with the betrayal of her beloved father. 'Dad was the one who discovered Harry. He should have been his coach. How could you take that away from him?'

'Who would have coached *you*? If your dad was travelling the international circuit with Harry?'

'You would have coached us,' said Brooke uncertainly.

'When? How?' If her children ever had children they might at least have an inkling of how Joy had staggered beneath the weight of her responsibilities through those difficult years.

'But it was Dad's *dream*,' said Brooke. 'You took away his dream.'

'What about your dreams?' Joy held out her hands to indicate all four of her children.

'It didn't matter, we were never going to make it anyway,' said Brooke.

'But you didn't *know* that back then!' cried Joy. 'This is what you all forget. You all wanted it. You like to pretend you were doing it for us, but *you damn well were not.*' The fury rose within her chest. She knew her children better than they knew themselves and she saw their childhoods so much more clearly than they could. 'You all wanted it. I know you did. The *sacrifices* you all made.'

Her voice broke. She remembered the weeping blisters on Amy's right palm ('It's like she's been doing *manual labour*!' said Joy's mother, disgusted); the sad complicated resignation on Logan's face when he told Hien he'd have to miss his eighteenth

349

birthday party because he'd be away competing in a tournament in Alice Springs; Troy at twelve, his cheek cushioned on the placemat at the dinner table where he'd fallen asleep while he waited for dessert; Brooke, tiny and determined on the court in her pyjamas and sneakers, getting in some practice before breakfast.

The pain, the exhaustion, the relentless travel; the parties and dances and school events they all missed: what if her children had endured all that and then seen their father by another player's side as he won the grand slam titles they'd all dreamed of winning?

It would have been unendurable.

Back then it was a choice between her children's happiness and her husband's dream, and she was a mother, so there was no choice, not really. She chose her children.

Remembering the day she'd done it was like remembering the day she'd committed a crime, a tiny crime without a weapon, as fast and simple as extinguishing the flame of a candle between her thumb and her finger: a fierce tingle of pain instantly gone.

She'd picked up the phone when no-one was at home and called Harry's dad, Elias Haddad. Elias was betting everything on his son's tennis. He'd given up his job so he could be his manager. He was living on his savings.

Harry's mother and sister did not figure in Joy's thinking back then. They'd never existed for her.

'Elias, I need to tell you something in strictest confidence, something my husband would never tell you,' she'd said, and she spoke fast, without letting him speak, her eyes on a funny photo that sat on her desk of her sons, nose to nose, funny because they were glowering at each other like two boxers.

She'd always got on well with Elias. He was chatty and charming in that European way. She'd been able to convince him not to call the police when Troy attacked Harry. She said it would serve no purpose and take up Harry's training time. She apologised profusely on Troy's behalf. She pretended it was about jealousy and he seemed to accept that.

Now she said, 'If you and Harry are serious about his tennis career, and I know you are, you need to leave Delaneys.'

'*Leave* you guys?' he said, and the surprise and alarm in his voice pulled her up short, but she barrelled on.

'Yes, leave. Move to Melbourne. I'm going to give you the name of someone at Tennis Australia. Call her as soon as you put down the phone. She's seen Harry play. He'll get noticed. He'll get the wildcard entries at the Open. He'll be anointed. He'll become one of the chosen ones. It's all about the politics, Elias.'

She and Stan had always told the children there were no such thing as the 'chosen ones', there were no favourites on the circuit, it didn't matter where you lived, or who you knew or who your parents knew, all that mattered was how you played – but there were politics in tennis. There were politics in everything.

'More importantly, he'll get the kind of coaching he needs, the kind we can't give him. We'd love to keep him, of course we would, and please don't mention it to Stan, because I'm afraid my husband can't be objective about this. He wants what's best for Harry, but he also wants what's best for himself, and that's keeping Harry. But the truth is, Delaneys is holding him back, Elias, and I can't sit here and let that happen to your son. It's time to take the next step.'

She knew that Elias would instinctively understand who to charm and when, just as his son was able to strategise so brilliantly on the court. Elias might even have come to the decision to move Harry on from Delaneys himself if she hadn't suggested it.

Elias did everything Joy told him to do and he played it perfectly. He never said a word to Stan about Joy's betrayal. He winked at Joy whenever he saw her, as if they'd enjoyed a secret tryst. It made her feel as if she *had* slept with him.

She later learned that Elias was a ladies' man who often juggled multiple beautiful women, so keeping secrets came easily to him.

For a long time she'd assumed Stan would discover the truth, and she'd been ready for it, ready to defend herself, but he never did, and after a while she let her guilt (not regret, she never once regretted it) drift gently into nothingness like the tiny black curl of smoke from that snuffed candle.

She'd worried that Harry's memoir might reveal her secret. It had never occurred to her that her house guest, who had pretended so convincingly that she didn't even recognise Harry's name, would reveal it.

'How did you know this?' she said to Savannah.

'My mother told me,' said Savannah. 'Dad couldn't send any child support money for about six months. He said it cost a lot to relocate to Melbourne, and my mother said, "Why are you doing that?" And he said, "Joy Delaney said it was the right thing to do." I remember it word for word. Mum had to get a second job to help pay for my ballet lessons.'

'"Joy Delaney said it was the right thing to do",' repeated Amy. 'Wow, Mum. That's . . .' She shook her head. 'Wow.'

After all these years, it was not Stan but their daughter looking at her with accusing eyes. She wanted to shout, *But I did it for you!* She tried to speak reasonably but she couldn't keep the emotion out of her voice. 'I was *not* going to let you watch your father take some other kid to the top!'

'Better some other kid than no-one at all,' said Logan. 'Harry would have won more grand slam titles by now if he'd stayed with Dad. He's never won a French Open title.'

'Harry never had the patience for clay,' said Joy querulously.

'Dad would have *given* him the patience. He's never been as consistent as he should have been,' said Logan. 'He needed Dad.'

'*You* needed him,' said Joy. 'You all needed him.'

'No,' said Logan. 'I didn't.'

God almighty, she couldn't make him see. He was looking at this from the perspective of the thirty-seven-year-old man who had left his tennis career behind, not the seventeen-year-old boy who still saw tennis in his future.

'Fine then, *I* needed him,' said Joy. 'I had four children, all playing competitive tennis, and a business to run. I couldn't do it on my own. You must remember what it was like.'

But she could see by their faces that they were blissfully oblivious to what it had been like.

She thought of a night when Troy had been playing all the way out at Homebush in a tournament that ran so far behind schedule he didn't even get onto the court until midnight. Stan was with Troy, Joy was at home with the other kids. Logan was worryingly sick with a temperature. She didn't sleep that night. She baked thirty cupcakes for Brooke's birthday the next day in between tending to Logan, she did three loads of laundry, she did the accounts and she did Troy's history assignment on the Great Wall of China. She got seven out of ten for the assignment (she was still furious about that; she'd deserved a nine). When she thought of that long night, it was like remembering an extraordinarily tough match where she'd prevailed. Except there was no trophy or applause. The only recognition you got for surviving a night like that came from other mothers. Only they understood the epic nature of your trivial achievements.

What had been the point of it all?

And yet, how could she have done any of it differently?

When it came to tennis at the level her children played, you were either in or you were out, and *they* wanted in. It would have been easier if they'd all been a little less talented, a little less driven, if they'd reached number one in the local district but gone no further.

'Anyway, might I remind you that you all hated Harry Haddad,' said Joy. 'With a passion.' She glanced at Savannah, who had closed the lid of the wooden chest that contained all her secrets and was now sitting on top of it, as if she were waiting for a bus. 'Sorry, Savannah, but they did hate your brother.'

'Oh, that's okay, I hated him too,' said Savannah. 'For years, whenever his face came on the television, I screamed.'

'You *literally* screamed?' said Amy with interest.

'I literally screamed,' said Savannah.

'I didn't hate Harry,' said Logan. 'I envied him, but I never hated him. I would have liked to have seen Dad keep coaching him.'

'That's what you think now, Logan,' said Joy impatiently. 'But when you were a teenager you thought very differently.'

'*I* hated him,' said Troy. He leaned against the wall, his head perilously close to the sharp corner of the framed print of a crying mermaid that had always hung in Amy's room, which Joy found depressing but Amy loved. Troy blazed rage and venom straight at Savannah. 'I think you did the right thing, Mum, because obviously these charming people have no problem cheating, lying, scamming –'

'Okay, that's enough now,' said Joy.

'What? We need to show good manners to *her*?'

Troy had such passionate yet fluid convictions about justice and morality. His teenage drug-dealing empire was perfectly acceptable but Savannah's scamming him for money was not; cheating at tennis was an unforgivable sin, but then he'd gone right ahead and cheated on his lovely wife.

'Look, if you're going to get all worked up about it, I'll transfer the money back to you,' said Savannah to Troy. 'I just needed some cash to re-establish myself.' She sounded as if she were talking to a sibling about a loan she hadn't repaid. Was this her way of admitting that she'd lied to Troy when she made those dreadful accusations about Stan? What if Troy had actually refused to pay up? What would she have done next?

Had Savannah understood the power of Joy's secret she'd just shared? Would *Joy* have paid up if she'd attempted to blackmail *her?* Possibly.

Joy's head spun. She couldn't align Savannah the sly black-mailer with the Savannah who had nursed Joy so tenderly when she came home from the hospital.

'*Keep* it,' said Troy viciously. 'We just want you out of our lives.'

'That was my intention,' said Savannah. She stood and picked up her handbag, the new one Joy had bought for her with the crossover strap. 'I mean, to get out of your lives. This was only ever temporary.'

She sounded like she was trying not to cry and Joy knew perfectly well that it could be fake emotion, or someone else's emotion she was channelling for her own purposes, but her heart still broke for her.

Only ever temporary. Was that the way this child lived her whole life? This child who had been starving in their midst and they'd shouted at her, ignored her, refused to help her. Joy remembered how she'd slammed the laundry door with her foot. She couldn't see the child's face in her memory, just the outline of a little girl, her features a blur, but she could certainly remember the savagery with which she'd slammed the door in a child's face.

They hadn't known she was hungry. How could they have known? But Joy prided herself on being observant. She wanted to go back in time and do all the things the sort of person she thought she was would have done: feed the kid, listen to her, rescue her from her awful childhood.

'Well,' said Joy. 'You don't need to go *right* away –'

'Mum,' said Brooke. 'I think she probably does need to go right away.'

'Yep,' said Savannah. She looked at Joy's children. 'It's been a blast, guys.'

'Where will you go?' asked Amy.

'She's fine,' said Troy abruptly. 'She's got money.'

'I am fine,' said Savannah. 'I'll be back at some point to pick up my stuff.' She smiled radiantly at Joy, and now she was a dinner party guest taking her leave. 'Thank you so much for your hospitality.'

'It's been my pleasure,' said Joy automatically, but truthfully, because up until tonight it *had* been her pleasure. Her absolute pleasure.

For an excruciating moment they all held their positions, as if they were actors in a terrible theatre production and someone had forgotten their lines. Joy wouldn't have been surprised to hear an audience member cough.

'I'm very sorry,' said Savannah suddenly, her eyes bright with unshed tears. Joy would never know if they were real or fake, if she truly was or wasn't sorry, because Savannah suddenly patted the side of her handbag decisively, drew herself up, and left the room, left the house, exit stage left, just like Stan. She disappeared into the dark night from where she'd first come.

chapter forty-seven

Now

'That was the last time I saw Savannah,' said Troy Delaney.

'Did she return the money?' asked Christina.

Detective Senior Constable Christina Khoury was in what her mother would describe as a 'tetchy' mood.

She didn't have a body like she'd thought she'd had the day before. The call had come through almost immediately: *Not yours. Skeletal remains.*

This woman had died at least thirty years previously, back when Christina was a child, trying to decide whether she wanted to be a police officer or a marine biologist when she grew up, and why had she not stuck with marine biology? She could have been floating about looking at starfish right now.

Furthermore, a member of Joy Delaney's tennis club, a Fiona Reid, had just called in with the wonderful news that she'd *seen* Joy, yesterday afternoon, getting off the train at Central, looking as hale and healthy as could be, although sadly she hadn't seemed to hear her name when Fiona called out to her.

Because it wasn't *her*, you fool, thought Christina.

Meanwhile a psychic had just gone public with the news that

her feeling was that Joy was alive, but being held captive, somewhere near water, or possibly in the desert.

Christina *did* still have her motive. Joy Delaney's hairdresser, Narelle Longford, had contacted police the moment she heard about yesterday's discovery of the body, and she had shared all the information that her client had ever shared with her, including the story of a decades-old secret, revealed last year by their young house guest, who was not in fact a random stranger at all.

Stan's children had shared precisely none of this with Christina. They *knew* it made their father look bad and had chosen to say nothing up until now.

Christina studied Joy Delaney's second son, a good-looking man buffed by money and success, no doubt adored by his mother, but a man who had fallen with absurd ease for a young woman's blackmail.

She and Ethan were talking to him in his luxury apartment. The blindingly beautiful views from the huge windows were an irritation, like distractingly loud music. She found herself wanting to say, 'Can't you turn that down a notch?'

'She actually did return the money,' said Troy. 'She sent me a cheque in the post. I tore it up. Never banked it.' He shifted slightly in his chair, which looked spindly and cheap to Christina, like an office chair from the 1950s, but which was apparently something to be impressed by, according to Ethan, who had asked Troy if it was a genuine something-or-other and it *was* a genuine something-or-other. Why even bother asking? Troy was the sort of guy who took pride in overpaying for everything. Even blackmail. 'I suspect it would have bounced but I don't know that for sure.'

'Why didn't you bank it?' asked Christina.

'After she left, I started to feel sorry for her,' said Troy. He tapped a beautifully manicured thumbnail against his teeth. 'She'd obviously had a troubled childhood, and we were all cruel to her when she came to our house as a child, *unwittingly* cruel to her, but still, we were, and the more I thought about her, the more I realised how much we had in common.'

'What did you have in common?'

'Both our fathers chose Harry Haddad over us,' said Troy. He smiled wryly as if he wanted to give the impression that it didn't matter now but he couldn't quite pull it off, the childish pain still visible. 'She said something about how painful it was whenever Harry was on television, and I feel exactly the same way: I always change the channel whenever I see that guy's smug face.'

'Just to clarify: is anyone in your family in contact with Harry Haddad?' asked Christina.

'Not that I know of,' said Troy, the distaste clear on his face.

'And this Savannah is estranged from her brother? As far as you know?'

'As far as I know. I would think if she had anything to do with her brother she'd go to *him* for money.'

That didn't necessarily follow. Christina wrote down: *Interview Harry Haddad.*

It would probably tell them nothing, and celebrities took their time returning phone calls, but it was another box that needed ticking.

'So Savannah left . . . and your parents never heard from her again?'

'About a month after she left, this young couple showed up with a van and said Savannah had sent them to collect her stuff. Mum said they were "hippie types". She said they barely said a word, and they seemed terrified of Mum, so God knows what weird story Savannah fed them.'

'And that was it? No other contact from her?'

'As far as I know,' said Troy. His knees jiggled. He pressed his hands to his thighs to still them, as if they belonged to someone else.

'I assume there must have been some fallout after this revelation about what your mother had done. Presumably your father felt . . .' She paused, in the hope that he might fill in the word. He said nothing so she gave him some options. 'Angry? Hurt?'

Troy didn't pick a word. He said carefully, 'Possibly.'

'That moment he first heard,' said Christina. 'What did he do? Did he lose his temper? Shout? Swear?'

'My father never shouts when he is truly angry,' said Troy. 'He left. He just walked off. That is his . . . ah, coping mechanism, I guess.'

'Where did he go?'

'Well, this time he didn't get very far. He was walking. About ten minutes from the house. He fell. A pothole. He dislocated his kneecap. Tore his meniscus. Fortunately someone we knew was driving by and drove him home. He already had problem knees so that . . . was pretty bad.'

'No more tennis?' asked Ethan.

'He was told no tennis for at least six months.' Troy unconsciously put one hand to his own knee. 'Although he always defies expectations.'

'That must have upset him,' said Christina.

'Tennis is his life,' said Troy, with feeling.

'So no more tennis for your mother either, then,' said Christina, thinking of how often people had gone on about the wondrousness of the Delaneys' marriage because they played doubles.

'Well, actually, my mother started playing in a singles comp,' said Troy.

'Without your father,' said Christina.

'My mother was a top-ranked singles player when she was a teenager,' said Troy obliviously. He seemed to be missing the symbolism. 'She competed in her first Australian nationals when she was only fourteen, she beat Margaret —'

'Got it, got it,' said Christina, before she heard the woman's full CV. 'So your mother is out playing tennis while your father is stuck at home doing nothing, unable to play the sport he loves, feeling betrayed by his wife: I would assume it wasn't exactly a happy household.'

'I guess not,' said Troy. 'I don't know, I was busy with my own life.' He looked up at the ceiling for a moment and then back at Christina. 'I thought everything had gone back to normal, although I will admit –'

He stopped and she saw him swallow: an involuntary, convulsive swallow.

'On Christmas Day, I did think, it kind of shocked me, that I would think this –'

He stopped again, and Christina gritted her teeth. Up until now he'd been answering her questions in a comfortable, urbane manner, like a successful man being interviewed for a magazine profile, but now his veneer had slipped. She wanted to grab him by his stylish linen shirt and yell, *Just tell me! Your dad did it! We all know he did it!*

His hands were locked as if in prayer. 'For the first time in my life I thought . . .'

He looked at her pleadingly, as if he needed exoneration.

'What did you think?' Christina weighted her voice with authority.

'That my parents might truly hate each other.' He turned his gaze back to his shiny harbour view. 'It was mutual, by the way. The hatred was mutual.'

chapter forty-eight

'I told the police what happened on Christmas Day.'

'What do you mean? Nothing happened on Christmas Day.'

'Oh, come on, Brooke.'

'Nothing *relevant* happened.'

Jacob Azinovic could hear voices, loud and clear, as he walked around the side of the Delaney house carrying a slow-cooked lamb casserole.

'I need you to take this over to Stan Delaney for me,' his mother had said when he came over to check out the mysterious 'beeping' sound her car had been making, although it was suspiciously silent when Jacob drove it.

'Why do I have to take it over?' protested Jacob. This was the real reason he'd been summoned: to walk over the road and deliver a casserole.

'Jacob,' said Caro. 'It's possible that man murdered his wife.'

'Then why are you cooking for him?'

'Innocent until proven guilty,' said Caro. 'Stan has been very nice to me since your father died. Joy would expect me to send over a meal.'

'Not if Stan killed her, she wouldn't,' said Jacob, but his mother's eyes had welled with tears, so he'd sighed and picked up the baking dish and headed out the door.

'I overcooked it,' his mother called out, as he left. 'Just in case.'

No-one answered when he knocked on the Delaneys' front door but he could see that the driveway was filled with cars, so he'd come around the side of the house.

All four Delaney children were there, sitting at a table on the back veranda, talking animatedly and loudly. Jacob felt that familiar sense of awed trepidation he used to feel when he'd seen them together as children. There was a kind of glamorous violence to the Delaney siblings. At any moment a monumental battle could erupt.

'They know all about Savannah now,' said Troy. His luxuriant dark curly hair looked like he'd been running his fingers through it. Troy was the first boy Jacob had ever loved. His first experience of a flirtatious straight boy. 'They know what Mum and Dad were arguing about now. They know Dad has a motive.'

Jacob cleared his throat to make his presence known and shifted the casserole. It was hot against his forearms.

'Don't use the word "motive",' said Brooke. 'It is not a motive! Did *you* tell them about Savannah? I thought we'd agreed not to mention the Harry Haddad connection at all.'

'I never agreed to anything, but it wasn't me. It was Mum's hairdresser,' said Troy. 'They're trying to get in touch with Harry.'

'I don't see what Harry could tell them,' said Logan. He rubbed his eyes with his knuckles. 'Savannah was estranged from him.'

'Did you think it was Mum?' asked Amy. She spoke in a dreamy kind of voice. 'When you heard about the body on the news?'

Oh God, this was an awful conversation to overhear. Still no-one noticed Jacob.

'Hi, guys,' he said, with a crack in his voice. Not nearly loud enough. He'd forgotten how you had to up your volume when all the Delaneys were together.

'No, I did not think it was her,' said Logan. 'Not for a minute. She's fine.'

'It's too long now,' said Troy. 'She's been gone too long. We need to forget the whole "Mum is making a point" theory.'

'All we can do is support Dad,' said Brooke.

'Not if he murdered our mother, we can't,' said Troy.

Brooke said, 'Shhhh!' She pointed at the back door of the house. Presumably Stan was inside. 'Don't say things like that. People can *tell* you have suspicions, or doubts, or whatever the hell you've got. They're analysing our body language online. When we had the media conference you and Amy stepped away from Dad. It looked bad.'

'I was not stepping away from Dad,' said Amy. 'I felt dizzy. I thought I was going to faint.'

'If you're so worried about *optics*, maybe you should have got Dad to join the search party,' said Troy to Brooke.

'Dad thought it was a waste of time,' said Brooke. 'He said there wasn't a snowflake's chance in hell Mum would have ridden in the reserve, because she wrote to the council saying it was the wrong place for a bike track and she never forgave them for not listening to her.'

'Mum does get offended when the council don't listen to her recommendations,' commented Amy.

'Do you even *care* about Mum?' Troy suddenly turned on Brooke, and Jacob flinched at the fury on his face. 'Are you even *worried*?'

'Of course she cares,' said Amy. 'Don't be so mean to her.'

'I'm *frantic* about Mum.' Brooke spoke through clenched teeth at her brother. She didn't seem at all intimidated by Troy's fury.

'It seems like you're more worried about setting Dad up with a fucking lawyer!'

'It's just in case,' said Logan to Troy. 'Dad doesn't even want a lawyer.'

'In case *what*?' cried Troy. 'In case he's guilty of murder?'

Jacob was frozen on the spot, his hands slippery under the baking dish.

'She's my mother too,' hissed Brooke. She slammed her fist so hard on the table that it rocked and Logan had to catch the side to stop it falling. 'You live half your life in America and don't even call her for weeks on end!'

'I call her all the time!'

'You do not!'

'Well, the truth is *none* of us had called her lately,' murmured Amy at the same time as Logan sighed heavily and said, 'This is getting us nowhere.'

Troy stood up abruptly. He did a double-take when he saw Jacob standing on the lawn like a loon. 'Hi, Jacob.'

'Sorry,' said Jacob idiotically. 'I didn't mean to interrupt. Mum asked me to bring this casserole for your dad.' He held it out as proof and the glass lid wobbled alarmingly. *My mother overcooked it on the off-chance your dad is a murderer.*

'Whoa.' Troy stepped off the veranda and grabbed the baking dish from him. 'That's really nice of your mum, tell her thank you.'

'I'll get Dad for you,' said Amy. 'We're all just waiting for him to clean up. He's inside, uh, painting the bathroom.'

'Like you do,' said Troy. He held the baking dish easily under one arm like a football. 'When your wife is missing. Great time to renovate.'

'Jesus, Troy,' said Logan under his breath.

'Don't disturb your dad. I'll leave you to it.' Jacob backed away fast. 'I hope – I hope you get good news soon.' He held up two tightly crossed fingers. Like a fool.

The four Delaney siblings looked back at him gravely. They did not look like people expecting good news anytime soon. They looked like people waiting for a funeral to start.

As he walked back to his mother's place he wondered what could have happened last Christmas that was either relevant or irrelevant to the police.

He'd been here visiting his mother at Christmas. He had not heard or seen anything untoward from across the road.

His thoughts turned to a long-ago Christmas Day, when he was around ten or eleven and he somehow ended up at the Delaneys' place, umpiring a late-afternoon doubles match between the four siblings, who had all received various types of tennis gear for Christmas that they wanted to try out.

'Don't let my awful children take advantage of you, Jacob!' Joy had called out, but Jacob loved umpiring the Delaney matches. He knew all the rules because his dad was a sports nut, and so Jacob was a sports nut too. He felt as powerful as God up there on the high umpire's chair, with a bird's-eye view, able to see every mistake. He put on a loud, grave voice, imitating the umpires on TV, and the Delaneys didn't even make fun of him. They appreciated the effort.

It was Logan and Brooke playing Troy and Amy, and at that time they were evenly matched, although they shouldn't have been, because Brooke, although clearly talented, was just a little kid and Amy was a teen, an incredible player, but Amy was hampered by Troy, who made stupid errors in between flashes of brilliance, and they were up against Logan, who at fourteen had the power and speed of a man, and made the court look small.

The match went on and on, until Jacob's dad came over to collect him because dinner was on the table, but then his dad, being his dad, got caught up in the match.

Joy and Stan set up picnic chairs. The two grandmothers tottered out in high heels carrying gin and tonics and cigarettes. Stan gave Jacob's dad a beer. The sky turned pink. The four children played as if lives were at stake.

Jacob couldn't remember who won. He just remembered their passion and their talent. He still loved witnessing the combination of passion and talent, in any endeavour, whether it was sport or musical theatre. The grown-ups were respectfully silent during each rally and then applauded like they were watching a grand slam. The Delaney kids fed off their applause. They punched the air. They roared with delight. They fell to their knees. It felt like Jacob was part of something big and important.

'Remarkable family,' Jacob's dad marvelled on their way back across the road to a cold dinner and a rather cross mother. 'Your umpiring was top-notch, Jacob.'

It occurred to Jacob that a man who could take such pleasure in watching someone else's children compete in a backyard tennis match would probably have quite liked at least one athletic child of his own, rather than the two uncoordinated, academic kids he got.

It said something about his dad that it had taken Jacob thirty-four years for that thought to occur to him.

Your umpiring was top-notch, Jacob.

Just when he thought he had a handle on this grief business, it walloped him, as if he'd only just got the news. He pressed the back of a hand that still smelled like lamb casserole to his mouth and a small white butterfly fluttered by so close he felt its wings brush against his cheek.

His mother believed every passing butterfly was his dad stopping to say hello, which was convenient, because there were plenty of butterflies in this leafy suburb.

Hi, Dad, thought Jacob. He didn't believe the butterfly was his dad, but still. Just in case. He watched the butterfly sail up above his mother's front door. It hovered under the eaves, right next to the small metal bracket where his mother's security camera usually hung. It had been smashed by a hailstone in the storm a couple of weeks back.

Yeah, I know, Dad, thanks for the reminder, I'm getting it fixed. I'll pick it up —

Then he stopped in his tracks. He turned around and looked back at the Delaneys' house and wondered what mistakes that camera might have witnessed from way up there with its bird's-eye view.

chapter forty-nine

Christmas Day

'That is the creepiest Santa I've ever seen,' said Troy to Amy.

They sat side by side drinking champagne on the three-seater dark brown leather couch in their parents' living room, watching a miniature Santa Claus gyrate his hips to 'Santa Claus Rock' on the coffee table.

'He's leering at me,' said Amy.

'Don't turn him off,' said Logan as he set up a stepladder under a light fitting to change a globe. 'I suggested Santa might appreciate a break and Mum called me a Grinch.'

It was the first time they'd all been together since the dramatic confrontation with Savannah back in October, and it was also the first time in years that the Delaneys had celebrated Christmas with just the immediate family: no in-laws, no partners, no random friends or second cousins.

No strangers who turned out not to be strangers.

In fact, thought Amy, as she chugged back her second glass of champagne on an empty stomach – an extremely empty stomach – it was possible this was their first Delaney Christmas *ever* with just the six of them, because growing up they'd always had the two grandmothers at Christmas lunch, gently lobbing passive-aggressive compliments back and forth across the table.

It felt pointless celebrating without other people, as if the whole objective had always been to perform the festivities for an audience. Why bother with any of it now? No-one was religious and there were no children to become sugared-up and adorably excited about Santa.

Yet Amy's mother appeared to be on a crazed mission to make this the Christmas-iest Christmas of Delaney family history. She'd decorated the already cluttered house with a quite extraordinary volume of newly purchased Christmas decorations. Shimmering lengths of tinsel had been thrown indiscriminately along windowsills. A series of identical grinning snowmen ornaments were precariously perched on top of the signed tennis ball collection. A nativity scene had been crammed in the middle of the tennis trophies, so that Amy could see the surprised face of baby Jesus reflected in a Bundaberg Seniors Mixed Doubles Tournament trophy. Baubles hung from doorhandles. There was reindeer-shaped soap in the bathroom. Steffi had been forced to wear jingly gold bells tied to her collar, which she clearly found mortifying. Right now she sat beneath the coffee table with her head between her paws, morosely munching on a piece of Christmas wrapping paper with the gift label still visible. It said, *To: Troy! From: Mum and Dad. With love!*

Joy wore a new red dress and flashing Christmas tree earrings and was whirling about the kitchen, preparing an incredibly elaborate hot lunch that was clearly beyond her capabilities. *No-one* was allowed to help her with *anything*. They had been instructed they must not bring anything except themselves and alcohol. They were 'busy people with their own lives'. 'I'm not a busy person with my own life,' Amy had protested, but she hadn't even been allowed to make brownies.

When they'd arrived, three hours ago, they'd been told to remain in the living room, where they should all *sit back and relax*. It was extremely stressful.

'Why didn't you bring your toy boy along today?' Troy removed a piece of red tinsel from Amy's hair. He himself had a fetching dusting of gold glitter on his cheekbone, but Amy didn't tell him. She thought it suited him. He looked like a rock star.

'He's just a friend,' said Amy.

'Sure he is,' said Troy.

Simon's parents lived in the country, on a *cattle farm*, of all the horrifying places to live, and Simon had gone to spend the Christmas break with them. He had invited Amy to come but meeting his family at Christmas would obviously give him the impression she was a normal girlfriend and she very nearly had a panic attack just imagining all that endless space.

'I feel like we're missing someone.' Troy looked about him with dissatisfaction, holding his champagne glass by the stem. 'It doesn't feel like Christmas, in spite of all this . . . horror.' He gestured at the decorations.

'I know,' said Amy. 'I was just thinking the same thing. I keep looking about for the missing person.'

'I think it's Indira who is missing,' said Troy. 'I miss Indira.'

'Me too,' said Amy. Indira was a great Christmas guest, because she hadn't celebrated it growing up and therefore had no rules or expectations or baggage about the holiday. She always got a little drunk and sang carols beautifully. None of the Delaneys could hold a note, so they were rapturous in their appreciation. Also, she would have found a way to convince Joy to let her into the kitchen to help.

'Did you hear that?' Troy called across the room to Logan. 'We miss your girlfriend!'

Logan ignored them as he unscrewed the old light globe.

'Get Indira back!' cried Amy. 'I command it, peasant!'

One of their favourite games when they were kids involved Amy's siblings agreeing to be her 'peasants'. Well, it was one of her favourite games. They all had to do what she commanded and fetch her things. She could never quite believe she got away

370

with it. She could still remember the sick, delicious feeling of power as she watched Brooke obediently make her bed.

Logan didn't even bother to respond. Her power was long gone.

Troy lowered his voice. 'I don't especially miss Grant.'

'I miss his roast potatoes,' said Amy.

'He was so fucking proud of them,' said Troy.

'Deservedly so,' said Amy. 'Hey, have you noticed how Brooke is –'

'I can *hear* you both,' said Brooke from the floor next to the couch, where she was lying flat on her back on the purple floral carpet doing some weird kind of pretzel-like stretch. Brooke had worn a summer dress to please their mother, who said, 'Oh! That looks nice, although I thought you'd wear your lovely green one today.' Amy had at least made an effort to get the colour code right by wearing a vintage green miniskirt and a red singlet top. Her mother said, 'My goodness, you look like a gangster's girlfriend!' The boys wore the same clothes they always wore, and their mother told both of them they looked gorgeous.

'Eavesdropping peasant.' Amy kicked her sister with her foot.

'You've forgotten the revolution.' Brooke stretched one hamstring and then the other. 'We are no longer your peasants.'

She was Brooke again. That's what Amy had been going to say. *Have you noticed how Brooke is Brooke again?* She was back doing random yoga poses and floor stretches. She snorted when she laughed. She talked about lowbrow stuff like *The Bachelor*. She actually looked taller. Maybe she'd been subconsciously hunching for Grant. 'Girls, you must never hunch for a boy!' their mother used to cry, which was all very well for her.

Brooke sat up, her dress bunched up around her knees.

'Bum shuffle,' ordered Amy. 'Be cute. Like you used to be.'

'She's still cute,' said Troy.

Brooke tried to shuffle along the carpet on her bottom but couldn't do it. 'I'll get carpet burn,' she said. She put her hands flat on the monstrous carpet. 'When Dad dies, how fast do you think Mum will tear this up?'

'His body will still be warm,' said Troy.

Amy shuddered. 'That's horrible.'

'Mum should just get people in and do it,' said Troy. 'Imagine how much better this room would look with beautiful floorboards.'

'Dad keeps saying he's happy to tear it up,' said Logan. 'I've said I'll do it but then he always changes his mind at the last minute.'

'It's because Grandma was so proud of it,' said Amy. 'They used to call this the Good Room. She worked all those hours to save up to get this carpet after Dad's father left, and she thought this colour was so fashionable.'

'Grandma *chose* this colour,' marvelled Brooke. 'Imagine actually choosing it.'

She stretched her legs either side of her in a V-shape and dropped her forehead to the horrible carpet.

'Ouch.' Amy shuddered. 'Don't do that.'

'You three all need to stretch more,' said Brooke without lifting her head. 'Hey, did I tell you I've joined a basketball team?'

'Seriously?' said Logan from his perch.

'Thought I'd try a new sport,' said Brooke into the carpet.

Amy and her brothers all exchanged glances. There *was* no other sport besides tennis.

'I always wondered how I'd go in a team sport,' said Troy. 'Tennis is lonely.'

'Because you're such a team player,' said Logan.

'I'm good at basketball,' said Brooke.

'Of course you are,' said Amy.

There was an ominous clatter and crash from the kitchen.

'Do you think we should try again to help, Mum?' Brooke stretched even lower, her voice muffled by the carpet. 'I'm pretty hungry.'

'Yes, I'm actually feeling quite faint.' Troy put the back of his hand to his forehead.

'She yelled at me last time I went into the kitchen.' Logan hopped down from the ladder. 'Do you think she'd notice if we ordered a pizza?'

'I opened the oven to check the turkey and she *smacked* me across the back.' Brooke sat back up, her face flushed. 'She literally smacked me.' She pointed at Troy. 'You've got glitter on your face.'

'Leave it. It looks nice,' said Amy.

'What's Dad doing?' interrupted Brooke.

'He's in his office,' answered Amy. 'Watching re-runs of Harry's matches.' She'd stood at the door and watched him, his head bent, his massive shoulders hunched, murmuring to himself as he took notes for God knew what purpose.

'Obviously thrilled to spend Christmas with his beloved family,' said Troy.

'It's because of Harry's comeback. He's obsessed,' said Amy.

'This seems to be a new level of obsession,' said Logan. 'Now he knows what Mum did.'

'Yep. He'll never forgive her for taking away his golden boy,' said Troy lightly. He refilled his champagne glass and held up the flute to the light.

'They aren't talking,' said Brooke. 'They're not even looking at each other.'

'It's upsetting,' said Amy, and she thought she spoke idly, the way anyone would speak if their parents weren't talking on Christmas Day, but she saw her siblings straighten and tense. Looks were exchanged. Unspoken warnings shared. This was the way it had been ever since the year of suicidal thoughts. She'd been fourteen. Everybody had suicidal thoughts at fourteen. Unfortunately Amy had written long heartfelt goodbye letters to each member of her family, which had been discovered, roundly mocked and never, ever forgotten. Brooke said she still had hers 'on file', which was mortifying. (Amy had misspelled the word 'melancholy'.) Such was the paradoxical nature of sibling relationships: they could tease her for the sappiness and spelling of her suicide notes while being terrified she'd write new ones.

'You mustn't get worked up about it,' said Brooke carefully, as though Amy were teetering on the edge of a bridge.

'I'm not suicidal, it's just upsetting!' snapped Amy.

Brooke held up her hands. 'Got it.'

'I'm not ten! If they get a divorce, they get a divorce!' She could hardly bear to think of it. Her parents living in different homes, trying out new hairstyles and hobbies, new *relationships*? In truth she felt exactly the same way she would have felt if they'd divorced when she was ten.

'Surely they're too old to divorce,' said Brooke. 'What would be the point?'

'They're not *that* old,' said Logan. 'It happens.'

'I should have got them a marriage counselling gift certificate for Christmas,' said Troy thoughtfully.

He'd got their mother a bike. You could tell it was a bike, even though every inch of it was beautifully wrapped in gold paper. 'A bike!' their mother had cried, both hands to her heart as he carried it in. 'How did you know I wanted a bike?'

Troy mysteriously always knew what everyone wanted.

'I must *eat*,' said Amy. 'Brooke, go tell Mum we have to eat something now because you're getting a migraine.'

'You tell her you have to eat because you're having a panic attack,' retorted Brooke.

'Tell her Logan is hungry,' said Troy. 'She won't want *Logan* to be hungry.'

'I told her I was hungry an hour ago,' said Logan.

Steffi came out from under the coffee table and put her head on Amy's lap.

'What's the latest with Claire?' Amy asked Troy as she stroked Steffi's soft ears. Troy's ex-wife had been back in Australia trying to get pregnant with their frozen embryos and so far she'd been through one round with no luck.

'She's having a break, trying again in the new year,' said Troy. 'There are four more left.'

'Do you hope that she *does* get pregnant?' asked Amy. 'Or that she doesn't?'

'I want it for her. I don't want it for me. I don't want that guy bringing up my biological child. I really, really don't want that.' He paused. 'Did I tell you I met him?'

'The cardiologist?' asked Brooke. 'What's he like?'

They all looked at Troy, waiting for his answer, staunchly on his side in spite of their sniping, in spite of his past mistakes, suddenly, mysteriously, as close as siblings could be. Amy remembered that awful day when their father got out of the car on the highway. One moment they'd all been fighting, hating each other as hard as you can possibly hate a sibling, and then suddenly, the car was silent and Troy was holding Brooke's hand and they were looking at each other, waiting for their mother's response, united in their horror.

'He's an arrogant twat,' said Troy.

'That's surgeons for you,' said Brooke.

'He's not right for her,' said Troy. 'He calls Claire *baby*. She's trying to have a baby and he calls her baby.'

Brooke said, 'I mean, I guess that's a common term of –'

The kitchen fire alarm began to beep. An acrid smell filled the house and their father limped heavily into the room, radiating grumpiness. One of the grinning snowmen toppled from the shelf and onto the carpet.

'What's going on?' demanded Stan. He looked at them all as if they were children.

'It's fine!' Joy shrieked from the kitchen. 'Everything is fine! Just relax! Everybody stay right where you are!'

★

Joy threw a tea towel up at the smoke detector on her kitchen ceiling to try to make it stop beeping. She wished Logan had never installed the damned thing. It was so sensitive. So judgemental of her cooking.

375

'It's not an actual fire,' she told the smoke detector. She caught the tea towel and tossed it up again. It was a bad throw. It landed splat on her face. She twisted it into a ball and threw it again. 'It's just a bit of smoke, you stupid thing! Stop overreacting.'

She'd been doing walnuts in butter and brown sugar like Savannah had done on Father's Day (she'd told Joy that salad was a 'cinch'!) and then she'd been distracted trying to stir the stupid lumps out of the gravy and next thing the walnuts were black smoking chunks of nuclear waste. No warning, no middle ground!

Lunch kept slipping further and further away. Her children wouldn't stop interrupting to ask if they could help, and she didn't want their help, because then they'd all get involved and start making annoying suggestions and ordering her around: *Don't bother with the walnuts, Mum, isn't it time to put the potatoes on?*

It felt like she was stuck in one of those recurring nightmares she still had where she was trying to get one of her children to a match on time but her car was moving in slow motion. She'd wake with her foot still desperately pressing an imaginary accelerator.

She threw the saucepan straight in the bin. It was ruined forever. Everything was ruined forever. What in the world was she trying to prove with this elaborate lunch and all these fancy, fiddly side dishes? No-one in her family even *liked* turkey. Or walnuts. She'd created a picture in her head of a glittering red, gold and green Christmas Day that would somehow magically make them a family again.

'Are we ever going to eat today?'

Stan was in the kitchen, glowering at her. It was the first time he'd spoken directly to her in weeks, and this was what he chose to say.

'Well, that's lovely,' she said. 'Not "Can I do anything to help?" but "Are we ever going to eat today?"'

'Everyone has been offering to help and you refuse to accept,' said Stan.

She said, 'Everyone has not offered to help. *You* have not offered to help.'

'I am very happy to do anything if it will finally get lunch on the table. I am at your disposal.'

I am at your disposal.

It was like seeing his damned mother come back to life. She used to sit in this kitchen exhaling a long stream of cigarette smoke with amused malicious eyes while Joy cooked: feeling stupid and banal and talking too much.

Joy didn't know she was going to do it before she did it.

She picked up the first of his mother's sneering china cats and threw it with the power of a first serve against the wall, decapitating it cleanly. She picked up the second one and did the same. It caught the edge of the kitchen cupboard and sent a glittering shower of hand-painted china across the bench.

There was silence.

'Feel better?' drawled Stan with his mother's cruel contempt. 'Or do I need to pass you another ornament?'

The smoke alarm once again began to beep its thin, sharp, insistent warning of danger ahead.

chapter fifty

Now

'So then my father stomped out of the kitchen – well, he sort of stomp-limped because of his bad knee – and went back into his office and slammed the door. It turned out Mum had smashed these two ornaments that belonged to my father's mother.'

'Oh dear. Did they have sentimental value to your father?' asked Roger Strout.

'Spot on, Roger,' said Amy.

Sometimes he suspected she was gently teasing him. Roger Strout was a former automotive fleet sales executive who had accepted a redundancy package two years ago, completed a Diploma of Counselling and was now offering talk therapy six days a week. His ex-wife thought that was appalling because who in their right mind would accept help from *Roger*, of all people? No wonder there was a mental health crisis in this country. In fact, a lot of people not in their right mind would accept help from Roger, of all people, because yes, there was a mental health crisis in this country, and people from all walks of life were desperate for help. He was booked up three months in advance. He was well aware of the limitations of his qualifications and experience and scrupulous about never describing his clients as his patients, because it wasn't a doctor–patient relationship: it was a collaboration.

Right now Roger and Amy sat opposite each other in the matching oversized fabric-covered wing chairs with the brass stud detailing on the arms that all clients touched with their fingertips when they were about to tell him something important.

Amy's blue-dyed hair was tied back in the tightest, tidiest ponytail he'd ever seen her wear, as if this was one area of her life over which she could maintain control.

At their last appointment she'd mentioned that her mother had sent an unexpected text message saying she was going 'off-grid'. Amy had spent the session talking about how she'd like to go off-grid herself, maybe move to a small country town where everyone knew her name, except she really hated the country. She hadn't shown up for the appointment after that, and then, last week, Roger had got the shock of his life when he saw Amy with her siblings on the local evening news appealing for information about their missing mother.

'So then my father refused to eat Christmas lunch with us, which my mother finally served at around four pm, by which time we were all starving and quite drunk, and well . . . it was a very dysfunctional Christmas Day. But you know, that happens in lots of families, doesn't it?'

'Christmas can be stressful,' said Roger, who had begun Christmas Day with an early-morning screaming match with his ex-wife about the agreed handover time for their two children. Festive indeed.

'None of us were exactly in a rush for another family event and we were all busy and distracted over January. I'm not saying we *lost contact* with our parents. I mean, how often do you visit your parents, Roger?'

Roger made a noncommittal sound. Amy preferred not to play by the therapy rules and instead pretended they were old friends catching up for a chat. She tried to catch him out by shooting abrupt personal questions at him, which he normally managed to dodge. (The answer was that he had dinner with his parents every Sunday night without fail.)

'But you're an only child,' she said.

He had no memory of sharing this information.

'See, because there are four of us, we all assumed that someone had been over to the house. Brooke and Logan are *always* over there, except apparently they weren't for a few weeks, which they could have mentioned.'

She said this with the cheerful, childish disdain with which siblings often spoke about each other. Roger had a client who was an extremely well-spoken university lecturer, except for when she talked about her older sister, when she morphed into a freckled, pigtailed kid: 'My sister gets *everything*, Roger.'

'Normally Mum is the one organising family events, or she drops by, or suggests coffee, and so it took us a while to notice she wasn't in touch,' continued Amy. 'Also, it's not like Mum and Dad are *incapacitated*. They're so active. They're more active than me.' Amy plucked at the fabric of her pants. 'Mum isn't even seventy yet. They keep describing her in the papers as an "elderly" woman. She's not elderly! They should try returning her first serve when she's in a bad mood.'

She smiled tremulously at the thought of her mother's serve.

'My brothers and sister and I worked out that when we got that text from Mum, it had been a whole week since any of us had had any contact from her, which seems wrong. I mean, she is a *little* bit elderly.'

She used her fingertips to massage her cheeks. 'My jaw aches. I've been clenching it ever since we filed the missing persons report.' She opened and shut her mouth a few times. 'I keep thinking about my rabbit dream.' She looked at him expectantly.

'Your rabbit dream?' said Roger. You sure had to be on your toes with Amy.

'You know. My recurring rabbit dream?'

'Oh, yes, I remember,' said Roger. 'Where you forget to feed your rabbit.'

'I forget that I *have* a rabbit, and in my dream, I suddenly remember – oh my God, I have a rabbit! – and I'm walking out to the rabbit hutch in the backyard and I know the rabbit is going to be dead.' She shuddered as if at a real memory of a terrible mistake.

She lowered her voice and met his eyes. 'Sometimes it's not a rabbit, it's a *puppy*, which is worse, although I don't know why; that's so unfair to rabbits.'

She put a hand to her collarbone as her chest rose and fell rapidly.

'Your parents don't require you to feed them, Amy,' said Roger. 'They're not bunnies or puppies or children. They're grown-ups. It was your mother's prerogative to go off-grid.'

Assuming she actually sent the text. Roger had read the news stories. He knew her mother's phone had been found in the house, meaning someone else could have sent the text.

He wondered if his limitations were about to be tested beyond their capabilities, because it seemed possible, if not probable, that Amy's father had killed her mother. Even someone with the most robust mental health would find that traumatic.

'By the way, you'll be pleased to hear I broke up with my flatmate,' she said abruptly. 'Not that we were ever really going out. It was just sex.' She shot him a look as if she were hoping to shock him.

'Why would you think I'd be pleased about that?' asked Roger.

'He's far too nice for me,' said Amy. 'He's been so *supportive* about my missing mother. I felt like I was building up this debt I could never pay off. Like a mortgage. I could never have a mortgage.'

'Well, you know,' said Roger, 'a relationship is about –'

Amy said, 'I wasn't worried at first. About Mum. When we didn't hear from her. I was *pleased*! I thought, Good for you. Your turn now.'

Roger took a moment. He didn't get it.

'What do you mean, "Your turn now?"'

'It was like what my dad used to do. When I was a kid, I always used to think, Why doesn't *she* just walk out?'

Roger wrote down, *Father: walking out?*

But he didn't speak. He could sense the words banked up in her.

'I was angry every time Dad left.' She massaged her jaw. 'But I was even angrier with Mum for putting up with it.'

Roger waited.

'But I don't know. What if Dad *did* do . . . what people are saying?' She looked at him imploringly. 'What if it was an accident? Because my grandfather – what he did to my grandmother – it could be genetic! Because that *was* a terrible thing that Mum did. Harry was a once-in-a-lifetime opportunity for my dad. You only get one chance like that! I always knew how much Harry leaving hurt Dad, I knew he never really got over it, I could *see* it whenever Harry's name came up, and then we find out that it was actually Mum! All along it was Mum!'

Roger wrote down, *Grandfather? Harry? One chance?*

He couldn't grab on to a thread of the conversation so he could make sense of it.

'But if Dad did – I mean, I couldn't forgive him. What if he *asks* for my forgiveness? How could I forgive him? But he's my dad! How can I abandon him? What if he asks me to be a character witness? In court?'

She was rolling down a steep slippery slope of potential catastrophes. 'Whose witness would I be? How do I choose a side? Do I visit him in jail? How can you visit your mother's murderer in jail? You can't!'

The words dried up. All he could hear was ragged, desperate panic. Her eyes met his in mute terror. Watching someone have a panic attack was like looking into the eyes of someone trapped behind glass, drowning right in front of you.

'Breathe with me.' Roger put down his notepad and picked up the carved wooden figure of an elephant that sat next to the tissue box.

'Focus on this. Feel the curve of its trunk. Focus on the smoothness, the roughness.' He watched her hands trace the elephant's textured surface.

'Tiger,' whispered Amy, and for a moment he didn't get it. He thought, It's an elephant, not a tiger. Was it something to do with the bunny dream? But then he remembered how at their very first session, she'd teased him about how every therapist she'd ever seen wanted to talk about the tiger when they described the fight-or-flight response.

The sabre-toothed tiger. She was trying to tell him it was here. Leaping for her throat.

chapter fifty-one

'No criminal record,' said Christina. 'No evidence of violence or threats of violence. No life insurance policy.'

'There's still a financial benefit,' Ethan pointed out. 'They were cashed up from selling the tennis school. He'd be in a better position financially than if they divorced.'

'I'm not talking about the Delaneys. I'm saying you could have said all of the above about this charmer.' She jabbed a finger at the newspaper on her desk.

The body found in bushland had been identified as Polly Perkins. Polly was a woman who'd lived in a suburb close to Joy Delaney. Thirty years ago, Polly's husband told everyone his wife had left him and gone back to New Zealand. She'd left a 'cold, hurtful' note. The neighbouring women had been sad for him. They'd brought around casseroles and carrot cake.

The truth was that Professor Andrew Perkins had hit his first wife, Polly, over the head with a new Sunbeam steam iron, after he had expressly forbidden her from buying it because he was under 'significant financial stress at the time'. His full, frank confession included the rueful admission that he 'really hadn't intended to hit her quite that hard'. He'd buried his wife's body in bushland within a short drive of his home. If it wasn't for the landslide caused by the storm, Polly would be there still.

Polly had been estranged from a scattered dysfunctional family, but there had been a missing persons report filed by her best friend in New Zealand. Over the years this friend had valiantly tried to get the Australian police interested in her missing friend, to little avail. Records showed just one visit by police officers to the Perkins house, three years after Polly 'left'. The two officers had enjoyed some carrot cake baked by the kind neighbour who had become Andrew Perkins's second wife.

The second wife had used the murder weapon to iron her husband's shirts for a good twenty years before being given permission to buy a new one.

She had this week told police about an ongoing pattern of financial, verbal and physical abuse that had left her a prisoner in her home.

'This man enjoyed thirty years of freedom after he murdered his wife. He could easily have gone to his grave without justice.' Christina pressed her thumb on Polly's husband's murderous, well-fed face. 'We may not have Joy Delaney's body yet, but –'

Her phone rang. It was probably just as well. There had been too much emotion in her voice. It was Constable Pete Novak, the ground search coordinator. 'We've found an item of clothing in the bush reserve behind the Delaneys' house that you'll want to see. I'm sending you a picture now.'

She opened her email and clicked on the photo attached. It was a t-shirt screen-printed with a distinctive design of three flowers: orange, red and yellow. Gerberas.

'Is that –?'

'Yes,' said Pete. 'It's covered in blood.'

chapter fifty-two

'Thank you for coming in today, Mr Delaney,' said Christina.

Ethan noted that her manner was businesslike: not at all aggressive. She seemed to be speaking with the friendly detached authority of a medical specialist who has asked a patient to come back in for a serious follow-up appointment. 'You know Constable Lim, of course.'

She indicated Ethan. Stan looked over at Ethan and nodded, folding his arms across his barrel chest. 'Yup.'

Stan Delaney's wife had been missing now for nineteen days. The scratches on his face were completely healed. Ethan noted that he'd shaved for this interview and dressed in a business shirt. No tie. The shirt was ironed. He looked like a respectable member of the community. He had no legal representation. It was difficult to imagine this man having anything to do with that blood-soaked t-shirt.

They were in the small windowless ERISP room at the station. ERISP stood for Electronic Record of Interview with a Suspected Person, and it meant that this entire interview was being recorded on both an audio and video disc. Ethan sat in one corner, observing and keeping an eye on the recording equipment.

'You really want to be a cop?' his brother had said to him

when he first mentioned going into the police force. 'Directing traffic?'

Ethan's brother was an actuary. He was sitting in a city office right now solving mathematical equations while Ethan was helping solve a possible murder, and his brother thought *he'd* made the better choice of career.

Christina did something quick and complicated with her hair to make it tighter at the back. She said, 'Mr Delaney, I'd like to go through the timeline one more time.'

'Okay.' Stan nodded. He sat up, uncrossed his arms and placed closed fists on his thighs. *Bring it on*, he seemed to be saying. 'What do you want to know?'

'Stan Delaney is formidable on the court,' one of his fellow club members had told Christina and Ethan, a man who was keen to let them know that he believed Stan had buried his wife's body under their tennis court. 'He's ruthless. Calculating. Ferocious. He gets this look on his face that makes your blood run cold.'

Christina looked down at her notes as if to check them, although Ethan knew for a fact that she knew the timeline by heart.

'You woke up that morning – Valentine's Day – and you didn't see your wife?'

Ethan had been intimidated by Detective Christina Khoury when he first started working with her. He thought she thought he was a moron. She had a way of looking at him as if she were sizing him up and finding him wanting. But he'd got used to that look now. She gave the same look to her morning coffee each day and she loved her coffee.

(Ethan's aunt said that he and his brother were intimidated by women because they were subconsciously terrified of displeasing them due to the fact their mother had walked out when they were little kids. Ethan and his brother both agreed that was total crap. They didn't say this to their aunt's face, of course.)

'We were sleeping in separate rooms.' Stan answered Christina's question with steady eyes.

'Was that a new development?' asked Christina.

'Relatively new, yes.'

She checked her notes. 'And you went out to buy milk first thing in the morning?'

'Yes,' said Stan. 'We were out of milk. I also bought the paper.'

'Right,' said Christina. 'And you came home but you didn't see Mrs Delaney.'

'Not right away. I was reading . . . something in my office.'

That was new. *Reading what?*

Ethan leaned forward. So did Christina. 'What were you reading?'

'Just some paperwork.'

'What sort of paperwork?'

Stan shrugged. 'Nothing of importance.'

Ethan saw the lie and he knew Christina saw it too. He watched her wait. She was still. He wondered if her heart was racing like his. Stan said nothing. Perhaps his was the fastest racing heart in this small room.

'Right,' said Christina after a moment. 'So you were reading this "paperwork" and then you heard the front door.'

'Yes,' said Stan. 'I don't know where she'd been. But I heard her come in. And then I went to talk to her, in the kitchen. She was drinking a glass of water. She seemed . . . worked up about something.'

'And that's when you argued.'

'That's right.'

'About what?'

He crossed his arms again. Defensive. 'It was just an ordinary argument between a husband and wife.'

'Considering the fact that your wife left your home and has now been missing for nearly three weeks, I'd say this was more than an ordinary argument between a husband and wife, Mr Delaney.'

For the first time Ethan heard aggression in her voice: a hint of something bigger and more menacing beneath it, like a quick glimpse of a shark's fin.

But Stan didn't even blink.

Christina said, 'So, that morning, after this "ordinary" argument, you left the house and you didn't come back until what time?'

'Around ten o'clock that night. Like I've told you. Many times now.'

'And where did you go that day?'

'I just drove. Like I've told you. Many times.'

'You just drove.'

'I was upset.'

'What about?'

Ethan could see Stan's frustration rising like boiling water, which was exactly what Christina wanted. She was slowly turning up the temperature.

'I was upset because I'd argued with my wife.'

'But you don't remember what you argued about.'

He unfolded his arms once more and leaned towards her. He was a big man. 'No, that's not right. I *never* said that. I do remember what we argued about, but it's personal. My marriage is private. It's none of your business. It's not relevant to your investigation.'

It took a certain type of man to say to a police detective: 'It's none of your business.'

Christina said, 'If you're worried about your wife, perhaps you could let us determine what's relevant.'

Stan shrugged in the manner of his oldest son. Said nothing.

'So you came back and she was gone.'

'Yes.'

'But you didn't call anyone. You didn't call a single one of your children. You didn't call a single friend. You didn't call her.'

He lifted his chin a fraction. 'We'd argued. Like I told you. I knew she was angry with me. I assumed she'd gone to stay with someone – and that she'd be back the next day.'

'But she wasn't.'

'No, she wasn't,' said Stan.

'Was there any infidelity in your marriage?' she asked.

His nostrils flared. 'No.'

Christina flipped a page in her notebook. For show. 'It's my understanding your youngest daughter once caught your wife with another man at a party.'

'That was a long time ago. Joy drank too much punch and kissed Dennis Christos. It was hardly a great love affair. Old mate is dead now anyway. According to my wife I killed him.' Stan frowned as he realised what he'd just said. 'I didn't *literally* kill him. He had a heart attack.' He sniffed. 'He should never have kissed my wife either, by the by, but as I said, that was a lifetime ago.'

Grudges can last a lifetime, thought Ethan.

Stan jerked his chin at Christina's notebook. 'Did my daughter tell you that? About Joy kissing Dennis at the party?'

'Your former son-in-law, Grant Willis.'

His brow cleared. 'Right. Well, that makes more sense.'

'You mean because your daughter wants to protect you?'

He said nothing.

Christina said, 'I'm guessing all your children want to protect you.'

'I don't need protection,' said Stan. 'Because I've done nothing wrong.'

'The young woman who stayed with you last year,' said Christina. 'I believe she was a former student's younger sister. Your most famous student's sister.'

His face hardened. 'There was no *affair*, if that's what you're thinking. I know that's what people have been saying. It's laughable.'

'So it's recently come to our attention that while Savannah was staying with you, she revealed certain information. Information that I understand came as a shock to you.'

He squeezed his lower lip between his thumb and his finger. 'Who told you that?'

Christina didn't answer. Ethan watched him trying to work out which of his children had handed over a potential motive for murder.

'Your wife betrayed you, didn't she? She told Harry Haddad's father that he'd be better off with another coach.'

'I wouldn't use the word "betrayed",' he said.

'Wouldn't you? I understand that's exactly the word you *did* use.' They held each other's gaze. It felt perversely intimate, as if they were about to kiss.

Stan Delaney's eyes, brown and dark lashed, were young and wary in an old man's face. Was it a young man's violent rage that had been responsible for this old man's unthinkable actions?

'What do you mean?' His voice quavered. He was cracking. At last.

'You said to your wife that you'd never felt so betrayed.'

'Who *told* you that?' Stan's jaw shifted back and forth as though he was grinding his teeth. Ethan could no longer see the young man, only the old man. An old man wondering which of his children thought he was capable of murder.

'I'm hearing that your wife may not have been faithful. I'm hearing that she betrayed you professionally.' Christina was going in for the kill now. 'You lost your temper. Justifiably so. Harry Haddad could have and should have been your greatest professional success. Your wife stole that opportunity from you and kept it a secret.'

She pushed the Polaroid of the bloodied t-shirt across the table. 'Mr Delaney, we found this t-shirt buried in bushland near the back of your house,' she said. 'Have you seen it before?'

The colour drained from his face.

'Buried,' repeated Stan Delaney. 'You think I *buried* Joy's t-shirt?'

'Did you?'

'No.'

'Do you recognise the shirt?'

'It's my wife's shirt. I'm sure you know that,' said Stan. He pushed the picture away from him, contemptuously, as if it meant nothing to him. 'It's covered in my wife's blood. You probably know that too.'

Christina's tone was now almost jocular. 'Mr Delaney, this is not looking great for you. I really think it would be in your best interests to turn your mind to your last interaction with your wife.'

Stan sighed. He tipped back his head, stuck his thumbs in his pants pockets and studied the ceiling. 'I think it might be in my best interests to shut up and get myself a lawyer.'

chapter fifty-three

Valentine's Day

It was seven am and Joy couldn't see the point in getting out of bed. There was nothing pressing to do. It would just be another day like yesterday and the day before that. The smoke haze outside her window was as grey and sombre as a midwinter sky, except for the blood-red summer sun that burned like a cigarette end.

Joy had never experienced asthma, but she had recently found herself taking small, shallow, lady-like sips of air. Was it the smoke or the state of her marriage?

It had been months since Savannah had left and it didn't feel like anything was lessening or softening. The opposite: their anger was hardening and solidifying.

She and Stan had been through bad times before. The difference was that there were no distractions now: no work, no children. When they were younger there hadn't been time to obsess and brood over how the other person had wronged them. They'd been too tired to keep sharpening the edges of their hurt feelings.

Now they were stuck in this big empty silent house and there was no way to escape the invisible yet tangible conflict between them. Joy felt like she could trace its outlines in the air.

January had been especially bad because of the Australian Open. Harry Haddad's comeback had crashed and burned after a 'shock loss' (some went as far as to say an 'embarrassing loss') in the first round to an unseeded nineteen-year-old Canadian. Ten double-faults and over eighty unforced errors! Harry and his new coach, Nicole Lenoir-Jourdan, were parting ways. Joy hadn't watched the match, but she'd walked past the living room and seen Stan gripping the sides of his chair, crackling with so much fury and distress it had felt like he was a live electrical wire. If she'd touched him she'd have gone flying.

Now, if one of them walked into the room and saw the other one there, they walked away again. They spoke only when necessary. They hadn't slept in the same bedroom since Savannah left.

Stan slept on a mattress on the floor of Logan's old room. Amy's bedroom would have been more comfortable, but perhaps he didn't want to sleep where Savannah had slept, so well done to him, that sure showed her. Joy bet his back hurt. She hoped it did hurt. Did that mean the love was finally gone? It seemed possible that not a droplet remained. She was as dry and desiccated as their desperate-for-rain front lawn.

She heard the sound of water running from somewhere in the house. She'd stopped cooking after Christmas as a test to see if Stan might offer to prepare something, to put some toast in the toaster or to order takeaway, but he hadn't said a word.

They were quietly feeding themselves as if they were flatmates, slipping in and out of the kitchen, polishing the benchtops, rinsing their plates, leaving behind as little evidence of their presence as possible, as if this were one of the rules of the competition. Stan appeared to be working his way through the cans of spaghetti and baked beans in the pantry. Joy mostly ate toast; sometimes she boiled an egg.

She felt fragile and shaky, exhausted and constantly on the verge of tears. It reminded her of the weeks after she'd just had a baby or lost a loved one.

Joy didn't know how Stan was spending his days. He seemed

to be doing something in his office. When she walked past she caught glimpses of him frowning over his glasses as he importantly turned the page on some paperwork, although God knew what paperwork it could have been. Joy took care of the paperwork. Divorce papers? Also, why did she call it *his* office? When the children were little they always called it 'Daddy's office' even though Joy was the one who handled all the business of the business.

Yet they all had to maintain the pretence that because Stan was the man, whatever he was doing was automatically more important and deserved priority over any contribution from the little lady.

Well, fuck you, Stan.

The swearing in her head was a new and satisfying development. When she was thirty she'd assumed that by this time of her life nothing would matter all that much, her emotions would be muted and soft, as soft as the skin of an old lady's face. The violence of her thoughts startled her and woke her up. She assumed these words would not make their way from her brain to her tongue, but you never knew.

Imagine if her children heard her talk like that out loud. That would show them.

She was conducting an experiment. She'd stopped calling her children. She was sick of the harried impatient way they answered her calls. She was sick of being the one to organise every family event. It had now been seven days since she had spoken to any one of her offspring. She would have assumed that her most dutiful children, Logan and/or Brooke, would have checked in by now, but no.

Hypothesis: My children don't care.

Conclusion: My children don't care.

Her friends were quiet and busy with their own lives too. Caro had her daughter, Petra, visiting from Copenhagen with her children. Childish laughter floated from Caro's garden into Joy's window. Caro shouldn't be letting those children play outside in this smoky air. Two other friends had become first-time grandmothers: one baby boy, one baby girl. Joy had sent them *Congratulations on your grandson/granddaughter!* cards. She kept a stack of them in a drawer and grimly selected the correct gender each time she got the happy news.

She tried to work out what to do with her day. Her eyes traced a horrible brownish stain on the bedroom ceiling. She'd never noticed it before. It looked like blood, but she knew it was just rainwater from a long-ago storm. It hadn't rained in forever.

She must get up. She didn't move. Her hands clutched at the fitted sheet. *Come on, Joy.* Two of her fingernails were broken and kept getting caught irritatingly against the sheet. She couldn't find the nail scissors, even though she knew she'd bought a new pair just two weeks ago. Her fingernails broke so easily now. Like elderly bones. Like her elderly heart. She was not elderly. She wasn't even seventy. Before Christmas she'd beaten a fifty-year-old, a good player, 6–4, 6–2 but she hadn't been back to the club this year. She didn't seem to have the energy.

She did not feel *suicidal*, absolutely not, but for the first time ever she found herself thinking that maybe she'd had enough. It wasn't worth the bother anymore. She wanted her grandparents. She wanted her mother.

She imagined their faces lighting up when she walked through the arrival gates of the afterlife. It would be nice to see them again. She would run into their arms. She'd have to wear something nice for her mother.

Today was Valentine's Day. A day that celebrated love. She and Stan had never really taken much notice of Valentine's Day. It was an American holiday but every year there seemed to be more fuss about it: red roses and chocolates and teddy bears. Men in suits carrying bouquets. Joy didn't want red roses but she would like a husband who still shared her bed.

She rolled over onto her stomach and pressed her face into her pillow. If she started crying she might never stop.

'Get up,' she said into the pillow. 'Get up now.'

She thought of her mother describing a morning when Joy was a baby. Beautiful, no-nonsense Pearl Becker woke up one morning and couldn't get out of bed. She could barely lift her head from her pillow. 'It was like I had blocks of concrete tied to me,' she told Joy. When she heard the milkman at the front door (those were the days!) she called out to him to please get help, and so the doctor came around to examine her. A doctor doing a house visit: those sure were the days. The doctor said she probably had some kind of 'vitamin deficiency' and told her that she needed to 'get up and be strong for her baby'.

Of course those weren't really the days, because now, with the benefit of modern knowledge, any layperson would diagnose her mother's depression, although Pearl refused to accept that. 'Oh, no, it was something *physical*, Joy, I had nothing to be sad about!' she said. 'I had you! A beautiful baby! You would have looked better if you didn't have that big round head, as bald as a cue ball, but you were a sweet little thing.' Her mother specialised in the tiny razor-sharp dig wrapped in a soft compliment, so you didn't notice the blood until afterwards.

'And I had a handsome husband!' That was before the handsome husband went off to 'meet a friend' and never returned.

Joy's limbs felt as heavy as perhaps her mother's had felt that long-ago morning, yet her heart raced. Was this a glimpse of depression coupled with anxiety? Was this how Amy suffered? A dull ache crept across her forehead. She never got headaches. The universe must have decided it was time she experienced what both her daughters endured.

Why had her daughters had to suffer these invisible illnesses that no-one seemed to understand?

'Might I suggest a firmer hand,' said their family GP with a droll wag of his finger in Amy's face. And then: 'Is this one a bit of a hypochondriac maybe? Baby of the family? Likes the attention?' He'd winked at Joy over the top of Brooke's pain-stricken, dead-white face. Another daughter's eyes begging Joy for relief she couldn't give.

It was easy when she took the boys to see him. Their illnesses were masculine, visible and curable: coughs and blocked noses, rashes and broken bones.

The GP didn't know what he didn't know about mental health and migraines. Even the specialists didn't seem to know much more, and they were even more expensive and patronising. But why had Joy been so polite in the face of their ignorance? So meek and grateful? *Thank you, Doctor. I'm sure you're right, Doctor.* And then she'd get back in the car with a miserable daughter beside her, and the girls misinterpreted her frustration at her own impotence as anger at them, and they blamed themselves just as she blamed herself.

That GP was dead now. So was at least one of those specialists, as far as she knew.

Useless rage directed at long since dead men propelled her out of bed and into the shower. She gathered and stoked the rage as she showered. There was only her shampoo and body wash in the shower stall now. No evidence of a husband. Stan was using the other bathroom.

Perhaps it was time to finally accept defeat on this marriage: to meet at the net, shake hands, clap each other respectfully on the shoulder, wave to the fans and walk away.

She scrubbed her head hard. Her broken fingernails gouged her scalp.

She thought of all the truisms she and Stan had passed on to their children and their students.

You can still fight back from match point down.

If you want to overcome a losing streak, you re-evaluate your game.

She was a fighter. She was a winner. She was Joy Delaney. She would not give up on this marriage. She would take decisive, aggressive action today.

She would make an apple crumble, that's what she'd do. Stan might at times be obtuse but he would understand the symbolism of Joy making his mother's signature dish. She would try out

Savannah's suggestion. There was a bottle of whiskey in the back of the pantry.

She took two Panadol for her headache. She brushed her teeth for twice as long as usual. She blow-dried her hair using the big round brush Narelle said she should use but that she avoided because it made her wrist ache. She put on a flattering dress, one that Stan had once lavishly described as 'very nice'. Lipstick.

She walked out of the bedroom feeling peculiarly self-conscious. The house was silent. Was he even here?

'Stan?' she called out. Her voice cracked. Surely he would answer her. '*Stan?*'

No answer. She walked to the front room, pulled back the curtain. The car was gone. He was out early. She wondered where. Well. It was stupid to feel hurt that he had not told her he was going out, because this was the way they were living right now, but still her heart felt newly hurt, as tender and soft as bruised fruit.

She went to the kitchen, put the jug on for a cup of tea and opened the refrigerator to get out the apples for the crumble.

She'd bought five plump green Granny Smith apples when she was in the shops on Thursday, but now there was only one left, rolling about sadly in the crisper.

Stan had managed to eat *four apples* in two days.

She considered going back to bed and aborting the mission.

No. She rallied. She would pop down to the mini-mart by the railway station and pick up some more. They always opened early.

Except Stan had the car and it would take forever to walk there.

She made a low growling sound of frustration.

Steffi, who was lying in her favourite cool spot by the back door, lifted her head enquiringly, her tail thumping against the floor.

'I'm trying, Steffi,' said Joy. 'It's just that he's eaten all the apples and taken the car.'

Inspiration struck. She would change into shorts and *ride her brand new bike* to the mini-mart! So far she had only been for one little spin around the cul-de-sac. She loved the *idea* of the bike, but she was actually a bit nervous about traffic. She would face her fears! It was exhilarating to face your fears. Or so everyone said.

Half an hour later she stood on trembling legs in the mini-mart, plunking down the money for four overpriced Granny Smith apples. She was friendly as usual to the mini-mart man even though he scowled at her as usual (why did he hate her so?). She placed the apples in her wicker basket and began the ride home. She had to really work the pedals to get up the hill. In all the years she'd lived here she had never noticed the Mount Everest–like incline of this particular street.

Someone beeped their horn, making her heart leap. The bike swerved and the front wheel banged violently against the gutter. She straightened the handles, turned the corner, looked down and saw that the front tyre was completely flat.

'For goodness sake, what *next*?'

She threw the bike to the ground, hard, like a child. She stood, hands on hips, breathing heavily, looking at the bike and the apples. She kicked one of the apples like a ball. It rolled a listless short distance. She was not going to make an apple crumble today. Or ever again.

So that was the end of that.

You can choose the right shot, you can have a good swing and good technique, you can do everything right, and it can still go wrong. No player, no matter how good, makes one hundred per cent of their shots.

Some days you lose. They'd drummed that into the children too. You can be number one in the world, you can win and win and win, but it's inevitable: eventually you will lose.

She walked the rest of the way home, carrying her helmet by the strap. The car was in the driveway. She would go back and collect the bike once she'd calmed and cooled down. Inside, the

house was silent, but she could feel the skulking, sulking presence of her husband. Her shirt stuck to her sweaty body and her
mood flared as scratchy and hissy as Caro's awful thieving cat.
She went to the kitchen, got herself a glass of water and drank
deeply.

'You should probably read this.'

Stan's voice, suddenly so deep and loud behind her, made her
jump. The glass banged painfully against her teeth. She turned
to look at him. He threw some kind of bound document onto
the table.

'What is it?' she said.

'It's Harry Haddad's memoir,' said Stan. 'This is a preview
copy, I think you call it. He's sent it to us to read. I'm in it. We're
both in it.'

'Right,' she said.

She almost said, 'Whatever,' like a teenager. She'd forgotten
all about that damned memoir. It didn't matter now. The ugly
little secret was out.

'He admits he used to cheat when he played as a kid,' said
Stan. He tapped his finger on the document. She read the title:
Game to Harry.

'He *admits* it?' She put the glass down and slowly sank into a
chair at the table, pulling Harry's life story towards her. If Harry
was publicly admitting that he once cheated then it must have
been more than a few bad calls.

'Yes,' said Stan. 'It's not that surprising –'

'I beg your *pardon?*' She looked up at him. She couldn't believe
he would say that. 'What do you mean, it's not surprising? You
didn't believe Troy. You accused him of lying.'

'I did not,' said Stan. 'I never said he lied. I told him it was an
unfortunate reality of the game. I told him he would sometimes
face kids who made bad calls and that he shouldn't focus on his
opponent but on his own game.'

'Rubbish!' She wanted to grab the back of his head and
force him to look in the right direction where he could see his

past clearly. 'You took Harry's side! You didn't support your own son!'

'*My* son assaulted another player! Of course I didn't support him. Are you crazy?'

'Don't you *dare* call me crazy.' She was electrified with rage: against her husband, against those long-ago doctors who couldn't help her daughters, against the rude mini-mart man. Her hair did *not* look nice right now, it was all flat and sweaty, and her legs still wobbled from that bike ride up Mount bloody Everest from her failed mission to get apples to make her horrible husband's nasty mother's apple crumble. 'Troy lost his temper because he didn't have your support!'

'Troy was given every opportunity. They were *all* given every opportunity. They have no idea how lucky they were.'

She felt the criticism of her children like a physical blow. 'They played their *hearts* out!'

He didn't listen. His mind was still on Harry. His mind had always been on Harry: Harry's talent, Harry's potential. Harry, Harry, Harry.

'Do you want to know why that poor kid cheated?' he roared. He picked up the bound document and shook it violently at her. 'Because his father told him his sister had cancer.'

The words jolted Joy, like a change in direction so sudden it could rupture an Achilles tendon. She thought she already knew everything that Stan had to say in this argument.

She said faintly, 'He told him Savannah had cancer?'

'Like father, like daughter.' He smiled with grim satisfaction, as if he'd predicted exactly this bizarre outcome, and pushed the manuscript across the table towards her. 'He told Harry that he had to win prize money so his sister could get some kind of life-saving medicine. Dumb kid thought he was playing to save his sister's life. No wonder he cheated. If he'd stayed with me, I would have found out and put a stop to it, but I never got that opportunity because *you* made a unilateral decision to send him away!'

His hands were splayed like claws, like he wanted to strangle her.

She could not think about Harry now. She focused instead on the information she'd had back then.

'Your children needed your support!' she shouted back. '*I* needed your support!'

'You had no right! Coaching was my *profession*!' Stan towered over her and she was not frightened, she was exhilarated, because the fractured shell of their marriage was finally cracking open like a coconut. She wanted it all out. She wanted to finally say everything she'd never said.

'What about *my* profession?' She banged her chest with her fist. 'What about me? What about my career? My sacrifice?'

'Your sacrifice?' His disbelief was like a public shaming. As if *she* had anything to sacrifice. She wasn't worth anything: not a smile from the mini-mart man, not a phone call from her children.

'*I gave up my tennis for you,*' she said. Finally she'd said it out loud. All these years it had been there, never on the tip of her tongue, not at the back of her head, but right at the centre of her chest, beneath her collarbone, between her breasts, right where she continued to bang her fist, over and over.

What about me, what about me, what about me?

She'd never wanted his gratitude, just his acknowledgement. Just once. Because otherwise, what had been the point of her entire life? Of all those lamb chops she'd grilled? Of all that spaghetti bolognaise? My God, she despised spaghetti bolognaise. Night after night after night, plate after plate after plate. The laundry, the ironing, the mopping, the sweeping, the driving. She'd never resented it at the time but now she resented every moment, every single bloody lamb chop.

He said quietly, 'I never asked you to give anything up, Joy.'

But that was the point. He didn't have to ask her.

'If you wanted it, you would have done it,' he said. The anger had gone from his voice. She could see that familiar deathly stillness coming over him. He was removing himself from the situation: first mentally, then physically.

She knew what came next, what always came next. In a moment she'd be alone in this big silent house with her thoughts and regrets.

Stan said, 'If you'd really wanted it, nothing would have stopped you.'

She couldn't speak. Did he not see that the only thing that could have stopped her was her love for him?

Then he delivered his final damning judgement. 'You were never going to rank in the top ten, Joy. If I thought you could have got there, I would never have let you stop.'

The air whooshed from her like a fist to the stomach. He would never have *let* her stop. As if her sacrifice had been his considered decision.

If she had been the one to be injured it wouldn't have occurred to him to give up his career.

He was wrong, and there was no way in the world that she could go back in time and prove it, to him or to herself.

Instead, she reacted instinctively. 'You weren't good enough to coach Harry. He was better off without you. You would have held him back! He needed a better coach than you!'

It wasn't true. She believed Stan to be one of the best coaches in the country, maybe the world. She knew what *he* could have been without the tethers of a family, but didn't he know what *she* could have been? How far she could have flown?

He put Harry's memoir back on the table. He patted the pocket of his jeans, pulled out the car keys.

She dug deep for the most glittering pieces of vitriol she could find. 'I was the one who made Delaneys a success. Everyone knows it. If it wasn't for me, you'd have *nothing*, you'd be *nothing* but a washed-up, useless . . . *nothing*!'

The words bounced off him. He turned to walk away and she could not stand it. It was not fair that he got to leave. It had never been fair. It had never been right. And yet she'd endured it, over and over again, and her children had endured it, and it was unacceptable, inexcusable behaviour and she would no longer accept, she would no longer excuse. This time he would stay.

She ran after him, and even as she ran, part of herself registered the shame and indignity and inappropriateness of her actions. She floated up to the skylight and observed herself: a small sweaty senior citizen running out of her nice kitchen and down the hallway towards the front door after her husband, shouting incoherently, alongside an old dog, barking confusedly, trying to work out where the danger lay because there were no strangers in the house, so what could there be to fear?

Joy reached for the back of her husband's checked blue and white shirt, the shirt she'd ironed, to wrench him back, to make him stay. Steffi ran in crazed panting circles around them. Stan swung around and the dog tripped him. He lurched forward, nearly falling. One hand grabbed at the wall, causing the framed photo of Brooke with her Under 8s regional trophy to swing and bang and crack. Joy's outstretched hand, clawing for his shirt, instead raked down Stan's cheek, drawing instant blood with her vicious broken nails.

He grabbed her, his fingers painful on her shoulders.

She froze because his face was no longer his. It was an unfamiliar mask of ugly rage.

Her heart stopped. The world stopped.

For the first time in her sixty-nine years she felt the fear: the fear every woman knows is always waiting for her, the possibility that lurks and scuttles in the shadows of her mind, even if she's spent her entire life being so tenderly loved and protected by good men.

chapter fifty-four

Now

'Let's see it one last time,' said Christina.

Ethan pressed play and they sat, side by side at his desk, transfixed by the jerky but clear colour footage from the CCTV provided by the neighbours who lived two doors away in the same cul-de-sac as the Delaneys. The camera had been smashed by a hailstone in the big storm two days after Joy had disappeared and Caro Azinovic's son, who had installed the camera for his widowed mother, had been getting it fixed. He was the one who had brought police this damning video revealing a fish-eye view of the front of his mother's house. It captured, accidentally, a pie-shaped sliver of the Delaneys' driveway.

Christina and Ethan watched Stan Delaney emerge from the front door of his home, at two minutes past midnight on the day after his wife disappeared, struggling to carry an unwieldy, floppy object wrapped in a blanket to his car.

He opened the boot of his car, dumped the object, leaned in to rearrange it, reached up with both hands to slam the boot shut, and then he stood – for exactly three minutes and forty-seven seconds – both hands flat on the car, his head bowed, like a man in solemn, reverent prayer, before he finally lifted his head and walked off camera.

It was eerie and powerful to watch.

'Jesus,' said Ethan. 'The way he stands there, for all that time. It's so . . . my God.'

'I know it is,' said Christina. She would get her confession today. She could feel it. She would play this footage to Stan Delaney and she would not say a word or make a sound for the entire length of the video. She would watch him watch himself bow his head over his wife's body. She knew he was not a churchgoer, but she knew he'd been brought up Catholic, as had she, and she recognised the stance of a man in prayer, a man who longs to confess his sins.

Tonight she and Nico would go to meet their parish priest to discuss the holy sacrament of marriage and she would try not to think about the fact that Joy and Stan Delaney had once made the same vows that she and Nico would make next spring. She would not think about a young Joy Delaney or Polly Perkins promising their husbands to have and to hold, for better, for worse, for richer, for poorer, in sickness and health, until death do us part, until you carry my body out to the car in the dead of the night and dispose of it somewhere it will never be found, until I speak too loudly, until I spend too much money on a new iron, until I hold back your career for the sake of our family, until I kiss another man at a party, until I displease you in some way I cannot yet imagine.

'Christina?' said Ethan.

'Sorry,' said Christina. 'What were you saying?'

He said, 'Nothing really. Just that I didn't pick it. That first day we interviewed him, I knew he was hiding stuff from us, but when he looked at that photo of his wife, I thought, No way did he do it. He loves her.'

'I never thought he didn't love her.' Christina adjusted her engagement ring so the diamond was centred again on her finger.

But she'd always known he'd killed her.

That was the cruel knowledge that she would carry down the aisle on her wedding day along with her bridal bouquet of white roses and blush-pink gardenias: it was possible for both things to be true.

chapter fifty-five

Valentine's Day

Stan Delaney had always known that women had the power to draw blood with their words. It was his mother's favourite hobby: to knife the soft stupid defenceless egos of her husband and her son.

Don't tell the boy he's going to play at Wimbledon one day, he's dumb enough to believe it. The two of you are as dumb as dog shit.

Not every day, just most days. Not when she was drunk, when she was sober. That's when she got nasty.

She'd jab her finger at the side of her head and smile her beautiful smile at her husband and say, *The lights are on, but nobody's home, isn't that right, my love?*

Stan's father had no arsenal of clever words with which to defend himself. He quailed and recoiled. He smiled stupidly as if his wife had made a joke that was too clever for him. He shut down and went silent. He took it and took it.

He took it and took it until one day he didn't take it anymore.

Fourteen-year-old Stan ran to his mother where she lay crumpled and still on the floor, and it was good that he did that. He could always tell himself that his first instinctive response had been to run to his mother, to put his body between her and his father, but he also could never forget the first tiny, terrible, traitorous thought that came into his head:

She deserved it.

So faint, so tiny, he sometimes pretended he'd imagined he thought it. It happened so fast, but it also happened so slowly, and it was so long ago, who knew what he'd really thought at that moment? You couldn't rely on memory. It was an unreliable source.

*

Stan was just like his father. He'd always known it. Not clever and quick like his mother. Not clever and quick like his wife. Not good at school. Thick as a brick. Not the sharpest tool in the shed.

*

At the age of seventy, he felt his wife's flesh beneath his hands as his father's colossal rage and humiliation, his pain and hurt, ballooned within his chest and exploded behind his eyes.

chapter fifty-six

Now

'I think they're going to arrest my dad any day now,' said Claire Geer's ex-husband, his eyes on the early-morning glitter-blue of Sydney Harbour. There was a croissant flake on his lower lip, and something so childlike and anguished about the way he said 'my dad'.

They sat side by side, with takeaway coffees and almond croissants in white paper bags, on a park bench overlooking the ferry stop where Troy had kissed her for the first time. She wondered if Troy remembered this, if he'd even deliberately suggested this location for that reason. Surely not. He had big, terrible things on his mind right now.

Claire reached over and moved the crumb from his lip with her fingertip. 'Why do you think that?'

'We heard the police have CCTV footage from the neighbours across the street.' He stopped. 'That apparently shows something . . . very bad. I can't even imagine what.'

His voice shook.

'Jesus,' said Claire. The coffee tasted sour in her mouth. She rested the takeaway cup on the bench next to her and looked at their bare legs, stretched out side by side in front of them. They both wore shorts. Their legs looked like the legs of a couple with a sunshiny weekend ahead of them, not a divorced couple with seedy infidelity behind them and a potential tragedy in front of them, not to mention an awkward procreation arrangement.

Claire Geer was thirty-four years old. She had long curly red hair that everyone commented on, a world history degree that didn't interest potential employers or anyone really except for her father (he was a history teacher), and an unexpectedly fulfilling career in the US in health administration, or not that unexpected because she was the kind of girl who made the best of things, whose school reports and job references always mentioned her 'positive attitude'. 'I bet you were a cheerleader,' her new husband had said when they first met, and of course that wasn't a thing in Australia and Claire couldn't even do a cartwheel, but she'd let him categorise her as a sunny, sweet Aussie girl. She was *nearly* the girl he believed her to be. She was a people-pleaser, as sunny and sweet as an Australian summer. No need to mention the humidity or mosquitoes, the bushfires or hailstorms. She loved Geoff dearly, but not in the helpless, hopeless way she'd loved Troy. The point of history was to learn from it, not repeat it.

She would have happily never seen Troy Delaney ever again, or even returned to Australia. The wounds had healed nicely, no visible scars, and she'd found a new life, a new love, so she could once again watch romantic comedies without scoffing.

But here she was, in Sydney, sitting next to her ex-husband.

She knew that Troy had only consented to her trying to get pregnant with their embryos as a form of penance. She'd seen the instant, instinctive horror on his face when she'd put it to him in New York last year.

She also knew her husband, Geoff, did not want her pregnant with her ex-husband's child. He didn't want a family that badly. She'd seen the exact same instinctive horrified response on Geoff's face when she'd put it to him.

Both men were doing it for her: one out of guilt and one out of love. It was the first time in her life she'd asked more of someone than they wanted to give, more than she maybe deserved, but the truth was that she didn't think twice when it became clear it was her only option. She couldn't long for her own biological child and leave five possibilities frozen for eternity.

She'd been in Australia now since last November, trying to get pregnant, while Geoff had stayed in Texas, except for a two-week trip at Christmas. It had been a strange, surreal time: the longest period in her life since she'd graduated that she hadn't had a full-time job. She was reading and doing a lot of walking. She'd met with her ex-husband a handful of times: always for businesslike coffee, and they seemed to have found an acceptable, companionable rhythm. She'd even introduced him to Geoff when he visited in December – it seemed the polite, grown-up thing to do considering their arrangement – but it had been weird and clunky, awful really, and she could tell the two men hated each other. Both men had been at their worst: show-offy and insecure.

But now Troy's mother was missing, none of that mattered.

'I just don't believe it,' she said. 'I know I haven't seen your parents in years but it just doesn't seem possible to me.'

She remembered the toast that Stan had given at their wedding.

'In my profession, love means zero,' Stan had said, champagne glass in hand, and he'd waited a moment to be sure everyone got the joke, nodding happily as all the guests groaned. Then he said, 'But in life, love means everything. Love wins the match. I'm not the sharpest tool in the shed, but I made the smartest decision of my life when I married Troy's mother, and I reckon Troy just made the smartest decision of his life when he married this beautiful girl right here. Don't ever let her go, mate, and welcome to the family, sweetheart.'

Then he raised his glass to Claire and sat down and kissed Joy, his hand at the back of her head, pulling her to him as if they were the young bride and groom.

It was impossible to imagine that man hurting his wife – that man would have died for his wife – but then again, it had been impossible to imagine his son, with whom she'd been so besotted, cheating on Claire for no good reason.

That's what had been so painful. They weren't in a rut. They weren't having 'issues'. He didn't fall in love with someone else. He wasn't even drunk or high. He just randomly, arbitrarily, idiotically broke her heart.

Unimaginable things happened every single day and there wasn't always a good reason.

'Brooke has found Dad a good criminal lawyer. We know exactly what to do when the call comes through,' said Troy. 'Brooke is standing by Dad. She said that even if he did it, she'll stand by him. Brooke says one moment of madness doesn't nullify a lifetime of love, but I think it does, I think it does nullify it, don't you?'

Claire lifted her hands. 'You're in an impossible situation, Troy.'

'Brooke and I aren't talking,' said Troy painfully.

'You'll work it out,' said Claire. 'It's all too raw at the moment.'

'Dad never gave me an inch.' He made a harsh jarring sound that only just resembled a laugh. 'He can hardly expect me to forgive him for killing my mother.'

'I don't think he would expect your forgiveness,' said Claire. 'If this happened, if there really was a moment of madness, he would never forgive himself.'

Troy glanced sidelong at her. 'He was so angry with me. For what I did. To you.'

'Ancient history,' said Claire. It wasn't. Technically it was 'contemporary history', a subset of modern history. She crumpled her empty croissant bag into a ball.

A ferry sounded its sonorous horn as it lumbered across the water towards them.

'That's where I kissed you for the first time,' said Troy, his eyes on the ferry stop.

'Don't,' said Claire sharply.

'Sorry,' said Troy. 'I just didn't want you to think I'd forgotten.'

They watched the ferry bump clumsily to a stop. The passengers emerged across the gangway. A savage-eyed seagull stalked towards them in the hope of something better than croissant crumbs.

'This one worked,' said Claire quietly.

He said nothing. She thought he didn't get it.

'I know it did,' said Troy finally, without looking at her. 'Congratulations. I'm really happy for you.'

'You *know*?' She swung sideways to look at him. 'How do you know?'

'I just knew. The moment I saw you. Something about your face. And you're not drinking your coffee.'

'That's not why. It just tastes really strange today.'

'It tastes strange today because you're pregnant,' said Troy. 'It's great coffee.'

She looked with astonishment at the takeaway coffee cup. 'I can't believe you worked that out before me.'

'I know you,' said Troy quietly. He lifted a hand quickly, as if to accept a fair penalty by the ref. 'Sorry. I mean, I *knew* you. I once knew you.'

They sat in silence and watched the ferry heading back out towards the horizon, and the grief for what could have been and what could now never be bowed their heads.

'I wish I could tell my mother about this,' said Troy.

'I wish I could tell your mother about it too,' said Claire.

She wished so many things were different about this moment, except for the baby, who would be cherished, who had been created out of modern medicine and love, reluctant, guilty, complicated love, but still love.

Somehow it would all work out. She would make sure of it.

chapter fifty-seven

'Troy thinks Dad is going to be arrested today,' said Logan.

'What does Troy know?' said Indira Mallick, and she realised she'd automatically slipped into the role of supporting Logan in the ongoing competition between him and his younger brother, although only Troy openly wanted to win.

Indira and Logan sat at the glass-topped table where they used to eat dinner each night.

She'd told Logan that she was here in Sydney for a friend's baby shower, and it was true, but she would never have flown all this way for an awful baby shower. She'd come for Logan. 'You're still in love with him,' accused a friend as they cooed, 'So *cute!*' each time the guest of honour opened another gift and held it up above the proud pregnant curve of her stomach. Indira had informed her sternly that her ex-boyfriend's mother was missing. She was here as a friend.

'How is Amy coping?' she asked Logan.

'She's okay. I think she's actually in a session right now with her therapist, or counsellor, or whatever we're meant to call him,' said Logan.

'That's good,' said Indira. 'She should probably –'

She stopped herself. She was no longer a part of the Delaney family and therefore no longer entitled to an opinion about how Amy should manage her mental health.

Amy had once told Indira that she was pigeonholed because she was easily offended when she was a child and now everyone assumed she was still easily offended, which was offensive. Indira had sympathised because she too was pigeonholed by her family as the 'clumsy one', even though she was no longer especially clumsy.

She picked up one of the 'missing person' flyers on Logan's table. It was too busy, with too many different typefaces. It broke her heart that she hadn't been the one to design it. The photo showed Joy wearing a t-shirt that Indira had given her. It was screen-printed with three big gerberas. She and Joy had a shared fondness for the flower. They bought little gerbera-themed gifts for each other.

'Do you want any help putting these flyers up?' she asked Logan.

'It's okay,' said Logan. 'They're everywhere. I feel like we've done everything possible to get the word out there. She's just . . . vanished.'

Indira looked at Joy's smiling face. Logan's mother would never deliberately stay out of contact for this long. She was the sort of person who kept effortlessly in touch with everyone. Even after Indira broke up with Logan, Joy had continued to send the occasional non-intrusive text or email, filled with exclamation marks and emojis.

Logan didn't seem at all like his mother, but in this they were alike: he was good at keeping in touch with people too. He was the friend who went around to people's houses and helped build their back deck or fix their drainage problem. He was the friend people called when they'd locked themselves out of their house, or when an appliance exploded. She should never have called him passive. Passive people didn't spend entire weekends helping their friends build back decks.

He was a good person.

She experienced the truth of this like a physical injury. A literal twist of the heart.

'Are you okay?' asked Logan.

'Don't worry about *me*,' said Indira. 'I'm worried about you.'

She put her hand on top of his. He looked terrible. He was always scruffy – scruffiness was part of his identity, it was how he differentiated himself from his brother (that was her theory, of which he did not approve) but this was a new level of scruffiness. His eyes were red, his skin blotchy, his jeans sagged around his waist like an old man's trousers. He must have lost weight.

Seven months ago, she'd broken up with Logan because she'd felt trapped, pleasantly trapped, but trapped nonetheless, in a perfectly nice life, living in this perfectly adequate townhouse, going to the same perfectly adequate Mexican restaurant every Friday night. It wasn't that she loved change. The thing she most disliked in Logan was the thing she most disliked in herself. She too loved the seductiveness of a daily routine.

Logan didn't chase her to the airport like a scene in a movie. Naturally he didn't.

But then: *nothing happened*. Her life didn't magically become different. She was still Indira. Just alone and lonely. She missed him. She missed sex. She had assumed sex was like chocolate – if it wasn't in the house she wouldn't think about it.

It had begun to occur to her that she wasn't trapped because of *Logan*; she'd been trapped in her own Indira self, like everyone was trapped in their own selves.

'What about Troy and Brooke? How are they?' She could feel the question everyone was surely asking unpleasant and sour in her mouth: *Do you think your dad did it?*

'Troy and Brooke aren't speaking,' said Logan. 'It's like Troy thinks he's proving his loyalty to Mum, and Brooke thinks she's proving her loyalty to Dad.'

'And you?' said Indira. 'What about you? Are you okay?'

'I'll be fine.' He suddenly flipped his hand over and held on to hers. She watched his face. A muscle in his jaw shuddered. He squeezed her hand once, tightly, and then he returned it to her, carefully and gently across the table.

She held the released, rejected hand with her other hand as if to comfort it.

Logan tugged hard on his earlobe. 'Are you happy?'

'I'm fine,' she said. 'You don't need to talk about me right now, not when you're going through this terrible thing.'

'Are you painting?'

'Am I *painting*?' She gave a half-laugh. 'I'm all talk and no action when it comes to painting, you know that.'

'That's because you need a studio,' said Logan urgently.

'Sure, Logan,' said Indira. 'That's what I need.'

'You need somewhere like this,' said Logan. 'Just for example.'

He opened his laptop and clicked on a real estate website.

'What's this?' Indira pulled the laptop towards her and her elbow knocked against the cup of tea she'd been drinking. Logan caught it before it spilled, with practised ease, as if he'd known that was going to happen.

'It's a three-bedroom house,' said Logan. 'It has a granny flat out the back. The light is beautiful.'

Indira stared without comprehension at the screen.

'Sorry, Logan, I don't quite get –'

'I looked at it just before Mum went missing.' Logan tapped his finger on the screen. 'It's further out from the city but it would be worth it for more space.'

Had his anxiety about his mother made him lose his mind?

'I also bought you a ring,' he said. 'It's in my sock drawer.'

She stared at him.

'Obviously I'm not proposing. Not *now*. Not when my father is about to be arrested for murdering my mother. It's just that you're here, looking . . .'

He gestured up and down at her body as if it were obvious what he wanted to say. She looked down at herself, mystified. She was wearing a comfortable shift dress that he must have seen a hundred times before. Her nose was red around the nostrils from a cold last week.

'Looking so bloody beautiful,' he said, and his voice broke on the word 'beautiful'. Indira was stunned. She had never seen him cry. Not even close.

When they first started dating, he used to call her beautiful all the time and she'd snap at him because it embarrassed her, it made her feel as if she needed to urgently call out to a derisive audience, *Don't laugh, I know it's not true!* So eventually he stopped saying it.

She'd successfully trained her beautiful boyfriend not to call her beautiful.

Logan rested his head in his hands. His voice was muffled. 'Sorry. I don't know why I said that. It just came out. I'm so tired.'

'It's okay.' She put her hand on the back of his neck and leaned in close to his ear. 'Everything is going to be okay.'

She didn't know that, of course. All she knew was that right now she was going to make him eat, and then sleep, and then she was going to stay by his side for whatever horrendous or wondrous things lay ahead.

chapter fifty-eight

'Beautiful day,' commented Ethan to Christina as they drove towards Stan Delaney's home to arrest him for his wife's murder.

'It is.' Christina looked out the car window at the cloudless blue sky.

'How do you think he'll react?' asked Ethan. Ethan's shirt today was an exquisite teal blue. The colour of a bridesmaid's dress. Christina looked down and saw a small stain like old blood on her shirt. That's what happened when you got dressed in the dark so as not to wake your partner. It was probably tomato sauce.

'My bet is he'll be calm,' said Christina. 'He will have been given legal advice not to say a word.'

Her phone began to ring with an unfamiliar number. 'Detective Khoury,' she answered, pre-emptively brusque. Nico told her she sounded too angry on the phone. He said not everyone was a potential criminal. He was wrong. Everyone was so a potential criminal. Or a potential victim.

'Hi there, Detective Khoury. How are you?' It was the posh velvety tone of a man who was confident that his social status was superior to that of the vast majority of the population.

Christina was irritated. 'Who is this?'

'This is Dr Henry Edgeworth. I understand you've been

trying to reach me. I've just returned from overseas.' Most people sounded nervous when returning a phone call from the police, but not this wanker.

'Yes, that's right,' said Christina. Took your bloody time, mate. 'It's in relation to a missing woman. Joy Delaney.'

'Delaney,' he repeated. His silk-smooth voice snagged.

'There was a phone call from your apartment to her on the fourteenth of February this year.'

Christina felt Ethan's attention on her half of the conversation. He would have worked out that it was the plastic surgeon finally returning their call.

'I'm afraid I can't help you,' he said. 'I don't know anyone by that name.'

'Can you explain why our phone records show a phone call from the landline at your apartment on that day that lasted forty minutes?'

'Perhaps you've got the wrong Dr Edgeworth.'

'Right,' said Christina. 'Or is it possible that someone else could have made a phone call from your apartment? A family member? Your wife?'

He was guarded now. 'My wife and children never stay at the apartment. We have a family home in the eastern suburbs. The apartment is just a small one-bedroom near the hospital for when I'm working late. It's more convenient.'

Yeah, I bet it's more convenient, thought Christina.

'We have no doubt that the call came from your apartment. We also believe it's probable that Joy Delaney met with foul play,' said Christina. 'So I really need you to think carefully about this.'

Another pause. 'Is this the old lady? I saw the husband on the news.'

'That's right,' said Christina.

'Well.' He cleared his throat. 'Well, alright, I can tell you that I did have someone staying at the apartment a few weeks back. A . . . family friend.'

Girlfriend. Definitely a girlfriend.

'So, now I think about it, I'm guessing *she* was the one who called this lady,' said Dr Edgeworth. His voice grew in confidence. 'In fact, I'd say she definitely did. I expect they're related.'

Christina said, 'Why would you expect that?'

'Well, as it happens, this girl's name was Savannah Delaney.'

'Savannah *Delaney*,' repeated Christina, looking at Ethan. His eyebrows had popped.

Right from the beginning she'd known that Savannah was at the very centre of this investigation, and yet they still hadn't managed to locate the damned woman.

'Maybe she's her niece or something? She said her mother was dead.'

'When did you last have contact with her?'

'Not for a while now,' said Dr Edgeworth. 'Actually, the last time we spoke was probably . . . let me think . . . Valentine's Day.'

chapter fifty-nine

Simon Barrington's breath quickened as he stared at the words on his laptop screen. Was it a coincidence? Was he misremembering the words in Amy's mother's text? Did this mean nothing or everything? Had he just accidentally cracked the case of the disappearance of Joy Delaney?

He was sitting at the dining room table. He knew Amy was at home. She'd just walked in the door and given him a silent, stiff wave before running up the stairs to her room.

She was so fragile right now, like a delicate glass version of herself.

'You knew this wasn't ever going to be a thing, right?' she'd told him when they 'broke up' a few days ago, although Simon wasn't sure if there was anything to break. She made it sound as if there were blindingly obvious ethical considerations that prevented them from being together, as if they were married politicians from opposing parties, not flatmates with a larger than conventional age gap. They could have given it a shot.

But he said, 'Sure, I knew that,' because he didn't want anything to be difficult for her right now, and she was looking at him with such desperate entreaty.

'I'm hard work,' she told him. 'I'm hard work even when my mother isn't missing.'

He could have quoted his dad's favourite Kris Kristofferson song and told her that loving her was easier than anything he'd ever do again. He could have said, 'Let me help get you through this.' He could have said a lot of things, but he just said, mildly, 'I like hard work. I'm a hard worker.' Then he felt bad because she'd looked like she was about to cry, so he'd said, 'It's fine, Amy. Don't worry about me. Focus on your mother.'

There were footsteps on the stairs again. Was she going straight back out?

'Amy?' he called.

She came into the dining room.

'Hi,' she said. She looked pale and tired, but composed. 'I'm on my way out. My brother is picking me up. He thinks my dad might get arrested today.' She smiled without it reaching her eyes. 'Lucky I got in a quick session with my shrink. I'm good to go.'

'That text message your mother sent,' said Simon. 'Did it mention the number twenty-one?'

Amy looked startled. 'I think it did. But they were just random nonsense words. She did that when she texted without glasses.'

She tapped at her phone and showed him the text message. The wording was exactly as he remembered.

'Well, this might not be anything,' said Simon. 'But I was just thinking about Savannah, and how it turned out she was Harry Haddad's sister, so then I was Googling Harry, and I was looking at his charity work and I noticed this.'

He moved the laptop around so she could see the words.

She looked at the screen, then at her mother's text message and back at the screen again.

He saw her catch her breath.

chapter sixty

'Does this change anything?' Ethan frowned. 'That Joy talked to Savannah on the day she disappeared? And that was also the last day Dr Edgeworth had contact with Savannah?'

They'd stopped at an intersection, and he looked over at Christina, his hands on the wheel, trust and respect in his eyes, as if this was a question with a right or wrong answer, and that Christina, with her years of experience, would know the answer, and all he had to do was ask for it. He thought she had some special knowledge and that one day he would attain that knowledge, and for a vertiginous moment she felt like a kid, pretending she was an experienced detective. *I'm just little Chrissie Khoury, Ethan, what the hell would I know?*

'What do you think?' she said. Good mentoring.

'Well,' said Ethan. 'Is it possible that Joy and Savannah are somewhere together?'

'It's possible,' said Christina. 'Anything is possible without a body.'

'Call us when you've got a body,' the guys in Homicide said.

Accept nothing. Believe nothing. Check everything. Should they turn around?

'It doesn't change the evidence,' she said. 'The scratch marks, the bloodied t-shirt, the CCTV footage, the motive. We've got plenty.'

Their interview with Savannah's famous brother had told them exactly nothing. Harry Haddad spoke with fond respect of his former coaches, Joy and Stan Delaney, but said he hadn't spoken to his sister in many years. He thought his father might have once had an email address for her, but he wasn't sure. Harry was estranged from his mother, and had no contact details for her either. 'My mother remarried multiple times,' he said. 'I'm not even sure what surname she's decided to use these days.' His tone, initially warm and helpful, had begun to fray as he discussed his complicated family history.

Savannah was an optical illusion. A distraction. Her only relevance was that she'd given Stan a motive to murder his wife.

'So we're still going to arrest him,' said Ethan.

'We're still going to arrest him,' said Christina. 'And then we're going to track down this Savannah, whoever the fuck she is, and arrest her too.'

'For what?'

'For pissing me off,' said Christina.

Ethan grinned. 'Fair enough.'

chapter sixty-one

Caro Azinovic sat in the front room of her house, drinking a cup of tea while she enjoyed an overdue telephone call with her daughter in Denmark.

She watched a white car pull up outside the Delaneys' house and a man and a woman emerge. They both wore suits. There was something purposeful and foreboding about the way they walked towards the front door.

She thought of the security camera footage she and her son had given to the police.

'Oh dear God,' her son had said as they watched it together.

'You can't actually see what he's carrying,' Caro had said.

'At that time of night?' said Jacob. 'It doesn't look good, Mum.'

Caro and her daughter had only exchanged a few brief emails since she'd been in Sydney last month and they were overdue for a catch-up. Petra was up very late on the other side of the world because she was upset about a complicated issue regarding her son's school and Caro listened sympathetically. She'd thought the Danish were so socially advanced that there wouldn't be such a thing as schoolyard politics over there, but apparently it was universal.

'I think the police might be at Joy's house right now,' she told Petra when she finally finished her story.

'Why would the police be there?'

Caro filled her in on the dreadful details.

Her daughter sounded panicked. 'But, Mum, why didn't you tell me any of this before?'

'Well, this is the first time we've properly talked since you went back, so it didn't even occur to me. To be honest I've been so het up about it all I –'

'Mum, you need to tell me the name of whoever is in charge of the investigation. *Right now.*'

'But why?'

'Because I saw Joy Delaney on Valentine's Day.'

chapter sixty-two

The street was deathly quiet as they pulled into the driveway. Not even the sound of a leaf blower in the distance.

As they walked towards the house Christina's phone began to ring, a strident sound in the silence. She flicked it to voicemail.

'Good morning,' sighed Stan Delaney when he opened the door to them, as if they were unwelcome but expected visitors, which Christina guessed was exactly what they were. He was unshaven today, bare feet, in shorts and a black t-shirt. 'Come in.'

He led them down the hallway, past the framed photos. There was a faded gap where the framed photo they'd seized had hung. The house smelled of toast.

They went into the living room where they'd had all their previous discussions. Stan gestured at the couch.

'You haven't found her, have you?' he said suddenly.

Afterwards Christina would think back to that moment and wonder if *this* was when she should have known that something wasn't right, because while his face most certainly showed fear, which she'd expect, it also showed hope, and why would he be hopeful?

Yet even if she'd stopped to second-guess herself she would have been reassured by the good solid evidence that had led her to this point. Her gut instinct had been supported by piece after piece of compelling evidence.

This was not the time for second-guessing.

She spoke clearly. 'Stan Delaney, you're under arrest for the murder of Joy Margaret Delaney.'

He didn't flinch. His face hardened and smoothed, as if he were slowly but perceptibly turning to stone.

'You don't have to say or do anything unless you want to. Anything you do say or do will be –'

Ethan said, 'Christina.' He had his head tilted as if he were listening to something. 'I think there might be –'

She ignored him and continued speaking to Stan. 'Anything you do say or do will be recorded and may later be used as evidence. Do you understand that?'

'Yes,' said Stan. 'I understand that.'

'Detective Khoury,' said Ethan formally, a bit louder.

'What?' She felt a spasm of irritation.

Ethan lifted his chin to indicate something in the hallway behind her.

Christina turned around at the same time as a small woman with white shoulder-length hair came into the room, removing a backpack from her shoulders. A set of keys dangled from her finger.

Christina had been thinking so much about this woman and her life and her choices, it was as discombobulating as seeing a glamorous movie star in the flesh.

Stan Delaney walked like a man in a dream towards his wife and lifted her right off her feet. Her keys crashed to the floor.

Stan cried, his hand cradling the back of his wife's head. He cried like a man cries when he has little or no experience of crying: dry sobs that racked his body.

It was the first time Christina had seen Stan Delaney, the man she wanted to convict for his wife's murder, display even a modicum of emotion.

'What in the *world*?' said Joy Delaney.

chapter sixty-three

Valentine's Day

Stan Delaney felt his colossal rage and humiliation, his pain and hurt, balloon within his chest and explode behind his eyes. But he was not his father. Just like his father had not been his father that day, the day his body finally reacted to the daily onslaught of cruelty.

That one action had defined the rest of his father's life and the rest of Stan's life.

He might be as stupid as his father, as thick as a brick, but he would never make his father's mistake. He would never hurt a woman, not any woman, but especially not this woman, not the fair-haired tiny girl with the springy walk who had materialised like a miracle at that party all those years ago and smiled up at him with gleaming, combative eyes. He'd known, before that song finished its last silly synthetic beat, that she was the only girl for him.

More than fifty years later, he dropped his violently trembling hands. He turned away.

He didn't slam the door. He closed it with a gentle click behind him.

chapter sixty-four

Now

'Your family has been very worried about you, Mrs Delaney.'

Christina managed to keep her voice steady as she thought of the time and resources she'd spent trying to prove this woman's murder. She thought of her boss's face.

Accept nothing. Believe nothing. Check everything.

She hadn't followed her own rules. They should have turned around once they got the information from the plastic surgeon about Savannah speaking to Joy on the same day she disappeared.

'But I don't understand,' said Joy Delaney. She stood next to her husband, holding his hand in hers, patting it distractedly. She looked well rested and tanned. 'Why would you call the police, Stan? You knew exactly where I was, I left you a note.'

'I never got a note,' said Stan shakily. He was a plant returning to life in front of Christina's eyes: back straightening, shoulders dropping. 'There was no note, Joy.' He exhaled hard. 'At first I thought you were just making a point, but this last week, you know, I really started to think something terrible had happened to you.'

'There *was so* a note!' insisted Joy. 'I put it on the fridge door so you couldn't possibly miss it.'

'There was no note on the fridge,' said Stan. 'Where have you *been*?'

'But I left it right there! It was a very nice note! I put a lot of thought into it.'

Stan said, 'Did you use the London Eye fridge magnet, Joy?'

'Oh,' said Joy. She grimaced. 'That was stupid. Oh dear.'

'This fridge magnet is top-heavy,' said Stan to Christina. He was almost chummy with her now. 'Bad design. It keeps falling off the fridge.'

'It's a pity because it's a lovely magnet,' said Joy. 'It has a picture of us on the London Eye.'

'You didn't see the note on the floor?' said Christina to Stan, still treating him as a man with something to hide.

'I did not,' said Stan.

'But surely you called the children, Stan! I texted them!' said Joy.

'The text made no sense, Joy,' said Stan. 'It was gibberish.'

Joy looked at Christina and Ethan. 'Has he even offered you a cup of tea?'

'We didn't expect a cup of tea,' said Christina. 'We were in the process of arresting him.'

The dog pattered into the room and happily licked Joy's shoes. Christina shuffled out of its way. She'd met Steffi a few times now, and the animal seemed harmless and cute enough, but she wasn't a pet person, and she had the strangest feeling that this one actively disliked her.

Joy fondled the dog's ears. 'Hello, Steffi, did you miss me?'

Stan said, 'You know, I've got a good idea what happened to that note.'

'Oh, *Steffi*,' said Joy.

'The dog eats paper,' Stan explained to Christina as Joy bent to pick up the keys she'd dropped and was suddenly transfixed by something she saw on the floor.

'*Stan*,' she said.

She put her hands flat to the floorboards and looked up at him.

434

'You like it?' He beamed.

'It looks beautiful,' she said rapturously. 'Oh my goodness, it looks beautiful.'

Joy straightened up again, her eyes still on the floor. 'We had this awful purple carpet in here.' She corrected herself quickly. 'Well, it wasn't awful, it was just – not really my style.'

Stan said, 'It's okay. It was awful.'

'Anyway, while I've been away, Stan pulled up all the carpet and polished the floorboards! Doesn't it look beautiful!'

'I sanded the floorboards myself,' said Stan.

Christina looked at Ethan, and knew that he too was replaying the CCTV footage they'd seen, not of a man carrying his wife's body but a man struggling to carry a roll of old carpet, a man finally doing a particular task his wife had probably been asking him to do for years. She thought of the witness who had seen him with bloodshot eyes and covered in dust, not because he'd buried his wife but because he'd been sanding back hardwood floors.

Joy's smile faded. 'I'm sorry, did you say you were about to arrest Stan? Arrest him for what?'

There was a moment of silence. Right now Stan Delaney couldn't look any sweeter or more innocent if he'd tried. He couldn't take his shining eyes off his wife.

Christina reminded herself that every one of her colleagues would have made an arrest based on the facts at her disposal.

'Speeding?' guessed Joy. 'He has got a terrible lead foot.'

'No, not speeding,' said Christina evenly. She closed her eyes and tapped a fingertip against her forehead. Her mother had recently got into 'tapping' for stress relief. 'We were arresting him for your murder.'

'Murder?' said Joy. Her eyes widened. 'You thought he murdered me?'

'The evidence was compelling,' said Christina, almost to herself.

'But how could it possibly be compelling?' Joy held out her arms wide. 'I'm *alive*!'

'Yes,' said Christina. 'You certainly appear to be.'

'Surely you spoke to our children,' said Joy to Christina. 'They would have set you straight. Didn't Stan give you their telephone numbers?'

'They had that t-shirt.' Stan spoke to Joy as if they were alone. 'The one we used to wrap up your foot when you cut it on the oyster that day at the beach. Remember? They found it "buried" out the back. They thought *I* buried it.'

'Of course I remember,' said Joy. 'I thought I put it in the bin. I bet Caro's damned cat ran off with it. Otis steals laundry all around the neighbourhood.' Her voice trailed. 'I don't understand. Are you saying you thought it was . . .' She looked at Christina with a sick expression. 'You thought it was my blood?'

'Well, it *was* your blood,' said Stan reasonably.

'But for goodness sake, Stan, surely you *explained*! It was very simple to explain!'

'Of course, I was going to explain, but by the time they found the shirt, it was obvious I was in trouble. I decided not to say anything until I had my lawyer with me,' said Stan.

'Your lawyer?' scoffed Joy. 'What lawyer? You don't have a lawyer!'

'Brooke found me a criminal lawyer. Nice young fella. Turns out his father was that Ross Marshall, who used to play at the club back in the eighties, remember him?'

Watching Stan talk, Christina was reminded oddly of herself. She wasn't a big talker. Nico was the talker. But when they were back together after any time apart, she suddenly became Chatty Cathy, desperate to tell him everything she'd been saving up.

'The one with the underhand serve?' asked Joy vaguely.

'That's the one!' said Stan. 'He plays lawn bowls now. Probably suits him better.'

'You can't genuinely have thought he murdered me,' said Joy to Christina.

'I had those scratches on my face,' said Stan. 'It looked like you scratched me.'

'That's because I did scratch you!' said Joy. She splayed her right hand to display her fingernails. 'I felt terrible about that.'

'So you didn't get it from a hedge,' said Christina to Stan. At least her instincts had been correct there.

He met Christina's eyes. 'I knew how that might have looked to you.'

He'd lied in a criminal investigation. She could charge him with perverting the course of justice. Depending on his wife's actions, she could charge her with public mischief. She was going to bloody well charge someone with something today.

Joy sank suddenly onto the couch. 'This is quite upsetting.'

'It has been quite upsetting, yes,' said Stan dryly. He sat next to her, so close their legs touched. The dog sat on the floor in between them, her tail sweeping back and forth.

Joy pulled a cushion out from behind her back and placed it on her lap. 'I hope people don't hear about this.' The dog rolled over on her back and displayed her tummy, which Joy began to rub with her foot.

'People have heard about it, sweetheart. There was a press conference,' said Stan. 'You're a missing person. It was on the news. There were helicopters. People tramping through the reserve looking for you.'

'Looking for me? Like I was hiding under a bush? Oh my Lord.'

'So let me get this straight. You're saying your dog ate the letter you left,' said Christina. 'And your neighbour's cat ran off with the bloodied t-shirt.'

'Lot of pets involved with this case, Detective Khoury,' commented Ethan soberly.

'So it seems, Constable Lim.' Christina shot him a look. His eyes danced. She bowed her head and squeezed the bridge of her nose while she considered the absurdity of this case.

Perhaps on the way home she and Ethan would rescue a kitten caught in a tree while the townspeople cheered.

'Why did you clean your car, Mr Delaney?' asked Christina. 'Two days after your wife went missing?'

Why did you insist on doing everything possible to make yourself look guilty?

'Joy has been saying for months that the car smells of sour milk,' said Stan.

'I spilled a banana milkshake,' said Joy.

'So I thought I'd surprise her.' He beamed at Joy. 'It smells like a brand new car now.'

'Oh, Stan.' Joy's hands went to her mouth in the classic gesture of a girl whose boyfriend has gone down on one knee. 'You paid someone to clean the car? Did it cost a fortune?'

'It was highway robbery,' said Stan. 'I also bought a mobile phone. Also highway robbery.'

'You did *not*,' said Joy. Her foot stopped rubbing. The dog looked up at her hopefully.

'I'll give you my number,' said Stan.

They were looking straight into each other's eyes.

'So you can always contact me,' said Stan. 'Always. I'll never turn it off. I'll always answer.'

Joy took his hand in hers. 'Okay,' she said. 'Okay, then.'

The words were not startling, but it felt somehow as if they were witnessing a startlingly intimate conversation and Christina found herself politely looking away from the couple and at the floorboards. Nico said there were good floorboards waiting beneath the vile carpet in the house they'd just bought. Amazing to think something beautiful could lie beneath the ugliness and all you had to do was peel it away.

She felt her irritation dissolve beneath a slow-moving but inexorable tide of elation. Joy Delaney was no longer missing, presumed dead: she was alive and in excellent health. Christina no longer had to spend her nights at the office preparing the brief of evidence, wondering resentfully which witness statements the DPP would ask them to retake because it was their job to doubt every piece of evidence.

Like she should have done.

She and Nico could share a bottle of wine tonight and sleep late tomorrow. They would have sex tonight and in the morning and probably the afternoon.

This wasn't a career case that would put her face on the front page of the newspaper. It was a cute dinner party story she'd tell with Nico's arm slung around the back of her chair. Or more likely Nico would tell it for her and she'd make small factual corrections.

She glanced at Ethan, who was smiling sentimentally at Joy and Stan as though he were father of the bloody bride. He caught her looking and abruptly adjusted his face.

'Perhaps we could speak privately, Mrs Delaney,' she said to Joy. 'You can tell us what's been going on and where you've been all this time.'

chapter sixty-five

Valentine's Day

He was gone. The air vibrated with the terrible words they'd hurled. Joy walked in a daze down the hallway, back into the kitchen and looked around her. Her empty water glass sat on the sink. She put it in the dishwasher. Closed the dishwasher. Wiped a single droplet of water off the sink.

Right then.

It used to be that when Stan left, the fast-running current of Joy's life picked her up and carried her through until he returned, but now there were no children to distract or console, no lessons to reschedule, no business to run. She had no idea what to do next. She didn't know how to fill her day. She didn't know how to fill her life.

The dusty bottle of whiskey still sat on the kitchen table. She poured herself a shot glass with shaking hands and drank it in one dramatic gulp like a person in a movie. She shuddered. Whiskey was awful but she enjoyed the slow warmth it created, like an electric blanket heating up cold sheets.

She saw a pair of nail scissors sitting innocently on top of the junk in the bowl on the sideboard, as if they had always been there, so she sat at the table and trimmed the two broken nails that had scratched Stan's face while she wondered if they could ever come back from this, or if they'd finally reached the end of their forgiveness, their love, their patience.

It occurred to her that she wanted to be *gone* when Stan came back.

For once, she wanted *him* at home waiting for her. But where could she go?

She was in the process of idly Googling answers to all her problems when her phone rang like a gift. Her heart lifted. She answered without looking at the name. Surely it would be one of the children, remembering at last that they had a mother. Her money was on Brooke.

'Hello?'

'Joy?'

She recognised the voice instantly. 'Savannah.' Her eyes went to Harry Haddad's memoir sitting on the table in front of her.

Should she hang up?

She had once answered a late-night call from a young man who Joy *knew* was trying to scam her, because he was telling her that she'd won some extraordinary prize and just needed to pay a 'nominal fee' for 'shipment' and Joy had let him rattle on for ages, just for the company. They'd ended up having an interesting chat about climate change, before she told him that he really needed to consider a more honourable choice of career, at which point he hung up on her.

She felt the same way about Savannah. She knew she should be wary, and she *was* wary, but she was also lonely.

'How are you, Savannah?' she asked. Cool but not cold. 'Where are you?'

'Great, Joy!' said Savannah. 'Excellent! Top of the world! How are *you* this morning?'

Oh dear. She seemed to be channelling the fast-talking energy of a door-to-door salesman who knows he only has seconds before the door is shut in his face.

Joy felt a sudden spurt of fury. 'You know, I'm not great, Savannah. I'm not actually having the best day, as it happens, I'm drinking whiskey in the morning, so if you're calling for another spot of blackmail –'

'I'm not,' said Savannah.

'Because I hope you know that what you did to us was unacceptable,' said Joy. 'If you'd gone public with those accusations about Stan you could have ruined our lives forever –'

'I returned the money,' said Savannah. 'And I never would have done that.'

'Well, I don't know what you would have done, do I?'

There was no answer. They sat in silence for a few moments and Joy remembered the day she came back from the hospital and how Savannah had brought a tray to her in bed, with a cup of tea and tiny triangles of cinnamon toast. My goodness, that toast had been nice.

'Okay then,' she said in the appeased, let's-move-on tone she used to employ with her children when their behaviour had been unacceptable, but there was nothing more to be said. 'Well. What have you been up to?'

'I'm in a sort of new relationship,' answered Savannah. 'He's a doctor. A plastic surgeon. Lots of money. I'm calling from his apartment. I'm kind of living here now.'

'That's wonderful news!' said Joy warmly. She was rehabilitating herself! She was turning her life around! 'I'm so happy for –'

'He's married,' interrupted Savannah. 'It's more of an affair than a relationship.'

'Oh,' said Joy sadly.

'Joy.'

It was her. The act was gone. She sounded the way Joy's children used to sound when they called and as soon as she heard them speak she knew there was a crisis: the match had been lost, a heart had been broken.

She steeled herself as she used to steel herself for the blow to the stomach of her children's bad news. 'What is it? Tell me.'

'My brother has written a memoir,' said Savannah. 'My father emailed it to me. The publishers are sending it out to anyone who is mentioned in the book for fact-checking.'

'I know,' said Joy. 'We got a copy too.' She pulled the manuscript towards her and flicked the stack of pages with her thumb. 'Stan has read it. I haven't read it yet.'

'I wasn't going to read it,' said Savannah. 'I thought, What do I care? I don't want to read about your wonderful, successful life. But then . . . I got curious.'

'Well, of course,' said Joy.

'My dad told my brother I was sick,' said Savannah. She spoke mechanically now. 'That's how he motivated him. He thought he was playing to save my life.'

'Yes, Stan told me that,' said Joy. 'He was upset to hear it.' She said carefully, 'I assume you didn't know?'

'Of *course* I didn't know! I thought he was having a wonderful life. Eating steak while I starved. I hated him.'

'Oh, Savannah,' said Joy. 'I hope you know you're not responsible for what your father did.'

'You know how it started? I really was in hospital,' said Savannah. 'I ate a cupcake at school so my mother made me drink salt water until I vomited. I got dehydrated and collapsed after I performed.'

She spoke as if being forced to drink salt water was the sort of thing any mother would do. Joy put two fingertips to her forehead. Good Lord.

'So then my mother sent my dad a photo of me at the hospital with a drip in my arm. To make him feel bad so he'd send more money. My dad showed Harry that photo to make *him* feel bad, and that's when he started this whole . . . charade.'

'I see,' said Joy. 'So when did he finally realise you weren't sick?'

'It seems like there wasn't a big revelation. It just slowly crept up on him that he'd been duped, but by then his tennis career was properly taking off and then, ironically, he ends up with a child who really *does* get seriously sick. My niece.'

Joy heard Savannah sniff.

'I heard his daughter was sick and I did nothing. I *felt* nothing. Literally nothing. I'm no different from all those people who ignored me. I'm a terrible person, Joy.'

'No you're not.'

'Oh, I am,' said Savannah. 'I really am.'

Joy stood up from the table. She picked up one of the framed photos of her children. It was Amy's thirtieth birthday. They stood in a line, arms around each other, smiling.

'You need to call your brother,' said Joy.

There was a long pause. Savannah sniffed again.

'I talked to my dad. He says Harry wouldn't be where he was today if my father hadn't given him such a good incentive to win in the early days. My dad thinks it's *funny*. Isn't that sick? My family is so sick.'

'Yes,' said Joy. 'It's awful. Tennis parents can be . . . awful.'

'Anyway, so I wanted to tell you I'm going away,' said Savannah.

She'd changed tone again. Brusque.

'I've actually signed up for one of Harry's cancer charity things. It's stupid, I know, it's not like that will change anything, but I wanted to *do* something. For him. To atone. When I feel bad I like to . . . take action.'

'Sure,' said Joy. 'I understand.' She kind of understood. She wasn't one to wallow.

'It starts tonight. It's called the 21-Day Off-Grid Challenge to End Childhood Cancer. You stay in these tiny solar-powered cabins in the middle of nowhere without phones or wi-fi. You don't even get the address of where you're staying until the day you leave. I thought, well, it's not just supporting Harry's charity, it might clear my mind. Like a . . . circuit-breaker.'

'I don't understand. How does doing this end childhood cancer?'

'Oh, well, it doesn't, obviously. But you pay a fortune and a percentage goes to cancer research,' said Savannah. 'People sponsor you. It's for wealthy people. They post about it on Instagram.' She put on a posh accent. '*I'm just so humbled to be able to do my bit for this important cause.* You know the type. Obviously, *I'm* not wealthy, but I am very cashed up at the moment.' She paused. 'Don't ask.'

'I will not ask,' said Joy. 'I hope you're not going anywhere near the fires?'

'Opposite direction,' said Savannah. 'It's a five-hour drive. A place called Orroroo Gully. Orroroo means "wind through the trees", so that sounds nice, I guess? It's got waterfalls and lakes and wildlife or whatever.'

'Oh, I think it sounds wonderful, Savannah,' said Joy.

'Yeah,' said Savannah. 'Although . . . I don't know. I'm having second thoughts. I might get lonely. I might lose my mind. I might seriously lose my mind.'

Joy put down the framed photo. She looked at the walls that trapped her and thought of waterfalls and lakes and wildlife.

'What if I came with you?'

'Yes,' said Savannah. 'Yes, please, Joy.'

★

Once the decision was made, Joy was a whirl of nervous energy. She wanted to be gone before Stan came back. She wanted him to return to an empty house. She'd never made a decision this significant without first consulting Stan. It was exhilarating. It was terrifying. It would show him. It would show the children. Everyone would be very surprised. Her friends would be surprised too. It would be nice to be surprising for once.

This would be a *circuit-breaker.* She was enamoured of Savannah's phrase and kept murmuring it as she got ready. This was exactly what she needed right now. For a circuit to be broken.

Stan would miss her. Or he wouldn't miss her. If they didn't miss each other, then the decision would be made.

She couldn't find her phone, even though she'd just been talking on it. She couldn't find her glasses, even though she'd been wearing them just minutes ago. She couldn't find her wallet.

She found her phone. She texted the children without her glasses, the words blurry on the screen. Nobody texted or called straight back, as if the fact that their mother was going off-grid for three weeks was of little interest.

She found her wallet. She found her glasses. She dragged out an old promotional backpack from the bottom of the cupboard and shoved in casual clothes. Something warm for at night. Shorts and t-shirts, swimmers and runners, underwear and PJs, a brand new toothbrush still in its packaging. Savannah said they would swim and do bushwalks each day, rest and read. No need for fancy clothes. No need for much at all. It was about minimalism, apparently. It was about reconnecting with your true self. It was possibly a load of nonsense, but Joy could always come home early if she got bored.

She sat down and wrote Stan a letter.

Dear Stan,

I'm so sorry for saying those terrible things.

Delaneys would have been nothing without you. I ran the business but you were the business, Stan! You were 'the talent'. Nobody could coach like you. Nobody could get the best out of a player like you. Even the hopeless ones. Especially the hopeless ones! You never gave a half-hearted lesson. (I did! I admit it!) I loved watching you coach even more than I loved watching you play. It was like seeing an artist at work. I probably never told you that before. I should have.

I'm sorry for what I did. I'm sorry for sending Harry away. I wanted our children to have the best coach in Australia and that was you. It was wrong for you but right for our children and I chose them. You were right when you said if I'd really wanted to make it with my own tennis I would have done it. But I was good enough, Stan. I was so. I know it. You know it too. I never regretted that decision, I think I just wanted it acknowledged, but, oh well, it doesn't really matter now.

There is something important I need to say. It was hard to live like that, all those years, Stan, knowing that you could walk out the door at any moment.

Each time it happened it made my heart freeze a bit more until I thought it would freeze solid.

So now it's my turn to walk out.

I'm going away with Savannah. I know you're still angry with her and rightly so, but she's just a mixed-up kid, and I feel we have a kind of responsibility.

We're doing Harry's '21-Day Off-Grid Challenge to End Childhood Cancer'. It's not costing us anything. She's already paid. It's for charity, which is nice. I'm staying in a 'tiny, sustainable, solar-powered house' with her. (I do hope you've been exaggerating about my snoring.) There's a phone number you can call if there's an emergency but otherwise I will be properly 'OFF-GRID'.

When I come home maybe we can come up with a new strategy for how to be happy for this part of our life. We're so good at strategy. I think we can do it.

So I guess the ball is in your court, my darling. That's a good one, hey?

Love, Joy

PS My bike got a puncture and I left it under a tree in front of the O'Briens' old house. Will you please pick it up for me?
PPS I'm sorry for scratching you. My nails keep breaking. I think I need more calcium.

She carefully put the note on the refrigerator door with the London Eye magnet, right up high, where it would be impossible for him to miss it. She would not do to him what he'd done to her all those times. There would be no mystery as to her whereabouts.

Now her phone, which she'd had just five minutes ago, was missing again. She spent a few precious minutes looking for it before giving up. She didn't need a phone. That was the point of this 'challenge'. She was 'unplugging'. She was going 'off-grid'.

She filled up the dog's food and water bowls and told her where she was going and asked her to please take care of Stan. Steffi gave a low growl of disapproval.

'No, Steffi, I think it *is* a good idea,' said Joy, and she slung her backpack over her shoulder and felt as young and adventurous as if she were off to go backpacking around Europe.

★

The moment she closed the front door, her phone, which she'd knocked onto the floor as she swept up her backpack and then kicked under the bed as she left the room, began to buzz and vibrate with confused text messages from her children: *Huh? Mum, this message makes no sense!*

Her plan was to walk to the bus stop and catch the 401 into town, where Savannah would pick her up in a fancy car her married boyfriend was lending her.

Caro's daughter was pulling out of her driveway at the same time as Joy left the house. Petra opened her window to say hello, and when she found out that Joy was catching a bus into the city, she offered Joy a lift because she happened to be going to a literary lecture at the State Library, which was excellent luck. Not a nice day to be outside. On the way into the city they had a very nice chat about Copenhagen, where Petra lived now, and was flying back to the very next morning, with two small children. The children were with Caro right now seeing a movie, a last-day excursion with their beloved grandma. They talked about how everyone rode bikes in Denmark and wore flat comfy shoes and Joy asked if Petra had met Princess Mary (she hadn't) and she told her how just this morning she'd tried to be one of those lovely relaxed European ladies on a bike but it hadn't turned out so well.

Meanwhile, back at the house, the London Eye fridge magnet slid slowly, inevitably towards the kitchen floor, taking Joy's letter with it.

Steffi lifted her head from her paws, pattered across the floor and leisurely devoured the whole delicious sheet of paper.

Five minutes after Caro's daughter dropped Joy off, she got a frantic call from her mother saying that her son had fallen over on their way into the cinema and she was taking him to the hospital because she was worried his arm was broken.

Petra missed her lecture and drove straight to the hospital. Her son's arm was not broken, only bruised, and they were able to make their flight the next day, no problem, but with all the drama, it was not surprising that she entirely forgot to mention to her mother that she'd given her neighbour a lift into the city, at least not until three weeks later, when Petra was back in Denmark and her mother said that Joy Delaney had been missing for three weeks.

chapter sixty-six

Now

Amy had no aptitude for languages but she did do French in high school and she could remember the satisfaction of watching a paragraph of nonsensical words magically morph into sensible sentences, and that was exactly what was happening to her now as she studied her mother's nonsensical text message.

Going OFF-GRID for a little while! I'm dancing daffodils 21 Dog Champagne to end Czechoslovakia! Spangle Moot! Love, Mum.

The words became:

Going OFF-GRID for a little while. I'm doing Harry's 21-Day Challenge to End Childhood Cancer. Sponsor Me! Love, Mum.

She read the message out loud. Once. Twice.

'Do you think that's where she could be?' said Simon, in another one of his crisp white t-shirts, looking up at her anxiously. 'It's possible?'

Amy nodded. 'It's possible.' It made sense. It made perfect sense.

At this moment, everything made perfect, exquisite sense.

'It's also possible I love you,' she whispered, without meeting his eyes or moving her lips, as if she were operating a ventriloquist's doll, as if it might not count if she didn't say it properly. In a minute this beautiful clarity would be gone.

Another man would have said, 'What did you just say?' and she wouldn't have said it again. Another man would have tried to hug her or kiss her and she would have stood as stiff as a board in his arms, because right now she couldn't be touched.

But Simon Barrington wasn't another man.

He didn't move or smile or try to make eye contact. He looked straight ahead at his laptop screen and said, formally and clearly and quite loudly, as if he were making a legally binding declaration to a government official: 'I love you too, Amy.'

It wasn't the first time she'd heard those words from a man, it was just the first time she believed them.

★

Minutes later the phones of the four Delaney children dinged simultaneously in locations across Sydney, and each phone was snatched up with fumbling, frightened fingers as they read a five-word text from an unknown number.

It said:

Your mother is home.
Dad.

Stan's first ever text from his brand new phone turned out to be his most memorable.

chapter sixty-seven

When Joy's children saw her again they each hugged her in a way they hadn't hugged her since childhood. They were the fierce, desperate hugs that once followed nightmares, when she could feel the rapid hammer of fragile hearts in tiny chests as they clung to her.

Both her sons lifted her clear off the floor, just like their father did.

Both her sons cried, just like their father did.

Neither of her daughters shed a tear. They scolded her, like frightened mothers scold lost children on their return. 'You must promise to never *ever* do anything like that again, Mum! You must wear your glasses when you send a text! You must never leave the house without your phone!'

She enjoyed being told off by them. She could hear the rhythms of her own voice, her mother's voice, her grandmother's voice, every relieved cranky woman from the beginning of time.

*

It was nice to hold on to the memories of those fierce, desperate hugs when the hugging stopped.

chapter sixty-eight

Joy could remember people in late January talking about some kind of dreadful virus creeping across the world, but she was too distracted by her crumbling marriage to take much notice, and besides, she never caught colds. She had an excellent immune system.

By the time she was 'back on the grid' the world had spun off its axis, and it was hard not to feel personally responsible, as if the moment she stopped supervising, chaos was the consequence. It was just like when she took her eyes off Troy as a toddler: the mayhem and destruction that followed!

Suddenly, everyone was 'social distancing', especially around Stan and Joy, who were supposedly 'elderly' and 'at risk'. When they went for a walk, younger people leaped elaborately out of the way, off footpaths and into gutters.

'If my time's up, my time's up,' Stan told the children, and the children groaned and said all their friends' parents were making similarly foolhardy comments, and Joy and Stan exchanged smiles and made solemn promises to behave.

Those first weeks after Joy returned home were like being on a honeymoon in the middle of an apocalypse.

They couldn't stop touching each other or watching the news, which for the first time in Joy's lifetime was global and enormous, yet personal and specific. You couldn't shrug it off. You couldn't say it was very sad but life goes on, because life didn't go on.

They couldn't stop saying they couldn't believe it.

Prince Charles got the virus! No-one was safe. Not even royalty.

'Lockdown' took the pressure off retirement. Now their only responsibility was to stay home and stay safe, not to partake in a daily repertoire of wholesome, bracing activities. Now it wasn't just their lives that had stopped, but everyone's lives. Now it wasn't just her formerly bustling home that had fallen silent but formerly bustling cities all around the world. People heard birdsong in places where they had once only heard traffic. Skies cleared. If only this beautiful global pause could have happened without the relentless suffering.

Joy kept thinking about her grandmother's first husband, who had died of the Spanish flu a hundred years ago after he made the 'silly decision to go meet his friend down at the docks'. It had always sounded like a fairy tale to Joy, and a necessary piece of her history. *Of course* that first husband had to make the silly decision to meet his friend at the docks, so Joy's grandmother could go on to marry Joy's beautiful grandfather and Joy would then come to be Joy.

For the first time ever, it occurred to Joy that her grandmother's first husband probably would have preferred not to die of the Spanish flu, thank you very much, just like Joy would prefer not to die of this one. She wanted to see what happened next. Her grandparents and mother would have to wait at that arrivals gate for a little longer.

★

It took a while for Joy to fully comprehend what her family had been through while she was gone.

Stan told her that all four children initially withheld

information from the police that they knew would make Stan appear guilty. He'd seen their doubt and fear increase exponentially as the days passed without their mother's return. Their questions became increasingly pointed.

'I started to feel guilty,' said Stan. 'I started to feel as if I had hurt you. I had dreams that . . .' He stopped. 'The dreams were bad.'

The children referred to their confused loyalties both obliquely and overtly.

In the middle of an impassioned lecture about hand sanitising and face masks, Brooke suddenly said, apropos of nothing, 'I found that criminal lawyer for Dad because I knew he was innocent, Mum. Not because I thought he was guilty. I hope you both know that.'

Oh, my darling, thought Joy. *You never could lie.*

Once, after Troy dropped off a lavish twenty-four pack of toilet paper he'd naturally managed to procure during the bizarre panic-buying frenzy, and when he and Joy were alone, sitting on the back veranda at a safe social distance, he said, 'I thought Dad might have done it, Mum. I actually thought it. And I was angry with Brooke because she was supporting him.'

He sounded just like when he was a little boy, confessing something unspeakable, and Joy said, 'It doesn't matter, darling, just put it out of your mind.' Putting things out of your mind wasn't the modern way, but where else could he put it?

Troy and Brooke patched up their differences, thank God, in the way that siblings and spouses sometimes did, with actions, rather than words.

Brooke bought Troy a box of chocolates.

Troy bought Brooke a car.

★

Joy and Stan didn't talk at all about Harry Haddad, until one day when they were watching the news and it was announced that

Wimbledon would be cancelled because of the pandemic, the first time that had happened since World War II.

'I understand why you did what you did,' said Stan quietly.

He didn't say he forgave her, but she took it as forgiveness.

A younger couple might have spent months in counselling talking it through but she knew they were done with it. Move on. Once you've hit a ball there's no point watching to see where it's going. You can't change its flight path now. You have to think about your next move. Not what you should have done. What you do now.

She had betrayed him. He chose to still love her.

There was nothing more to say.

★

There were awful possibilities that kept her up at night.

For example, what if she and Savannah had been in an accident and their car had disappeared forever beneath the murky depths of some lake, and Stan had then been arrested and charged with her murder? What if he'd languished in jail for the rest of his life and only Brooke had visited him?

In the early days she made a lot of phone calls to that pretty, impatient and unsmiling Detective Christina Khoury.

Joy was mildly obsessed with her. 'Leave the woman alone,' Stan said. He looked traumatised whenever her name came up, which was why Joy felt a strange desire to continue convincing Christina of Stan's innocence, even though his innocence was undisputed.

She needed the detective to know that her husband was *one hundred per cent* innocent. He absolutely did not murder her.

'We did have a strong circumstantial case, Mrs Delaney,' said Christina grimly.

But then Christina softened, and reminded her of all the reasons why her various fears would never have eventuated. For one thing, she said dryly, Joy and Savannah had not crossed any lakes on their drive so it was unlikely they would have ended up at the bottom of one. Furthermore, Savannah's married lover or boyfriend or fling or whatever you wanted to call him (her *mark*?), Dr Henry Edgeworth, would have finally led them to Savannah and Savannah would have led them to Harry's Off-Grid Challenge. More importantly, they would also have got that better-late-than-never statement from Caro's daughter in Copenhagen. The case wasn't built on truth so it would have inevitably collapsed like a stack of cards.

'Your husband would never have been convicted,' Christina told her.

Then Joy asked her if the pandemic was affecting her wedding plans and Christina said that her wedding was going ahead, but it was going to be a much smaller event than originally planned.

'What a pity!' said Joy sympathetically.

'Such a pity,' said Christina, but she sounded like she might actually be smiling.

★

'What did you and Savannah *do* all that time you were away?' Amy asked Joy. 'That's a long time to spend together. Did you get bored?'

'Did you play games?' asked Brooke, because that's what the Delaneys would have done. There always had to be a competition going on. Someone always had to be winning and someone always losing. 'Did you . . . argue?'

Joy understood that her daughters felt conflicted about the time she'd spent with Savannah, because Joy had never spent that much time alone with either of them, and they all three knew that if they had, they would have driven each other right around the bend.

'Oh yes, it got *very* boring at times,' Joy told her daughters. 'And we did annoy each other sometimes, yes.'

It wasn't true. She and Savannah had got on just fine.

Probably because Savannah wasn't her daughter, although she did feel maternal towards her, and she wasn't really her friend, although it was like a friendship. She felt fond of Savannah but she didn't adore her in the fierce, complex way she loved her daughters, which meant, paradoxically, that she could spend three weeks with her no problem at all. Two tiny women in a tiny house.

Now when she looked back on those twenty-one days she first had to work her way through feelings of shame for the dreadful hullabaloo she'd caused, but once she got past that, she remembered that time like a sun-dappled dream, a holiday from her life and a holiday from herself, or the self that she'd become.

The wooden house where they'd stayed was surrounded by a four-hundred-year-old rainforest, waterfalls and walking trails. Kangaroos and wallabies regularly streaked past the oversized window, like passing cars on a quiet suburban street.

Joy slept deeply and dreamlessly in a single bed. There were no mirrors in the house, and without evidence of her own face, or a husband or children, it felt strangely as though she were once again Joy Becker, with most of her life ahead of her, not most of it behind her.

Every couple of nights someone delivered a basket of food to their doorstep. It was simple fresh food: fruit and eggs and bread and vegetables. Not much meat. All curated to give the wealthy guests their rustic 'back to basics' experience but knowing it was curated didn't seem to matter.

She and Savannah took long walks on their own and sometimes together. They read, for hours at a time. The house had a shelf full of very old paperbacks, none of which had been published after 1970. Time slowed and softened like a long hot summer from childhood.

She noticed that Savannah seemed to settle on one personality and stick with it. It seemed to be the personality of a young, reflective, quiet girl. All those strange little quirks of speech vanished. Sometimes they shared stories of their childhoods.

Just happy stories. Savannah spoke about when she and Harry were brother and sister, before tennis, before ballet, before their parents' divorce, when an afternoon in a fort made of bedsheets could last as long as a holiday. Joy talked about her grandparents. One day she told Savannah that her grandmother always called her underwear her 'unmentionables', and Savannah got the most delightful case of the giggles.

Then there were days when she and Savannah exchanged no more than a handful of words.

Joy loved the silence. She knew that she didn't have the personality to do this on her own – she wouldn't have lasted – but having Savannah there, half-stranger, half-friend, was the perfect compromise.

For the first time in decades she stopped.

She thought she'd stopped when she and Stan retired, but she hadn't stopped at all. She'd kept on running hopelessly towards some unspecified, unattainable goal.

She found that the less she thought, the more often she found simple truths appearing right in front of her.

For example, she had given up her dream of a professional tennis career with clear eyes. No-one could have convinced her to do otherwise, even if she found a way to travel back through time and tap herself on the shoulder and say, 'He's just a boy.'

He was never just a boy. He was Stan. She wanted him and she wanted his babies. She believed that Stan would not have been able to bear his wife's success. She was probably wrong about that, because that was before Stan had ever coached. She didn't know the man he would become and the pleasure he would take in seeing other players succeed. She was a girl of her time and she was a girl whose father had walked out and never returned. She believed men's egos were as fragile as eggs. She believed that you needed to do everything possible to make sure that your man returned home.

She made the right choice for the girl she was then.

One day Joy might have a granddaughter who played tennis – all her grandchildren would play, it was impossible to imagine otherwise – and it wouldn't occur to that precious girl of the future to give up her dreams of competitive tennis, or anything else, for a boy.

Also Joy wouldn't let her.

★

One morning, while Savannah was still asleep and Joy sat on the veranda and drank a cup of tea and watched the sun rise – it was the same sun, but it seemed to move so much more slowly and elegantly than it did at home – she thought: I didn't send Harry away only for the sake of the children, I sent him away because I was angry with Stan for the times he walked out, and I was angry because I was tired and because I felt responsible for everything: from Troy's drug-dealing to Brooke's headaches to tonight's dinner and tomorrow's laundry. It was secret petty marital point-scoring and she would never admit that to Stan, because if he was going to forgive her he would need to believe that her motives had been nothing but motherly, but there was relief in admitting it to herself.

Surely Joy's clever granddaughter would know how to have it all without actually doing it all.

★

'Why go away with *her*, of all people?' asked her family. 'After what she did to you? How could you *forgive* her?"

Joy said, 'She just happened to call at the right time.'

That was true but it was also true that Joy enjoyed not only her cooking but her company, and that Savannah's intentions might not have been pure when she banged on their door that night, but most of her actions had been kind, excluding of course her unkind blackmail of poor Troy, but when Joy weighed that up against Savannah's childhood and her family's own actions that long-ago day when they'd all been so heedlessly cruel to a child in need, she found that she could forgive if not forget.

Forgiveness comes easier with age, Joy explained, full of her own wisdom and grace, but her children laughed at that and helpfully listed the many people Joy had still not forgiven, decades after the event, like that one very rude local council member and the teacher who only gave Joy seven out of ten for the Great Wall of China assignment she'd done for Troy.

The difference was that none of those people had ever made Joy minestrone or cinnamon toast.

There was only one time in the twenty-one days that Joy suddenly questioned why she was spending time with this person, and that was when Savannah admitted to other tiny, peculiar acts of revenge against Joy's family.

For example, she'd called Logan's college and complained about him.

'I didn't *exactly* accuse him of sexual harassment,' she said, and she said she was pretty sure they hadn't taken much notice. She'd also made a number of online bookings at Brooke's physiotherapy practice so that she'd get a whole lot of no-shows.

Joy was incensed on behalf of both her children.

'You were risking their livelihoods!' she cried.

'I could have done much worse,' said Savannah. 'I've done worse.'

'Oh, well done to *you*, Savannah!' snapped Joy. 'Should I thank you for not doing worse?'

Savannah bowed her head as Joy continued, 'So obviously you blackmailed Troy. What about Amy? What did you do to her?'

'Nothing much. I just made brownies on Father's Day,' said Savannah, as if it were obvious.

'But how in the world did you know that would upset her?'

'You'd told me they were her signature dish,' said Savannah.

Joy hadn't remembered this. She'd been an old chook

twittering away while Savannah took careful notes. She found herself unable to look at Savannah, because she felt, just for a moment, like slapping her.

'And me?' Joy suddenly remembered herself, because wasn't she the worst offender on that day? She'd been the only grown-up.

'I tried to seduce your husband,' said Savannah. 'While you were sick in hospital.'

'Oh,' said Joy. 'That. But you wouldn't have *really* . . .'

'Yes, I would have,' said Savannah. 'Like I said, I've done worse, Joy. I've done far worse. I'm not a nice person.' It was twilight and they were sitting on the balcony watching hundreds of black bats swoop across a huge orange sky. Joy breathed, and felt her anger rise and fall, and when she was calm again she said, 'I think you are a nice person. You're a nice person who has done some not so nice things. Like all of us.'

'I might have broken up your marriage,' said Savannah.

'Well, yes,' said Joy. 'That was a terrible thing to do. You must promise to never do anything like that ever again, because some marriages couldn't survive an accusation like that, but you know, I never believed for one moment that Stan harassed you.'

'I didn't mean that,' said Savannah. 'I meant what I told him about you and sending Harry away.'

It was true that Savannah may well have ended her marriage with *that* revelation. 'Well, yes, but that wasn't a secret anyone asked you to keep,' Joy said to her. 'That was entirely my own doing. To be honest, I never expected it to stay a secret as long as it did.'

Savannah sighed as if Joy really didn't get it. 'Okay, but I'm not a nice person.'

It felt like she was trying to tell Joy something more than she was saying, as if there was a hidden message in her words, and if Joy concentrated hard enough she'd be able to decipher it, but all she saw was a very damaged young girl who had been dealt an awful hand in life, who had come to her house and cooked and cleaned for her.

Joy waited for Savannah to tell her whatever she wanted to tell her. She could feel her desire to speak, the way she'd once felt her children's desires to confess some terrible action or unspeakable thought, and mostly, if she was patient and gave them the space, they finally told her what they wanted to say.

But Savannah sat, one hand wrapped tightly around the key on the chain at her neck and watched the sky darken until the bats vanished into the inky blackness, and when she finally opened her mouth all she said was, 'I think I'll make a tomato and basil frittata for our dinner.'

A part of Joy was relieved. Savannah wasn't her child. She didn't want to know her secrets. She didn't need to know.

When the twenty-one days were up and they said goodbye to their tiny house in the wilderness, Savannah drove them back to Sydney.

'What are you going to do now?' asked Joy.

'I might call my brother,' said Savannah. 'Tell him I did his "challenge", for what it's worth, and then I don't know what I'll do. Make another new life somewhere? What about you?'

'Oh,' said Joy, 'I guess I'll just go home.'

For the first time she understood what a privilege it was to be able to say that.

★

'Who cooked for you while I was gone?' Joy asked Stan once, when they were eating dinner.

'Caro sent over a horrible chewy lamb casserole. Brooke brought around some meals,' said Stan. 'But I told her I could cook for myself. Not sure where this "Stan can't boil an egg" thing came from. I taught *you* to boil an egg.'

'You did not,' said Joy.

'I did so,' said Stan.

The memory floated to the surface of her mind, perfectly preserved, like an ancient artefact.

He did in fact teach her how to boil the perfect soft-boiled egg, and that was when he told her that as a kid he'd often had to cook for himself after his father left and his mother was 'napping', and Joy had been overcome with a girlish, sensual desire to *feed her man*, to nurture him like a real woman would, to mother him the way he hadn't been mothered, and she'd kept him out of the kitchen, shoo-ed him away until he stayed away, and as the years went by, cooking stopped feeling sensual and womanly and loving and became drudgery.

'Maybe we could take turns with the cooking,' she said. 'During lockdown.'

'Sure,' said Stan.

'Careful what you wish for,' warned Debbie Christos, who still had bad memories of the year Dennis decided to become a Cordon Bleu chef and spent hours preparing distressing fiddly French dishes often involving innocent ducklings.

Stan wasn't interested in ducklings, thank goodness, but it turned out he could cook a perfectly adequate roast dinner.

When he put the plate down in front of her, he'd set up his new phone to play 'You Ain't Seen Nothing Yet' from 1974, when they were entirely different people, and also exactly the same.

'Haven't I?' asked Joy.

'Nope,' said Stan.

*

Sometimes, at two am, it was always two am for some reason, Joy would sit bolt upright in bed because a kind of horror had seeped into her dreams and she would find herself thinking about Stan in handcuffs, and the lines of coffins on the TV news, and Polly Perkins, who had not gone on to live happily ever after in New Zealand as Joy had always believed, but whose body had been discovered while Joy was away, and people had briefly thought it might have been Joy's body, and she would find herself thinking about all the women who assumed their lives were just like hers, far too ordinary to end in newsworthy violence and yet they had, and all the ordinary people, just like her and Stan, who had been planning 'active retirements' and whose lives were now ending cruelly, abruptly and far too soon.

She tried the 'techniques' suggested by Amy, who was handling lockdown far better than her friends because they had never experienced the permanent low-level sense of existential dread that Amy had been experiencing since she was eight years old.

Eight! Joy wasn't completely sure what existential dread was but it sure didn't sound good.

First, she tried Amy's breathing exercises but they always reminded her of being in labour, and as her labours had all been very aggressive and fast – those four children of hers *barrelling* their way into the world – that wasn't exactly relaxing.

Amy also suggested 'practising gratitude', which was a technique where you listed all the things for which you were grateful, and Joy was good at that.

There were many things for which to be grateful. For example, Indira and Logan were not only back together but were also engaged. The ring was awful! But Indira seemed to like it, and the girls said Joy should absolutely not say a word about the ring's awfulness, so she was keeping her lips zipped. She just hoped that one day, years from now, when their marriage went through a bad patch, Indira wouldn't suddenly shout, 'I've always hated this ring!' Joy could hardly bear to think of poor Logan's hurt feelings if that happened. 'Yeah, I think he'll live, Mum,' said Troy.

Brooke's clinic was still afloat, thank goodness, because physiotherapy was considered an essential service and Brooke said people were giving themselves dreadful injuries trying to do their own exercise routines at home and undertaking overly ambitious DIY projects, so that was great news.

Troy's ex-wife, Claire, was pregnant with Troy's baby, and because of the pandemic she had decided she wanted to make a life in Australia and her Poor Husband had reluctantly agreed to move here. Troy had decided he wanted to share custody of his child, and Claire had agreed. The Poor Husband wasn't too happy about that.

'Stop calling him the Poor Husband, Mum,' said her children with blithe partisan cruelty. 'It's Troy's biological child.'

(Joy's first grandchild was due Christmas Eve. That son of hers always did give the very best gifts.)

Joy hadn't met the Poor Husband yet, but she was going to be particularly nice to him when she did, because she had a terrible secret suspicion.

She remembered one particular match when Troy was playing against his nemesis, Harry Haddad, and Harry sent a cross-court shot so impossibly wide any other player would have let it go, but Troy went for it. He had to run almost onto the next court, but he not only made that impossible shot, he also won that impossible point, and the small crowd of spectators whooped like they'd gone down a rollercoaster. Even Harry grudgingly clapped one hand against his strings.

Troy always went for the impossible shots.

Well, Claire wasn't a tennis ball.

She was a sensible, intelligent girl who would make her own life choices, and if Troy did somehow charm her out of her marriage, it wouldn't be Joy's fault, would it?

There was nothing Joy could do to change the outcome of her children's lives, any more than she could have changed the outcome of their matches, no matter how hard she bit her lip, which she used to do, sometimes until it bled, or how much Stan muttered instructions they couldn't hear.

Sometimes their children would do everything exactly as they'd taught them, and sometimes they would do all the things they'd told them not to do, and seeing them suffer the tiniest disappointments would be more painful than their own most significant losses, but then other times they would do something so extraordinary, so unexpected and beautiful, so entirely of their own choice and their own making, it was like a splash of icy water on a hot day.

Those were the glorious moments.

That's how she finally made herself fall back to sleep: by remembering all the glorious moments, one after the other after the other, her children's ecstatic faces looking for their parents in the stands, looking for their approval, looking for their love, knowing it was there, knowing – she hoped they knew this – that it would always be there, even long after she and Stan were gone, because love like that was infinite.

chapter sixty-nine

At first Brooke thought she imagined the sweet fragrance that drifted like a memory into her consciousness as she cleaned her exercise equipment with antibacterial spray.

She was cleaning with even more desperate vigour than usual because her last patient had mentioned, at the very end of his session, that he'd woken with a sore throat this morning 'but he was pretty sure it wasn't COVID'. Then he'd coughed. Straight in her face.

People were idiots. People were *heroes* – she had friends working in Intensive Care Units right now, facing far more than the occasional head-on cough – but people were idiots. She had learned, when her mother was missing, that it was possible to simultaneously hold antithetical beliefs. She had existed in the centre of a Venn diagram. She loved her father. She loved her mother. If her father had been responsible for her mother's death, she would have stood by him. She knew she was the only one of her siblings who had stared directly at the solar eclipse of this possibility. Troy *thought* he had faced it but he had only done so by pretending that he didn't love their father.

It was not that Brooke loved her father more, or that she loved her mother less. The body could find balance between opposing forces. The mind could do the same.

She could see her decade with Grant as a failure, or she could see it as a success. It was a relatively short marriage that was now ending in a mildly acrimonious divorce. It was also a long-term relationship with many happy memories that ended exactly when it should have ended.

She sniffed. What was the smell? It was so familiar. So *obvious*. And yet obviously not obvious, because she couldn't put a name to it. She studied the label on the bottle. It was the same brand she always used, but overlaid with the comforting antiseptic smell was something else: like baking.

Was it the café next door? They were only doing takeaway coffees now. No table service. It was sad to see the tables and chairs piled up on top of each other gathering dust in the corner and the red masking-tape crosses on the floor to keep everyone apart.

'Hey, did you guys ever find your mother?' one of the young waitresses asked Brooke just this morning as she handed over her coffee.

'We did,' said Brooke. 'She's fine. She's good. Great, in fact.'

There had only been a small paragraph in the newspaper about Joy's return. There was a touch of chagrin in the tone of the reporting. People didn't want the old lady to be dead, but it was kind of disappointing that she was alive.

'Oh, I'm so happy to hear that!' The waitress's eyes sparkled above her mask, entirely disproving Brooke's theory. 'It's so great to hear some good news for a change. Stay safe!'

'Thank you,' said Brooke. People were awful. People were wonderful. 'You stay safe too.'

Brooke was a self-employed single woman living through a pandemic. She couldn't date. She couldn't play basketball. She couldn't go out to dinner with friends. Instead there were drinks over Zoom and sudden, intense, beautiful moments of human connection like this (although also awkward: were they going to say 'Stay safe!' to each other every single day now?).

No, she was not imagining that smell. It was from childhood.

Like cut grass. It was normally accompanied by cigarette smoke and Chanel N°5.

She put down her spray and walked out to the reception area like she was in a dream, and there it was, sitting on top of her desk.

An apple crumble. Still warm from the oven. Like it had come from another dimension. From heaven or hell or the past. It was wrapped tightly in aluminium foil. There was a sheet of handwritten paper sticky-taped to the foil. The writing was neat and childlike. There was no heading. It began: *Four medium apples, peeled, cored and diced.*

She opened the door of her office to look outside but saw no-one except for a masked elderly lady pushing a shopping trolley and frowning ferociously in Brooke's direction, as if daring her to approach.

Brooke went back inside. She peeled back the foil and breathed in deeply. She didn't need to taste a single mouthful to know that Savannah had cracked the recipe.

chapter seventy

It was a cold blue sunlit August morning. Hard to imagine a deadly virus in this crystal-clear air.

Stan Delaney diligently went through the stretching routine prescribed by his daughter to protect his crappy knees before he went on the court. He and his wife were going to have a hit. Just a gentle hit.

'You two have never had a gentle hit in your lives,' Brooke said.

Joy was next to him doing her own Brooke-prescribed routine when his mobile phone rang.

'For heaven's sake.' Joy rolled her eyes. She complained that he was too attached to his phone. He had it in his pocket all the time and placed it right next to his plate when they ate. She said that was poor etiquette. He thought that was the point of the damned thing.

Stan peered at the screen. 'It's Logan.'

'Quick, quick, answer it, then!' Joy would never let a call from one of their children go unanswered, especially not now, after everything that had happened. They might laugh over it one day, but their laughs would always be tinged with horror.

'Dad,' said Logan. Stan clenched the phone tight. Logan didn't sound like himself. 'Yeah, mate?' He steeled himself for death or disaster.

'You remember my friend Hien?'

'Of course I remember him.' A car accident? Did Hien have the virus?

'He has a son. Six years old. Hien has been asking me to come and watch him play tennis for months now, and I've been putting it off, but this morning I thought, Oh, to hell with it, the kid has been stuck at home doing online learning. So anyway, I finally did, and, Dad –'

He paused, and in the pause, hope rushed like mercury through Stan's veins.

Logan said, 'I've never seen anything like it.'

Stan watched the hair on his arms stand up. 'He's pretty good then, is he?'

'Yeah, Dad, he's pretty damned good.'

The first time Stan saw Harry Haddad play – a kid who had never set foot on a court before – it was like seeing one of the world's natural wonders. Only a coach sounded the way Logan sounded right now, and Stan knew that Logan was a natural-born coach even if the fool boy didn't seem to know it himself.

'So, I know it's been a long time,' said Logan tentatively.

Don't ask me.

Please don't ask me.

Do it yourself, son, do it yourself, please say you want to do it yourself.

Logan lowered his voice as though he were sharing a shameful secret and said, 'I think I want to coach him.'

It was the high of an ace or a perfectly executed smash.

Stan silently fist-punched the air.

'What?' said Joy. 'What is it?'

Stan waved her quiet. He kept his voice controlled.

'He'd be lucky to have you,' he said.

There was silence and the next time Logan spoke his voice had firmed. 'You think I can do it?'

'I know you can do it.'

'He listens,' Logan said.

'Yeah,' said Stan. 'It's satisfying when they listen.'

The true talents were thirsty for anything you could give them. They listened and applied. They flourished before your eyes.

'I think he's going to go all the way, Dad.'

'He might,' said Stan. 'You never know. He might.'

He wanted to say that it didn't matter if the kid did or didn't go all the way, that all that really mattered was that Logan was participating in his life again. He wanted to say that being a coach wasn't second best or a fallback or a compromise and that Logan could still be part of the beautiful world of tennis, that everyone counted, not just the stars but the coaches and umpires, the weekend warriors and social players, the crazy-eyed parents and the screaming fans whose roars of appreciation lifted the stars to heights they would never otherwise reach.

But that would have taken more words than he had to spare, so he hung up and told Joy, who had a lot of words to spare about Hien, and Hien's mother, who'd never played tennis as far as Joy knew but did have an athletic way about her, so Joy bet that was where the grandson had inherited his talent, and she hoped the boy wasn't naughty, because Hien had been very naughty as a child.

Eventually Joy ran out of words, and they went out on the court and began to warm up and Stan's crook knee felt good. They moved to the baselines, got into a rhythm as easy and familiar as sex, and Stan found himself thinking of his own father and their secret Friday afternoon matches, which had gone on for years, like the secret assignations of a double agent.

Of course, they couldn't play on the backyard court his dad had built with his own hands. After he left, his dad had never crossed the threshold of his own home ever again.

They met instead at a crummy local court surrounded by scrubby bushland near a seedy scout hall. The surface was cracked, the net sagged, but the tennis was beautiful.

Stan's father said that one day he'd see his son play at Wimbledon. He said it as if he'd been given inside information.

When Stan was sixteen his father died on a train platform waiting for the six forty-five am to Central. Instantly dead. Just like old mate Dennis Christos. 'No great loss,' said his mother, who believed that Stan had not seen his father for years and would not have comforted her son for his loss even if she'd known the truth. She was not a mother who gave comfort. When his boys were children and got fevers and Joy tended to them, her hand stroking their hair, Stan sometimes felt a deplorable ache of envy. His sons accepted their mother's love in such a cavalier fashion, as if it was their birthright, and maybe sometimes he was tougher on them, Troy especially, because of his envy.

For many decades he rarely thought of his father and he never spoke of him, not until the day he and Joy went to Wimbledon and he heard his father's voice, so clear and deep in his ear, as if he were sitting right next to him, 'Well, isn't this something for a boy from the bush.'

That was the first time in Stan's life that he could remember his body overreacting to a *feeling*, to a mere thought in his bloody head. He never told Joy what he felt that day. They both pretended it was some strange, unspecified illness that had struck him down. How could he tell her that being at Wimbledon didn't just cause him to grieve his own lost career, and his children's lost careers, but the long-ago loss of the kind, loving man who so notoriously assaulted his mother?

It was his father who taught him to be on guard for the ghastly apparition of a man's temper.

'This is what you do,' he told him, more than once, as they sat sweating companionably in the shade after each Friday afternoon match. 'If you ever lose your temper with a woman or child, you must leave. Walk out the door. Don't stop to think. Don't say a word. Don't come back until you're calm again. Just walk away. Like I should have done.'

Stan took that advice literally, precisely, with death-like seriousness. He believed a man's temper to be his most hideous flaw. When Troy jumped the net and attacked Harry Haddad all those years ago, Stan knew he'd failed, and when Troy made stupid decision after stupid decision, Stan wiped his hands of him. He had done what he told his children and students to never do: he'd given up. You never give up. You fight to the last ball. The match isn't over until the last point is played. But he gave up on his son.

Recently, he'd begun listening to one of Joy's podcasts about trading. Joy said it was boring and she was right, but Stan persevered and yesterday he'd called Troy and said, 'How's work?'

'Work is good, Dad,' said Troy tersely.

Stan took a breath, took courage, and said, 'I guess the market is like your opponent. Is that it? You're competing against the market? Trying to predict what it does next?'

There had been such a long silence that Stan felt the colour rise on his face. Had he said something so unbelievably stupid that Troy was rolling about laughing? Because his old man was as thick as a brick?

But then Troy said slowly, 'Yeah, Dad, it's exactly like that.'

'Right,' said Stan. 'So –'

Troy interrupted him. He said, 'You know when I got really good at this, Dad?' and he didn't wait for Stan to answer. He said it all in a rush. 'When I stopped being a show pony. When I put my ego away. When I got consistent and strategic.'

He said, and it was hard to understand him because his voice went a bit wonky for a moment, 'Every single thing you taught me on the court, Dad, I use every single day of my life.'

He'd never taught the boy to get fucking pedicures, but still, it was nice to hear that.

It had been bloody nice to hear that.

A plane flew above, and Stan tipped back his head and watched it streak across the sky. It was possible he might never step on board a plane again, which was fine with him, he was happy down here.

Joy came to the net. She wore her hair in a young girl's ponytail when she played. She still had the best legs he'd ever seen.

Her volley still needed work but she wouldn't listen. Her cheeks were flushed from exertion and the cold air. She loved the sport as much as he did, as much as he loved her, which was more than she would ever know. He'd had no interest in playing doubles until he met her. They were better players together than apart.

Each time she fell out of love with him, he saw it happen and waited it out. He never stopped loving her, even those times when he felt deeply hurt and betrayed by her, even in that bad year when they talked about separating, he'd just gone along with it, waiting for her to come back to him, thanking God and his dad up above each time she did.

Joy shielded her eyes to watch the plane disappear on the horizon. She dropped her hand and looked back at Stan.

She said, 'Let's play.'

chapter seventy-one

'If you hear the cabin crew say, "Evacuate, evacuate, evacuate,"' said the flight attendant, 'first check that the area outside the aircraft is safe.'

She said 'evacuate, evacuate, evacuate' in such a bored, bureaucratic monotone, it was funny. You couldn't find the horror in the words.

The girl in 12F stopped listening to her exit row responsibilities. No plane would crash during a pandemic. That would be too many disasters for the nightly news. Anyway, in the unlikely event of an emergency the muscly guy seated next to her would shove her aside and fling the exit door free.

She tugged at her mask. It itched.

Everyone fiddled incessantly with their masks, trying to adjust to this strange new world, only their frazzled eyes visible. Glasses fogged up. Some people kept pulling their masks down under their noses for refreshing sniffs of germ-scented air. Two women across the aisle scrubbed at their tray tables and armrests with disinfectant wipes as if they were cleaning up a crime scene.

The girl looked like a member of a nineties girl grunge band. Her hair was dyed inky black and shaved on one side. She wore ripped black jeans, chunky buckled motorcycle boots and a lot of clanking jewellery that had set off the metal detectors at the airport: a bangle coiled with snakes, a skull necklace.

The girl was flying to Adelaide to visit her mother.

Her flight had been delayed multiple times so as to ensure bad moods for all. By the time she picked up her car rental and drove out to her childhood home, it would be past nine. She assumed her mother would be tucked up in bed, warm and cosy, don't let those bed bugs bite, just as she'd left her in the gold-tinged light of dawn many months before.

'Bye, Mum!' she'd called. 'Love you!' There had been no answer.

The night before that morning, she'd cooked dinner for her mother, as she always did when she visited. A tiny exquisite calorie-controlled meal on a big white plate. Two herb-encrusted lamb cutlets (all fat excised with surgical precision). Eight green beans. One small, perfectly shaped scoop of mashed potato. Her mother still watched what she ate. You must never stop watching! Insidious calories can creep onto your plate and onto your body. Sometimes calories can find you in your dreams.

Her mother, dressed as though for church, although she'd never been to church, polished off everything on that big white plate. Afterwards, she picked at the pieces of meat between her teeth with a toothpick while proclaiming the meal to be 'quite good'.

Then her mother showered for a long time, cleaned her teeth and changed into her nightie and dressing-gown, after which she sat on the couch to watch television with a small glass of vodka (the lowest calorie alcohol, no carbs, fat or sugar) and two yellow sleeping tablets. The doctor had said she should take only one tablet thirty minutes before bed, but what did he know? The girl's mother said, 'You should make your own decisions when it comes to your health.' She took two tablets every night and slept like the dead.

The girl stood in the kitchen for a long time staring at her mother's plate before she scraped the gnawed bones into the bin.

Then she went out to the living room and spoke to the back of her mother's head. 'Didn't you teach me to *never* eat everything on my plate?'

Her mother said, 'You've got that topsy-turvy! You teach your children to eat everything on their plates.'

The girl said, 'Your rule was the opposite. Never *ever* finish everything on your plate.'

She looked at the shelves where all her ribbons and medals and trophies were displayed. She picked up a trophy. It was one of her least prestigious – just second place in a 'tiny dancer' regional competition – but it was one of the largest and most impressive-looking. A gold-plated pirouetting ballerina on a chunky white marble base.

The girl remembered dancing for that trophy because she remembered everything. She remembered her mother's tiny smile for her tiny ballerina. The tiny smile was the girl's tiny reward for the blistered toes and bruised toenails, the shin pain, the ankle pain, the back pain, but above all, the pain of unrelenting hunger.

She said to her mother, 'Don't you remember? If I forgot to leave something on my plate you locked me in my room. Good dancers must learn to control their calories.'

Her mother continued to watch the flickering television. 'I don't know why we're talking about this now.'

The girl didn't know why she was talking about it now either. It had not been her plan. She was here to say goodbye. She was moving interstate with her new boyfriend. He was Irish, a painter. He thought she was normal. He thought it was sweet that she'd been a ballerina. His sister had been a ballerina too. The girl knew his sister's ballet experience had been entirely different from her own.

The girl said, 'Sometimes you locked me in my room with only water. I had to ration the water. That was a terrible thing to do to a little girl. I thought I would be there forever. I thought I would die. I think I might have come close to dying. A few times.'

Nothing.

'I have an eating disorder,' said the girl. 'I've got issues with my thyroid, my iron levels, my teeth, my digestion, my brain, my personality. I'm not . . . right.' She paused. 'You *wrecked* me.'

Canned laughter rose and fell from the television.

Finally her mother spoke. She sounded a little impatient, a little amused. 'You always were such a liar, Savannah. You had a *television* in your room. Like a little princess in a castle! Just look at all those *trophies*! Don't you think I had better things to do than drive you around to ballet recitals across the country? I had a life of my own, you know!'

So that's how she lived with it. She did it the way so many people lived with their regrets and mistakes. They simply rewrote their stories. Her mother had recreated herself as a devoted mother: as if ballet had been her daughter's favourite extracurricular activity, not her own obsession.

'You were only moderately talented,' said her mother after a long pause. Her words were beginning to slacken as the two sleeping tablets did their job. 'You weren't a protégé like your brother. I knew that from the beginning.'

Your father got the protégé.

The girl folded herself up. Neatly. Geometrically. Like origami.

She went back into the kitchen and cleaned with swift hard tiny graceful movements. She scrubbed at a congealed spot of grease on the stove with a dishcloth, pulled tight over her thumb, until it was gone. She swept the floor. She cleaned the sink until it shone.

She went back out to her loving mother and found her sound asleep on the couch, head tipped back, her mouth open in a perfect oval shape, like one of those fairground attractions.

Her mother had said earlier that day that sometimes the sleeping tablets worked too fast and she fell asleep on the couch and woke with an aching lower back. She said this as if it were somehow the girl's fault.

So the girl took charge. She picked up the remote and turned off the television. 'Let's get you to bed, sleepy-head! No sore back for you!'

She had to drag her under her armpits, but her mother was as light as air, as light as a tiny ballerina. She dragged her to the closest bedroom, which happened to be the one that had once belonged to the girl, the one with the old-fashioned lock on the door.

These days it was illegal to have bedroom doors that could be locked from the outside. A safety issue.

There seemed to be no safety issues when the girl was growing up.

The girl heaved her mother onto her old bed. She pulled the sheets up tight and smooth over her chest and under her mother's chin.

Once she was done she found she was breathing fast yet with a controlled kind of exhilaration, as if she had performed something extraordinary yet ordinary, remarkable yet required, like thirty-two fouetté turns en pointe.

'Sleep tight, don't let the bed bugs bite.' She kissed her mother on her forehead. She felt her breath warm on her cheek. At the doorway she said, 'Now, you know I do need to lock this door. That's the rule. You gnawed on those bones like a disgusting little pig!'

The girl found the key to the bedroom door where her mother had always kept it, in the little trinket dish an ex-husband had given her as a gift. It had a cartoon of a man and a woman hugging on it. Hearts floated above their heads. It said: *Love is . . . being loved back.*

He'd been one of the nicer husbands, he'd taught the girl to cook, and then he was gone, taking his surname along with his cooking utensils. If he'd stayed, he would not have let what happened to her happen.

There were many people who would have stopped it, if only they'd known, if only they'd looked a little harder or bothered to ask a question or listen.

There were teachers and other ballet parents and doctors who could have noticed. Like the plastic surgeon who had seen her when she was a child. Dr Henry Edgeworth. Her mother took her for an appointment to see how much it would cost to pin back her 'unfortunate ears'. (It cost too much.) 'I'm hungry,' the girl whispered to the doctor as he studied her unfortunate earlobes, and he chuckled as if it were funny that he was examining a malnourished child.

He'd recently paid an expensive price for that kindly chuckle, although he thought he'd paid a bargain price for an affair with a trashy young girl he met at a nightclub. Either way was fair.

While her mother slumbered that night, the girl went to the supermarket. She bought six boxes of Optimum Nutrition Protein Crunch Bars. They looked delicious! She bought a shrink-wrapped pallet of bottles of water. She carried the supplies into the bedroom and left them on the floor near the bed. Her mother breathed peacefully through her mouth.

She wrote her mother a friendly note. *This looks like a lot but you will need to ration carefully. Remember: self-discipline!*

She relocked the door.

The girl left that night for Sydney. It was back when there were no border closures, when you could move across the country with your new Irish boyfriend and not think about it.

She hadn't expected to be gone as long as she was. She got busy! Life! Her relationship didn't work out but she met new people and visited old friends and acquaintances. She tied up some loose ends. She had a few cash windfalls. She even did some charity work. She 'reached out', as the Americans said, to her famously successful brother, and he was kind, and they agreed they would get together once this crazy world returned to normal. He said he never wanted to see either of their psychotic, fucked-up parents again, and she understood. Neither did she, really, but she was a devoted daughter just like her mother had been a devoted mother.

She kept the key on a chain around her neck. It seemed

important, essential even, to keep it close. It demonstrated her love.

'Going back home?' asked her muscle-bound seatmate as the plane began to taxi towards the runway. It was a time when people everywhere were going back home. The man had gentle dog-like eyes over the top of his mask.

The flight attendant demonstrated what to do if an oxygen mask fell from the ceiling. First remove your mask. The virus will no longer be your main concern!

'I'm visiting my mother,' said the girl.

There were many ways a resourceful senior citizen could have, should have, may have, probably had freed herself from a locked bedroom. Kicked down a door. Banged on the window. Called out to a neighbour. *Shouted* to a neighbour – the bedroom was on the second floor and faced a brick wall, but still, it was possible. A child could study a window made of thick glass effectively locked by layers of ancient impenetrable paint between the sash and the frame and find no way to break or open it, but a *grown-up* could find a clever solution. *If I was a grown-up I could get myself out of here*: that's what the little girl had once thought. She had longed to be a grown-up, with money and food and agency, but she was a kid, just a kid who dreamed of a beanstalk she could climb to get out of that room and into the sky. She didn't want the giant's gold. She wanted the giant's dinner.

She still felt helpless and trapped, no matter what actions she took in her increasingly desperate attempts to make the pain stop. She knew her memories did not fade like other people's seemed to fade and she accepted that, but she didn't get why the pain *intensified* the older she got and the further away she got from those times.

'Me too,' said the guy next to her. 'Is your mother on her own?'

'Yes,' said the girl. She knew what he meant, but she thought, We're all on our own. Even when you're surrounded by people or sharing a bed with a loving lover, you're alone.

A friendly neighbour might have called in to check on her mother after a week or two or three had passed, although if you required the concern of friendly neighbours, it helped to be a friendly neighbour yourself.

So maybe not.

Or perhaps her mother was in bed right now, peacefully unwrapping her last delicious nutritious protein bar, sipping from her last bottle of water, floating away on a choppy endless sea of television, just as her spoiled daughter once did when she slipped free of the cruel hunger pains and into other realities and other lives.

Perhaps her mother had created a sitcom version of herself.

The girl imagined a plump, smiling version of her mother bustling to greet her, wiping her hands on her apron, pulling her close. 'I woke up that morning and had a good old laugh! You locked me in, you little minx!'

Perhaps the house would smell of sugar and butter and love.

Perhaps it would not.

'My mother and I are going to isolate together,' said the guy. 'She has autoimmune issues, so she has to be careful. It's scary.'

'Yes,' said the girl. 'So scary.' She touched the key around her neck. 'We have to keep our parents locked up right now.'

A demented laugh rose in her chest and caught in the air between her mouth and her mask. She breathed fabric in and out and thought of a plastic bag pulled tight around her head. Her seatmate didn't notice. He didn't know the truth about the girl seated next to him, sharing his exit row responsibilities. Masks were so great. So useful and protective. Nobody knew what went on behind them. She could be any type of person she chose to be, any type of person he needed her to be.

The pilot's voice crackled over the intercom. 'Cabin crew, please prepare for take-off.'

She pulled her seatbelt tighter, the way a nervous flyer does, and she felt him notice and she felt him care, the way nice, well-brought-up boys care about fragile, frightened girls. He needed fragility. She could give him fragility. She wasn't dressed right – girl next door would have been better – but it was all in your delivery.

The engines roared. That moment before take-off always seemed impossible. Against the laws of nature. But things happened all the time that were seemingly against the laws of nature.

The plane lifted into the sky.

The girl looked down at the patchwork quilt of suburbia below: miniature houses with tiny backyards and swimming pools, matchbox cars travelling along winding streets past sports-grounds and tennis courts.

From here above the clouds, life looked so peaceful and manageable: *Jump in your matchbox car and drive to that cute little city to earn your living! Go to those dear little shops and buy your dinner! Love and feed your children! Follow your dreams and pay your taxes!* Why was it so impossibly hard for some people to do those things, yet so easy for others?

Her seatmate was describing his mother. 'She's a homebody. Not exactly active.'

'My mother is the opposite,' said the girl.

She saw a woman who looked just like her, running her a bath, checking the temperature with her hand, sloshing the water back and forth to get it just right. She saw her standing at her bedroom door late at night with an extra blanket because it had 'suddenly got so chilly'. She saw her pulling a dress off a rack that was 'just her colour' and then clapping her hands with delight when she walked out of the change room. She saw a woman furiously scolding her for her behaviour, but then moving on, as if it was possible for even the most terrible of actions to be forgiven.

The girl said, 'My mother plays tennis.'

acknowledgements

Thank you as always to my incredible editors of many years: Cate Paterson in Australia, Amy Einhorn in the US and Maxine Hitchcock in the UK. Thank you also to Danielle Walker, Brianne Collins, Kathleen Cook, Conor Mintzer, Joel Richardson and Alex Lloyd for your invaluable editorial comments and suggestions.

Thank you to my sisters and fellow authors Jaclyn Moriarty and Nicola Moriarty for reading the very first draft of this book and my sisters Katrina Harrington and Fiona Ostric for reading the very last draft. Special thanks to Jaci for texting me the writing prompt that began this novel.

While writing *Apples Never Fall* I needed to learn about competitive tennis, tennis coaching, police investigations, trading, physiotherapy, life in the seventies, accounting and ballet. I am hugely grateful to the following people who gave so generously and patiently of their time and expertise: Matthew Futterman, Mike Lowers, James Harb, Paul Francis (please support his wonderful charity, The Humpty Dumpty Foundation), Rob Who-Knows-Who-He-Is, Mark Davidson, Kim Ivey, Rob Collins, Elina Reddy and Yan Levinski, Elena DeCinque (via Marisa Colonna), Dr Teresa Lee, Cameron Duncan, Scott Harrington and Julie and George Gates. Thank you to Beau Loughhead, who contributed absolutely nothing to this book, but I feel guilty every time I see him because I forgot to thank him for a real-life anecdote I put to fictional use in a previous novel.

There is a certain kind of thoughtful, well-connected person who, upon learning that you are researching a particular topic, texts you the very next day with an introduction to someone with the exact qualifications you need. Thank you Lisa Faddy, Jackie Aloisio and Charles Anderson for being those sorts of people.

Thank you Molly (Cherie Penney's dog) and Daisy (our family's Chocolate Labrador) for helping inspire the character of Steffi.

In spite of all this generous expertise, I know there will be mistakes and they are all mine. Before you point them out, please note that I have taken some artistic licence with the real world particularly in relation to timing. (For example, the song 'Popcorn' was released when Joy was nineteen, not seventeen.) However there was nothing fictitious about Australia's catastrophic fires early in 2020. The *Authors for Fireys* Campaign raised funds for bushfire relief and Sulin Ho and Nicole Jourdan-Lenoir both donated to this wonderful initiative to have their names appear as characters in this book. Simon Barrington was also the winning bidder at a Rural Aid Charity auction to have a character in this book named after him. Thank you Sulin, Nicole and Simon for your donations and your names.

Thank you Caroline Lee for superb narration of my audio books.

Thank you to my remarkable translators around the world.

Thank you to fellow Australian authors Ber Carroll and Dianne Blacklock for being my 'office mates' for more than a decade now. Thank you to my wonderful publicists, Tracey Cheetham in Australia, Gaby Young in the UK and Pat Eisemann in the US. Thank you to my fantastic literary and film agents: Fiona Inglis and Benjamin Paz in Australia, Faye Bender in the US, Jonathan Lloyd and Kate Cooper in the UK and Jerry Kalajian in LA.

Thank you, with all my heart, to my readers, indisputably the loveliest readers in the world. I'm grateful every day for your support. The 2020 pandemic means that I will sadly not meet as many of you as I normally would when launching a new book. I will never ever complain about travel again and I'll see you in real life for the next one.

Thank you to my family for everything. Thank you Adam for coffee delivered each day before I even open my eyes, thank you to my beautiful daughter Anna AKA THE BEST DAUGHTER IN DA WORLD AND FAV CHILD IN UR FACE GEORGE (this is what happens when you leave a document open on your computer for a passing eleven-year-old. I decided I would leave her words for posterity as it seemed appropriate for a book about sibling rivalry) and my beautiful son George (get her back next time, George).

Thank you to a shy yet chatty little girl called Diane, the only kid in her class photo holding a doll, who grew up to become a gorgeous blonde bombshell, mother of six, grandmother of twelve, foster mother to many more. This one is just for you, with lots of love and gratitude that I got you as my Mum. Finally, thank you to my father. It's my first book without you here, but you'll stay in my acknowledgements forever Dad-Man.

★

The following references were helpful to me in writing this book *Late to the Ball* by Gerald Marzorati, *Rafa My Story* by Rafael Nadal with John Carli, *Unbreakable* by Jelena Dokic with Jessica Halloran, *The Golden Era* by Rod Laver with Larry Writer, *Margaret Court The Autobiography* by Margaret Court, *Home The Evonne Goolagong Story* by Evonne Goolagong Cawley & Phil Jarratt, *A Spanish Love Affair* by Susan Joy Alexander (I gave Joy a similar experience to Susan's real life experience of one particular match with a biased umpire at White City.) *Counselling: Recognising Our Profession in its Own Right* (2019), an article by Fiona Griffith, with thanks to Melissa Shadforth for passing on.

The Migraine Guy Podcast is the name of a real podcast but everything Joy hears is fictional. *This Dementia Life* and *Chat with Traders* are also the names of real podcasts.